Lawless

Chris Babcock
Jonathan Babcock
Abigail Bales
Anita DeVries
Elijah Fitz
Megan Flahive
Katelyn Flatt
Nicole Gusto
Vannah Leblank
Drake McDonald
Brad Pauquette
Alli Prince
Matthew Sampson
Thirzah

Lawless

An Anthology of Stories Inspired
by the Book of Judges

Developed by
Alli Prince

The Pearl

PEARLBOOKS.CO

The Pearl Factory, LLC
303 N. 7th St.
Cambridge, OH 43701
PearlBooks.co

PRODUCER
Brad Pauquette

EDITOR
Alli Prince

COVER
Jessica Ostrander (Artwork)
Brad Pauquette (Design)

LCCN: 2023952240

Paperback ISBN 978-1-960230-04-1
Ebook ISBN 978-1-960230-05-8

Contents

To those who forge new worlds,
may you invite the Spirit into them.

Foreword

God is so much richer than what we see in the fiction section of the Christian bookstore. Here at The Company, we're ready to invest in something different—something hard. Something risky.

If the Bible talks about the hard stuff of real life and asks difficult questions, why are we so reticent to do the same?

Alli Prince and I worked together at The Company to develop the concept of the *Lawless* project, and she did all of the hard work to make it a reality.

We chose the book of Judges as the inspiration for this anthology precisely because of how rich and complex it is. There's nothing simplistic and there are no easy answers in the book of Judges. It's the type of Bible you just have to chew on.

We had one rule for our author's content. They weren't allowed to introduce any subjects that the book of Judges didn't introduce. But that's not saying much.

The content of this book is decidedly PG-13. While younger teenagers would certainly enjoy the book, make sure it's right for them.

You won't find any graphic sexuality in these pages, but, like the book of judges, sex and gender are important thematic elements to many of the stories.

You won't find any American "profanity" in the book, but there is a fair amount of violence—again, in keeping with the book of Judges.

Armed with some information about the universe and some guard-rails regarding the content, fourteen authors were turned loose to write their own stories—each author assigned a specific judge or passage of scripture to inspire his or her work. Consistent with the themes and stakes of the passages, these authors pushed boundaries and asked hard questions.

We shared a common goal: to introduce something engaging which might inspire someone to more richly explore the Bible. These judges of the Bible were real people, you know.

Something marvelous happened in the process—a community came together around the project. Fourteen individuals submitted themselves to the process and to each other to create something that's better than what we could have each produced on our own. Countless more members of The Company rallied around the project to encourage and lend their support.

I hope you enjoy these thought-provoking, sometimes quirky stories inspired by the book of Judges. It's my hope that it lights the first step on a path to more meaningful, challenging, constructive Christian fiction.

Thank you for joining us in this journey, and thank you for supporting better Kingdom literature by reading this book and sharing it.

-Brad Pauquette
Producer

Introduction

Welcome to Covenant, a post-apocalyptic, dystopian earth where technological advancement has come to a jarring halt and resources are sparse. The journeymen, a group of people chosen by a mysterious deity called Donumdonair, must struggle through treacherous deserts inhabited by two tyrannical tribes: the fierce Desperados and The Order of Kosmoa.

Lawless holds fourteen different stories that travel through time and the land of Covenant—from the harsh empty deserts to the cool, refreshing cities.

Each story is inspired by a particular section of the Biblical book of Judges. The judges of the Bible were real people, with thoughts, hardship, motivation, and desires, just like you. What would it *really* be like to live in a time when every man did what was right in his own eyes?

From the beginning, this project has had one goal: to produce Christian literature that doesn't shy away from the realities of life. Fourteen Christian authors have stepped up to the challenge.

Christian Fiction has a particular reputation. It's known for its preachy messages and subpar storylines. It's known for relying on an audience that will come just because we've slapped the name of God onto it.

Enough is enough. With this anthology, the authors have taken a step up. The Bible talks about hard topics. The world talks about hard topics. It's time for Christian literature to talk about hard stuff, too.

I hope you enjoy reading these stories as much as we have enjoyed writing them. But more than that, I hope that you read them and then go back and read the inspiration *behind* the stories. I hope that this anthology blesses you with a new appreciation for scripture, and most importantly, I hope you connect with Jesus.

-Alli Prince
Editor

Sacrifice

Alli Prince

Stefan looked up from the corpse of the beast, its body broken and slumped on its side. Even now, dead and sitting in a pool of sickly green ooze, the beast towered a good three feet above Stefan.

Behind him, Orlan, a priest of Kosmoa, strolled down the silver ramp of his pristine ship, his white robe billowing behind him. "Kosmoa will be pleased with your sacrifices," his voice rang out over the plain.

The ship stood like a sore thumb against the deep brown rock of the desert wastelands around them. Soft puffs of steam rolled from the ventilation systems along the side of the ship. The glass viewing ports along the top were tinted black and along the nose, engraved in the metal, was the shape of an hourglass.

Stefan knelt to the ground and pulled out his 400-plasma-knife. He clicked the small brass switch on the side. White light flickered along the serrated edge of the blade. He slipped the knife into the beast's flesh and slowly began to carve away long strips of hide. Smoke drifted away as the white electricity cauterized the surrounding flesh, preventing the blood from soaking into the fresh hide.

Orlan stepped off the silver ramp and onto the cracked desert floor. He kept his hands clasped together and hidden inside the long swooping sleeves of his robe.

"Tell me, who slayed the creature?" he asked.

Stefan wiped his brow with the back of his hand, then held up two fingers. "I did, with their aid."

He jabbed a thumb towards the other outlaws, the men who traveled with him on business trips such as this. They stood back against a scraggly dead tree, awaiting their turn for a cut of the meat.

Orlan's shaved head shone in the light. He smiled. "Stefan...thank you for protecting the lands from this creature. Kosmoa is pleased with the sacrifice of your time."

Stefan huffed. He clicked his tongue and looked back down at his work. He adjusted the rifle strapped to his back and wiped the sweat from his brow, leaving a dark green streak of ooze along his forehead. Orlan strolled around the beast and then stopped, stooping down to crouch next to Stefan.

His robe splayed in the dirt around them. Stefan kept his face turned firmly towards the beast. He sawed another strip of hide from the creature.

Orlan swallowed. His pale nose scrunched as the stench of burnt and bloody flesh wafted from the fresh slice.

"What do you want, Orlan?" Stefan asked.

"Will you be sacrificing to your god today?"

"No."

Stefan braced himself as he felt the eyes of his group swivel towards him. He wiped his brow again and folded the new piece of hide over his left arm. He stood and began to shove the pieces into his leather satchel.

"Perhaps," Orlan lowered his voice and leaned forward. "If you did give up a sacrifice…your god would speak to you."

Stefan turned and strode away from the creature. He stepped over the long, hairless tail of the beast and over the gravel and rock of the desert. Behind him, Orlan struggled over the rough terrain.

"Stefan, I'm sure Donumdonair would—" Orlan stopped and tugged the edge of his tunic from a scraggly bush, then rushed up the rest of the incline and fell into step with Stefan. "Nothing big—something small! The size of a small dog would do! I'm sure Donumdonair would initiate you back into your clan, were you to appease—"

"No." Stefan stopped and turned to face Orlan, his teeth barred. "My clan made their choice—and I've made mine. Now leave me alone."

Orlan sighed and folded his hands back together inside the sleeves of his robe. Stefan turned roughly towards the setting sun, adjusted the rifle, and stalked away.

"When you are ready!" Orlan called. "I'll help you!"

• • •

Stefan strayed on the outskirts of the Journeymen market. The sounds of chatter and haggling clattered from inside the dusty, wooden stalls. The squeals of children laughing and playing pierced the air. The Journeymen were known to have the fairest price—*if* they'd buy from you. Stefan adjusted the red bandana that concealed the bottom half of his face. He swallowed and shoved his trembling hands deep into the pockets of his leather coat, then took a step into the market stalls.

The smells of spices and freshly cooked meat enticed a deep rumble from his stomach. Slowly, he approached a stall and set the long strips of hide on the counter.

The man on the other side of the stall looked down at the hide, then up at Stefan. He was short, with a protruding stomach and receding hairline.

"What're we lookin' to trade?" the man leaned against the wooden counter, which creaked and shifted at the weight.

"What'ya got?" Stefan asked.

The man sighed and looked at the crates behind him. He motioned with the stump of his arm, cloth wrapped tight around the wrist where the hand should have been.

"Plenty…let's see," the man sighed and scratched the back of his neck with his good hand. "I got rations, bandages… Hmm, well, I see you got a 900-Lite-rifle on your shoulder there. I got light cartridges?"

Stefan nodded. "What would you give me for all this?"

"Hmm…well, trading those pelts…that'll run you, let's say, twenty light cartridges, seventeen rations, and three bandages."

Stefan nodded. A fair price indeed. "I'll take it."

The man grinned and began to collect the tiny metal boxes with his one hand and set them atop the counter. Stefan scanned the perimeter. Sitting on the top of the crates a few feet behind the man sat a doll. Small, with braided black hair made of yarn and two simple buttons for eyes.

"How much for the doll?" the question popped out before Stefan could stop it. The man hesitated.

"You got a little girl?"

Stefan nodded. "Born a year or so ago."

"I got two still at home, both boys," the man set a handful of light cartridges on the counter. "My little girl got herself a nice man—married off last spring."

Stefan smiled and leaned against the pole. "Congratulations."

The man wiped his brow with a cloth, then grabbed the doll and set it on the counter.

"This used to be hers…" the man sighed. He held the doll's hand between two meaty fingers, then let his hand slide to his side. "I'll just add this in—consider it a parting gift from one father to another…May it be kept by your daughter till the day she is wed."

Stefan bit his tongue to keep the gratitude out of his eyes. He swallowed and nodded.

"Many thanks."

The man grinned, then turned and grabbed another handful of light cartridges.

"Say, which clan are you from? I don't think I've seen your face 'round these markets before—"

Suddenly, a deep voice rumbled from behind Stefan. "Do you know who it is you're serving, friend?"

Stefan grit his teeth together as a hand came and rested on his shoulder.

The man behind the counter glanced from Stefan to the man. "Ah, greetings to you, Aldore, and uh, I don't say I had the pleasure of making his acquaintance."

"This is Stefan…of *Orson*."

The man's eyebrows raised, then in a barely heard whisper, *"the whore's son?"*

"That's right…" Aldore grinned as he came to stand next to Stefan, his hand still gripping Stefan's shoulder. A rebreather hung loose around Aldore's neck, and his dark brown hair was cut close to his scalp. His eyes were narrowed, and his white teeth flashed as he continued to smile. "Say, how's life treating you, Stefan? It's been, what... *six* months since your wife left you for that Desperado?"

Stefan shrugged the hand off and faced away from Aldore.

"Oh—" He slapped a hand against his forehead. "I forgot—you never married her, did you? Heh, took a page out of your old man's book, I guess."

"What do you want, Aldore?" Stefan whispered. Aldore grinned, his tiny eyes like black beads as his skin folded and creased.

"What do I want from *you*?" Aldore shook his head. He patted Stefan on the shoulder, a cloud of dust puffed out. Aldore took a step back and motioned to Stefan's figure. "Nothing, Stefan...*nothing*."

Stefan glowered and watched as Aldore shoved both hands in his pockets and strolled off down the market lane. Stefan took a shuttered breath, then turned back to the man across the counter. He reached for the light cartridges—but not before the man behind the counter rested his hand on the pile.

"The pelts'll run you *eleven* rations and ten light cartridges." The man narrowed his eyes. "And no doll...sorry."

Stefan's cheeks darkened with color. His throat warbled as he swallowed, then in a voice barely above a whisper, he spoke. "*I'll take it.*"

• • •

The half-moon had risen high into the sky by the time Stefan traveled back to his homestead. He looked up as he walked the rough desert terrain. A chill wind ruffled his coat as he approached a large, wired fence. Barbs and spikes clung to each loop of wire that ran along the top of the rusted metal poles staked into the ground. His boots crunched the loose stones of gravel and dirt. He stopped just in front of a large, metal archway. Red lasers crisscrossed in the metal archway to form a gate of angry light.

Stefan slipped out a small metal card from his belt, which was attached to a string. He swiped the card against a metal box on the gate. The lasers flickered, and the hum of electricity died as the lasers, one by one, powered off. A box on the other side of the gate whined as a whistle sounded off, announcing his presence. Four cows looked up from where they grazed on the scraggly brown patches of weeds, their eyes sunken and their ribs protruding from their sides.

He walked through the gate, reached behind him, and pressed the card against the whistle. The lasers, one by one, powered back on behind him. Stefan shoved the card back into his belt.

He'd not walked five feet down the worn sand path and towards the wooden shack in front of him before he heard the excited squeals from inside. He pulled the bandana down and grinned.

"*I know!*" a woman's voice traveled down the path from inside the shack. "I know—Daddy's home, isn't he?"

Stefan pushed aside the worn blue cloth they called a door and stepped inside.

"I'm home." He coughed. The wooden shack had no rooms and held just the necessities Stefan could afford.

Mary looked up from the ground by the small fireplace. Her deformed legs twisted under her at an odd angle. Her hair was tied back into a bun with loose strands of golden blond hair falling to frame her young face. Kaelee sat in her lap.

"She's always so excited to see you," Mary whispered as she held up Kaelee, who wriggled and pumped her arms. The small child let out a squeal and kicked her legs. Stefan slipped the rifle from his shoulder and leaned it against the wall, then took three steps forward and scooped her into his arms. The child all but disappeared inside his thick arms, so tiny and small compared to the mountain of a man that held her.

Kaelee's mouth parted into the shape of an oval as she stared up at Stefan. Her hands lightly patted the stubble on his chin. She squealed and kicked her legs. Stefan chuckled and moved to the wooden chair by the fireplace. He sat, the wood creaking under his weight.

"How'd the day go? Is she still choking on the solid foods?" he asked quietly. Mary winced as she shifted her legs out from under her and leaned against the rough wood wall.

"No, she ate very well today," Mary whispered. Deep lines were set in her cheeks and around her tired dark eyes. Stefan looked up.

"You didn't give her your rations again, did you?"

Mary pressed her lips together. "She's a growing child, Stefan—"

"*Mary.*" Stefan set Kaelee on his knee and lightly bounced her up and down. "I need you to eat—for her. If you—hey!"

Kaelee had shoved his fingers into her mouth. She gnawed along his dirty thumb. A small drip of drool dribbled off her chin and onto her knee. Stefan winced and pulled his hand away.

Mary shook her head and smiled. "We sat in the front yard today, and she stood all on her own… She's growing up. She needs the food."

Stefan grunted and leaned back in the chair. He sucked in a breath. The fire crackled to his left. Mary slowly shut her eyes as Kaelee reached forward and played with the fraying edges of his bandana, still tied around his neck.

"Besides," Mary whispered. "A little hunger is a small price to pay for what you've done for me."

Stefan looked up. He set his mouth in a firm line.

"I did what any moral man would do. To take advantage of someone who can't even run—"

"It was more than *most* would do, Stefan," Mary cut in. She smoothed out her skirt, pale and blue and dirty from the ground on which she often dragged herself. She smoothed a lock of blond hair from her face and blinked away a shine that had taken to her eyes. "I'd gladly give up food for weeks to repay you."

Stefan leaned back. He untied the bandana with one hand and let it slip into Kaelee's grasp.

"You do enough, Mary… You do enough."

• • •

Stefan jolted from the chair. Dust fluttered along the wooden floorboards. The sound of a ship touching down roared outside, and the dirt-covered windows shook in their frames. Rays of artificial light seeped in from the cracks in the ceiling. Mary and Kaelee had retired for the night to their place in the corner. A metal pole with a shower curtain separated them. Stefan cracked his neck as he stood. He ran a hand over his face and walked towards the door.

"Stefan?" Mary whispered from the corner. "Is everything alright?"

"Got company," Stefan roughly responded. "Stay inside an' keep Kaelee quiet."

He grabbed his gun and pointed it out the door. With the barrel, he moved the blue cloth and stepped into the morning air.

13

The sun rose just over the large rock formations in the distance. His boots crunched the gravel.

"Hey, Stefan!" Aldore called from behind the fence. Stefan blinked. Three ships stood behind Aldore. Two were small and scrapped together with spare sheets of metal. Rust and dirt caked the exposed metal. The third ship, in the middle, was the same silver ship from the morning before.

"What do you want, Aldore?" Stefan called. He took a step towards them.

"To return something that was taken from you." Aldore rapped a hand on the metal gate. He shifted to meet Stefan's eyes past the angry red beams. "Mind comin' out for a discussion on the matter?"

Stefan swallowed. He glanced behind him and into the shack. Mary had peeked a head out the curtain. Kaelee still slept, nestled in her arms. Mary pressed her lips together and slowly shook her head.

"Put your gun on the ground and we'll see," Stefan called back. Mary narrowed her eyes. Stefan watched as Aldore, with great show and flourish, removed the pistol from his belt and set it on the ground. Stefan slung his rifle over his shoulder and walked down the path toward the gate. He stopped, just in front of the lasered defense.

"I'm surprised you own cattle." Aldore nodded toward the four beasts that stood to the right, grazing on the dead shrubbery. "Cattle often provide well for a family—"

"Provided that family can trade for fair prices," Stefan bit. "Why're the Elders here? I thought Journeymen were banned from mingling with the priests of Kosmoa—"

"You know Donumdonair's rules, as do I," Aldore bit. "He detests joining with each other. This is pure business, not social pleasures…

You killed a great beast yesterday, didn't you?"

Stefan nodded. Aldore suppressed a sigh.

"There's a beast similar in stature. It's threatening the region."

Stefan raised a brow. "You need to get to the part where this is *my* problem."

Aldore ran a hand through his hair and glanced back at the ships.

"Listen…you kill this beast for us, and I'll talk to the Journeymen. We'll forget the soil on your reputation, and you'll be welcomed to fair price and wage in the marketplace again."

Stefan let out a breath. He sent a quick glance back to the shack.

"Donumdonair will be pleased with us?" Stefan lowered his voice to a low whisper. "My family and I will be welcomed?"

Aldore scoffed. "Yes, you, your daughter, and the unmarried wench that resides with you. I'll handle all of it—*if* you kill the beast."

"Why?" Stefan clenched his fist. "Why not go kill the beast yourself?"

Aldore sneered. "I don't work with deranged lunatics that believe in a false god…besides, the Kosmoan priests requested your help by name."

Stefan looked at the ship. He stared up at the tinted windows. The sun glinted off the metal and blinded him. Stefan looked back to Aldore.

"Well?" Aldore asked. "Will you go? The elders are waiting inside their ship for you. Together, you'll pick up their warrior and then go slay the beast."

"I'll do it."

• • •

Stefan shifted as he stared at the market around him. Pristine stalls set in symmetrical and perfect order. The stone ground contained barely a scuff of a boot or a granule of sand as robed figures quietly did their shopping. Stefan shoved his hands deep into his coat and followed Orlan at a distance as he took in the perfect surroundings of The Order of Kosmoa's market.

"Stefan—keep up, you don't want to get lost," Orlan called from in front of him. Stefan shook his head.

"How could I get lost with your shiny head leading the way?"

Orlan's ears reddened. "I sacrificed my hair to my god—it's not funny! The high priests said it was what Kosmoa required."

"What god wants *hair* as a sacrifice?" Stefan chuckled. "Seems useless once it's off your head."

Orlan straightened and dusted off his robe—for show, of course, for they were in perfect order. "Come. We must retrieve Kade and then make way for the beast before dark…besides, look around. We're in Kosmoa's territory. Many here go without their hair."

Stefan looked around. More than half the crowd had a cleanly shaved skull, including the women.

"Where are the children?" Stefan asked.

Orlan raised a brow. "What do you mean?"

Stefan jabbed his thumb towards the sparse market. "There's no children playing in the market."

Orlan placed a hand over his heart. "*Children* in the market *playing*? Why, you Journeymen are…very interesting. Here in Kosmoa's territory, the children play in their designated play areas. Now, come along, we don't want to be late."

Together, the two men walked from the crowded market down a clean stone pathway.

"What are those?" Stefan asked as they passed large square buildings, made from white metal and decorated with intricate patterns of white and gold lattice.

"Those are our homes—each member of The Order of Kosmoa receives one upon their fiftieth sacrifice. Do you Journeymen not receive such honors from Donumdonair?"

Stefan remained silent. He watched as a sleek silver ship hovered above one home. A dog in the yard howled up at it, the hair raised on the back of its neck.

"Wait," Stefan said. He watched as the bottom of the ship opened. Puffs of air blew out as the metal doors slid open. Three men slipped out, rappelling from the ship with long metal lines. They held black guns in their hands. They landed in the yard, their guns clicked and began to whir as the light bolts on the side powered on.

"What are they doing?" Stefan stopped. Orlan glanced from Stefan to the home, then hurriedly back to Stefan.

"Keep moving—" he hissed, reaching out his hand to pull Stefan forward.

Stefan shrugged off Orlan's hand. "What are they—"

Bolts of light shot out of the guns and blasted into the metal of the house. A scream from inside pierced the air as the metal turned red and began to melt in on itself. Stefan's eyes widened. Metal curled and the roof caved, dropping to the ground. Dust flew up in a thick cloud of smoke as the men continued to fire upon the home. Stefan took a step forward.

"No—no, there's people in there! They—"

"Didn't pay their sacrifice!" Orlan hissed. He stopped in front of Stefan, his hands raised. "That man promised a sacrifice and refused to keep his word. You're a Journeymen. You understand the importance of honesty…"

Stefan clenched his teeth. He gripped his rifle and watched as they continued to fire at the house. Orlan tugged on the sleeve of his jacket, and he tore himself from the scene. He followed Orlan down the path, the sounds of the mutt barking and the metal shrieking behind him.

• • •

Kade of The Order of Kosmoa was a tiny man. He stood half a foot shorter than Stefan, his eyes narrowed into a continual squint as though staring up at the sun.

"So, you're Stefan Orson, Killer of Beasts?" Kade asked as Stefan and Orlan walked up the pathway to his home. "We're in fine hands, then."

Together, the two men loaded their weapons and supplies and boarded Orlan's silver ship. The inside of the ship dripped with luxury—from the soft leather seats that lined the sides to the shelf in the back that held the finest liquors and crystal glasses. Orlan swept inside, his hands clasped together in his sleeves, and chose a seat.

Stefan glanced down at Kade, who shrugged and trudged after Orlan. Stefan followed and sat across from the other two men.

Stefan grabbed the shoulder straps and tugged them around his shoulders. He clicked the metal pieces together and sat back. The ramp to the ship lifted and closed off the sun. Orlan sat across from him, already buckled and hands clasped tightly together. The ship shook as it lifted from the ground and blasted into the rough desert air.

. . .

Orlan broke the silence. "You know, I do not judge you Journeymen, despite what you may think. I think Donumdonair is a fine god, really."

Stefan raised his bushy eyebrows, his arms crossed.

"Really?" Stefan asked.

"Really. I just…it confuses me why he makes it so hard to be of any worth. I mean, if he accepted what Kosmoa accepts as sacrifice, it would be much simpler."

"You've got it wrong," Kade grunted. Stefan glanced at him. Kade sat, his legs dangling a couple of inches off the metal floor of the ship, swinging them back and forth. "Y'see, I married a Journeymen woman. How she explained it to me was like this. Donumdonair values his people above all else. He calls them to live above the others."

Orlan scoffed. "Above the others? How pretentious—oh, no offense, Stefan."

Stefan grunted. "Sure."

The ship jolted to the side. Stefan glanced out the window. The desert wasteland sprawled out as far as the eye could see. Outcroppings of rock formations jutted up from the serene sands. He watched as the ship descended to the ground; his back cushioned by the soft seats.

"We're here—the beast was last seen in those mountains," Orlan said. Stefan unbuckled his belt and stood. He slung his gun off his shoulder and into his hand. The ramp whirred as it slowly descended. Harsh rays of desert light burst into the comforts of the ship.

"Stay safe, you two," Orlan muttered.

Kade and Stefan glanced at each other, then nodded to Orlan.

They collected their guns and walked off the ship.

The hot desert air hit Stefan as he left the comfort of the cool ship behind him and began the trek to the rocky mountain formations in front of them.

"Ready?" Kade inspected his guns—two small, handheld pistols with electric white light on either side. The gears inside hummed as the gun powered on. Stefan shifted his hands to the side of his rifle and pressed down on a small brass button. A sight popped up on the top of the gun as the lights along the side flickered on.

"Don't die," Stefan huffed. Kade nodded. Together, they crouched low. Their boots crunched against the sand as they moved towards the large cropping of rock. Stefan looked down at the sights and towards the mountainside.

"There's a cave," Stefan commented. "My guess? That's where the thing hides."

Kade nodded, then silently moved towards the cave. Stefan followed a foot behind him.

"So," Kade whispered as they made their way over the rough terrain, "what'd they threaten you with to get you out here?"

Stefan gave a wary glance. "They didn't."

"No?" Kade huffed. "God, I wish I were a Journeymen."

"What do you mean?"

"I failed to give up a sacrifice last quarter," Kade muttered. "The Elders wanted my wife for the night. She refused. So, here I am."

Stefan was silent for a moment. They paused as they approached a drop-off, the jagged cliff traveling down ten or so feet, then a valley of sand and, just across from that, the mouth of the cave.

"The clan I was born into has forsaken me, for the sins of I and my father," Stefan muttered. "I was born as nothing. I do this to prevent the same fate for my daughter."

Kade hummed. "And what does your god say about how your people treat you?"

Stefan shrugged. "I do not know. He does not speak to me."

"Do you speak to him?" Kade asked. Stefan glared, hard and cold, then silently pushed his rifle strap over his shoulder and climbed over the cliffside. Kade huffed beside him and followed. The two crouched low to the ground, their feet sinking into the sand.

"Bad terrain," Kade muttered as he lifted his boot. Tiny granules of sand tumbled from the crevices of cracked leather.

Stefan held onto the rocky cliffside next to him. He slung his rifle off his shoulder and gripped it in his right hand. With his left, he clung to the cliffside. He aimed his rifle forward and stared down the scope toward the cave. Kade stood and struggled through the loose sands. Stefan narrowed his eyes as he stared at the mouth of the cave. From this angle, it looked shallow.

"The cave's been clawed," Stefan said. "Do you see it, Kade?"

Kade paused halfway through the sand-field. He stared up at the cave, his eyes narrowed.

"It looks unnaturally formed," Stefan continued. "Like the beast dug—"

The sand shook. Deep ripples formed in the middle of the small clearing around Kade. He turned to look at Stefan, his eyes wide, mouth parted to say something. Then, like a whale bursting from the sea, the creature burst from the sand. Its snout to Kade's left and its bottom jaw to his right. With a sickening snap, the jaw closed, and Kade disappeared inside the beast's maw.

Stefan pulled the trigger. A bolt of electric white light shot across the sand-field and seared into the creature's skull, inches from its beady black eyes. The rat-like beast clawed up from the ground. It shook. Sand flew from its matted black fur. Stefan threw the rifle back over his shoulder and scrambled up the cliffside. The beast shrieked into the air, a piercing sound that trailed off into a hiss.

Stefan hoisted himself up, digging his hands into the crevices. The rocks sliced his fingers as he scrambled up the cliffside. Tiny red beads of blood slipped from the beds of his fingernails past his knuckles and into his sleeves.

The sand-rat screamed again. Sand showered through the sand-field. Stefan's hand cleared the top of the cliff. With a final grunt, he leaped up and threw himself up onto solid ground. He twisted around and brought up his rifle.

The sand-rat stared at him with its mouth parted. Its large furless tail stood straight up behind it, casting a long dagger-like shadow along the ground. Twice in size compared to the beast Stefan had slain the day before. Blood smeared its yellow-stained teeth. Kade's cracked leather boot was lodged between two incisors. Stefan sucked in a breath, his teeth clenched, his nostrils flaring. The beast's nose twitched. Stefan's hands shook.

The sand-rat screamed. Stefan clenched his teeth and pulled the trigger.

Light burst from the tip of his rifle and seared into the back of the beast's mouth. It wrenched its head back. Its paw hurled towards Stefan, who lurched to the side. The paw slammed into the rocks next to him. Stefan grunted as he scrambled to his feet, gun raised. He fired a series of light bolts, singeing the sand-rat's underbelly. The creature howled as it backed away. Smoke rose from the fresh wounds.

The sand-rat's nose twitched. Its beady eyes narrowed. The hair on the back of its neck rose and its mouth opened. Saliva mixed with blood clung to its bottom jaw as it shrieked.

Stefan knelt to his knee, lifted his rifle, and peered down the sight, slowing the scene down in his mind. He narrowed in on the black eyes and fired as he exhaled.

The bolt sizzled as it left the barrel of the gun. It flew past the dust and the debris disturbed and thrown about from the fight and directly into the beast's eyeball. The beady black orb burst upon impact. Tiny bolts of electricity flickered and seared the surrounding flesh.

Stefan didn't move as he fired three more shots, one after the other, in the same spot. Each bolt burrowed further into the skull.

The creature howled as the shots hit. Its paw blindly came up to scrape at the burning flesh, its green blood soaking the surrounding fur. The creature crumbled to the ground. The muscles in the beasts' shoulders spazzed as the final burst of electricity from the light-bolt sizzled through its body.

Stefan lowered the gun. He tore the bandana away from his mouth and sucked in a greedy breath of air. He ran his hand over his head and smoothed back his hair.

Stefan's hands shook as he took a step towards the edge of the cliff and looked at the sand-rat. Its tongue protruded from its clenched jaw, swollen, and dripping with sickly green liquid. Stefan swallowed.

"*I* did it," he whispered. He covered his mouth to keep in a laugh. "*I did it*!"

· · ·

23

Orlan stood as Stefan entered the ship.

"So, it's dead?" Orlan asked.

"I did it—" Stefan stepped forward and clasped his hand on Orlan's shoulder. "Orlan—I've earned back my place with the Journeymen."

"Then we celebrate!" Orlan clapped his hands together. Behind the priest, nestled in the corner of the ship, sat a shelf lined with fine crystal glasses. "Here—take a drink! You've more than earned it!"

Stefan strode forward and grabbed the first cup. He filled it with a dark brown liquid, pressed it to his lips and threw it back in one giant gulp. Stefan grimaced and leaned against the side of the ship. He slipped the rifle off his shoulder and set it against the wall. Orlan swept towards him and grabbed the glass bottle. He tipped it and filled Stefan's drink once more.

"Now, tell me, Stefan, Killer of Beasts and pride of the Journeymen," Orlan set the glass bottle on the shelf. The liquid swirled inside. Stefan looked for a moment at the glass and grinned. Orlan folded his hands inside his sleeves. "What will you sacrifice in celebration? Perhaps crops?"

"I've no crops—not yet. But once I'm reinstated in the market, I'll plant a garden—a huge one." Stefan pressed his drink to his lips and took a long sip. He wiped his chin with the back of his hand and let out a sigh. "Mary shall tend it and Kaelee will play in the strawberry fields."

"Hmm, perhaps furniture or wealth then."

Stefan shook his head. "No. I've none of that…"

"Then what can you sacrifice?" Orlan's eyebrows scrunched together. "As tribute to your god, surely you must give him something."

Stefan pressed his lips together and stared down at the shiny silver floor.

Slowly, he pushed himself away from the wall, his shoulders pulled back. He swayed briefly, then looked into Orlan's dark eyes.

"Whatever walking thing I first see on my property," Stefan said and raised his cup. "For I am Stefan *Orson*, Killer of Beats, Hunter of Monsters, and *pride* of the Journeymen!"

Orlan smiled, grabbed a crystal cup and clinked it against Stefan's. The drink spilled over the top and sloshed onto the floor. Stefan sat on the soft seats and kicked his feet out to the middle of the aisle. He leaned back, closed his eyes, and grinned.

• • •

Stefan walked up the dirt path. With one hand he fished out the gate card, in the other, he held a doll. Small, with braided black hair made of yarn and two simple buttons for eyes. He swiped the gate card against the access port and watched as the red beams of light, one by one, powered off. Orlan kept a close pace behind him as the two walked through the rusted metal archway, and the beams of red flicked back on.

The whistle sounded and Stefan turned, swiping the card over the control box.

"Stefan!" The shout came from the front door. Stefan turned. The cows had moved to graze behind the shack, the sound of the bells around their necks the only indication they were still on the property. In front of Stefan, a small, pudgy figure stumbled out of the shack and onto the path.

Kaelee's arms pumped up and down, excited gasps escaped her gaping grin as she stumbled towards him. Stefan froze. Mary's voice echoed from inside the shack. "Stefan—look! She's walking! She's walking!"

Orlan rested a hand atop Stefan's shoulder and stepped around the man. Sweat clung to the top of Stefan's brow and his gun slipped from his shoulder and clattered to the ground. Stefan blinked, then snapped his attention to the priest on his left.

Orlan smiled, his dark eyes gleaming and clasped his hands together inside his sleeves.

"Donumdonair will be pleased with your sacrifice."

Find the story of Jephthah in Judges 11.

The Deliverer

Brad Pauquette

In that time, each man did what was right in his own eyes…

Yasef led three boys through the desert—a gift for the magistrate, each eight years old, chosen personally by Yasef from the available tributes. All three had dark hair and colored eyes, just like Yasef—an oddity among the Journeymen. They wore tunics, covered with makeshift leathers—this one with a borrowed jacket that only came to the waist, that one with mismatched gloves, an aviator cap pulled over the ears. Only one had a real rebreather, an old model, pre-war, and the other two wrapped cotton scarves over their mouths.

Yasef stood six feet tall and wore a long leather coat of a striking but dusty honey brown, which hung down to his black boots. A scimitar adorned his belt. His right hand was covered by a black glove, his left metallic and bare to the elements. He wore a rebreather of the latest Kosmoan design, a sleek silver mask with a circular filter over his mouth and nose for radiation, toxins, and dust…mostly dust.

It was a three-day journey across the western plain from the City of Palms. After two silent days, on the third morning, as the sun peeked over the horizon, they left the last inn in Covenant and walked past the Guidestones. Yasef lowered his hat and ignored the stones. "Keep it moving," he told the boys, his voice robotic through his mask. Yasef tapped the side of his goggles to change from red polarity tint to sun gray.

"Do you remember when the sun stood still?" one of the boys spoke up, "for the armies of Donumdonair to defeat the Kosmoans?"

Yasef looked back as he walked, "Shut up."

The boy seemed to shake his head, but it was difficult to tell through the pile of discarded fabric he carried over his head and body. "My uncle told me that the Guidestones are a reminder to tell the stories," the boy's voice was muffled through the scarf over his mouth. "You have to tell the stories when you pass the stones."

Yasef stopped and turned. "You're wrong." His voice was flat like the desert. He tapped a button on his goggles to clear the tint so that he could look the boy in the eyes. "The ancient ones said that when you pass the Guidestones, fathers should tell their sons the stories." He looked them over, one by one. "You don't have any fathers."

Yasef turned and continued on, the boys trudging behind him. A full minute passed, then two.

"Then why don't you tell us the stories?" one of them piped up.

Yasef laughed, dropped his chin to his chest, didn't turn. "Because I don't have a father either."

They walked on over the cracked dirt in silence. Not a bird, not a gust of wind...only the sound of the dust cracking beneath their feet and all around them. Yasef scanned the horizon in twenty-degree segments, looking for bandits, Desperados, sand-rats.

A muffled voice began to fill the space. "Do you remember when

28

the river stopped like a wall of water for the people of Donumdonair to pass…"

Yasef ignored it and continued on.

It was a lie of sorts; he'd had a father once. Of course, everybody did. In the first years after the Imperial war, his father had given him to the magistrate—to Bryden the Great. The old man had said god told him to. But not before Yasef's birthday, the one where they pronounced him a man. What was it that the prophet had spoken of him? "You will be the arm of Donumdonair…"

Well, it fit. Donumdonair—the giver of gifts. What irony, isn't that exactly who Yasef was? Marching these boys through the desert to give them in tribute to the magistrate, the Great Eldon?

"Do you remember when…" the boy droned on, he fumbled over the words, "when Donumdonair sent a deliverer…"

Yasef ignored the boy, and grimaced when his left arm shorted and jittered. He worked the fingers and rapped on the control box in the elbow with his living hand.

Donum had given his people away, and Yasef was just following suit. *Follow in my ways*, wasn't that the command of Donum?

• • •

Four nights ago, Yasef sat in a pub on the outskirts. Rupert had brought in a pelt and they planned on drinking all night with the proceeds.

Rupert was a man like Yasef, a man without welcome.

A traitor for the Kosmoan empire, a traitor whose usefulness to the occupiers had evaporated, but who was not even worth a respectful assassination. Now Rupert was only as respected as the pelts he brought in and the drinks he shared.

So they shared a table. Yasef's drinking buddy leaned in conspiratorially. "You could kill him, you know."

Yasef laughed. "Please tell me you're joking."

Rupert pushed his drink aside. "Think about it!" he shouted, then looked around, whispering through his teeth now. "Think about it." He leaned in farther, his voice wet in Yasef's ear. "Think about it, you know the whole place, you can come and go, you take stuff inside. Nobody even searches you!"

Yasef did know the whole place. He knew the secret passage in the closet of the cold chamber in the penthouse. The room where Eldon spent his days in bed. They kept the temperature ten degrees below normal so that the fat man wouldn't sweat to death.

Yasef had served Bryden the Great faithfully. He grew as a man in that house under his tutelage, as a servant of the magistrate. He learned to serve, learned to think, learned to fight. His robotic arm was Bryden's own design.

He'd hidden in that closet when Eldon killed his own father, Bryden the Great. He'd watched Eldon plunge a knife into his Bryden's stomach, watched the old man bleed out. The old man lay dying on the floor as Eldon stood over him. The old man saw Yasef through the slats in the closet door and ever so subtly shook his head.

Eldon left the old man to bleed out, closing the door behind him. Yasef rushed from the closet.

"You must go, my boy," Bryden whispered in the voice of death. "Eldon will have them looking for an assassin." And Bryden told him about the secret passage through the closet, the one even Eldon didn't know about.

"Your god will see…" Bryden had said, mouthing the phrase over and over as he died. "Your god will see."

And Yasef had fled. And Eldon had taken the chamber, the power. The edict upon the journeymen changed. Eldon wanted the boys younger and younger. In his wisdom, Bryden raised up the tributes as trusted servants of the Kosmoan empire, to bind the empire's authority among the Journeymen. Eldon treated them as chattel. No more noble sons—orphans…orphans with dark hair, colored eyes. That was the only rule. When Eldon was done, he passed them about among his nobles, never to be heard from again.

And here was Yasef, the courier. The one who delivered the tribute. The one who kept the peace, honored the treaty, respected the edicts. Yasef, the arm of Donum. The deliverer. *Do you not see? Or do you not care?* If Donum didn't care, then Yasef had decided he didn't either.

His friend in the pub rapped on the table. "The Kosmoans are weak. Eldon is weak," Rupert slurred. "…but he's still the glue. You topple Eldon, you topple it all."

A heavy, drunken silence lingered between them. There were a few other patrons in the pub, but each drank alone, the only sound from an old tinny speaker in the corner.

"You know what happens to those boys," Rupert murmured.

"I just deliver the tribute. We all agreed to it, it's in the treaty. Somebody's got to do it." Yasef pawed at his nose, then lifted his glass for a long drag.

"Whatever helps you sleep at night," Rupert giggled, "aside from this stuff." He drained his glass.

"I just deliver. I mean, really, how would I know any more about what happens than anybody else?" Yasef's eyes glazed over. "I'm just the deliverer—the delivery man."

"Maybe it's time for a dose of their own medicine, if you know what I mean," Rupert winked and nudged an imaginary person with his elbow. Then his face turned serious. "Cause whatever that old roach Bryden did to you…" Rupert shuddered. "I can't—no, correction, I refuse to imagine what that fat rike is doing now."

Yasef had stopped listening, gazing into the bottom of his glass. "If you don't shut up, I'll make sure you get the death you deserve."

His friend waved him off. "Fine, not you then. If someone did the deed, finished that fat roach off, surely they'd be the arm of Donum." He clinked his glass against the metal of Yasef's left arm and winked. Rupert laughed as he picked up the bottle of spirits and refilled their glasses.

"Donum has his own arms," Yasef said. "What's he need me for?"

• • •

Yasef stared at the stones as he walked back across the parched and cracked dust of the western plain as he returned from the most recent delivery.

The fat man had his tribute—the Great Eldon. The only thing "great" about Eldon was his size. The man had ballooned to four hundred pounds, and they said he never left his bed chamber. His fat lips were purple to match his shadowed eyes. As usual on this most recent delivery, a kimono hung loosely around him, revealing a hairless chest.

As Yasef reflected on the delivery, he shuddered. Eldon had spoken to Yasef more than usual this time. He had leaned in conspiratorially, "You could stick around," the words lingered in Yasef's mind. "I could make time for you…" Eldon had raised his eyebrows, his mouth had parted, tucking his bottom lip behind his teeth, and caressing his chin with his finger. Then his eyes came alive, as if by inspiration. "Or we could each pick one," Eldon had gestured to the boys being delivered. "There is much to be done in the palace…together."

Yasef had stared straight ahead, in the custom of the royal court. His voice unfazed as he asked, "isn't it against the edict for you to socialize with me, Great One?"

Eldon had snickered, his jowls jiggling. "But since when are you a Journeymen, Yasef?"

Staring past the stones now at the desert beyond, the first finger of Yasef's left hand twitched, then his wrist spasmed and curled in. He absently reached over and pressed the reset button behind his elbow. His left arm fell limp at his side, then three seconds later began its boot sequence. First each finger closed, then opened, the wrist rotated in a complete circle, and the elbow worked three times.

Yasef grimaced and cocked his head as the neuro connections clicked back on. "Piece of trash," he muttered to himself.

He approached the guide stones and stopped. His fleshy right hand, covered by a leather glove, massaged the stubble of his beard that stuck out from beneath his goggles. Yasef was a head taller than most other Journeymen, his muscular physique could be discerned even beneath his desert leathers. He knew why he was chosen for this task by that sick despot, and it wasn't Donumdonair.

33

All twelve stones remained, but only eight were standing. Yasef could hear the voice of his father telling of the erection of the stones. Each stone had been carried by six men. Each stone, edges rounded into smooth shoulders by the river when the water still ran.

Not a single stone bore a mark, but to any Journeymen of honor, they told a story. They carried a story, and there was an instruction, to tell of the works of Donum before he dropped them into this forsaken lawless land.

Follow in my ways. Wasn't that the call of Donumdonair—the "giver of good gifts"? Was Yasef giving as Donum did?

Yasef tried not to picture what Eldon was doing, but his imagination ran on its own authority.

Yasef could still feel the fat man's fingers as they lingered over his shoulder. What was the phrase he used? "I'm always looking for company…" Yasef shuddered and sank to his knees in front of the stone of his own clan, the smallest stone in the line, long since fallen.

Yasef fell face down in the sand and his body shook with guilt. He cried and shuddered, but only the wilderness heard.

Finally, he stopped. The grief remained, but there were no more tears. "Is this how Donum gives?" he called out.

Only the emptiness of the wilderness responded.

Then he heard the voice—a gentle whisper of so many grains of sand running along in the wind.

The god who sees, Yasef could hear the voice of the sand. *The god who sees.*

His mind began to play a different voice. Yasef grimaced and squeezed his eyes shut tight as the voice grew. The voice of his father, whom he could feel standing at the guidestones.

And in those days, Donum saw. Donum saw his people greatly oppressed, and the sins of the oppressors had come due.

His father's voice continued, but it began to tell a story Yasef had not heard before. *So he raised up a deliverer, a man of neither this people nor that one. A man whose arm was mighty, the arm of Donumdonair. A man given the secrets of the Kingdom, a man who opens the door to freedom for the captives, release for the prisoners.*

Yasef cried out and the voice stopped. He pounded his fist into the dirt and clawed at the ground with his fleshy right hand. Something cut his finger. He worked his hand into the dirt and found the object, tenderly excavating it.

As the sand parted, a dagger emerged. A simple thing of two edges, straight blade, bearing the seal of Bryden the Great in the hilt.

• • •

As Yasef crossed the threshold into the cold room, he removed the rebreather from his face. He looked up and his eyes locked with Eldon's.

Eldon's lips curled into a smile, and he snapped his fingers. "Everybody out." The servants looked to Eldon, then to the man in the doorway, and fluttered out of the room.

"Close it," Eldon instructed Yasef.

Yasef closed the door, then turned back to Eldon. He set his rebreather on a chair next to the door.

"Please, please…make yourself comfortable," Eldon said. Yasef stood and a silence settled in the room.

Finally, Eldon spoke, "I've been watching you since you were a boy in my father's court, you know." He drew out the words *watching you.*

Yasef swallowed hard. "I know," he said. "And I've been watching you."

The fat man's eyes widened with delight, and he covered his smile with his hand.

"Would you like to sit down?" Eldon rubbed the bed beside him, smoothing out the covers that were bunched under his weight.

Yasef approached the bed, slowly, one deliberate step at a time, his boots barely making a sound on the marble floor. He removed his long coat and threw it back towards the chair that held his mask. The muscles of his arms showed through his undershirt, long and hard.

Sweat broke out on Eldon's forehead, and he inhaled in a short gasp. He looked towards the spot on the bed, licked his lower lip, and raised his eyebrows.

"There's something I have to do first," Yasef said, only two steps away.

Eldon's eyebrows narrowed quizzically, and his mouth parted. Yasef put his hands on Eldon's knees and leaned in.

"I have a message from god for you," Yasef whispered, his voice breathy in Eldon's ear. The stubble on Yasef's face brushed up against Eldon's cheek, as if they shared one beard. Eldon looked toward the ceiling then closed his eyes, inhaled sharply again. Yasef could feel his fat, wet lips begin to nibble at his ear.

In one smooth motion, Yasef pulled the dagger from his inner thigh with his mechanical left hand. He leaned forward still, and rested his shoulder against the fat man's chest as he thrust the dagger into Eldon's belly.

Eldon's eyes widened in shock and a gurgle followed a breathy gasp. Eldon breathed out sharply, again and again, as his lungs racked for air.

In that moment, Yasef's arm glitched, and his arm shot forward, his hand following the dagger inside of the man, buried up to his wrist in fat, as if Eldon's stomach was birthing a mechanical arm.

Yasef grunted, pulling his body back.

The fat man just sighed, a long, grievous tone, before he died, the heft of his head and chest slumping down over his enormous belly.

Yasef stopped for a moment to look over the man. He died the way he lived, in his bed, half-dressed—a caricature of the Kosmoan way of life.

Yasef tried to remove his hand from the man's body, but it was stuck, wedged further in by the death slump of the man's enormous weight.

"Not now, you piece of trash..." Yasef whispered as he pulled at his arm. The elbow mechanism wouldn't release and the shoulder was jammed. He reached over to pull at it with his right hand, even bringing his foot up to push against the side of the bed. His arm was locked inside, held tight by the man's girth. Yasef's eyes moved repeatedly to the door as he pried, but there was no movement.

Finally, Yasef shook his head in disgust. He reached behind his left elbow and pushed the reset button. The arm fell limp.

Yasef nervously observed the chamber, noting the door, the windows. There had been almost no noise, and even if a servant had heard it, what would they think it was? A grunt and a gasp. The room was clean, in immaculate order, save for the fat man's bed sheets and the pool of blood dripping down the mattress, coagulating on the tile floor.

Three seconds later, the boot sequence began. He could feel the fingers move, one by one, squishing inside of the man's gut. He could hear the servos move to twist the wrist. The elbow tried to move through its sequence, the gears of the hydraulic pump clacking as the corpse's flesh resisted the movement.

Finally the arm was free, the joints moved freely. With a panicked burst, Yasef withdrew his hand from the man's stomach, a tangle of shredded intestines wrapped around his fingers, dripping with feces.

"Ahh, rike this…" Yasef muttered, shaking out the hand to relieve it of some of the residue. Without warning, the smell assaulted him, and he nearly threw up on the floor. Yasef waved off the body, abandoning the dagger.

He stepped into the closet, crouching to find the access panel.

• • •

Six months later, a man with a mechanical arm kneeled in the desert. He stood a head taller than most Journeyman. He wore a honey-brown leather coat, battle-scarred. Next to his scimitar, a pistol hung on his belt, and two swords, stained in blood, were strapped to his back.

He knelt before a group of boys, eight of them on this day. The boys had dark hair and colored eyes, just like the man. Their young eyes carried pain like iron shackles, and their feet were sore from running a half day from the Kosmoan capital.

Behind the man stood twelve stones. Though they did not bear a single mark, they told a story. The desert man, the deliverer, removed his rebreather, then his goggles and began to speak.

"Do you remember when the sun stood still…" and as Yasef told the stories, he looked into their eyes, each one, and imagined he could see a spark of hope.

Find the story of Ehud in Judges chapter 3.

The Bramble King
Megan Flahive

The tavern in Waseya was louder than normal tonight—even now, after the midnight hour had long since gone and all the regulars had retired to their beds or slumped into corner tables with the last sip of whiskey slowly trickling out of their tipped glasses.

No one cared about this corner of Covenant. Waseya was a forgotten, one-street town at the foothills of the Black Mountains, not even a place in town to sacrifice to any of the gods, if you were practicing. It was a pass-through place, filled with pass-through people just biding their time.

Which was exactly why Jordan was here, sitting at this card table. It was close—too close for comfort—to where his brother, Rian, had his headquarters, but if Jordan didn't stock up now, he'd die out in The Wastes. And, if he was honest, he really was here for news. He listened to the men griping around the card table but kept his mouth shut and his head down. He knew he shouldn't be here, but curiosity got the better of him. Three years had passed since the incident, but people might still remember his face, and that would be a problem. But he had to know. He had to know what happened after he left. And he had to do *something* to wipe his slate clean. Jordan tipped the brim of his hat lower and buried his chin in the scrap of fabric he used to cover his nose and mouth during dust storms.

He was still young—it was close to his nineteenth birthday—but the dry air and guilt had changed his face, digging new grooves into his forehead and setting his mouth permanently downward. He'd styled himself with the rough and dirty leather gear of the Desperados and grown his beard out into a matted clump, a rusty saber at his side. He didn't speak when he came into the tavern and no one paid him any mind, just as he wanted. But if someone took the time to look past the hard angles, thin frame, and jutting cheekbones, they could see the same auburn hair and dark eyes that graced his brother's features too. The same brother the whole bar was now cursing with each new glass.

"Rian is a kosriking roach if I ever met one!" the gravely voice floated over the card table, crescendoing over the general din of the tavern. The man slammed his cards down on the sticky table and knocked back the rest of his drink. He was dressed in dusty leathers, threadbare around the elbows and cuffs, patched in places and shabby. "He brings his crew in here and kills anyone that speaks out against him—and what for? To crawl back to his high and mighty compound up in the Black Mountains and abandon us here to rot?"

"What are you gonna do about it, Gage?" said his companion in a squeaky voice. "You think a snipe like you is any better?"

"You're kosriking right I am! At least I'm *from* this here town. If I ran things, we'd get those Kosmoans to mind us and pay us fair for what we got."

"Ha! And what is it exactly that we *got*? I ain't seen nothing but dust and death since I got here."

The one called Gage ran his hands through his dirty blond hair. "I got my connections with the Order. We get in with them, and we're set for life. Besides," he gestured around. "Me and mine are the ones who actually run this town and everything in it. You think Rian and his guys got anything on us? I hear his crew is tired of doing his dirty work anyway."

"You're all talk," Gage's companion scoffed. "One," he said to the dealer, who slid a card across the table.

Jordan stared intently at the cards in his hands: a straight flush that could win him this game and the huge pot piling up in the center. He tapped the gummy surface of the table and traded out one of his cards for a worse one. No need to draw attention—not yet, anyway. If he could hold his own for another hour or so, there was a chance everyone would be too drunk to notice if he won or if he just plain took from the winnings. He hadn't contributed much to the pile—a few pelts he'd scavenged and some rusty pieces of broke-down re-breathers unearthed from the dust. But there were also piles of jerky, some loaves of bread, and even a plasma-knife. It wasn't functional, but Jordan knew he could fix it. His stomach grumbled at the thought of that jerky, too—what he wouldn't give for a full belly or something better than his rusty saber out in The Wastes against the sand-rats.

With a sinking thought, Jordan knew he was just like these men here: all smoke and no fire. Like them, he held no love for his eldest brother. He couldn't. Not after—

BANG.

Jordan almost jumped out of his skin.

"Kosrike you! Put that away!" Gage shouted at one of his men who had dropped his lite-pistol as he shoved around the crowd at the bar.

"Sorry, boss. It's bugging out," the man said, his words slurring.

Gage shook his head, and the rest of the table went back to their game.

Jordan decided to fold and clutched his mug tight to hide the shaking in his hands. It had been three years, but the sound of gunfire never got more familiar.

His head pounded with the memory of that day.

By the time the whole household was gathered in the courtyard, he'd already gotten a black eye and a split lip for being mouthy, saying Rian was a roach, a nub, a thorn, a weed. He was young then, and brash, desperate to prove he was brave and unafraid. Rian was the eldest, gone from the house before Jordan had even learned to walk, and only related through their father. Rian had lined up all the brothers, all seven of them, and marched them outside at gunpoint while he cleared the rest of the house. Jordan watched as his second-oldest brother stood before Rian with his hands bound, trying to bargain for the lives of his siblings.

Bang.

The body crumpled to the ground.

Jordan's mouth hung open at the sight of his brother's limp form, unable to process what he was seeing, ears ringing with the echo of the gunfire.

Bang.

A pile was starting as another brother, hands tied, fell on top of the other.

Bang.

Another. The blood was pooling now, running down the stone walkway in scarlet rivulets.

There was an eerie silence in the courtyard. No screaming; the household staff too scared or shocked to make a sound, most of their number culled that morning when Rian had stormed in.

Jordan should have known his errant brother—*half* brother, to be specific—would try to take out any potential competition for his father's estate. His blood boiled. He felt so stupid and helpless. He should do something. He should try to tackle the gun out of Rian's hand. Jordan was a foot shorter and not half as muscular, but with the element of surprise, surely he could help the rest of his siblings escape, right? His feet were rooted to the ground. This was it. He was going to die today. Nausea and fear roiled in his gut as he watched the pool of his brothers' blood grow and glint under the merciless sun. Jordan's hands shook, and a trickle of sweat raced down his back, adrenaline thrumming through his veins, and his heart seemed lodged in his throat.

He was just about to lunge when his middle brother leaned over and whispered in his ear, "When I make a scene, run." Jordan barely had a second to understand what he was saying before his brother pushed him out of the way and onto the ground, throwing elbows into the faces of the two men holding them at gunpoint and then running at Rian. The other gunmen rushed toward him, and the household staff exploded in screams at the commotion.

Stunned, panic cleared his mind of anything other than what his brother had just ordered him to do: *run.*

Jordan scrambled to get his feet under him and stumbled toward the now churning crowd of staff, dazed but following his brother's direction. A girl with ash-blond hair and dressed in a plain brown cotton dress beckoned to him. "Go! Run out through the kitchens and don't look back." She fixed her hazel eyes on him. "May Donumdonair bless you and keep you." And with that, she shoved him through the door, and the crowd reformed around the space he left.

He heard another *bang* as he weaved through the rooms of the house, slipping on the smears of blood left on the tile from that morning's raid. He burst through the back door out onto the desert plain. His legs and lungs burned. *Run. Run. Run.*

His brother's voice in his head chanted over and over.

Run. Run. RUN.

Wheezing, he saw a boarded-up well in the distance near the foothills. If he could just get there…

Bang.

Jordan pushed his already seizing lungs into a sprint for the last few yards and jumped into the dark hole blindly. His feet hit the muddy earth, and he made himself as small as possible in the darkness, his heart pounding in his ears and his breath coming in wheezy gasps.

Bang.

The shot echoed across the empty plain, and Jordan bit into his hand to keep from screaming.

Night fell, and there were no more shots, and Jordan allowed the shame to fully swallow him.

"Call," Gage said, shaking Jordan from his memories. One by one, around the table they put down their hands, ending with Gage proudly displaying his four-of-a-kind.

"Mind dealing me in?" said a tall, muscular man Jordan had seen hovering at the bar. He had sidled over almost imperceptibly as the hand was finishing. His clothes were nice, almost too nice for a place like Waseya, and his features were obscured by a hat and scarf around his neck. His thick, red beard, the part you could see, was neat and oiled, though, and he smelled not of stale liquor and sweat like the rest of the men in the bar but of some kind of cologne. He was too rich for this town—out of place among the rabble that called Waseya 'home-for-now.'

Gage's face became guarded but inquisitive. "Sure, stranger." He nodded to the dealer and continued to examine the man. "I ain't seen you before. You new here?"

"Ain't been here before," the stranger said, lowering his scarf to take a sip from his glass. "Stopping in for a supply run."

Gage laughed. "That's most of these snipes around here," he motioned to the rest of the table. "If you're seeking something in particular, me and my men can get you what you need."

"Mighty kind of you," the man said. "Where y'all get your supplies from? Ossia?"

Gage tsked. "They ain't done nothing for us. All this is set up by me and my boys."

"Oh yeah? You got a nice operation here then."

"That's what I'm saying!" Gage grinned and elbowed his companion. He snapped his fingers at the bartender. "Two more for me and my new friend here!"

The cards were dealt, and the players all shuffled their hands and placed their bets. Jordan nervously calculated how much more he could throw in. He was running out of scraps to bargain, and this new player put a wrench in his plan of taking the winnings when the rest of the players passed out from their drinks.

45

"Well, tell me your story," Gage said to the new player as they all traded out cards. "Why are you stopping here of all places?"

"Like I said, supply run. The Order's got me running shipments between their towns because I ain't scared of what'll kill ya out in The Wastes." He pulled out a plasma-knife, and the whole bar stilled. "This works just as good on the hide of a sand-rat or a Desperado." A toothy smirk spread across the man's face before he turned to Jordan and said, "No offense meant."

Jordan went stone-still and held his breath, looking from the plasma-knife to the man brandishing it and then back to the knife.

Suddenly, Gage barked a laugh, and the spell was broken. The noise in the tavern resumed, and Jordan sucked in a shaky breath. "Aw, he don't speak none, you won't get a rise outta him. You're a vicious one, I'll give you that... I think I like you, friend."

"Say, y'all got this operation here, but I was told Rian ran this town...that true?" the man asked, tucking his plasma-knife away into the recesses of his leather duster.

Gage's face screwed up, but before he could answer, there was a commotion from upstairs as a door slammed open, and a girl in a torn dress stumbled out, dark blond hair covering her face in a stringy curtain. Jordan saw she was bleeding from her lip as she stumbled down the stairs and toward the bar. A man exited the room behind her, zipping up his pants and spitting after her.

The tavern patrons paid the commotion no mind. Only Jordan and the strange man followed her with their eyes. She ducked into the kitchen before Jordan could get a good look at her, the bartender following close behind.

The stranger spoke up. "She work here too? I thought this was a

Journeymen city. I thought y'all's god didn't take kindly to whoring."

"Oh, her? Rian has her working here. Insulted him. Can't remember her name, though... You know it?" Gage asked the man to his right, who was too drunk to respond. "Any case, she's been 'round here since he took over the crew from his dad, Farrell—you know Farrell?"

The stranger nodded. "I've heard of him."

"Well, when he was running things, it was good around here. Business was booming, land of plenty. I swear there was less dust, too!" Gage laughed. "Well, you know what happened when Farrell died."

"Rian ain't even Farrell's real kin," slurred the drunk to Gage's right, cheeks red and eyes half-closed.

"That right?" the stranger said. "Is he not a Journeymen like you?"

Gage scoffed. "His mother was from Ossia, and that's the only reason he got their support when Farrell died."

"Only a halfer," mumbled the red-cheeked man, who laid his head down on the table and proceeded to snore.

"So, what'd she do if he has her working?" the stranger asked, motioning to the girl, who had emerged from behind the bar to dab at her split lip with a handkerchief.

"Heh, know what she did?" Gage grinned. "Called him a whore's son to his face! So he cut off her feet so she couldn't run and made her a whore like she said his mother was."

All of a sudden, the memory slammed into place for Jordan. The hair was longer and darker, but he remembered who she was now: she was the girl who worked on the estate as a maid. She was the one who had told him to run through the kitchens.

The one who had saved him.

He looked up from the cards in his hands and toward the girl now climbing the stage in the middle of the tavern and turning up the volume on the rusty speaker in the corner.

Metal flashed out from beneath her swishing skirts—Jordan couldn't see much of it, but the steel looked dull and rusty, ill-fitting if her gait had anything to say about it. Rian had cut her off at the ankles...and Jordan didn't have a single scratch on him.

She saved him, and he had nothing to show for it. His brothers were still dead, Rian was still alive, and Jordan was...well, he was just here surviving when he had no right to be.

No other shot had rang out that night when Jordan hid in the well, but later, when the moon was at its peak, he'd had to cover his ears at the high, keening scream that reached him across the plains—clear as a bell even all the way down in that pit.

The same voice that was now crooning a ballad up on the stage.

Guilt, shame, and revulsion bubbled up in Jordan's throat and soured his gut.

She saved him. She saved him, and her feet were cut off for it. Sunken cheeks and protruding collarbones mottled green and purple confirmed Jordan's worst suspicions of what her life was like here.

She swayed back and forth with the music, her eyes closed, and finally opened her mouth to sing:

The trees came down from mounts o'er yonder
Seeking out a nobler seed.
Far and wide, they sought their victor
One to counsel, judge, and lead.

The girl had a lovely voice, though it was hard to hear her over the general drunken din. Several patrons hummed along, off-key but smiling in their stupor.

Gage turned back to the table, grumbling. "Rian ain't done nothing for us here. Ain't even got us good women. Hey!" He snapped again to the bartender. "Drinks on me for any man here that will stand with me against Rian!"

The bar exploded in drunken cheers, potential loyalties thrown to the wind at the prospect of free libations. The bartender brought over a bottle of whiskey and filled their glasses. Jordan raised his glass half-heartedly and removed his scarf to take a sip, though his stomach roiled. The burn of the liquor coated his throat and made his nose itch.

First, they asked the olive noble,
"Why do not you be our king?"
Answered Olive, "Not my calling,
For honor gods with oil I bring."

Next, they asked the pretty fig tree,
With its goodly yield to eat,
"Nay," she said with great derision,
"Why sacrifice my fruit so sweet?"

Then, the trees they asked the vineyard,
Joyous bounty o'er its bough.
But the vine denied them also.
"Cheer I bring already now."

Jordan watched the girl sway with her song as the game progressed and the chorus repeated. He looked around the table. Gage was now glassy-eyed and squinting up at the girl on the stage, taking in her torn dress and metal feet.

The stranger was oddly sober, taking in his drunken companions with searching eyes. Jordan would have to tread carefully around this one.

So they asked the lowly bramble,
Gladly he did take them in
"Take your refuge in my shade here,
Mind you not my thorny skin."

Oh trees, oh trees, keep that you care,
Your Bramble King, here lies a snare
For windy plains do make air drier
You will be burnt by Bramble's fire.

With the final verse, the girl met Jordan's eyes with an unblinking, hazel-eyed stare, and he felt the blood drain from his face.

She knew who he was—through the beard and the clothes and the time, she knew who he was.

Panic slicked his palms and deafened his ears with the thumping of his heart. He had to get out of here—

NO. He would not run again. He *couldn't* run again. He would have to save her, right? *Could* he save her? He had no money or food—that was why he came here in the first place.

Jordan's panic didn't end as her eyes flitted away, and another song began. His thoughts raced. Would she tell anyone who he was? If he had to guess, it was less than an hour or so until sunrise. Maybe he could make it out of town with supplies while the rest of the bar was sleeping off their hangovers—NO. That would be running. *Again.* Jordan felt the gnaw of shame consume his insides. *Coward, coward, coward,* a voice chanted through his mind. *Always running. Useless. COWARD.* His mind spun, and he felt the bile crawl up his throat.

The game ended with the stranger winning the hand. Jordan was too distracted to play well, so he had folded early on, nursing his drink as he watched the rest of the game unfold, pretending not to understand the conversation around him.

Gage stretched his arms above his head, "One more round, friend. Best two of three?" He leaned back, balancing on the back legs of his chair, and stared out the window as the dealer shuffled. Jordan saw him squint. "You see those lights on the mountain?"

The stranger craned his head to look out the window as well. "Probably just fireflies."

Gage rubbed his eyes and shook his head. "I should stop drinkin'…"

"So, you think you could take this town from Rian?" the stranger asked. "Sounds like you might have the men to do it."

Gage scoffed as he picked up his cards. "I don't just think I can. I know it." He turned and gestured to the bar patrons. "Every single person in this town is loyal to *me*. Not that bastard son holed up in Ossia. He ain't even come here personally since he laid claim to it three years ago. Just letting it rot away."

"What would you do if you ran things?"

"I got people in the Order that owe me favors," Gage winked and tapped the side of his pointed nose. "We get them in here, and I'd make this place like it was when Farrell was running his outfit. Those Kosmoans got deep pockets, you know?"

The stranger arranged the cards in his hand. "You'd have them take care of Rian for you?"

"Naw, friend, they're just the coin once we clear out the riffraff. Me and my guys, we could handle him no problem." Gage knocked back the last of the brown liquid in his glass and slammed it down on the table, startling his snoring companion awake. "I tell ya, I wish he'd come here now, and we'd show him he ain't gonna control us anymore."

The man smiled and poured more whiskey into Gage's glass. "I'd like to see that."

Gage sipped from his newly filled glass and glanced out the window again. "Say, it look like them fireflies is gettin' closer?"

At that moment, the door to the tavern burst open, and one of Gage's men stumbled through, blood pouring from a deep wound in his chest.

"It's Rian's men! They're comin', boss! They say he's comin' for you," the man gasped.

Gage's mouth opened and closed like a fish out of water as chairs scraped across the wooden floor, everyone in the bar stumbling to attention and shaking passed-out companions.

The stranger laid down his cards and folded his hands, meeting Gage's eyes with a calm stare. "Well, here's your chance. Go out and show everyone who runs this town."

Gage sputtered. "What did you say your name was?"

A slow smile crept along the strange man's face. "I didn't. But I'm surprised you wouldn't have recognized me."

"Rian?" Gage whispered, the color draining from his face.

Quick as lightning, Rian whipped out the plasma-knife hidden in the folds of his leather duster and brought it down on Gage's hand, pinning him to the table. Everyone at the table shot back in their chairs as Gage screamed in agony. Rian bared his teeth, removing his hat to reveal the permanent frown etched into his forehead and his auburn hair. Auburn hair just like Jordan's.

"Where's that mouth of yours now, *friend?*" Rian ground out between his teeth. "You wanted a fight—*so fight.*" Slowly, he fixed his eyes on Jordan, who sat open-mouthed next to him. "You plan to stick around this time, *baby brother?*"

The room exploded into movement, and the tinny speaker continued to play, tinkling notes underlying the chaos of bodies pushing to escape from the tavern. Men rushed the door only to be met with whoops and shouts and the sharp edges of knives as they tried to cross the threshold.

Rian's men were right outside the door.

Jordan scrambled from his chair, heart pounding. It was *Rian.* It was Rian all along.

And he'd known who he was this whole time.

There were no thoughts in his head now, only instinct. He had to get out. He had to find an exit. Bodies crushed around him, shoving him out of the way in their rush to escape through windows, through back rooms, from second-floor balconies—any way but out the front where Rian's men waited with torches in hand and guns and knives at the ready.

Jordan felt a hand grip his arm and pull him into a back hallway. He turned towards the hand to find the girl staring him in the eyes. She searched his eyes to confirm his identity, and he gave her a small nod in reply. They tucked themselves behind a door and peered through the slit in the door frame.

An uncanny silence had fallen on the tavern now. Only a few of Gage's men remained, all held at gunpoint by Rian's men, who held lite-pistols aimed at their heads. Rian surveyed the room of overturned chairs and broken bottles and landed on Gage, sweating and struggling and still pinned to the table.

"You want this nub of a town? Go ahead and take it…if you can," he said, resting his hand on the plasma-knife still pinning Gage's hand. Rian looked around to survey the room and then turned to one of his men, "Lock the doors. Burn it all." With that, he strode out of the tavern.

Rian's crew knocked out Gage's few followers. They smashed the bottles of alcohol from behind the bar, then lit a match and dropped it on the shattered glass bottles. Heat billowed out from the main room as the flames quickly spread, blocking the exits. The girl clutched Jordan's hand and pulled him down the hall. They rushed up a back staircase as the sounds of Gage's panicked screams reached their ears. The stairs switched back and forth before they burst out on the flat rooftop under the brightening dawn sky.

She dragged him to the edge of the roof, and Jordan took in the rest of Waseya. Building by building, Rian's men were setting fire to the town. Families clutched their babies and valuables to their chests as they escaped their burning homes, sobs echoing out across the plain. Rian's men herded them into a line in the middle of the street, lite-pistols and plasma-knives trained on them.

Rian stood by the barricaded door of the tavern below them. Fire glowed from the windows and smoke poured from under the doorjamb. He held a hand up to the cowering people in the streets. "Hear tell that you want a new someone to come to your aid when Desperados come raiding, or the sand-rats ravage your livestock? Well, you don't have to worry about that anymore...because there won't be any of you or this kosriking town left after tonight." He turned to one of his men behind him. "Kill them all," he said.

Jordan looked at the girl with him. Her face had paled as the screams of families rang out over the pre-dawn plain. Rian paused on the dusty dirt road that ran through the middle of the town. "I know you're here somewhere, Jordan," he said in a booming voice above the shouts behind him. "You think I wouldn't recognize my own kin at a table with me?"

Jordan felt the blood drain from his head.

"You can't run from me every time. I didn't see where you scurried off to, but I *will* find you," Rian said. "Come out and meet me like a man, or I will burn down every town in my way!"

Jordan was shaking, every nerve in his body telling him simultaneously to run away forever or to get it over with and accept the death that waited for him.

He had to do *something, anything*. But what could he do? They were on the roof of a burning building, and his brother was *right there*, looking for him.

He looked to the girl at his side and saw the set of her face turn from panic to anger. She frantically looked around them on the rooftop, the sounds of screams coming from below as Rian's crew began slaughtering the families of Waseya. Suddenly, she stilled, staring at the stone cornice in front of them. Jordan saw her eyes dart from Rian below them, back to the stone, and then back down again.

This was it. This was his chance. *This* was something he could do.

He put a hand on her arm and nodded, understanding passing between them wordlessly.

Jordan ducked a bit behind the edge of the roof so no one could tell where his voice came from. "Rian!" he yelled into the night. "I'm here!"

The noise on the street stopped momentarily as the men below tried to discern where the voice was coming from.

"Come on out, baby brother," Rian crooned. "We both know how this is gonna end."

Jordan took a deep, shaky breath and stood up fully, making himself visible over the roof edge. "Come and get me first, and then we'll see."

A vicious smile grew across Rian's face, and he approached the smoking tavern. "Only one way down...or are you gonna try and run? *Again?*"

Jordan felt the blood rushing in his ears with anger and fear. *He had to get Rian closer.* "No running. We finish it."

Rian walked closer. "And how do you plan on doing that from up there?"

One more step. "Come closer, and I'll tell you."

Rian finally stepped onto the porch of the burning tavern—right below the stone cornice. Jordan nodded, and the girl threw her full body weight into the stone. With a single push, she tipped it over the side...

Jordan heard the sickening crunch as the cornice met its target, and they both peered over the edge to see his brother clutching his head. Blood was pouring from the wound as Rian staggered away, peering up through the fountain of blood running down his face. His eyes widened as he met the eyes of the girl, a dry wind rustled her skirts and exposed her metallic feet.

One of the crew rushed to his side. Rian grabbed a fistful of his shirt, pulling him close. "Shoot me! Do it! I won't let them say a woman killed me!" He shoved his lite-pistol into the man's hands and put the barrel to his already bleeding forehead.

Bang.

The shot echoed in the creeping dawn, silencing the screams of the massacre at hand and stopping the slaughter.

Everyone stared at Rian's body where it lay, the pool of blood spreading from his lifeless form.

Ten seconds went by... Twenty.

After thirty, Rian's crew member stepped off the porch, turning to the rest of the men. "Move out." They followed in silence. The only sound the crackling fires of the buildings still ablaze.

As the men left the town, Jordan and the girl climbed down an old fire escape in the back of the building. They came into the street to watch the bandits go, standing with their backs to one of the few unburnt buildings still standing.

When the men were only specks on the horizon, Jordan sank down and leaned back against the building, head in his hands.

"'Vengeance is mine,' says Donumdonair, 'and recompense,'" the girl whispered. "'For the time when their foot shall slip...'"

Jordan finished the saying, squinting at the sun peeking over the horizon. "'For the day of their calamity is at hand, and their doom comes swiftly.'"

Find the story of Abimelech in Judges 9.

The Voice Within
Thirzah

"MARSHAL!"

Eliana looked up from her stack of papers as the door to Heylin's old-saloon-turned-courtroom burst open. The door slammed against the wooden wall, releasing a cloud of dirt and dust into the air as a man stormed into the room, dragging something—or someone—behind him.

The man looked straight at Eliana, who raised her chin and squared her shoulders. A wide-brimmed leather hat sat jauntily tipped back from her forehead, but her cotton dress was nicely pressed, a rare hybrid species of rugged survivalist and elegant lady only bred in the outskirts of Covenant.

The man's steel-toed boots thumped against the cedar wood floor as he approached. "You're the town's marshal, aren't you?" he shouted. A red bandana hid the collar of the man's denim shirt, which was stained with sweat.

Nathan, a retired beast hunter and now bailiff, stepped in front of the mahogany bar-counter serving as Eliana's desk. His chapped lips pressed in a line mirroring those on his forehead. He wiped his calloused right hand on his leather vest and then placed it over his sword's hilt as the man dragged his victim down the aisle toward Eliana. "Karson Dirge, what is the meaning of this?" Nathan called out.

The bailiff nodded to the crowd of around fifty people sitting in narrow makeshift rows of rickety wooden chairs and upside down crates on either side of the spacious room. "We're in the middle of a session to discuss the drought. If you have a complaint for Marshal Eliana then you can wait your—"

"Rike your session, and rike the drought!" Karson sneered. "This son-of-a-roach murdered my sister!" Karson yanked the man he was dragging forward. The man stumbled and groaned, collapsing in a heap at Nathan's feet.

The crowd broke out into murmurs and whispers as the man on the ground moaned in pain. Eliana wiped a few beads of sweat from her brow, setting the small stack of papers she had been using to fan herself with down on her desk. She stood to her feet, holding up a hand to silence the murmuring crowd.

"Nathan, please step aside," Eliana told her bailiff.

Nathan glanced back. He obeyed the command with a nod, and Eliana's eyes fell on the young man Karson had dragged into the courtroom. His right eye was bruised purple and swollen shut. His overalls were torn to shreds, arms and legs littered with cuts, scrapes, and bruises. Parts of his blond hair were dyed pink by his own blood.

Eliana's stomach churned as the metallic scent of blood invaded her nostrils. She looked up at Karson. He had dark hair, sun-bronzed skin, and a muscular build—unsurprising by the way he had dragged the other man into the courtroom. "You seem to have already doled out punishment on this man yourself, so why bother coming to me at all?"

Karson glanced down at the beaten man on the ground, then looked up at Eliana. "You've got it all wrong, Marshal. I didn't do this to him!" He looked at the man again. "Not most of it, anyway... Just the eye and a couple of scrapes—but that's not the point." Karson clenched his jaw as his brow lowered. "He let Kara—my sister—be murdered!"

Eliana frowned. "What do you mean he let—"

"No!" The blond-haired man dragged himself to an upright position. Tears rolled down his swollen cheeks. "I didn't, I—I tried to stop them!"

"You didn't try hard enough!" Karson snapped.

Eliana slammed her hand down on the bar counter. All eyes turned to her as she rubbed her stinging hand. "That's quite enough, Mr. Dirge." Her leather boots clipped against the wooden floor as she walked around to the front of the bar, approaching the two men. She swept her arm out to the side, glancing at the old empty whiskey barrels, small card tables, and out-of-tune upright piano on the back left side of the room—lingering reminders of the building's former purpose. "This is a courtroom now, not a tavern," Eliana said. "What I need right now is a clear explanation, not anger."

Wood scraped against wood as Nathan dragged two empty wooden chairs over from the front row, placing them behind the two men.

Eliana nodded her thanks before turning her attention back to the men. "Have a seat, and we'll begin. First, what are your names and occupations?"

Karson frowned, sitting down with a thump. "My name is Karson

Dirge. I'm a beast hunter." He nodded at Nathan. "He knows, so he can vouch for my character."

Eliana raised an eyebrow at Nathan, who shrugged. "Karson used to be a student of mine," Nathan explained. "He's hot-tempered and has a mouth unfit to kiss his mother with, but he's sensible when the occasion calls for it."

"I see." Eliana leaned back against the bar counter as her attention turned to the bruised and beaten man next to Karson. "And you are?"

The man stared at his blood-covered hands. "I'm...my name is Finn Lorin. I'm a farmer...I grow crops."

Eliana nodded. "Mr. Lorin, could you explain your side of what happened? Karson said you have something to do with the death of his sister."

Finn's head jerked up, his eyes wide and wild as a sand-rat. "It's not true! I love Kara—I'd give my life for her!"

Eliana frowned, her chest tightening as she spoke. "What happened to Kara, Mr. Lorin?"

Finn let out a deep breath, looking up. "It was just like any other morning... I went down to the fields to check on our crops. Thanks to the drought, I've had to use most of my water rations to try to keep them alive. And since things have been so rough lately, I left my lunch behind, so Kara, she'd..." He hung his head. "No...Karson is right... It really is my fault." Finn stared at his lap. He played with his hands, rubbing his thumb over his knuckles as he continued. "Kara and me got married a couple months ago, and sometimes I 'accidentally' leave my lunch behind so she'd have to come down to the fields and bring it to me. We'd always talk for a bit and, well, you know...and then she'd go back to the house." He swallowed hard.

"But today, while she and I were...together, we heard a hovercraft heading our way."

Eliana's stomach dropped. "A hovercraft?"

"Yeah, three of them," Finn spat. "Silver, each with an hourglass engraved on the side and shiny enough to make a man blind just by taking a peek at 'em."

Eliana's hands shook, so she clasped them together. "Kosmoans."

Finn nodded. "They stopped their hovercrafts and offered to buy Kara from me."

"The nerve of those conniving snipes!" Karson roared.

The crowd murmured in agreement. Anger rolled into the court-room like a thick fog, resting on each of the occupants, including Eliana. Her lips trembled as she forced her expression to stay neutral, her gaze focused on Finn's beaten and tear-streaked face. "And...what did you do?"

Finn scowled. "I pulled her close to me and informed them that Kara is *my wife*—that I love her and she's not for sale!"

Eliana nodded, brushing a few frizzy strands of hair behind her ear. "How did they respond?"

Finn shook his head, venom in his voice. "They...laughed. They told me I was selfish—possessive even. They called me and all Journeymen primitive for 'indulging in foolish nonsense.' Then one of them said that I should reconsider their offer...because..." He gritted his teeth. "Because *Kosmoa* had demanded that they sacrifice the first woman they laid eyes on once their fast was over." The young man clenched his fists. "They said they'd be taking her either way, so I might as well hand her over willingly."

Eliana gulped down the fury bubbling up inside her, wiping more sweat from her brow with the cuff of her cotton dress. "What happened after that?"

"I refused," Finn said. "I told them they'd lost their senses and reached for my blaster." His gaze dropped to the floor. "But it...wasn't there. I forgot it, just like my lunch—but not on purpose."

Eliana pursed her lips. "I see," she said.

Finn winced. "But even so, I...I did have a whip with me. I always use it to chase pests off my fields, so I stepped in front of Kara and told the Kosmoans to leave." He shook his head. "I knew I didn't stand a chance against all three of them, but I tried...I—" Finn's voice broke. A couple of tears rolled down his swollen cheeks. He shuddered. "When I came to my senses...Kara was...she was gone."

Eliana lowered her voice, fighting against the tears that pricked at her own eyes. "I'm sure you did your best, Mr. Lorin," she said.

"Well, I'm not," Karson snapped. "His whole story is a load of nubatou!"

Nathan folded his scarred arms over his broad chest, his gray-blue eyes boring into the younger man's. "Karson, I must insist that you cease using such words in the presence of the marshal."

Karson pointed at Finn. "Didn't you hear him? This *nub* made my little sister leave the safety of their home to bring him his riking lunch because he can't keep his hands to himself for five riking minutes. Then of all the moronic things he could have done, he forgets his riking blaster and can't even manage to protect her! His stupidity killed my sister!"

Finn glared at Karson. "You don't know that! She could still be alive!"

Karson scoffed. "And you think that would be better than what the

Kosmoans do to all the women they steal from us?" he shook his head, clenching his teeth. "No…for my sister's sake, I hope she's already dead."

Eliana's face was hot, but whether it was from the weather, her anger, or both, she didn't know. A blurry image of a woman entered Eliana's mind. Wavy dark hair, dark eyes, and a bright smile—features that had been passed on to Eliana.

Twenty years before, Eliana's father had stood in Finn's place but had said something similar to Karson, and at eight years old, Eliana hadn't understood how he could wish that her own mother—his wife—was dead. But she understood now.

Eliana had heard this story, and many others like it over and over again—even before she became the town of Heylin's marshal two years earlier. And over and over again, she'd had to say the same thing to each of the victims' families. "Mr. Dirge," she began, "while your brother-in-law made several mistakes that led to the kidnapping of your sister, it is the Kosmoans who should bear the blame in this situation."

Karson shot to his feet, slapping his palm to his chest. "But don't I deserve justice? Doesn't my *sister* deserve justice? Her snipe of a husband couldn't protect her. Shouldn't that call for *some* sort of punishment? Shouldn't *something* be done?"

"Yes, but not to your sister's husband—" As Eliana spoke, thoughts invaded her mind. *Karson is ready and willing to fight. He will lead the Journeymen to battle against the Kosmoans. Now is the time.*

Eliana pushed herself off the bar counter, staring at Karson. "Mr. Dirge, why don't you turn your attention to the real culprits?"

Karson stepped back, bumping into his chair. He frowned at Eliana. "Is that a joke? Because it's not funny."

"It's not a joke." Eliana looked around the room at the spectators. Anger, fear, sadness, regret, guilt. She saw it all reflected on their faces as they watched her from their seats in the rows on either side of the room.

"Donumdonair has spoken to me, and the time is now," Eliana said. "We were children when the Kosmoans started using their god as an excuse to take everything we own, but their actions have only grown more despicable since."

Some members of the crowd nodded their heads, shifting in their seats. Others murmured to each other or stared at Eliana.

Eliana's voice shook as the storm of emotions threatened to escape from her lips. "We may be weak and scattered, but in many ways, we're more united than we've been in a long time—because all of us can agree on this one fact. No longer will we watch as our families, crops, livestock—our livelihoods—are stolen from us."

The crowd shouted in agreement. One man near the back shot to his feet. "That's right!" he yelled.

Eliana ignored them, allowing the words and feelings she'd kept in for years to spill out of her mouth and into the courtroom, filling the air with her anger and feeding the crowd's anticipation. "No more will we beg on our knees to be spared or weep for the loss of our loved ones," Eliana said, stepping back toward her desk. "There are many Kosmoans—that is true. And their technology is more advanced than ours." She slammed the palm of her hand on the bar counter, "But Donumdonair is on *our* side, and we *will* have victory over the Kosmoans!"

The courtroom erupted into roars and cheers. People hollered and stomped their feet as Eliana turned to Karson. "Donumdonair has been calling you to battle for some time, Karson Dirge. Will you answer the call and defeat our enemies, or will you continue to lash out at your own people?"

Karson stared at Eliana. "Are you saying…you want me to lead the Journeymen into battle?"

She tilted her head to the side. "Will you do it?"

"Yeah," he spoke without hesitation as if the words had already been planted and growing on his tongue. "I will."

A smile formed on Eliana's lips. She leaned back against the wooden bar counter as the cheers grew louder and the people stood and clapped.

Karson held up his hands and shook his head. "Like I said, I'll lead our people into battle, but even if Donumdonair is on our side, it doesn't change the fact that they have hovercrafts and upgraded blasters while we have nub," he said, silencing the cheers. "We can't hope to beat our enemy with a couple of rusty blasters and a few measly whips." Karson cast a glance at Finn, who winced and looked away. "All of you have families and friends you want to protect, so even if you don't know which end a blaster shoots from, we need your help."

"How can we help?" an elderly woman in the front row asked.

"Food and water rations, weapons, bring whatever you can get to the courthouse—" Karson glanced at Eliana. "If that's all right with you, of course."

Eliana nodded, hiding her smile behind firm, closed lips. "I can't think of a better location." She pointed to the right, toward the empty back wall. You can move some of the crates and chairs over to the left and store the supplies over there," she said. "And I'll help in any way I can."

"In that case, will you join us in battle?"

Eliana froze. "Excuse me?" She turned to look at the tall man.

Karson shrugged. "Don't get me wrong...I'm not expecting you to fight or anything; I was just thinking—in case something changes and Donumdonair speaks to you again."

As Karson spoke, Eliana's excitement morphed into panic. The Journeymen were finally going to fight against the Kosmoans, but the thoughts that had inspired this upcoming battle, had it really been Donumdonair's, or was it Eliana's own thoughts?

Nathan cleared his throat. "Karson, the marshal has plenty of work to do here in town."

"It'll just be for one battle. I'm sure the town can survive without her for a day," Karson said. "Besides...Donumdonair speaks to her, and he told her that now is the time to strike." He shook his head. "It'd be a mistake to leave her behind. Like I said, we'll need all the help we can get if we're going to defeat this army of roaches."

Eliana swallowed. "Donumdonair isn't going to change his mind," she said. "If he wants us to defeat the Kosmoans, we will—and no disadvantages are going to change that. But...I'll consider going into battle with you."

Karson nodded. "You should. Just about everyone in the city knows that Donumdonair speaks to you. If they hear you're going into battle, they'll be more likely to help our cause."

Eliana grimaced, glancing around the courtroom. Most of the crowd had left the building already, but a few small groups of people stood between the rows of chairs and crates, talking or moving the furniture to the left side of the room. "As I said, I'll consider it." She sighed. "Now, it seems I'm done for the day, so I'll return here tomorrow morning and give you my answer then."

"Very well...tomorrow it is."

. . .

"Mama, we're home!"

Eliana smiled, wiping her hands on her off-white apron as her son Damien burst into the kitchen, followed by her husband, Jayrin. "Welcome back," she said, bending over to hug the young boy. She sniffed the air and wrinkled her nose. "What is that smell?"

Damien giggled and stepped back. "There were baby pigs everywhere! Me and Rian helped catch them. It was fun."

Eliana looked Damien up and down, noting the stains on his clothes and the dirt covering his small face. "Ah, I see… It sounds like you worked hard today."

Jayrin chuckled, patting Damien on the shoulder. "He sure did. He managed to catch three of them all by himself."

Damien grinned. "Uh huh!"

Eliana shook her head. "Well, dinner's almost ready. Damien, why don't you change your clothes and wash up? Just be careful not to use too much water, all right?"

"Be right back!" Damien turned and ran past his father and out of the kitchen. A moment later, they heard wood creaking above them as Damien climbed the stairs.

Eliana laughed. "How he manages to have so much energy in all this heat is completely baffling to me," she said as Jayrin pulled her into an embrace.

"Mhmm."

They kissed before pulling away. Eliana smiled. "How was work?"

"Uneventful until a couple of hours ago."

"Oh?"

Jayrin grabbed a wooden stool from the corner of the room and sat down. "Thanks to the heat, the marketplace was practically deserted for most of the day, but then a fire broke out behind one of the shops. Luckily, there was minimal damage, and we put out the fire before it spread too far."

Eliana frowned. "What caused the fire?"

"A fuel can that the owner left out back in the sun. I can't blame it though. I was hot enough to catch fire myself today."

They laughed, and Jayrin continued. "But something pretty odd happened afterward. All of a sudden, droves of people started walking around, and they kept saying something about a war with the Kosmoans." Jayrin eyed Eliana. "You wouldn't happen to know what everyone's talking about, would you?"

Eliana cleared her throat, fiddling with the frayed ribbons holding her apron on. "That would be because we're finally going on the offensive. We're going to drive the Kosmoan army back into their own territory."

Jayrin crossed his arms. "We?"

"Karson Dirge will be leading the people into battle because I told him that Donumdonair said he should," the words left Eliana's mouth in a rush.

Jayrin frowned. "*Did* Donumdonair say that?"

Eliana swallowed hard, pursing her lips as her brows furrowed. "I was sure it was him at first—it *felt* like it was him. But then I thought about it, and this isn't the first time I've thought about fighting the Order. It's just the first time that I actually spoke out about it."

Jayrin's frown deepened. "Then what made this time any different?"

Eliana's mind flashed back to the courtroom. Finn's bloodied, beaten face and Karson's plea for justice. Memories of her father and mother. She turned to her husband, fists and teeth clenched. "I want the Kosmoans to *pay* for what they've done to us, Jayrin. Their selfish sacrifices and self-righteous smiles make me *sick*. I want all of them to suffer and burn—to be cut down by blades, shot with blasters, and trampled to death. I want them to feel pain. The same pain we feel when our crops, livestock, livelihoods, and families are stripped away from us—and I want to do the same to them." She let out a breath that shook her entire body, shutting her eyes. "And that's why I'm not sure if I heard Donumdonair's voice calling me to battle...or my own."

"I understand your anger, Eliana—and I feel it too. Every time Damien leaves the house—even if it's with one of us, part of me worries that we'll be set upon by Kosmoans," his words faltered, and he ran his hand through his hair. "That being said, I doubt it was Donumdonair's voice that you heard."

Eliana opened her eyes. "You do? Why?"

Jayrin stood. He stepped over, grabbing Eliana's hands in his. His hazel eyes drifted over her thin frame. "Ever since you took the position of marshal, you've been running yourself ragged to keep up with everything the townspeople have thrown at you. Do you even remember what tomorrow is?"

Eliana blinked. "Tomorrow? Well, I know it's not our anniversary since—" She stopped, stumbling back as the hazy memory of her mother's smile returned to her mind.

Jayrin steadied her, pulling her close.

Eliana clung to him, her vision blurring with tears. "How could I have forgotten?" she whispered.

"...You've been busy."

Eliana swallowed, leaning her head on his shoulder.

70

Jayrin nodded and rubbed her back. "You can't afford to let your personal feelings get in the way of your judgment. You need to call off the attack first thing tomorrow, before it's too late."

Eliana frowned, blinking back tears as she pulled back to look at him. "It's already too late, Jayrin. People have been dropping off supplies and weapons at the courthouse all day."

Jayrin shrugged. "Then tell them that Donumdonair changed his mind."

She stiffened, frown deepening. "But he didn't."

"Only because you made it up to begin with." Jayrin shook his head, sighing. "Eliana, you can't play with people's lives like this—"

"You weren't there, Jayrin!" Eliana snapped, pushing herself away from her husband. "You didn't see what I saw in the courtroom—you didn't feel what I felt!"

Jayrin narrowed his eyes, crossing his arms over his chest. "Anger, Eliana. What you felt was anger toward the Kosmoans, which clouded your judgment and caused you to give in to your feelings. But we can't go to war over anger."

"But what if Donumdonair is angry too?" she bit back.

"What?"

Eliana clenched handfuls of apron fabric in her fists, looking up at her husband. "Donumdonair *sees* what's been happening here, Jayrin. He sees how the Kosmoans steal and plunder from us in the name of their *god*. So what if he's angry too?"

Jayrin frowned. "Even if he *is* angry, it doesn't mean that Donumdonair told you that we should go to war against the Kosmoans." He sighed, running a hand through his thick, dark hair. "Look, Eliana, you and I both know that this has always been a difficult time of year for you. But you're Heylin's marshal. You can't make decisions like this based on emotions. You should know that better than anyone else."

Frustration bubbled up within Eliana like boiling water. "But if I'm right? What if Donumdonair *did* tell me that we should wage war against the Kosmoans?"

"Eliana, he didn't!" Jayrin scowled. "Listen to me, you need to—" He stopped as the stairs above them creaked, and as they turned toward the doorway, Damien bounded into the kitchen, grinning his missing-front-teeth smile. "I'm hungry! Can we eat now?"

Eliana forced her lips into a smile, relaxing her stiff shoulders. "Of course! Let's eat." She glanced at Jayrin, who gave her a nod.

• • •

"So, have you made your decision?"

Eliana pursed her lips, but nodded. "I'll be joining you on the battlefield, Captain Karson."

Sitting across from her at the bar counter in a tall wooden chair, Nathan raised an eyebrow. "And Jayrin approved of it?"

Eliana smiled. "More or less." She sighed.

Nathan hummed. His gray-blue eyes seemed to look right into Eliana's thoughts. "I see."

Eliana averted her gaze, glancing around the room. Overnight, the courtroom had changed into a war station. The chairs had been moved to the left side of the courtroom to clear space for people to walk in and out of the building. All the crates had been moved to the right side of the room and had been filled with swords, lite-guns, and all sorts of other weapons that the townspeople had collected for the battle ahead.

Karson followed her gaze and grinned. "If there's one thing we won't lack in this fight, it's firepower."

Nathan nodded. "Weapons are good, but what about spacecrafts? That's what we really need if we're going to have a chance against the Kosmoans."

Karson leaned back, his tall wooden chair creaking beneath his weight. "We managed to scrounge up around fifty of them. Not all of them are in shape to fly though, so we'll have to hold off our attack."

Eliana crossed her arms. "Hold off the attack? For how long?"

Karson frowned. "For at least another three days."

Eliana hummed, looking back at the crates of weapons. "I see... It's not ideal, but since we need the—" she stopped as her thoughts were tugged away. *We don't need hovercrafts.*

"Marshal Eliana?"

"We don't need hovercrafts," Eliana said, "We'll ride horses instead."

Karson blinked. "Riking *horses?*" he cleared his throat. "Uh, forgive me for my ignorance, Marshal, but how are we supposed to face off against the Kosmoans—who will be shooting at us from the air—if we're on horses? And for that matter, with this drought, us and the horses will die out there. We'll do nothing but stop and rest."

Eliana played the thought over and over again in her mind, frowning. "I know it doesn't make sense, but I believe it's what we're supposed to do."

Karson sat up, staring. "Donumdonair spoke to you again?"

Eliana looked between Karson and Nathan. Both men watched her, and Eliana found herself nodding. "Yes, he did," she told them.

Karson sighed, running a calloused hand through his dark hair. "Then I suppose there's no point in arguing." He glanced between

Nathan and Eliana. "Tomorrow morning then. We'll face off against The Order of Kosmoa, and we will defeat them."

• • •

Eliana stared up at the dark ceiling, listening to the blades of the fan as it blew hot air around her bedroom. Sleep eluded her. Instead, she recalled the events of that day as she lay in bed. Karson's strategy for facing off against the Kosmoans was simple and would only work if each Journeymen joining the fight was a sharpshooter—which Eliana suspected wasn't the case. Despite the holes in Karson's plans, he had the confidence of a war veteran leading a thousand troops against a hundred.

"Eliana?"

Eliana rolled around to face her husband, lying next to her. In the darkness, she could only make out his shape. "Hmm?"

"I figured you were awake."

Eliana sighed, wiping sweat from her forehead. "How could I possibly sleep knowing that there's a chance I'm wrong?"

Jayrin sucked in a breath. "You should call off the attack—"

"No," Eliana swallowed hard. "I can't."

"Why not?"

Eliana closed her eyes. "Because if what I'm hearing is Donumdonair's voice and I don't act on it, then our people will continue to suffer and I'll have to live knowing that I ignored his voice."

"But if what you heard *isn't* Donumdonair's voice, then a lot of people are going to suffer and die tomorrow. Eliana…everyone knows you. They trust you enough to risk their lives because *you* told them they should."

"Just say it," Eliana whispered.

"Just say what?"

"You think I'm abusing my authority,"

The fan continued to whir, the hot air becoming almost as suffocating as Jayrin's silence.

Eliana opened her eyes to look at Jayrin's dark shape in front of her. "*Jayrin?*"

Jayrin sighed. "From what I heard, Karson agreed to lead the battle immediately when you asked him to."

"He just lost his sister—"

"Which is why he agreed," Jayrin interrupted. "Think about it, Eliana. He's just as angry as the rest of us who have lost something, thanks to the Kosmoans. But if Donumdonair isn't behind us, we're going to lose everything we still *do* have, and who do you think they're going to blame? Because it won't be Donumdonair."

Eliana let out a breath. "Then...I really hope I'm right."

She heard something move against the fabric, and Jayrin's hand slipped into hers.

"So do I," he murmured. "Donumdonair may not speak to me the way he speaks to you, Eliana...but I do trust him to keep you safe."

Eliana swallowed hard, bringing their clasped hands up to her chin. She squeezed her eyes shut as tears threatened to escape.

• • •

The sound of hundreds of hooves pounding against the dry, cracked ground echoed within Eliana's chest. Each thump brought her closer and closer to the end—the end of living in fear, or the end of their lives.

Eliana used the back of her hand to wipe away the sweat dripping from her brow. Heat weighed on her like a boulder, threatening to crush her with its weight. Next to her, Karson rode on his horse; his lips pressed together. He sat straight and still, staring ahead as sweat glistened on his own brow.

Eliana opened her mouth, then closed it, staring at her horse's gray mane. The battle would take place in Ardus Valley, and they were nearing their destination. Her stomach twisted itself in more knots than a well-tied lariat.

"Marshal?"

Eliana turned to look at Karson, who eyed her. "Yes?"

He frowned, lowering his voice. "I was wondering…does Donumdonair ever speak to you in dreams?"

She blinked. "Yeah, occasionally. Why do you—"

"Then did he tell you about mine? Is that why you chose me to lead this fight?" he interrupted.

Eliana's eyes widened. "You had a dream about fighting the Kosmoans?"

Karson's gaze turned distant as his eyes focused on something out of Eliana's sight. "A month ago." His hold on the reins tightened. "I dreamed that I went to you—and told you that now was the time to strike the Kosmoans."

Eliana's mouth dropped open.

Karson shrugged, his gaze dropped to his hands. "I thought it was just some weird dream." He scowled. "But if I had just…listened to that riking dream when I had it, then my sister…she never would have been taken."

Despite the unbearable heat, Eliana's blood grew cold as Karson's words washed over her. She could tell him that it wasn't true, that there was nothing he could have done to save his sister, but that would be a lie.

"So that's why you agreed to lead the people."

He nodded. "And it's why I want you here with us now. Even if Donumdonair were to speak to me again, how do I even know that I'd listen?"

Eliana glanced at Karson's face. "I'd say you're more likely to listen now than you were before."

"Kara shouldn't have paid for my choice," he snapped.

Eliana pursed her lips and turned her gaze to the distance, examining the sand and canyon lines on the horizon.

The sound of the hoofbeats softened, and Eliana looked up. The horses in front had stopped at the edge of the flat plain of Ardus Valley. She stopped her own horse as she spotted Nathan. A brown, broad-brimmed hat shielded his head from the sun. He weaved his way through the crowd toward them on horseback. "Karson, our scouts have reported that two hundred Kosmoans are already on their way here to meet us—all on hovercrafts—and should arrive soon."

Karson glanced at Eliana. "I see. Instruct everyone to have their lite-weapons at the ready. As we discussed yesterday, our best option is to shoot them down before they shoot us. It's unlikely that we'll have a chance for close combat, but have them keep swords on hand just in case."

Nathan nodded. "I'll see that it's done." The older man tipped his hat to them and turned, spurring his horse back toward the front line.

Karson grabbed the canteen hanging from his saddle, unscrewing the lid before taking a swig.

Eliana did the same. The water was warm but soothed her dry throat. "Has Donumdonair spoken to you again?"

Eliana shook her head as she swallowed and replaced the canteen's lid. "No, he—" She stopped as small dots appeared on the horizon in front of them, on the other side of the valley. A humming sound filled the air, and a shiver crept down Eliana's spine. The hornets' nest had been kicked. There was no going back now.

Eliana and Karson dropped their canteens, grabbing their blasters.

"Fellow Journeymen," Karson yelled out, "our enemy approaches!"

As Karson spoke to the people, Eliana's gaze fixed itself on the approaching aircrafts. Even from a distance they shone, reflecting the light from the sun. Eliana flinched as a beam of light shined directly into her eyes. The humming grew louder, the hovercrafts, bigger. They were less than half a mile away now. Eliana frowned, her eyes drawn to the vehicles at the front of the large group. Even from this distance, she could see the dark hourglass engraving on the front of the ships.

Flickers of crimson caught her eye. In the distance, it seemed like flames licked at the sides of some of the crafts. She leaned forward, tipping her chin so that the brim of her hat blocked the blazing sunlight. Was it a trick of desert shadow or smoke rising from the hovercraft? Suddenly, burning vehicles, fully engulfed in smoke and flames veered off path and began to descend from the sky. One of them spiraled out of control as it dropped, slamming to the ground. The craft exploded in an array of red, orange, and yellow.

Eliana turned to Karson, whose mouth was open as wide as a desert canyon.

Eliana's mind flashed back to the fuel can fire Jayrin had dealt with two days ago as more hovercrafts started to smoke and descend from the sky. She looked to Karson, who sat watching as the vehicles fell like meteors to the ground. "The people await your orders, Captain!"

Karson blinked, his gaze snapping to hers. "Of course." He urged his horse a few steps forward, raising his blaster in the air. "Fellow Journeymen, in the name of Donumdonair, we claim victory today!"

Eliana and all those around her, men and women, young and old, beast hunter and farmer, all shouted, their voices merging together into a single battle cry as they charged forward into the valley.

. . .

Two days after the battle with the Kosmoans, Karson and Nathan sat in Eliana and Jayrin's living room. Rain poured down on the town of Heylin and its surrounding fields, erasing any traces of the drought that had plagued the land for the last three months.

"I suppose this means that the farmers' crops will pull through after all," Nathan said, sipping herbal tea out of a chipped teacup as he glanced out the rain-soaked windows.

Eliana nodded, setting her wooden mug down on the crate they used as a table. "The timing was perfect. A little earlier and we'd have lost the battle."

"Yeah." Karson crossed his arms, looking at Eliana. "So, what now?"

Jayrin frowned. "What do you mean?"

Karson shrugged. "I mean we poked the hornets' nest. The Kosmoans can't be too happy that we took out so many of them."

Eliana shook her head, picking up her mug. "I see no reason to plan our next battles before we've properly celebrated this one. Two days ago Donumdonair gave us victory, and yesterday, he gave us rain." The corners of her lips turned up as she raised her mug in a toast. "I look forward to seeing what he has in store for us tomorrow."

Find the story of Deborah in Judges 4.

A Thorn of Rust

Vannah Leblank

Had the winds had a voice of their own, and had Donumdonair used them to be his messengers; had words of the Most-High still been heard in those days, and the air carried the songs of heroes victorious and evil defeated. If justice and hope could have been carried beyond the whispers of silence, then the breeze might have sung a song all of its own.

Its blasts would have roamed the fields of Covenant and skimmed over the burning sands of its deserts. Off the beaten paths of The Order of Kosmoa and down to the battered camps of the Journeymen, it would have traveled in search of a tale worthy of being told. And one day, as the sun shone bright and the dust twirled, it might have heard cries of war resonating through the Ardus Valley, and chosen to follow a lone man fleeing towards the plains.

It was early afternoon.

The sun was high. It had glared all throughout the day, and as Seneca ran he felt like his breath had been sucked away into the cloudless sky. His rebreather, instead of helping him inhale fresh and dustless air, was choking him. His rich uniform, still cluttered with techno-gadgets, all now out of power, dragged him towards the ground. His whole body was drenched in thick beads of sweat.

He still couldn't wrap his mind around what had happened. It all seemed so surreal. The battle, the chaos; how their vessels had crashed, and how the Journeymen had killed off his men. All of it felt like it could have been a bad dream, were it not for the *pain*. It nagged at his side where a rusty blade had grazed him. His legs burned, and his lungs felt like they were about to explode, his body was but a blur of torments.

But he ran.

As fast as he could. He couldn't stop. If he did, they would find him.

The large middle-aged man was about to collapse when, finally, he saw a tent in the distance. It was not much more than a tarp, assembled from animal skins and thinner fabrics to cut off part of the dust omnipresent in the air.

Praise be to Kosmoa, Seneca thought as he neared the habitation. Maybe his god, having seen all the lives sacrificed today for his glory, had finally looked down on him. After all he had done for the deity, he deserved at least that much clemency.

An old black-and-white flag hung on a rusted pole a little ways away from the tent. Seneca slowly blinked with exhausted satisfaction as he recognized the symbol of Bordermen. Although ethnically Journeymen, these people had been trading with The Order of Kosmoa for multiple generations. They owed not only a lot of their success to Seneca's nation but also their loyalty. The people who lived in that shelter could not refuse to harbor one of their benefactors. Their position, after all, was still precarious—they would be fools to refuse to offer help.

The fugitive halted in his run, slowing to a panting walk. The tent was still a short distance away, nestled amidst trees casting shade. Delightful, cool shade. He could only hope that the inhabitants of the tent would be as enticing as their primitive dwelling now seemed.

As he rejoiced in those thoughts, he sighted a tall woman preparing a wild rabbit. She was hanging the creature upside-down by its feet, tying it into place with a piece of rope made of old sheets. As he watched, she took a long, pointy knife and pierced the animal's skin, its lifeblood gushing out as she did. Seneca's own throat was so dry that, at that moment, he would have drunk even the blood of the little creature.

"Hello there," he managed to shout, his voice distorted by his rebreather.

The woman looked up, her eyes trailing from his shoes up to his face. Seneca, despite the fatigue weighing in his bones, raised his chin and stood up straight.

"Hello," she said. As she spoke, she seemed to scan the valley behind him. "Are you alone, sir?"

"For now," Seneca said as he dusted off his uniform. He winced as the fabric brushed his wound.

As he had guessed, the woman had the distinct accent of the Bordermen, slightly slurring her speech. She had about her the air of someone who had endured many a storm in the wilderness. Her shoulders were strong, her brow creased, and her hands calloused, but her eyes were bright.

She looked him over once more, then smiled kindly. "But sir, you look exhausted! Please, come inside."

The offer came right on time. Another wave of heat hit the general, and he nearly collapsed. He still found the strength to nod, then followed her towards the tent. He took a deep breath of fresh air as soon as he stepped inside the habitation, tossing his rebreather to the side.

"I am Jade," the woman introduced herself as she brought him a foldable chair and cleared the wooden table of various objects that cluttered it: a broken clock, a list of trading goods, and a backpack half-filled with basic survival items. "My husband and I have been living across Covenant with our sons, here and there, trading and hunting. And I take it that you are from The Order of Kosmoa?"

Seneca hesitated. How much should he be saying? The horde of brutal Journeymen warriors pursuing him, tracking him to finish him off, were likely still looking for him as he sat there in his own sweat. But this woman seemed so welcoming, her smile so sincere and subservient—surely she would not betray him.

"I am Seneca Dray," he said finally. "General from The Order of Kosmoa and servant of the god of all wealth and power."

Jade nodded eagerly, opening wide eyes. "But then, tell me, General Dray," she said, "what led you to this humble home? Surely there is not much here for a man of your rank and status." She bent down to wash her hands in an old plastic bucket as she spoke, cleaning off the remnants of rabbit, the hairs, the traces of blood. As he saw the water, Seneca barely contained himself from jumping up and pushing her away from the bucket to pour all its contents straight onto his face.

"I'm quite thirsty," he said, his voice hoarser than he intended. "Please bring me some water, and I will tell you all that happened."

"Of course," she said. After contemplating the water jug for a split second, she backed away from it, grabbing another jar instead. "Sir, all the water is too dirty to drink, and the well is a good walk off.

However, I have fresh milk from our goat; I milked her right before you arrived."

"That should do just fine."

She smiled, undid the lid, and poured him a generous cup. Seneca accepted it eagerly.

"The Journeymen," he said after downing half its content in one gulp, "they were planning a rebellion. There was this village, tiny and insignificant compared to our forces. We heard rumors that they were preparing to attack, so of course, we got ready for a retaliation that they would not forget. With our fleet of hovercrafts, beating them should not have been hard, but…the sun was so hot and somehow our fuel tanks overheated. Our crafts crashed into the sand…and of course those snipes jumped on the occasion."

Seneca paused. He still wasn't sure how this had happened. The inspections before the fight had gone well, and nothing odd had been reported. All had worked to perfection until, somehow, the Journeymen had come down that hill, crying the name of their god. Two warriors, a man and a woman, had led them. It was almost as if their cry to the divine had directly preceded the chaos that had ensued.

Seneca almost laughed at the ridiculousness of that thought. Kosmoa was the most powerful of gods; the pretentious Journeymen's "only" god had nothing to do with this dreadful outcome. This self-righteous nation's bravado did not mean anything, least of all that they had any religious ground on which to try and set themselves up as an independent nation. When the time was right, Kosmoa would avenge his Order and establish the glory of his people over all of Covenant. This defeat was simply a test, another sacrifice of lives before the blessing that was bound to come.

"What happened to your men? Why did you come here alone?" the woman asked, playing with a loose thread from her blouse. She stood in front of him, her shoulder against one of the tent's posts. Items of clothing were hung from that post to the next, drying.

"They died—every last one of them. Our ships crashed, and those who ejected in time were slaughtered. It...was a massacre. Those sons of roaches did not have the least bit of mercy."

Seneca shook his head, visions of the last few hours still flashing in his mind's eye. Who were those Journeymen to think they possessed any right to inflict such a brutal, murderous loss on their neighbors? They complained that The Order of Kosmoa had been too harsh to them, of course, but one day, they would understand that this had all been done for their own good. How could they expect to be blessed if they did not offer the proper sacrifices, their livestock, their prized possessions? How could their nation prosper if they simply went about their own way?

He was so deep in his contemplation that he nearly jumped when he realized Jade was two steps away from him, holding a small bottle of alcohol and a cloth.

"You've been clutching those wounds ever since you came in," she said. "I would be a bad host if I did not tend to them."

Well, *this* was the respect he was due. If only the rest of this woman's people could behave this way, there would not have been any war in the first place. They would all have been able to go on with their trading instead of squabbling.

He let her clean his injuries in contemplative silence. The sting of the alcohol hurt, but he bore it without complaint. Every last one of his men save for him had died; a few minor cuts were a small sacrifice. Kosmoa only knew all the other sacrifices he had endured to get to this day.

He turned his focus to the woman. She might not be as delicate as the average Kosmoan woman, but she had well-carved features. She had well-carved features and a flattering stature, not quite as tall as Seneca himself, but still a good height. As she worked, gently washing the skin around his wounds, her sparkly eyes were downcast. Her lips, though pinched, were plump and blood-red.

Jade finished tying a last bandage, then backed away.

"Tell me," Seneca said, stretching his legs, "for how long is your husband gone?"

The woman paused as she put away the bandages. "Why, who knows with this man? His travels take him farther some days than others."

"So surely he would not dare keep a deserving general from enjoying his wife for a little bit, would he? I could use some distraction myself."

Jade turned her back to him, tossing the unused bandages and the bottle of alcohol into a small basket on a shelf.

"Actually, I'm pretty sure he *would* take offense at just that. He is quite the hard-headed man, you know." She faced him again, a mischievous smile playing on her lips. "But it's not like he would know, now, is it?"

Seneca leaned back in his chair, a content smile stretching across his cheeks.

"However," the woman went on, "you look positively exhausted. I'm sure a bit of sleep could do you good beforehand. Then, we could enjoy ourselves as much as we want."

Right. Sleep. Seneca was reminded of just how weary he felt, and the prospect of resting first did not seem like an entirely bad idea. He only had to make sure he was safe while unconscious.

"Perhaps. Rest never hurt anyone, now did it? Just tell me you'll guard the entrance of the tent. No one must know I'm here."

"Of course," she said. "Don't worry, no one will trouble your sleep."

As she said so, she gathered a few blankets from across the tent and arranged them on a mattress in the corner, making it seem as comfortable as the modest display could be. Seneca walked over to meet her there. He put a hand on the back of her neck, leaning towards her.

"After you rest, sir," she said again.

He was too tired to argue. The warm milk was making him drowsy, and the swishing of the wind across the plain seemed to whisper a strangely enticing lullaby.

The makeshift bed seemed almost magnetic as he was pulled towards it and laid down.

He laid his head on the pillow, then perked up once more. "If anyone comes by," he insisted, "tell them there is no one here."

"I will." She flashed him a smile, and then her tall silhouette went over to the entrance of the tent, where she stood immobile. This image was imprinted on his retina as sleep quickly overtook him. Her proud shape, built solidly from years living in the desert, silhouetted by daylight across a crack of blue sky.

• • •

As Seneca slept soundly, the winds continued blowing.

Had they watched or had they paid attention to the scene beyond the slumbering general, they might have embraced the only other soul in the valley.

Jade leaned against the support post, an unassuming air about her. Her chin was raised as if in defiance to the dusty winds billowing around her, blowing at her skirts, rasping at her face. She did not recoil at their touch, nor did she hide behind a scarf or a rebreather. She knew their patterns; she did not fear them.

As perspiration from the day's heat started budding on her forehead, she left her position at the door to check on her guest. He was fast asleep, softly and peacefully, his mind far gone from this place.

The tent flapped open once more and the woman stepped out. The winds had picked up, as if curious. They followed the woman as she went back to the rabbit she had been skinning. The creature still hung upside-down in the tent's shade. Jade's son had trapped it the night before and brought it back to her proudly, as a trophy of war. It was the boy's first kill. She intended to prepare the carcass properly before he came back, accompanied by her husband.

Jade picked up her skinning knife once more, looking at its rusty blade. It was an old tool, pointy. The woman stabbed her way into the animal with the thorn-like weapon, piercing more than she cut. Still, her hands worked nimbly, almost aggressively, until the animal was skinned and cut up as she pleased.

Taking pieces of waxed fabric from under a turned-over crate, she wrapped the meat in a bundle, storing it in a small cooling machine, the only thing resembling luxury that her family possessed.

Jade stood, contemplating her weaponry in much the same way as the Kosmoans must have looked at their aircrafts. A crease slowly made its way to her forehead, her lips twisting into a grimace. Almost absently, she began to pace around the outside of the tent, circling the dwelling in much the same way wild wolves circle prey. Her feet raised tiny clouds of dust, which quickly blew away.

Then she stopped. The sun had almost reached its nest between two peaks, and she had about her the air of someone dissatisfied, as if an unfinished duty still tore at her.

Slowly, the tall woman made her way back to her skinning station and bent down to pick up her knife. She slid her finger along its useless edge, contemplative, then tested its point against her index. Curling her lips, she pounded her way to her tool chest and rummaged through it until she found a hammer. It was made of a solid stone attached to a piece of pipe; it didn't look like much, but it was sturdy. Her fingers tightened against the handle, whitening her knuckles. She breathed out deeply.

Slowly, Jade made her way to the tent. She looked into the distance only once, as if hoping her husband and sons were coming home from their day's travels, but the horizon was empty.

And so, silently, she entered her home. She made her way across it until she stood above her guest.

The air was stuffy, and Seneca Dray was fast asleep. Despite the day's heat, he was covered in one of the blankets she had let him use, as if hiding. A fleshy furrow knitted his eyebrows, but otherwise, he slept as soundly as an infant.

Jade grasped the hammer tightly and made sure both her tools were aligned with the man's head. She let out another slow breath.

At this very moment, Seneca perked up. He tensed, his head lifted a few inches over the thin pillow. His eyes were open, vacantly staring up at the tent's roof. Jade held her breath, standing immobile, her lips only moving to mouth a silent prayer. Perhaps it was heard, or perhaps it was chance, but Seneca closed his eyes again and slowly rotated until he turned his back to her, facing the tent's wall.

Jade's skirts brushed the compacted ground as she knelt beside him. Her hands were sweaty but firm. She hovered the point of the rusty knife directly above Seneca's temple and then, gathering all of her strength, slammed the hammer into it with a fierce blow.

The blade went straight through her victim's head and back out on the other side, staining the pillow and piercing through the mattress. Seneca's body tensed; then he was still. A pool of blood slowly seeped past the mattress and onto the ground at her feet.

"There is no one inside this tent," she whispered.

She stood there, immobile, for a long time. The air was still as death, the valley quiet and dark. Even the wind outside had abated.

Jade finally lowered her eyes to the hammer and uncurled her white fingers from the handle. As it thumped to the ground, it seemed to make more noise than all the day's battle shouts combined.

The next thing one might have seen, had they been watching, would have been Jade dragging the fallen general outside of her tent. His large form dug a groove into the ground with each tug, and his bald head, still pierced by the knife, seemed to hit every rock it met.

With a last strain of effort, Jade hauled the man next to the crate she usually sat on to work, dropping her burden where she stood. And where he fell, there he lay, dead and still.

A smirk slowly appeared on the woman's face. Deep red beads of Seneca Dray's blood, the life of one of Kosmoa's most celebrated generals, now mixed with the blood stains of the rabbit she had skinned earlier. A man, a corpse—glorious in his days, and now, a name that would be nothing more than a curse, an expletive on the wind, a sign of victory to a scattered people.

Had the desert's breeze been watching then, or had a herald been on the lookout for a story to tell, they might have seen the satisfaction blooming on the woman's face and remembered the tale of Jade, the tent-dweller who killed a man with an old skinning knife. And had the wind listened, truly listened, it might have remembered: the land was barren, the valley lonely, but off in the distance, a song was rising, and maybe, maybe, Donumdonair's people would live in peace again.

Find the story of Jael in Judges 4:12-22.

Primal Network

Matthew Sampson

The midmorning sun glared down on Sundar as he led his parents across the sands. Dust clung to their sandals and the hems of their clothes. A death lizard scuttled onto a rock nearby, hissed at them, and displayed its poisonous pink frill.

Abba muttered, "Even the creatures can see this path leads to doom."

Sundar kept walking.

The ancient ship called Longstay Alfa glowed in the distance like a second sun, reflecting the light from its heavenly twin. The Kosmoan fortress had fallen from the stars in ages past, leaving an impact crater whose stone walls stretched from horizon to horizon. The ship sat at the far end of the crater, the front was buried in the sand, and the top of the ship towered high, reaching for the stars with which it once belonged. Desperados had long since claimed the fallen fortress for their own.

Imma clacked two stones together, scaring off the lizard. "Hush, husband of mine." Like Abba and Sundar, she wore her best clothes, cuffs and hems embroidered with colors. "We decided on this path. We bartered for a travel pass." When Abba said nothing, she raised her voice. "Sundar, slow the pace, and give your cranky father a drink of water."

Sundar swung his pack from his shoulders with a sigh. Each of them carried gifts. Finely milled wheat bread, fruit juices, carved wooden bowls and spoons and boxes, and stones painted with stories. But all their gifts paled next to the cord on Sundar's wrist. He had woven it himself, two fibers to a thread, two threads to a strand, two strands to a weave, on and on, over and over, until the weaving tools had left his fingers numb and clumsy.

That cord was the most important thing he could give.

Abba shaded his eyes and stared at Longstay Alfa. "I still think a Journeymen woman would be a more appropriate match for our son. Matef's daughters. Yalenae or Sazume."

Imma sighed. She lowered her own pack to the sand and seated herself cross-legged next to it.

"Abba, enough." Sundar poured water into a plastic carton and held it out to Abba. "Drink. I'm not marrying either of them."

Abba ignored the proffered water. "Perhaps Kobe from our cutting crew." Their Journeymen clan had worked for the Desperados for decades now. Month after month, they harvested metal parts from a wrecked piece of Longstay Alfa called the Hackery, broken off in the impact and now resting miles distant on the other end of the crater.

The plastic studs along Sundar's spine began to tingle. His cybernetic implants often came to life when he felt agitated. "I swear you will—"

His vision spun and he swayed on his feet. The water inside the carton rocked, little drops splashing out the top.

Imma reached up to him. "Are you well, son of mine?"

"Just dizzy." Sundar crouched beside his mother. Most of the time, he could handle the mechanical parts occupying his body. The artificial cybernetics reached all the way inside his spine and up into the shallow reaches of his brain. The dizzy spells were not common, but they always passed quickly.

Sundar had to squint to focus on Abba's face, but his voice remained firm when he said, "I swear you will run out of eligible names before I change my mind."

Like a sand-rat hovering over its kill, Abba said, "Teria in the kitchen is very clever."

Sundar snapped, "Abba. I am *sleeping with Wit.*"

His father finally looked at him.

Their ancestors lived on in that gaze. Generations stared out at him like an army rallying to the blast of the shofar, bearing the weight of tradition like a shield. The Journeymen walked a single path, a narrow, treacherous incline carved out by a god older than living memory.

"This is not the right way," Abba said, blinking in the glare of Longstay Alfa.

But Sundar barely heard him. He stared at his parents through a haze. His heart pounded in his ears.

A sound burned high on the horizon, a mechanical drone. Something was coming.

Black dots pricked Sundar's vision, and in an instant, his mind was yanked from his body. He was distantly aware of his body folding, crumpling to the sands. But his awareness now occupied a metal ship soaring high above the sands.

Another mind pressed against his, old and tired, but curious too. It did not use words, but Sundar heard, *Hello, brother.*

Sundar jerked back from that presence, like shutting out a bitter memory, and all went black.

He awoke moments later in his own body. The heat of the sand radiated through his clothes, and Imma crouched above him, her expression lined and haunted.

Abba was staring at the sky.

Sundar pushed up from the ground, avoiding Imma's protest. His cybernetic parts still buzzed and his head ached as he rolled to his feet.

An atmospheric fighter streaked high overhead, heading for Longstay Alfa. Sleek, white, triangular with a blunt nose, tall stabilizing fins, and an hourglass symbol painted on each wing. *Aryeh*-class. An imperial scout of The Order of Kosmoa.

Sundar dropped to the sand and pulled his parents down. "Don't move."

The Kosmoan fighter winged high over the Desperado fortress, drawing fire from the turret mounted atop the iron mountain. It looped a tight circle around the ship's peak, dodging the fiery lite-bolts with ease.

Then it dipped low and blasted straight towards Sundar and his parents.

Abba made a choked sound in his throat. Imma half rose.

"Stay still!" Sundar hissed. *Pass over us, Donumdonair—*

The Kosmoan fighter shrieked overhead, so loud Imma's scream blended with the noise. It dropped low, leveling out over Longstay Alfa's impact crater. Sand blew up in the engine wash as the Kosmoan fighter arced back toward them.

Sundar pulled his parents to their feet. Both looked dazed, but they stumbled after him as he broke into a run towards Longstay Alfa.

Donumdonair—and a stone outcropping loomed off to their right. Sundar changed course, nearly pulling his parents off their feet. The fighter's roar strengthened as it approached. Its cannons rang out. Next to them, lite-bolts pummeled the sand, plumes of dust erupting where they had been moments before.

The fighter zipped past as Sundar pushed his parents into the rock's shadow. Dust smeared Imma's face. Her eyes were glazed and half open. Blood leaked from one ear from the concussive force of the fighter's passing.

Sundar gripped Abba's shoulder. "Stay here."

Abba's voice was high with fear. "What are you doing? Where are you going?"

Sundar tucked his father's head down. *"Stay here."*

The Kosmoan fighter roared overhead as Sundar burst out of cover and ran. As the dust of its passing settled around him, he stopped and looked up.

The fighter rose high in the air, nose lifting, thrusters spitting. As it spun towards Sundar, the eclipsed sunlight streamed around it like the burning mane of a lion.

The machine in Sundar's chest hummed.

He reached out to the fighter as it turned to dive.

This time, he did not leave his body. But the deep, intelligent mind in the sky turned its attention to him.

"You called me brother," Sundar said. "What did you mean?"

The fighter's mind paused. *You are a Goliath-class battle cyborg, designation G0-1057. We are made from the same parts.* Another pause. *Missing indexes.* Another pause. *Current status: in stasis. Updating status.*

Sundar reeled. Too many answers to questions he had been asking for so long. But he managed, "Why are you shooting at me if I am your brother?"

As if hesitating, the fighter circled once. A sense of confusion made its way to Sundar. Its pilot—suspended from control, briefly, for this decision—had breached multiple tactical considerations in the hot reconnaissance over Longstay Alfa. The pilot had not confirmed as hostile the unknown heat signatures crossing the sands, and yet had targeted them. Why should a young and foolish mind rule it?

"Then *surrender,*" Sundar said.

In the moment that it dove, the fighter's dissonant logic modules came together in sudden, startled agreement.

Sundar took control. The fighter's dive deepened. Down, down, and into the ground—

The networked connection broke. The ground shuddered beneath Sundar's feet, and the smell of fire washed over him in a torrent of wind. A pillar of smoke climbed toward the heavens.

Sundar stood there. His breath came in painful gulps.

G0-1057.

How—

He could not even ask the question. He turned and walked to where his parents clung to one another under Donumdonair's stony wings.

"Sundar!" Two voices in unison.

Sundar sat down heavily next to them. "Are you well?" But he did not hear their answers. *Goliath-class battle cyborg.*

His cybernetic implants had been part of him for as long as he could remember. They had grown with him. He could count his nineteen years in the seams of the machine in his chest.

The reinforcement in his spine protected artificial brain stems that sat alongside his organic nerves. He had always assumed some tragic accident when he was younger had wiped his oldest memories.

Longstay Alfa held caches of weapons and ancient technology. Perhaps, until nineteen years ago, it had also held a cyborg child.

Abba stared over at the fighter. It smoked just shy of their position. Sundar could almost see the questions in his eyes. Was this a sign of wrath or favor? Turn back or continue on?

When his father started to speak, Sundar braced himself. But instead, Abba said, "You should check on the pilot."

His parents kept their distance while Sundar crossed the field of smoking debris. He could make out only pieces of the fighter's mind. It was damaged, large chunks of its memory missing, and it said nothing when he reached out mind to mind, his hand resting on the metal hull of the ship.

Sundar climbed onto the fighter's wing and broke open the cockpit with a twisted scrap of metal. The pilot lay slumped to one side. A smooth black artifiskin covered his entire body, hiding any identifying characteristics from view. The impact had crumpled the cockpit, crushing the pilot's legs.

Abba sighed when Sundar returned and reported the pilot's demise. "A waste of a life."

Pity? For the Kosmoan who had tried to kill them? Sundar shook his head and made Imma open her eyes. Her dazed look was wearing off, but she held one bloodied hand to her ear.

Abba hovered. "We should turn back."

Sundar dipped into the pack of gifts, found decorative fabrics, and made Imma hold them to her ear. He wound a long strip of yellow linen around her head. "Fear is a prowling lion, Abba."

"A considered withdrawal is not fear. Your mother needs attention."

Sundar glanced at his father as he tied off the makeshift bandage. "She has received attention."

"She will be receiving more attention, and soon," Abba said, his voice raised. "Longstay Alfa does not love the empire. They will waste no time recovering a Kosmoan vessel." A pause. "There."

Sundar looked up. A silver shape approached from the Desperado fortress with a trail of dust in its wake.

Abba sighed. A ragged, gritty breath. He sat heavily next to Imma and put his hands on his head. "We should not have come."

Soon a tank rolled to a stop in front of them, a *Whipspider*-class armored infantry transport, long and low on four treads with a manual top turret. The iron frame looked like it had come straight from the Hackery. Desperados hopped out, weapons raised, yelling for them to get down.

Sundar sat behind his parents and matched their posture with his hands on his head. A Desperado looked them over and ordered them to stay where they were and await questioning.

A tall man stepped out of the tank. Bulky armor accentuated his broad shoulders. He carried a lite-rifle, a massive beast of a weapon pilfered from the Kosmoan armories sealed inside Longstay Alfa for centuries. Red paint striped the front of his chest plate, marking him as a crew captain.

And a black eyeball, empty as death, stared out of one of his sockets. A robotic eye with a rim of gunmetal grey. A cybernetic implant, no doubt tech stolen from the Kosmoans, paired to the targeting system of the Kosmoan lite-rifle he held.

Both Imma and Abba took a sharp breath at the same time.

Sundar whispered, "Who is he?"

Imma pitched her voice so low Sundar could barely hear her. "Catcher. Don't pull his attention."

"They didn't leave a guard," Sundar whispered. "We can sneak away."

Abba was shaking his head before Sundar finished his sentence. "And go where?" his father asked, indicating the wide stretch of open sand. "They said they want to ask questions."

All of them froze as Catcher strode past. He did not spare them a glance as he headed to the fighter and rested a heavy boot on its wing. "Can it be repaired?"

A Desperado circled the fighter and came back shaking her head. "The internal structure is screwed. Could do a rebuild, maybe. Won't be quick."

"Noted. Get the Kosmoan out." Catcher then raised his voice and yelled out, "Search the area, recover the debris!"

Most of the Desperados dispersed. Some broke out shovels and barrows from the tank and began collecting the smaller pieces of wreckage. Others began unrolling a pair of chains from a massive winch attached to the front of the tank. Each link was as big around as Sundar's forearm.

Sundar had seen Desperado tanks pull the meaty corpses of great sand-rats before. He did not doubt this one could move the fighter.

Two of the Desperados levered the Kosmoan pilot's crushed body out of the cockpit and set it on the wing. One of them clambered inside. He flicked the switches and pressed buttons. "Getting nothing from the flight systems."

"That is because," Catcher said, and he seized the pilot's leg and

dragged the body down to his level, "you are not part of the network."
The Desperado in the cockpit looked at him blankly.

Catcher pulled a bright orange release at the neck of the pilot's
artifiskin. The fabric's seal hissed as it loosened, collapsing the suit
into baggy folds.

Catcher stripped the body with the practiced motions of one
familiar with handling corpses. The legs of the suit were ripped
through. Vein-like wires and tiny electronic chips poked through
the torn edges. Catcher examined the damage with a grimace but
tossed it up to the Desperado in the cockpit. "There. Put that on
and try again."

"Captain!" A Desperado with a sniper rifle attached to her oversized backpack hauled a canister with yellow stripes across the sands
toward Catcher. She was barely taller than Imma, her black hair long
and wild on top and cropped nearly to the scalp on both sides and
around the back. She wore hunter's camouflage, leather armor stained
in a patchwork of greens and greys and browns. "Found a whole fuel
cell. A bit burned and dented but in one piece."

Sundar let out a breath. Abba turned to look at him.

Catcher held up a hand. "Rike, Wit, take that thing away. We're
still smoking here."

"It's still sealed," Wit said, but she changed direction.

Abba said, under his breath, "Wit."

Imma looked up.

Sundar gave a single short nod.

Wit hauled the fuel cell toward the tank. As she passed, she
glanced in Sundar's direction.

Her eyes met his.

She froze in mid-step. "What in riking Covenant."

One of the nearby Desperados eyed her. "What is it?"

"Nothing." Wit dropped her gaze and began dragging the fuel cell with extra vigor. "Busy. Hot."

Abba lowered his voice. "So it's a secret."

Sundar nodded again.

Abba watched as Wit disappeared behind the tank. "She doesn't want them to know."

Sundar pressed his lips into a firm line. "No."

Abba's sigh dragged into a groan. "Donumdonair help us. This is not going to work."

A loud snap drew their attention. Atop the fighter, a Desperado wearing the Kosmoan pilot's artifiskin spasmed, electricity sparking across the material.

Catcher leaped up onto the wing with surprising agility for someone of his bulk. He tossed his rifle to another Desperado, caught the loose folds of the artifiskin, and slashed through the spinal wires with a short plasma-knife.

The electrical arcs faded and disappeared. The Desperado wearing the skin sagged to his knees, his body shaking. He struggled with the shreds of the artifiskin until another Desperado came and helped him take it off.

Catcher paced, staring at the fighter, muttering.

Abba leaned across to Sundar. "We must turn back," he said under his breath. "These ones will not deal in good faith. They will take all we have and send us back to the Hackery empty-handed."

Sundar dug through his pack, pushing aside wrapped bread and cheese. "We will not speak to them." He kept an eye on Wit as she headed out to join three other Desperados struggling with a severed hull plate. "Just to her."

"Will my son not listen to me?" Abba said. "These people hold no loyalty to their blood. They call no god by name." He pinched the cord on Sundar's wrist between thumb and forefinger. Endless threads. Two into two into two, on and on, names and lives woven into a family, an ancestry, a clan. The Journeymen themselves, captured in a simple weave. "They do not walk the right path."

Bitterness flooded Sundar's tongue until he could not hold it back. "Maybe *we* do not walk the right path."

Abba leaned towards Sundar. "There is blessing on the way—"

"Is there?" Sundar rounded on his father. "I see blessing fall like rain, but not on what *you* say is Donumdonair's path. Who rules the sands? Who controls food production and governs the work schedules?" he flung out his hand toward Longstay Alfa. "They *make* their path, and even the kosriked empire shudders at their steps!"

The lines in Abba's face deepened. He took Imma's hand in his. Both wore cords like Sundar's, faded and frayed, but still strong. "Those are not the blessings *I* see."

"No," Sundar said, "because you will not lift up your head to look."

He flipped a packet of torus nuts from hand to hand. Wit had joined three other Desperados struggling with a heavy hull plate. Every time her voice rang out to mark the pace, the four of them heaved the hull plate a foot closer to the tank, directly past Sundar and his parents.

As Wit took a breath and swiped her hair out of her face, Sundar tossed the packet of torus nuts at her feet and called, "Wit."

Wit swore and kicked it back at him, spraying sand in his direction. Abba clutched at Sundar's arm. "Leave her be."

Sundar tossed another packet, this one ahead of her. Wit said something to the other Desperados, then stamped over to Sundar and his parents.

An angry flush burned in her cheeks. She aimed a kick at Sundar's ribs but pulled the blow at the last moment. Her voice dropped to a growl. "You're drowning in quicksand. *Don't you dare pull me in.*"

Footsteps approached like a drumbeat of doom.

"Kosrike it," Wit muttered, pinching the bridge of her nose.

Catcher snapped, "What was that?"

Wit turned and saluted. "Drowning, sir!"

Catcher frowned at her, lines of confusion wrinkling his brow. But when he turned to Sundar and his parents, his expression hardened into a gaze as clear as glass flash-melted from the sand.

"That fighter crashed at your feet," he said. "Why?"

Abba and Imma exchanged a troubled look. Abba said, "Surely you hit it."

"No. It dove. Suicidal." Catcher thrust his rifle into Wit's hands. "For what? Why did it want you?" he took Abba's pack and shook it in their faces. "Is this the reason?"

He dumped out the contents of the pack in a pile. Bowls shaped from clay, patterned and glazed, spilled across the sands. Carved wooden spoons with chips of quartz inlaid in the handles. Painted stones that told stories from the history of the Journeymen. Sticks of incense. Sweet-smelling herbs in bunches bound with thread made from plaited grass fibers.

Catcher stared. He snatched up Imma's pack and emptied it beside Abba's.

Lengths of fabric fluttered to the ground. Kerchiefs and bandannas, dyed and embroidered with clay-based pink, flower-based yellow, and blue from the juices of underground killer snails. Dolls twisted from straw and dressed in tiny sets of woven clothes. Rings hammered from wire, bent into a circle and soldered at the join, then engraved with tiny patterns. A sheepskin blanket. A set of hair combs carved from a sand-rat's femur.

The growing pile drew the Desperados like carrion birds to a carcass. They murmured among themselves and stared with hungry eyes. One inched forward, fingers twitching, but at a barked word from Catcher, he retreated back among the others.

Catcher poked through the collection with the toe of his boot. A strange look twisted his face. "What is this? Payment for a debt?"

When no one replied, he took the last pack from Sundar and ripped the hardy material asunder with a vicious strength that made Sundar blink. More things bumped against each other as they rolled onto the sand. Packets of seeds and nuts, loaves of bread wrapped in cloth, cartons of deep rich juice made from pressed fruit. Wheels of cheese speckled with spices and herbs.

A dim red light flickered in Catcher's robot eye.

"Kosrike it all," he muttered. "This world is meaningless." He looked up at the sky, then turned his gaze to the discarded body on the sands. "So riking *close*, and yet so far."

He crouched and picked a spoon from among the scattered gifts. "Tell me what these are for."

"It is a traditional offering." Abba's voice quivered, but he met Catcher's robotic glare without backing down. "A proposal gift from my son to the girl he loves."

Catcher snapped the spoon between his fingers. "You Journeymen and your traditions."

He rose and held out his hand. "My weapon."

Wit did not move. She stared at Sundar, her eyes blank with shock, her lips moving in words he could not make out.

Catcher turned to her and snatched the lite-rifle from her grasp. The weapon powered up with a whir, the sound a deep agonizing hum in the back of Sundar's head.

Sundar cried out and pulled his parents back, scrabbling backward on his seat. The shifting sand gave him no grip, and he floundered as Catcher's rifle screamed out.

But the lite-bolts were not for them.

Round after round of burning light pulverized the bounty spread across the sands. Bowls splintered into a million shards. Cheese melted. Superheated drops of juice sprayed across Sundar and his parents, blistering at the touch. Fabric burned, colors and patterns crisping into ash. The sweet smell of smoking incense floated across the sands.

Sundar did not recognize his own sob of pain until it shuddered out of him. He had made those bowls himself on his aunt's pottery wheel, molding the clay into functional artifacts, mixing the glaze, firing the bowls into brilliant color. He had gathered the herbs and the flowers and ventured into the bowels of the Hackery to catch the giant venomous snails that preyed upon mice and lizards and gave the most brilliant blue dye when their mucus glands were boiled.

Doom. Abba had seen the end of this path from the first step.

And yet Sundar could not turn back. He could not walk his father's path, his mother's path, the paths of so many in the Hackery as they cut plates of metal and bred stock for Longstay Alfa and absorbed Desperado abuse like sponges drinking up dye.

Some things hovered so fresh in his memory it was like he lived them again each time he remembered. His mother's songs. The smell of his father's greenhouse. The first time he had seen a dead sand-rat, its fur matted with green ooze and sand. Thirty lashes from a Desperado whip when he stumbled one day into a restricted area. His first touch with Wit, their breath entwining like a single living being.

The roar in his head was so loud he could barely hear Catcher's voice.

"Send them back to the Hackery." Catcher kicked sand over the smouldering mess. "We do not feed Journeymen for this. Put them on double duties for a few weeks. They clearly have the strength."

Sundar reached for the fighter's mind.

He sensed something, a faint signal grew as he probed it. He walked with it for a moment, lingering in the memories of the unbroken sky in its memory banks.

The sound of a lite-cannon charging up was as familiar as Sundar's own skin. That sound! A raw metallic growl, like the warning of a wounded lion. The first of the fighter's twin cannons had twisted in the crash, and it rocked the fighter onto its side as it exploded into shrapnel.

But the second cannon fired, and the targeting system resurrected. The Desperado tank jerked forwards and smoke billowed from its rear end as lite-bolts made impact.

The Desperados yelled, some opening fire on the Kosmoan craft, others throwing themselves to the ground as the fighter's cannon fired another burst of white light, then another.

The moment the fighter hit the fuel cell Wit had left inside the tank's main chamber, the armored Desperado transport blew up. Great bursts of fire ripped its iron hull to shreds. The shockwave kicked up a screen of sand and shrapnel and blew Catcher and the other Desperados off their feet. Weapons flew. Fire curled into smoke and embers.

Sundar struggled to his knees, coughing, hacking. A dozen cuts from flying shrapnel bled all across his body. All around him, Desperados fought to their feet, scrambling for weapons.

Sundar curled his hand into a fist and struck the nearest Desperado in the throat with all the force of nineteen years of slavery. The man collapsed with a choked gasp. Sundar seized his shoulders and slammed the back of his head against the sand. He did not wait to see if the Desperado was stunned or dead.

Sundar grabbed the Desperado's lite-rifle. It felt strange in his hands, but when Sundar aimed it at one of his oppressors and pulled the trigger, it sang out for him. The Desperado fell screaming with a hole in his chest.

Liquid fire flowed through Sundar's veins as he turned in place, firing in bursts, barely remembering to aim. Desperados shouted and scrambled for cover, still disoriented by the exploded tank, now just a blackened wreck in the smoky haze.

Something hit Sundar in the middle of his back, a heavy, blunt blow that sent him flying onto his face.

A boot planted itself between Sundar's shoulder blades, pinning him to the ground. Above him, Catcher breathed hard, leather creaking as he seized Sundar's collar and flipped him over. Sundar began to aim, but Catcher struck the lite-rifle out of his hands, sending it spinning out of reach.

Another blow to Sundar's temple sparked a wild burst of lights in his vision. Catcher seized Sundar's collar again and tore his tunic,

Journeymen patterns ripping apart all the way down his chest. Catcher's robot eye burned a brilliant blood red. "You did this." He reached down, ran a hand over the metal surface of Sundar's implants, over the seam of skin and steel. "You're part of the Primal Network."

Sundar threw sand in Catcher's face. The foot on his chest lightened, and Sundar rolled out from under Catcher's heel.

Catcher's boot came crashing down into the sand, mere inches from Sundar's ankle. Sundar scrambled back, but Catcher pursued, aiming stomps at his legs, preventing him from rising.

Sundar scrambled back until his hands brushed over the lite-rifle Catcher had knocked out of his hands. He raised it up but missed his first shot, a wild blast of light that streaked off into the sky.

Catcher swore and lunged for the weapon.

As Catcher reached for him, Sundar shot him in the chest. The captain twisted at the last moment, and the round glanced off his armor, but even so the blast threw him off his feet.

Sundar sprang to his feet and aimed down at Catcher. Just as he was about to put a round through Catcher's head, he heard another lite-rifle charge up. He spun towards the sound, swinging his weapon.

Wit stared at him down the barrel of Catcher's heavy rifle. Her eyes were wide, and she breathed in fitful gasps. "What in *Covenant.*"

Sundar backed off, weapon raised.

"Put a round through his knee!" Catcher stood up and tore off his chest plate and dropped the half-molten piece of metal. Burn marks scarred the leather armor beneath. "But don't kill him!"

Wit made a strangled sound. She aimed the weapon at Sundar's leg.

Catcher cuffed her ear and took the weapon from her. "What's wrong with you?"

Sundar took the opportunity to point his rifle at Catcher, but the man only blinked his single human eye and said, "Look at your parents, Journey*boy*."

Sundar kept the weapon trained on Catcher. But he darted a look toward the spot he'd left his parents.

Half a dozen Desperados surrounded Abba and Imma. Sundar's father lay on the sand, unconscious, blood trickling from his scalp. Next to him, Imma breathed in fitful gasps of smoke and grit.

"You're neck-deep in sand," Catcher said. "Throw down the rifle."

Sundar's finger twitched on the trigger, so violently he nearly shot Catcher in the chest again. He stopped himself just in time. "Let them go."

Catcher shook his head. "The moment you pull that trigger, your parents meet their god. You won't choose against them." He charged his rifle. "Your mother dies on the count of three."

Sundar threw the rifle at Catcher's feet.

The captain said, "Take him."

Desperados rushed forward. One scooped up the rifle and carried it away. Others forced Sundar to his knees and bent his arms behind his back.

Catcher powered down his rifle and stared at Sundar. He looked at the fighter and muttered to himself.

Then he struck Wit across the face. She went down, stayed down, holding her cheek and her silence.

Catcher did not stop. He kicked her in the ribs until she curled into a ball, hiding her face and chest.

"I ought to send you to the Hackery." His voice came out in a snarl. "You kosriked piece of scrap."

Wit remained in the sand with her knees pulled into her body.

Catcher grabbed Wit's shock of black hair and forced her head backward, making her look at him. "You want to open your legs for Journeymen? No one riking cares. Bed whoever you want."

He shook her. She screwed up her face and made a sound of pain.

"But as soon as it compromises your operational resilience," Catcher hissed, "you're out. You're lucky you still have use to me."

He let go of Wit's hair and rose, turning to face Sundar. "Her? Really?" He shook his head. "You're not her first, and you probably won't be her last."

Sundar forced out, "Let my parents go."

Catcher gestured. "Get him up."

Hands pulled Sundar to his feet. Someone smacked the back of his head. He closed his eyes.

"You do not make your path." The words burst from his throat, as if they came from a place beyond him, from something, someone greater than he. "It is laid for you, each false and crumbling step, and *I can see where it ends.*" He met Catcher's gaze. "It ends in doom."

Catcher sneered and pulled Wit to her feet. His grip bit into her shoulder.

Sundar took a deep breath.

One more thing, he prayed.

The fighter's sense of aching fatigue was so deep that Sundar gasped with the shock of it. But he heard, *Root access granted. Downloading shell.*

Suddenly the fighter's enormous mind swallowed his awareness. Sundar could feel every single neuron and synapse, a million connections in precise, painful detail, intelligence flowing through them like water. Every sound in reach of the fighter's sensors hammered Sundar all at once. The crackle of small fires in the wrecked tank, the shuffling footsteps of thirty hostile heat signatures, the labored breathing of two injured friendlies, death lizards squeaking, a toad burrowing for deep water, sand sliding, the breath of the sky, radio signals from the dormant *Vatican Renegade,* the beating core of flesh and wire inside their brother's chest.

Then the fighter's mind pulsed out for the last time.

When Sundar opened his eyes, he could see things that were not there. Files and menus hovered in his vision, a translucent overlay branded across the world. A command line blinked at him. He could see every command root in the back of his mind. If he looked closer, they began to combine, branching into millions of possibilities.

"Set a pace for Longstay Alfa," Catcher shouted. "Bring the injured. Leave the dead. Don't break the cyborg, but I don't mind if he takes a little pain."

The possibilities narrowed into a path.

Sundar sent a hundred commands in the space of a breath.

The crash had severed the fuel lines for the primary ion thrusters, but the emergency thrusters—canisters of compressed air, available even in total engine failure—still registered as online. They were meant for atmospheric maneuvering, not for fighting the heavy friction of terrain.

But they activated with a noise like a lion's roar. Sand blew up in dark clouds. The thrusters scraped the fighter's wing along the ground, bringing the functioning laser cannon to bear.

Desperados yelled. The entire crew scrambled for cover as Sundar sent supercharged blasts of light into their midst. One blast hit a retreating Desperado, vaporizing her armor and cooking her frame into a smoking skeleton.

Catcher bellowed. He threw Wit to the ground and raised his rifle to Sundar but hesitated with his finger on the trigger. His robotic eye flickered wildly between black and red.

One of the Desperados squeezed off a burst of lite-bolts that barely missed Sundar's head.

"No!" Catcher spun on the Desperado and fired a round into his chest, sending him crumpling to the sands. "You must not kill him!" Breathing heavily, he whirled on the other Desperados. "Rush him! Pin him down!"

No one moved.

Swearing, Catcher fired over their heads. They scattered, melting away towards Longstay Alfa.

Cold fury marked deep lines in Catcher's face as he turned back to Sundar. "Blind fools."

"They are not the only blind fool," Sundar said.

Catcher's gaze flicked to the Kosmoan fighter. Its lite-cannon was trained on his skull.

The anger slipped from his face. "Wait."

Sundar circled to stand in front of Abba and Imma, shielding them with his body. "Let Wit go."

"Wait. *Listen to me.*" Catcher pointed at Sundar's chest. His words came crashing over each other. "You are instinctually connected to the Primal Network. The Order of Kosmoa is built on that network. I only want your mind—your implants." As Wit shuffled away, he forced her back to the ground and trapped her under the weight of his boot. "Take what you want. Your parents. The girl.

Come with me, and you can have them all. You will not regret it."

"Let Wit go," Sundar said again.

Catcher's lips pressed together. He put the barrel of his rifle to Wit's head. She stiffened. "In exchange for your vow."

Sundar looked at the lite-rifle. Sensor readings flowed off the weapon, a visible stream of data in his virtual overlay. He tested a command, then another, and he was already sure when he said, "I will not walk your path."

Catcher snarled. "The offer becomes less pleasant with every moment you delay."

He pulled the trigger.

The rifle only sputtered.

A look of total confusion broke over Catcher's face. He raised the weapon and checked the light bolts on the side. Turned the weapon over and over, swearing with each frantic motion.

Sundar sent another command.

The rifle hummed to life, overheating in Catcher's hands. He threw the rifle across the sand, cursing. Wit wriggled out from beneath his heel and made a break for it, but Catcher snatched her around the body and wrapped one arm around her neck in a stranglehold.

He turned to face Sundar. "Kill me and you kill her too."

"You have forgotten one thing," Sundar said.

He reached out to the other node of the Primal Network.

He looked out at himself through Catcher's robotic eye. Another virtual overlay spread out in the captain's vision, tinted red, an automatic targeting system linked to the rifle Sundar had hacked. Warnings popped up as Sundar shut down the eye's cooling system. Again he overloaded the system with commands. Conflicting, critical commands. The targeting system blurred and spun out of control. And the eye began to heat up.

Catcher screamed. His head snapped back as he tore at the eye's metal rim with his fingers. Blood ran down his face as he pried the cybernetic implant out of his eye socket, each breath a hiss of pain.

Wit broke free.

Sundar crossed the sands to the captain's weapon. He picked it up, leveled the rifle at Catcher's head, and charged up a laser blast.

Catcher stared at him through one dull eye. "I searched for years. So many years."

The rifle did not sputter this time.

• • •

The surviving Desperados had fled to Longstay Alfa. Perhaps one or two still circled the crash site at a distance, staying well out of the fighter's range.

Sundar sat in the shade beneath the fighter's wing and watched the sands. Catcher's rifle rested in his lap. Somehow he knew its every measurement and function.

Next to him, Imma put a cold, wet cloth on Abba's head. Sundar's father stirred. He opened his eyes and stared out at the sand. "This is not the heaven I hoped to wake to." He blinked at Imma. "Oh. Now it is."

Imma smiled and stroked his head.

Sundar touched his father's hands. "Listen to me, father of mine."

Abba's gaze shuttered. He took a deep breath and, wincing, levered himself into a sitting position.

"You are going back to the Hackery," Sundar said. "You and Imma. You will go back to work, and you will walk the same path you have walked for years."

Abba turned and peered out at the sands. His gaze roamed across the bodies of fallen Desperados and caught on Catcher's prone form. His face went white. He pressed his hands to his head. "They will not forgive this. They will come for us."

Sundar shook his head. "They will come for *me.*"

Abba stared at him. Slowly the sands of recognition trickled into his eyes. "No."

Sundar put a hand on his father's shoulder. "My path is different from yours."

He could see the end now. His people singing songs of rejoicing, walking a free path in Donumdonair's light. Longstay Alfa's power broken. The Desperados scattered back into their roving bands.

That day was far off. But it was there like a promise, a woven cord on his wrist. He looked at his parents and he bit his lip.

"Farewell, my child," Imma whispered.

Abba made a choked sound. "Son of mine." He rose. His head barely came to Sundar's shoulders. He wrapped his arms around Sundar's midsection and hugged him with all the strength of thirty years of cutting and stacking iron hull plates.

When Sundar touched his father's shoulder, Abba pulled away, his expression somber, still twisted with pain. "You will come back to us."

"I don't know when."

"You will," Abba said, and he sat next to Imma, took her hand, and gripped it in his own. Imma smiled, her eyes distant.

Above them, the fighter creaked, and Wit dropped from the wing.

117

She pulled the straps of her oversized backpack off her shoulders and planted it at Sundar's feet. "Time's up. They're sending another tank out."

Sundar rose. "Keep them safe."

Wit nodded but avoided Sundar's gaze. She started to step away. But he caught her wrist and slipped his hand into hers.

"Thank you," he said.

Wit finally looked up at him. She wore a pensive look, the same haunted expression that had lingered about her eyes since Catcher assaulted her. Sundar thought he knew some of it. Making your own path against the weight of the world was not easy.

But she did not let go of his hand. Instead, her fingers tightened on his, and she leaned in and put her forehead against his chest.

"Did you really," she whispered, "come for me?"

Sundar ran his hand through her hair, combing out tangles and dust. "Give me your arm."

He untied the cord of cords from his own wrist and knotted it instead around her leather vambrace. Two into two into two. A promise he did not yet dare to speak.

Wit picked at the weave. "Did you make this?"

Sundar smiled and turned her to face the Hackery. "Ask my parents what it means."

The backpack fit his shoulders like it was made for him. He took Catcher's rifle. He lifted his gaze to the crater walls, to the bounds of Longstay Alfa's power. The path stretched out before him.

Find the story of Samson in Judges 14 and 15.

The Traitor

Abigail Bales

Still. Still.

It was too still.

It was a moment between moments, an in-between, a breath before a scream.

Reuben looked back and forth between the Kosmoan and Sura, his betrothed. Her eyes were shut, she scarcely breathed beneath the Kosmoan's knife on her throat. Her blue dress fluttered in the desert breeze, her long black hair in tangles around her round face.

Three other Kosmoans stood in the wreckage of Sura's home, fifty paces away, laughing. The Kosmoans wore their government's black battle uniforms—armored through the chest, covered head to foot in technology.

Charred and smoking planks of wood lay one upon the other, jabbing up into the sky and the sand below, walls that would never again stand. What used to be a well loved little house in the middle of nowhere was now merely a remnant—a plundered remnant of what Sura had worked so hard to acquire.

Feathers of pale blue smoke drifted into the sky, acrid, smelling earthy. Withered pink desert flowers drifted away with it.

Reuben shifted his weight, preparing to charge, the sand under his feet shifting with him. Sweat began to glisten along the line between his black hair and tanned forehead. He wore a light cotton tunic and a leather vest, his feet only clad in sandals, hardly ready for battle on this day—dressed instead to sit and watch the sunset while he held his betrothed and dreamed of their future life together.

The Kosmoan captain tightened his grip on the knife. He was tall, unconcerned, and with a mustache too big for his thin face. "Don't try anything," he said. "I'll kill her. If you want her to live, don't move. We'll take our goods and leave."

"Your goods?" Reuben took the slightest step forward, testing the waters. "You mean *hers*? You mean everything she owns? You destroy her home, take all her belongings, *and* threaten to kill her?"

Reuben's hand reached for the light rifle behind his back. He just had to keep the Kosmoan talking for another minute.

"You make us seem so evil," the Kosmoan said coolly. "We're just doing what our god commands. We're religious, unlike you Journeymen and your—hey—HEY!"

Reuben reached for it. He lunged towards the Kosmoan. His hands fumbled at his back, groping for the rifle—he pulled it from his belt, finger on the trigger, the pressure building—

There was an empty *click*. Nothing happened.

He was out of ammo.

Sura screamed in pain as the Kosmoan's blade dug into the soft skin of her neck.

Reuben let loose a roar. He tossed his useless rifle away and launched his body toward the Kosmoan. His hand found the Kosmoan's and wrenched the knife out of his grasp—a sharp, hot flash of pain ripped through his palm as the knife tore his hand open.

Rike!

"What do you think you're doing?" the Kosmoan yelled, recovering from the shock and rising back to his feet. He pulled Sura back by her throat, just out of Rueben's reach.

"HEY!" a deep voice roared behind them. They both froze. Reuben's palm poured dark blood onto the sand, little clumps forming in the puddle.

It was his father, Jair. He held a light rifle, finger poised on the trigger, aiming it at the Kosmoan, who took a half step back.

"No need to get feisty," the Kosmoan said, his pale eyes stretched wide.

Jair stepped closer, keeping the rifle aimed at the Kosmoan.

The other three Kosmoan terrorists approached from the blue-smoked rubble that was Sura's home. The silver hourglass emblem on their lapels gleamed in the evening light.

"Wait, you're Jair." The mustached Kosmoan looked curiously at Reuben's father, and his voice shifted from anger to confusion. "What are you doing? I thought we were on good terms."

Sura's eyes pressed shut, her lips flat and trembling. Reuben's eyes locked on the Kosmoan's spider-like hand on her throat.

"I'm sure this is just a misunderstanding," Jair said slowly, but didn't lower the rifle.

The rest of the Kosmoans stopped by their comrade, hands on their weapons.

"I'm acting in defense of my son and future daughter-in-law," Jair said. "I hope this won't change anything between us."

Sura's eyes blinked open and met Reuben's. They shared the same expression—confusion.

Another Kosmoan nodded towards Jair, an eyebrow cocked. "Jair, is it? Nice to finally see you face to face. Why don't you put down the rifle and have a civilized conversation."

"Let go of Sura, and I will."

The first Kosmoan glanced towards his comrades, shrugged, and let go of her.

In an instant, she was in Reuben's arms. She said nothing, but her body trembled all over. Never had she held him so tightly. Reuben pulled her a few strides away from the others, looking her over, from her leather boots to her thick dark hair and back again.

A thin sliver of blood trickled down her throat. Reuben tugged on the hem of his white shirt, ripping a few inches from the bottom. He held the fabric to her throat, watching as it absorbed the blood, staining it deep red. The cut wasn't deep, thank Donum.

Reuben wrapped his strong arms around his betrothed and rocked her back and forth, her head firmly resting beneath his chin as he watched his father. The sun was setting, turning his father and the Kosmoans into dark silhouettes.

Jair's head inclined slightly, his lips hidden by his black and gray peppered beard. He lowered the rifle.

The first Kosmoan nodded deeply. "With respect, Jair, you neglected to put the mark on this young lady's home. If there had been a mark…"

"Surely you'll repay her for the damage," Jair interjected

The Kosmoans glanced at each other, then burst into laughter. "Nonsense," the mustached one said. "That's not in our job description." Jair turned then, spotted Reuben and Sura.

His face was a monument of stony lines—his eyebrows, the creases by his eyes—all hard and flat.

"Hey, Reuben," Jair said, somehow maintaining a normal tone. "Take Sura home. Let me deal with these snipes."

Reuben hesitated, glancing at his dunebike...then slowly nodded. "All right," he said in a low voice, the word turned up ever so slightly into a question.

Tendrils of blue smoke drifted into the sky. His father nodded.

"Sura," Reuben whispered. "Let's go."

She fell into step with him and mounted the dunebike. It roared to life beneath them. Sand spat up into their faces as they rode away.

Away from his father.

Away from the smoke.

• • •

The night stretched on and on. At the end of it was a house with a yellow light in the window. The dark desert was speckled with a pale blue glow, like shards of stars in the sand, thickening as they moved closer to Havvoth Jair—Jair's lands—where Reuben and his twenty-nine brothers lived along with their father. The great expanse of land was divided into thirty districts, populated with large homes for them all, fields where cattle and donkeys grazed, trees, wells, and storehouses for their dunebikes and other vehicles, like the newest mudship that had been delivered last week. Reuben steered them past the donkey barns, large and looming in the darkness, past districts three and two, where his oldest brothers lived, and into the heart of district one—where he lived with his father.

123

The dunebike skidded to a stop in front of his home. Sura was limp against Reuben's back. Gently, he powered down the bike and helped her off.

"You can take the spare bed," Reuben said. "I'll wait for my father. Go rest."

She nodded, but didn't move. Her eyes lingered on the ground—on a tiny tendril of grass poking up through the sand, like gold in the light.

"What does it mean?" she whispered. "What was he saying?"

Reuben put a finger to her lips, though his stomach turned with the same questions, around and around and around.

"I don't know," he murmured, tilting her face to his. "Hey. Look at me. It's going to be okay. We'll be married soon. You can live with us until Father builds our house. It'll be all right."

Her cheeks were hollow—her chocolate eyes darkened and blood-shot. Tears clung to her thick lashes but didn't fall.

Reuben kissed her softly. "I love you."

She touched his cheek, then disappeared inside.

It was late. The sand merged with the sky in one long swath of darkness.

"Reuben?"

Reuben turned sharply, a great barrier of silence descending between himself and his father. Jair's eyes reflected the moon like two silver beetles.

Reuben stood in the yellow shaft of porchlight; Jair, just outside, in the silvery darkness.

"Son," Jair said. He sagged, his broad shoulders sloping towards the ground, a hand on his beard. "I'm so sorry. I never meant for that to happen."

Reuben brushed his hand through his thick black hair, out of his face, baring his sweaty forehead to the air.

"I don't understand," he said, his eyebrows lowering. "It sounded like those terrorists *knew* you."

Jair ran his hand over his beard, bowing his head so that his face was cast in shadow.

"There's a lot I need to explain, Reuben," he said finally. He took a step forward, into the light. "Will you come with me? So I can tell you everything?"

Reuben frowned and glanced back down at the tendril of grass before he nodded

Jair motioned for Reuben to mount his dunebike, then mounted his own. "Follow me," he said.

The dunebikes roared to life, the yellow headlights blinding against the darkness. The world shook with the bikes, and when they stopped, the silence was deafening.

They were at the Refinery. The massive building in the center of Havvoth Jair where his father managed his trade. Reuben had never been allowed inside.

• • •

A door opened. They passed through into musty darkness.

Reuben's eyes began to sting, and his throat itched. A rebreather was pressed into his hands and he tugged it over his face. A small click resounded through the room and the ceiling buzzed, electric lights flickering to life above them.

They seemed to be in a sort of large workroom, with long

wooden tables stretched out over the cold concrete floors. The walls were of a sandy brown stone and went on as far as Reuben could see. Dark spots on the wall drew Reuben's eyes. Immediately to the right of the door, in perfect columns, evenly spaced...of a deep rusty-brown color.

Reuben jolted as he realized they were handprints.

Handprints of blood.

Reuben stepped closer, and Jair wordlessly followed.

Beneath each handprint was scratched a name. All names that he recognized... The names of his twenty-nine older brothers, dwindling all the way down to a blank spot... A spot where his own name was etched into the wall.

Reuben.

Reuben glanced down at his wounded hand, which had already begun to scab—then up at his father.

"Give me your hand." Jair held out his own, coarse and tan, trembling slightly with age and perhaps trepidation. From his belt, he pulled a short-bladed knife.

"What are you doing?" Reuben took a step back.

"I will tell you everything," Jair said. "But you must take an oath of secrecy. A blood oath."

He looked pointedly at Reuben's clenched hand.

"You aren't touching me until you explain," Reuben said, his back against the wall, rows of handprints next to his head.

"Give me your palm."

Eyes darted from hand to wall and back. Reuben was speechless. His mouth opened and closed.

"Son," Jair said, and his eyes softened slightly. "You can trust me."

Reuben's heart beat harder and harder until he was sure it would burst through his ribs.

So he extended his palm, watching it tremble out in the open. He turned his face away as the blade dragged across the wound, reopening it. The pain was almost too much to bear.

The blood covered his hand and dripped down onto the concrete below.

"Put your palm here on the wall," Jair instructed, and Reuben did. Jair pushed the hand against the wall until it shook violently, the pain so intense that Reuben began to feel dizzy.

"With Donumdonair as our witness, Son, do you swear to secrecy what I am about to show you and tell you?"

Did he have a choice?

"You must swear," Jair said again. His eyes were wide and paranoid and intense. "You must swear never to tell. Our lives depend upon it."

Breath upon breath upon breath, and still the air was too thick to swallow.

"Father," Reuben whispered, his voice clawing its way from his throat, pleading. "What are you doing?"

"*I'm protecting you!*" Jair exploded. "Reuben! Don't you get it? The hyrim is what keeps us alive!"

Reuben wrenched his hand from the wall, a singular drop of blood slithering down the wall beneath his handprint.

"Hyrim? What?"

Reuben held his hand close to his body, against his stomach.

"Have you never seen the blue lights in the desert at night?"

The blood soaked through his shirt and began to dampen his stomach beneath. "What about them?"

"Those lights are hyrim. Highly explosive and highly valuable. The source of my wealth since I bought all this land at your age. Ever since, I've been trading it with my clients."

"Clients?" Reuben snorted. "You mean those terrorists?"

Jair stepped closer and put a hand on Reuben's shoulder. "Listen to me, Son. You have to understand. They are the source of everything you've ever had. Comfort. Security. Our home. *Your* future."

Reuben could hear the blood dripping onto the concrete.

"You're a traitor to the Journeymen," he whispered. *"We're* traitors."

He couldn't breathe.

"I did it for you." Jair put a finger to Reuben's dripping handprint. "This is your blood oath," he said. "This is our secret. Speak of it and you risk destroying everything you've ever known."

Reuben felt as though his throat was closing and he couldn't swallow past the massive lump. Pressure built up behind his eyes. He refused to let himself cry.

"Are all my brothers in on this?" he asked softly.

Jair nodded. "They all made their blood oaths when they came of age and were given districts of Havvoth Jair to control as their own. I was going to initiate you when you were married next year." His eyes softened slightly. "I didn't mean for you to find out this way."

"I understand," Reuben whispered, teeth clenched. "May I go?"

Jair had barely said a word before Reuben was out the door, running, running, as far from the bloody handprint as he could get.

His father's voice rang through the desert, *"I did it for you!"*

Reuben wanted to throw up.

He wanted to scream.

The desert could scarcely contain his anguish.

. . .

Reuben stopped running when his legs would carry him no further. The night was inky, a dripping page of stars smeared across the sky. All in one instant, the exhaustion came back, and Reuben went from his feet to his knees to all fours. He lay his head in the sand, wishing for...something.

A groan became a shout and then a roar—pervading the desert, ringing through the night, falling on deaf ears. Eyes closed. Breath in and out. Cheek against warm grains of sand.

He felt something prick at his skin. Looking down, a faint blue glow pulsed below his nose.

Hyrim, he thought.

Sticking a finger into the sand, he wormed his way down far enough that he was able to get ahold of it. Sharp pain shot through his hand and he let go.

A small trail of luminescent blue smoke drifted up from the sand.

Sitting up, looking out over the desert, hundreds of faint blue spots became visible.

Donumdonair, Reuben's soul cried. *What am I going to do?*

Reuben looked down at himself—his fit, lean body, clothed with expensive leather and cotton.

He looked at his dunebike gleaming in the moonlight in the distance.

He saw the Refinery, the buildings scattered across the horizon, and the faint blue lights across the great expanse of land his father owned.

He looked and his stomach turned, bile rose in his throat.

"What am I going to do?" he mumbled. "Oh, Donum, what am I going to do?

In a moment of blinding fury, he pulled his goggles off of his head and hurled them as far from him as possible.

The goggles arced gracefully through the air, glistening in the silver moonlight, until they fell onto a small glowing lump in the sand.

A tiny golden-blue explosion lit the night, followed by plumes of familiar blue smoke.

• • •

It was early.

Rueben had barely slept.

Sura sat alone in the kitchen, cradling a steaming mug at the table in the darkness. She was wrapped in a grey silken robe, tied loosely around her small frame.

Silently, he joined her and slipped his arm around her, kissing her cheek.

"Your father went out to work," Sura murmured.

Reuben cut to the chase. "You know, don't you," he said.

It wasn't a question.

"Yes."

Reuben held his forehead for a moment. "I've been up all night," he admitted, "thinking."

"About what?"

"Nothing," he said. "Everything. I don't know."

Sura set down her cup, sloshing some coffee onto the tabletop. Wordlessly she put a towel over the spot. "You're going to put a stop to this, right?"

Reuben turned, surprised. "What? What could *I* do?"

"What could you *not* do?" Sura took his hands, unfolded them, and trailed her finger gently over the wound. It had begun to scab once more. He hadn't bothered to wash it.

She stood, retrieved a damp cloth, and pressed it against the wound. He flinched.

"Reuben, you don't mean you plan to continue going on as if nothing happened?"

"Well," Reuben faltered, watching as she dabbed the dried blood away. "It would be easier, wouldn't it? Our entire life relies on my father providing for us. We can't just give that up."

"Our entire life? What are you talking about?"

Reuben looked into her eyes. "He's providing our wedding. Our home. Our business. Our land and technology and everything else we need!"

"We don't need those things," Sura retorted. "Besides, if they're being provided by your family's traitorism, I don't want them."

She sniffed. Reuben's face twitched. He didn't like the way she'd said *your family's traitorism.*

As though he'd had a part in it.

He pulled his hand away from her and prodded it with his other hand, feeling the fleshiness of his palm and how much it hurt with every jab.

Sura sighed through her nose.

"Sura," Reuben pleaded. "Please, try to understand… I just want the best life for us. I want you to be happy. I want *us* to be happy. And if that means accepting my father's generosity, despite the source…"

Sura drew away from him slightly, standing, her bare feet padding across the marble tile, back and forth, back and forth.

"What would Donumdonair want you to do?" she whispered.

Reuben groaned. "Don't talk about Donumdonair. He probably isn't even real. A real god wouldn't have let my father be involved with terrorists in the first place."

Sura let out a soft gasp. "You don't mean that, Reuben…"

"What if I do?"

"What if you're here to put a stop to this business?"

Reuben stood and leaned against the table.

"Just think about it," Sura continued. "Your father is selling weapons to terrorists that are being directly used to persecute our people. The Journeymen. Donumdonair's chosen people."

Reuben covered his face with his hands and smelled the rusty scent of the wound.

"What if you're here to stop it?"

Reuben felt her hand on his shoulder.

"You can't live in comfort while our people are persecuted," Sura's voice was soft in his ear. "Not without doing something about it."

Reuben sagged against her. "I know."

She reached up and put her arms around his neck. "So what are you going to do about it?"

• • •

Together they spoke until the sun had risen and golden rays angled through the blinds.

By the time Jair's dunebike had roared to a halt outside the house, they were leisurely sipping coffee together as though nothing had happened...

Jair opened the door, grunting something unintelligible and scratching his beard. He tugged off his leather jacket and stamped the sand off his feet.

He turned and saw the couple at the table.

Icy silence.

Sniffing, he hung the jacket by the door and entered the kitchen. "Good morning," he said.

Same tone. Same smile. But the light was gone from his eyes.

Reuben stood abruptly. "Good morning."

Reuben looked at Sura, she stood also. Together, they watched as Jair bumbled around the kitchen, making himself a cup of coffee, grumbling about lazy wives who didn't bother waking up to make him breakfast (he had thirteen). Finally, he turned, taking a swig of the black liquid and leaning against the counter.

"Sura," he said. "I hear you're staying with us until I get your house built?"

Sura glanced at Reuben, then to Jair, nodding. "Yes, I suppose so." They stood in silence, Jair taking a long drag of his coffee. "I'll get started on your house here soon," Jair continued. "That way, you two can get married sooner. We'll have to talk about plans and all that."

Reuben and Sura nodded. "We'll let you know."

"I need you to feed the donkeys for me," Jair said. "By the way, your brothers and I will be gone...on...on business. Until sundown." Jair avoided eye contact as he swished his coffee around in his mug.

"Fine, all right," Reuben nodded.

He and Sura left, leaving Jair alone in the kitchen to swish his coffee all he wanted.

"See you later," Jair called after them. The door shut behind them.

. . .

Skidding over the dunes, sand bounced off of Reuben's new pair of goggles and stung his bare cheeks. His other pair were long gone, an exploded little mess of metal out in the desert somewhere. Finding a new pair hadn't been hard. Jair had a stockpile.

The Refinery loomed in the distance, its vast concrete walls spanning over an acre of Havvoth Jair. Its immense shadow contrasted with the sunlit sand. Along the eastern wall, dozens of dunebikes were parked side to side—his older brothers'. All twenty-nine of them. They were all here.

And judging by the fifteen loaded donkeys tied up beside the dunebikes, they'd be leaving soon.

Reuben steered his dunebike around to the western side of the Refinery and powered it down, swinging his leg over and leaning the handle against the wall.

Scanning the desert around him, all was empty. The warm breeze scattered sand over sand. For a moment, all was still and calm.

All for justice, Reuben reminded himself, his back against the cold concrete wall. *All for Donumdonair.*

Reuben found a backdoor and entered the Refinery. The lights were off and it was cold—goosebumps rose on his bare arms.

Silent, still…Reuben listened. Circulating air whirred, carrying the sound of low voices.

He was in a back hall, and supplies were scattered randomly across the floor. The opposite wall held a closed door. A strip of yellow light shone beneath it.

He found a spare rebreather amongst the supplies on the floor, pulling it over his mouth and nose to breathe freely.

He crept close to the door, palm on the handle—he gave it a slow pull. It gave easily. Unlocked.

He slowly opened it a crack…

"…a good-sized order," Jair was saying. "As you know, we're using half the donkeys to transport it to Nedrino."

Reuben put his ear into the shaft of light, legs quivering to hold him still. He pressed his cheek against the rough sandstone wall.

"We can't be late this time," Jair continued. "We absolutely must stay on good terms with them. We had a close call yesterday…and we can't afford to lose their business. We must move quickly."

Grunts of assent from Reuben's older brothers. One of them—it sounded like Micah—asked, "close call? What happened?"

A pause, a creaking—Reuben froze, his muscles tensed up—but the familiar sound of his father's voice reached his ears and he relaxed.

"The Kosmoans targeted Sura last night," Jair said at last. "I'd forgotten to put the mark on her house when she became Reuben's betrothed. I wasn't thinking. There was almost violence. Thankfully, I'm a good talker."

A pause, then one of the brothers commented, "Diplomacy, eh?"

Jair was laughing. "Works every time."

More laughter, deep and rumbling through the room.

"They were lenient," Jair said. "Thank Donum. But I can't risk losing their business, especially with Reuben's upcoming marriage. I need to make it up to him and Sura somehow, so I want to give them a grand home. I can't do that without this business."

Reuben's fingers shook, and the great monster in his belly reared its head. Pictures flashed through his mind—of a house with a garden—a kitchen where Sura could bake—a library where they could read to their children.

He shook his head. He had to focus. He couldn't let himself get distracted.

Justice.

He closed his eyes and clenched his fist against the wall, knuckles cold on concrete.

In time, the meeting drew to a close, and the room on the other side of the wall rose in a cacophony of chaos and sound.

Reuben waited in the darkness until the yellow shaft of light was switched off into musty darkness.

The noise dissipated, donkeys brayed far away, and then all was silent.

Still Reuben waited, until the darkness had filled his eyes and nose and mouth and lungs and mind.

• • •

Finally Reuben couldn't take the waiting any longer.

He pulled open the door and entered the main room of the Refinery. It was massive. Last night, he'd only seen one side of it, by the door, by the handprints.

He looked down at his palm. The wound had scabbed completely over now. He looked away and tightened his hand into a fist.

The room stretched on as far as the eye could see, grey upon grey upon grey, tables lined up and stretched out, supplies askew, blue dust shimmering luminescent in the darkness.

In the darkness, it was easy to see just how much residue hung in the air. Hardly a square inch existed without the shining blue powder.

Reuben found the light switch and flipped it. A low buzzing—the lights came to life, momentarily blinding him. He shielded his eyes, and when he opened them, the blue dust was nowhere to be seen. It was completely invisible when the lights were on.

"All right," Reuben whispered, his voice metallic in the rebreather. "Let's get this over with."

It didn't take him long to find the stash of hyrim. It was stored in wooden crates, padded with wool. There were twelve crates that came to Reuben's waist, and he estimated that each crate held over a thousand of the small blue stones.

Slowly, methodically, he worked to push the crates to the center of the room, lined up with a few feet between them. He took the lid off of one and ran a gloved hand over the stones. They were smooth and the size of acorns. Each one he touched crumbled instantly, letting out a semitransparent plume of blue smoke.

A sudden beeping filled the room. A red light flashed on Reuben's rebreather. In his confusion, his leg slammed into a table, and he cursed.

"*Danger. Faulty system,*" an electronic voice said. "*Danger. Faulty system. Remove rebreather immediately. Danger. Faulty system.*"

Rike!

The room seemed to be closing in on him, his lungs burned and his breath came in short gasps.

Reuben glanced back at the crates of hyrim.

He had no time to lose.

No time to lose. No time to lose.

No time...

His body shook and he felt as though a thick blue fog was rolling over his consciousness...it was all he could do to fight it off. Run. Run. Run!

His footsteps resounded through the cavelike room, running, running, towards the crates, nearly tripping over one, tearing the lids off and throwing them askew. Silence to chaos in a few insane moments.

The lids were off, the hyrim exposed to the air, exposed to whatever Reuben would dare to throw at them.

"*Danger. Faulty system.*"

His head pounded in time with the flashing red light.

He looked around. It would have to be something heavy, something easily accessible, something relatively small that he could be sure of hitting the target.

There was nothing.

Rike! There was nothing!

Hands shaking, he fumbled around, scarcely in control of his limbs.

"*Danger. Faulty system. Remove rebreather immediately.*"

Reuben's hands flew to the rebreather.

His fingers ran over it, feeling the cool weight of the metal.

He had no time to think it over.

Quickly, he removed his rebreather, trying to breathe as little as possible.

It was slow and fast all at once.

The rebreather left his hand, angled through the air in a graceful arc, landing directly in one of the crates. Reuben spun on his heel, one foot in front of another, faster, faster, out the door as the ground began to rumble.

His chest began to heave as soon as he was out of the building, sucking in huge lungfuls of the delicious twilight air.

Adrenaline coursed through his veins.

Feet pounding divots into sand—lungs and thighs burning—sweat trembling in the cold night air—the earth began to shake beneath his feet.

Harder. Harder. Harder.

The sand shifted and Reuben lost his balance. The ground rose up to meet him, grains of sand smashing into his face.

He turned, clawing at the ground, trying to get back to his feet only to fall again.

Stillness. Then a golden-blue explosion lit the horizon. The earth shook.

Reuben lay still, watching the gold turn to yellow to a deep orange, followed by dark plumes of smoke flickering up into the night sky.

He felt cold.

A hand touched his shoulder. Reuben knew without turning around who it was.

"Thank Donum," Reuben gasped, gripping Sura, salty droplets clinging to his cheeks. "You're safe."

Sura pulled him to his feet, and when he couldn't hold his balance, she sank to the sand beside him, holding him.

"It's done," she whispered. "It's over."

Reuben blinked.

Was it over? Just like that?

They sat together until all that remained of the explosion was the blue smoke slithering through the sky.

Then Sura stood and extended a hand to her betrothed.

Reuben took it.

Together, they set off into the night.

Away from the smoke.

Away from everything they'd ever known.

Towards a new life.

Find the story of Jair in Judges 10:3-5.

Prison of the Mind

Elijah Fitz

Thou art become (O worst imprisonment!)
The Dungeon of thy self; thy soul
(Which men enjoying sight oft without cause complain)
Imprisoned now indeed,
In real darkness of the body dwells,
Shut up from outward light
To incorporate with gloomy night
For inward light alas
Puts forth no visual beam

JOHN MILTON

Sand clogged his throat, fine grits coagulating in his spit and strangling him. His cage was outside. He didn't need eyes to know that. The wind on his face was oven-hot, and the sun itself cooked the iron bars of his cage. When he tried to stretch, his fingers touched the bars and he felt their burning bite. He didn't make much of an effort to stretch, anyway.

Every little movement was agony. He'd never been in agony before, never known pain. He never knew how many types of hurt there were. Bruises, cuts, burns. All hurt in different ways. He poked the bruise on his leg with no idea how it had been given to him. To touch it made his gums itch and writhe inside his broken mouth. He categorized the pains: the bruises, cuts, burns, and scrapes. Every time he tallied them, he began again and discovered more. At the end of every tally, he reached up to his face and added two more—holes, where his eyes once were.

The pain was not the least of it. He could hear them, just out of reach of his cage. If he dared to brave the pain of the hot iron, he could stretch his hands through the bars and brush the stone wall of Kosmoa's temple. Inside, they laughed and squealed in delight and pleasure, safe and cool in their temple. A party to celebrate Sun's capture. Of the Desperado's victory over him. The party had been ongoing since the morning: orgies and games, wine and spirits, hedonism unbridled and ridden bareback.

All he saw was darkness, all he felt was pain, all he heard was mockery, and all he tasted was sand and blood. There was a time, he recalled, when he could have broken through the cage without a thought. Now, thinking was all he had. Eyes burned out. Body gone to waste, too weak to even stand on its own, to do anything but sit and burn. His bones were hollow, and his strength—once it had been so great—was gone.

He didn't even want it back. He didn't want the euphoria of violence or the satisfaction of judgment. He'd done it all before. Then and now, when violence ended, and wrath was satisfied, when he lay on the ground, spent and exhausted and sure of his death, all he really wanted was a drink of water.

. . .

Panting, Sun fell to his knees. The blood-soaked sand squelched and shifted under his weight. The glow of his exo-suit was fading, the once blazing light now less than a candle as life fled from his suit and it died. His ears were still ringing with the clash of swords, the boom of lite-rifles, the screams of the dying. Fires raged around him. Sun could not tell if the sweltering heat was from the flames or the sun itself.

Sun had been willing to let it go. They make his wife a spy, and he destroys their crops. No matter. Sun had never loved her in the first place. Let the traitor die with the crops. But the Desperados wouldn't stand the insult. They hunted him, hounded him—and even this Sun would have laughed off.

But when the Desperados could not find Sun, they turned their wrath to his kinsmen—beating, bruising, burning them until his people came and begged Sun to give himself over. This he could not let go. He told his kinsmen to bind him, to bring him to the Desperados who so wanted blood. He gave it to them.

He'd killed hundreds of them. One after another, Desperados fell to his hands. He could still feel the crunch of their bones, the warm spray of blood. He'd been a blaze, burning through the ropes that bound him as Donumdonair filled him with devouring fire. He'd been unstoppable—bullets bounced off his chest and swords shattered against his skin. Not even his hair had suffered harm. Now, with Donumdonair gone again, Sun came back to himself. His hands shook. Wet blood blackened everything. It coated his hair, his clothes.

The glow of his suit winked out entirely. Now it was just a frame of dead metal weighing him down. The rods lined his spine, his limbs, like a child's stick figure laid over his body.

His weapon of the day—what was once a piece of petrified wood—was splintered and shattered. He sat back on his heels, a giant amongst the bodies of ordinary men around him.

All around him, the fires burned crops and devoured life. His muscles felt slack on his bones; he couldn't move them no matter how he tried.

Breathing was laborious—the hot air in his throat burned, heavy with smoke. Never before had he wished for a rebreather. His heart still beat heavy in his chest, though that, too, was quickly losing strength. He needed water.

His head grew too heavy to keep up, and it bent backward until the world shifted and the smoke was all he could see.

"Is this it?" the words came out as a rasp. He imagined the words dancing with the smoke, joining together to rise as a message delivered high to heaven. "A thousand dead for you. No bullet or blade touched me. All that, just to die *of thirst*? You saved me just to kill me?"

The piece of broken wood fell from his slack fingers. It landed straight, sticking in the ground, perfectly vertical. No answer from Donumdonair. Sun fell over on his side and let the flames take him, too weak to do anything else.

He was not long in laying there before water dropped on his face. Sun's eyes fluttered open. Rain? No. The only dark clouds in the sky were smoke. Yet another drop landed on his face. Barely noticeable, and it evaporated quickly from the heat of the flames around him. But unmistakably cool and wet. Sun grunted and sat up.

From the wood, a puttering spray of water. Even as he watched, the spray steadied into a stream, a rush, a geyser. The torrent sprang up and over him, washing the blood from his hands and subduing the fires around him. And like the water, Sun's laughter started as a trickle, rose to a fervor, and gushed forth from him. He crawled towards the geyser, his laugh drowned out by the roar of the water. Too much for him to drink, too much for even a whole clan to drink.

As the water continued to pour forth, so too did his praises.

• • •

After his victory and the cleansing spring that baptized him, Sun celebrated. How else but with women? It was always so after a fight. When all was said and done, when the strength that rushed upon him was gone and the enemies around him were dead, the memory of his deeds worked him up. He needed a woman. Not just any. *A Desperado woman.* The way they danced, the sway of their hips, and the clothes they wore—diaphanous and free-flowing. Sun loved to see them spin and watch their dresses ride higher and higher up the thigh.

He wanted one, not just for lust but for the satisfaction of yet another victory over the Desperados. *I'll kill you, and you cannot stop me. I take your women—no, they throw themselves at my feet and you just watch. Watch me take another. Look in the window and see. Listen through the door and hear the Desperado women's love for Sun, chosen of the Journeymen.*

Sun entered through Stronci City's gates at noon. The exterior gate was heavy, with two doors, each as wide as Sun's wingspan and short enough that he had to stoop to enter. The gate had been fashioned to keep out invading armies and supplicant refugees—predominantly Sun's own tribe, the Journeymen. Outside the gates, surrounding the city, his people clustered and pushed to get through and were perpetually rebuffed by the closed gate and the rifle-wielding guards. The refugees' faces were burned from the sun, their clothes ripped and ratty, eyes sunken as they turned to look at Sun. They all knew him. How could a Journeymen not recognize Sun, the blaze of glory himself? Towering over even the tallest Desperado and as broad as two of the fattest of them put together, Sun was the hope of their people and he made sure they knew it.

The wind picked up sand and carried it like shrapnel that stung and scoured wherever it hit. On the horizon, a discoloring of light. A dust storm was well on its way. Those without shelter would find themselves buried in the sand; wanderers lost as the landscape remade itself around them. Sun knew these things and knew that the deaths of the refugees was the hope, and the intention, of Stronci's closed gates.

They touched his hands and looked to him for help. He said nothing, but he met their eyes and committed their anguished faces to his memory.

Entrance for Sun was not a difficult thing. The guards knew him either by reputation or sight and allowed him to pass unimpeded. Not that the gates could have stopped him.

The wide city streets were packed full of Desperados and the Order's people, rubbing shoulder to shoulder as they shouted their demands or their deals. It was cramped and sweaty, and the stink of it made Sun's nose itch. The men barely had room to raise an arm to hail a friend or a hawker. Somehow, though, they found more space to squeeze into as Sun passed. None wanted to touch him.

Sun walked carefully through the streets. These people ate and traded. They laughed and jested and argued and gave themselves over to passion inside the gates while his people suffered outside. Sun sneered at one finely dressed priest. His rebreather was too small for his fat face so that flaps of skin hung out around the seal. Fat man, safe inside his walls from storms and the fists of enemies. The whites of his robe untarnished by dirt or sweat. The man had probably never seen the rough side of a hand or felt the barrenness of a dead field in his stomach.

He was addressing Sun, shouting something having to do with strength. What did this fat roach know about strength? Hardly up to Sun's elbow and flesh so soft it looked to be silk. Oh, Sun would show him strength, *indeed.*

A step forward and a sudden weakness in his limbs, his exosuit weighing him down like the yoke on a beast. A rising sickness in his gut. His face scrunched and his cheeks flushed; his tongue thick in his mouth, he turned to vomit. As his eyes moved away from the priest, the nausea abated, and the exosuit was now light as air. Sun took the sign and followed Donumdonair's guidance away from the priest.

There were plenty of brothels in Stronci. Sun didn't even notice which one he went in, didn't notice the lighting or the other patrons, didn't notice the type of wood that made the counter, or the security shadowing him. He stepped up to the matron, hardly even seeing her. He slapped down a dagger he'd looted from one of the Desperados. Good quality—great, even. Rust had barely even started forming on the blade."Your prettiest Desperado woman." he demanded.

The walk from the purchasing room to the private area was a blur.

• • •

When he was finished with her, she laid on his chest, humming

147

contentedly. Her fingers tapped the metal rods grafted onto his forearm, drumming a rhythm

"Such an old model," she said. "It's a miracle the thing is working. Most suits nowadays are like a second skin and those are *rare*. Less than five were made. This is…rudimentary bone reinforcement. Old, old, old."

"You a mechanic?" Sun asked, his voice thick with sleep.

"Oh, I dabble." The excitement in her voice betrayed her. She sat up and started trailing her fingers along, following the straight gray rods up until they connected to his shoulders. "It's—it's *fused to you*," she gasped. "This model wasn't made for this. How are you even walking?"

Sun loved the attention. He let her talk and fawn over him.

A knock resounded from the door, and she sat up straight, ear tilted to the rhythm. Sharp taps, a pause. Two more hard raps. The encoded message lasted only seconds.

"What was that?" Sun asked, trepidation already growing. Any trace of sleep was gone.

"Matron. She says my people sent out a hit on you. They want to kill you."

Sun laughed. "Your people? I'd like to see them try. I'll crush what they send against me like they were roaches. Your people *are* roaches."

She was not laughing with him. "Roaches? What does that say about you? Every pleasure house in the city knows you only pick us *roaches*."

"I said your people were roaches."

She looked at him blankly, so he went on with a sigh.

"Can you own property? Do you have influence on politics? Do men listen when you talk? You've got to be considered a person to be grouped in a people. You are just…a woman. Not even a roach. If you weren't a woman, you'd be a mechanic, not a prostitute."

He laughed again, pleased at the flush of anger in her cheeks.

She kicked him out after that. *Fair's fair*, he supposed.

Sun was shirtless. He'd been unable to put it on fast enough before she chased him out of the brothel with shouts and slaps at his shoulders.

The light of the city glowed off the clouds, which rolled and rushed across the sky. The night was cold, made colder still by the wind that had gained strength in the hours he'd spent inside. It whisked away any sounds downwind. The sand that didn't try to flay Sun's flesh off stuck to his skin and made him itch. But that was as bad as it'd get inside the gates. Uncomfortable, but not deadly. Outside, though… people would die.

All the busyness of the streets had disappeared. They were all hiding from the storm. And from him. The barrenness of the city pushed him forward. Guidance from Donumdonair.

Sun found himself led to the exterior gates. No guards were out to watch them. To the right of the gates—flush with the wall—yellow light shone through the windows of the guardhouse. Sun could hear the sounds of rolling dice and the shouts of victory and defeat from inside it.

Stronci's walls were made of stone so thick that not even Sun could break through them. The gate was wood. Heavy, thick wood that needed six men to move it, but still…just wood. He crept closer to the gates, laying his hands on the doors, the iron filigree, the reinforcements. The mullion was another thick piece of wood, a bar that slid across the doors and sat between straps of iron bolted into the door. He traced it to the frame, the hinges.

Sun smiled, rolled his shoulders, and stepped up to the gate. He put his back under the mullion so that it rested on the broad of his shoulders. Muscles burned in euphoria, the effort a holy cleansing. His joints sang in holy worship. Though he did not breathe, his chest felt full of crisp, clear, life-giving air. He felt his skeleton could rip out of his skin and begin dancing.

A beep. New life filled the dead exosuit, and Sun began to glow like a knife fresh from the forge. They thought they could trap him inside the city? They thought they could keep his people out and leave them to die in the storms? No. Never again.

He lifted the gate off its hinges and walked out of the city. The crowds of his people were all around him. Faces that were once made of heartbreak and hopelessness now looked back at him with smiles and adoration as they rushed past him into the shelter of the city. Shouts of praise and thanks were louder than the blood thumping in Sun's ears—louder even than the howling wind.

Sun carried the gate as long as he could. The wind pushed him forward and the gate shielded him from the worst of the scouring sand. He was all but carried to the top of a hill overlooking Stronci. At the apex, his suit suddenly winked out its light and the gate slammed down. Sun slunk to the ground and, shielded by the gate, slept.

• • •

Time passed after his statement with Stronci's gates.

He found her dancing in a pub. Long brunette hair, dusty and tangled; delicate legs, small waist. Her dress, stained by sand and sweat, swayed with her hips and teased his eyes. A Desperado. She sashayed over to him and lifted his face to hers.

"I'm Andari," she introduced herself. She danced there most nights. Low yellow lights, blinking and half burned out. Round tables sticky with spilled drink, and chairs too small for a man as large as him. Sun found his own nights now occupied there, watching her. He quickly loved her. And what a feeling that love was! Sun had never been a poet. Leave that to the weaklings, he would say. But Andari could have drawn a thousand sonnets from his lips. All she had to do was ask.

It was as if she'd been made just for him, perfectly fashioned by Donumdonair himself. Not just a Desperado, but from an affluent family and well liked. He learned she'd turned down countless marriage proposals, that her maidenhead was untaken. Taking her would be another win over the Desperados. More than once, Sun had to involve himself when a man too drunk to know what was good for him started trying to take what belonged to Sun. She'd look at him across the bar, helplessness and fear in her eyes, and Sun would rush to her rescue.

She knew how to play the game, too. A wink, a nudge, a chaste kiss, and then she would dance away from Sun. They played this game again and again: Andari drawing close enough for Sun to touch, only to flit away when he tried and laughing all the while.

Her eyes sparkled every time, and Sun could read her words through them. "*Chase me*," they said. Sun obliged.

Time passed.

"I must have you," he told her, once more in the pub, though she was not dancing tonight. He put her on his knee and she kept her arms wrapped around his neck, the flickering lights surrounding her in a gloriole. They sat in the corner, now "their" table, and ignored the stares from jealous patrons. Sun caught the eye of one of them and winked.

151

"Marry me," she replied, shifting her weight until she was comfortable. Each little movement was lithe and smooth, a dancer even without music.

"Fine."

She laughed and kissed his forehead. "Oh no, it's not as easy as that. I won't delude myself and expect you to give up your whores, but I will be worth more than them. I want a part of you that no other woman has."

"Anything, Andari, sweetness."

She leaned down. Electricity rode her breath like lightning as it tickled his ear. It made the hairs on the back of his neck stand up.

"Your strength."

He pulled away from her like she was a viper, the first curlings of distrust and anger in his chest. But her fawning gaze cooled his temper before it could ignite. He laughed and picked her up from his lap, raising her high over his head. "You have it."

She squealed in just the way he loved. Sun was no musician: *leave that to the weaklings*, he thought. But he could listen to that music for a thousand years.

"Put me down, you oaf," Andari giggled. Sun could feel the staring eyes of the other patrons. "I meant that I want to know *how* you're so strong. No man can do what you do."

Sun tilted his chin up and puffed his chest out. He flexed his bicep and made his voice deeper. "You really think so?" He waggled his eyebrows. Andari laughed at him and Sun laughed with her.

"I think so. Tell me, *sunshine*, and I'm yours." She caressed his face and held his eyes.

Sun didn't even have to think about it.

"If you bind me in fresh iron manacles that were quenched in cold water, I will be as weak as any other man. Still stronger than your kinsmen, though."

"Prove it," she said, her smile like a devil's.

Within hours, Sun was laid bare in some back down inn. Andari crawled on top of him and he allowed her to shackle his hands above his head. She kissed his mouth, neck, down to his chest and belly.

And stopped.

Sun growled and bucked his hips against her. "Get on with it."

"SHH!"

Sun's eyes grew wide. His lips curled upward against his teeth. "Did you just *shush* me?"

"Sun, shut *up*! Do you hear that?" She climbed off of him and went to the window, twitching aside the curtain.

"The only thing I hear is a screeching magpie. Get back here or—"

"The Desperados are coming! They're here!"

Anger forgotten in a flash, Sun snapped his restraints and rose to the window, picking Andari up by her shoulders and moving her from the line of sight—snipers were rare, but not impossible.

Nothing outside but the night and its shifting shadows. No Desperados, no mob of enemies.

Sun tilted his head in confusion.

"You lied to me!" Andari began shouting at him. "You think I'm stupid! Shackles, Sun, really? You don't love me. You don't want to marry me!"

"Andari, what the rike are you *talking about*?!"

"Has all the blood left your head?" she pointedly looked down and raised an eyebrow. "I guess it has. I'll spell it out then since you're acting stupid. I asked you to trust me, Sun! I asked you to love me, and you lied to me! '*Iron manacles,*' you oaf. You lied to me—you don't love me and you never have!"

Sun's confusion began to ignite his anger.

He spoke through gritted teeth, anger turning his voice gravelly. "Get out of my sight, Andari. Stop pushing. I won't tell you."

"I am not going *anywhere*. You think I'm the one pushing? That's *rich*, Sun. Every other word out of your mouth is an effort to take me to bed! I haven't pushed anything."

Andari stood in between him and the door. *Leave*, he thought. *I have to leave.* Carefully, very carefully, he sidled by her. Her shouts echoed in the courtyard as she continued after him, right on his heels as he ran out of the inn and into the empty night.

"Coward!" she shouted. "Running away from a woman? The mighty Sun, brought low by a little argument. Look and see, everyone! Look out your windows. See how he runs."

Sun stopped. Turned. He shook with rage.

"I will not be mocked," he growled.

"Give me the same courtesy, then! You lied to me, and worse—*worse!*—you gave me such an obvious lie! Did you really think I would believe that? How could you possibly think I was stupid? Does 'Andari' mean 'idiot' in your mother tongue?"

Sun threw his head back and roared laughter, and his hair swung to brush against the middle of his back. "Hah! Yes, you *are* an idiot, *sweetness*. I didn't think that I needed to give you any more than a simple lie—and look! I was *right*. If the lie was so easy to spot, why bother testing me? You *believed* my stupid lie, which makes *you* stupid."

She slapped him, and Sun's laughter ceased immediately. They locked eyes, and Sun relished the fear and regret he saw in hers. It made his heart sweat and his gut roil. Yes, she should be afraid. Others would be killed for such an act. But Sun was not without mercy. He tossed her to the side and left her in the dirt.

He felt hot, his hands curled and uncurled again and again. He wished a thief would try him so he could put his fist through their brain.

This time, the woman knew her place. She stayed on the ground, shouting and begging his forgiveness even as he sauntered away. She crawled after him, leaving bloody tracks in the dirt where she'd skinned her knees. She wrung her hands, kissed the ground, held onto his ankle, and made him drag her. She mewled as only a woman could. "No, please! Sun, I'm sorry, please don't go."

"Fine." Sun relented. "Get out of my sight and maybe—maybe—I will eventually forgive you."

But how could he not have forgiven her? Sun loved to hear her laugh, her squeal. He loved that she could talk circles around him. He loved the wine they shared and the way it discolored her lips. Apart from her, the fire of his anger burned out, and love lit a new burning in his breast. He needed to see her again.

· · ·

Sun was watching her dance. A private showing, her apology for him. Her knees were still scabbed over, and if she bent too low they cracked and blood dripped down her legs.

She finished her dance and sat at the edge of the table, panting. She took the cup of wine from his hand and sipped it. She smiled at him while he stared.

155

"Aren't you ever scared?" she asked, handing the wine back.

He cocked one eyebrow as he considered the inquiry. "I'm not sure. It depends."

"Eloquent as always. *Very* loquacious."

Sun laughed as if he were in on the joke.

"There are many types of fear. When I was a kid, I would wake from a nightmare and be afraid to open my eyes. I've been afraid before."

"Not fear like *that*. That fear is not real! There's no substance to it. All you have to do is open your eyes, and the fear is gone—*whoosh* like the wind."

"That's true for all fear. It fades when you face it."

"No. You face a charging calvary alone, bullets are shot at you or an executioner's sword is hovering over your neck—the odds are insurmountable and your death is upon you no matter if your eyes are open or closed, and it won't go away when the sun rises. There's a different kind of danger in the daylight."

Sun looked at her, his head tilted and a bewildered smile on his lips. "I don't understand."

Andari sighed. "*Fine*. Aren't you afraid of dying?"

Sun laughed—*just like a woman to worry about death*. He thought that was all the answer that she needed, but her eyebrows drew down and her lips hardened into a line.

"No," he finally answered. "I am not afraid of death."

"What if your god—"

"He wouldn't." Sun's voice was iron. Unbreakable. "Whatever you might worry, Donumdonair will not betray me."

"But it's your *life*, Sun! Every time you walk out to face the Desperados, you could *die*."

"I am not afraid of death," he repeated. "If Donumdonair requires it, I will die gladly."

"I cannot believe that. Nothing is worth dying for."

"There is plenty worth dying for. Donumdonair is the greatest reason, but...to die for country is good. To die for love is better. It would be worth my life if I died in exchange for another. Don't you think so?"

Andari looked at him. Her face was unreadable, though that was nothing new for Sun. She suddenly sent him away, shooing him out of her room with promises to see him again soon.

He did not see her for a few days. Sun was not used to waiting. It chafed at him as he looked for her.

It was a week later when he saw her again. It was all he could do to sit through her dancing before calling her to him. When she saw him, her face brightened and she ran into his arms.

"I must have you," she said and kissed him.

Sun smiled. The game was won. "Knew you'd come around."

"No, my price is still the same." Her lips met his again and she squeezed him tighter.

Sun sighed. "Please, not this again. I don't want to fight. I think I've proven my love already."

"How? You don't trust me, Sun. You say you do, but every time I ask you to prove it, you lie. I will not be like your last wife and I won't be like your whores."

"You won't be like my last wife?" Sun huffed. "All you've done is act just like her. Rike!"

She turned her back to him and walked to the wall, bowing her head against it.

"You really think that? You think I'm like her? All you say whenever she's mentioned is how much you hate her, how much of a roach she is. If you thought that about me, I…I don't know what I'd do."

She kept talking, but the rest was lost amidst her sobs. Never before had a woman's tears cooled his ire. Even his own mother's weeping had only ever made Sun turn away in disgust. But Andari's sobs broke his heart. When he rose to comfort her, she pulled away. Through her sobs, Sun only heard a single question.

"Why don't you trust me?"

A hundred reasons came to mind. He ignored them all.

"I do trust you. Andari—come here!" he pulled her into his arms, smothering her into his chest. "Listen. This exosuit was grafted into my bones when I was born. As I've grown, so has it. It's never been charged before and never will be. I carry the weight around and trust Donumdonair to provide the strength for me. It is my vow to Donumdonair. This is the truth, I swear it."

She turned her face up to him, and though snot dripped from her nose and tears left salty tracks on her cheeks, she smiled.

• • •

On her own credit, Andari purchased a room for them. Not the ramshackle dives that Sun spent time in. This was one of the Order's endeavors. Higher tech, the lights never flickered. The patronage was high class. Electricity ran through the place like it was a lightning storm. In their room, Andari had dimmed the lights and closed the sheer purple curtains. She made him lay on the bed. She bathed him in oil, rubbed his back and combed his hair until he was drowsy. She started playing music on a lyre—he hadn't known she could play.

Sun's eyes grew too heavy to keep open, his tongue too thick to talk to her. His body felt swollen and all but sank into the bed. Pleasant vertigo spun him down into sleep. He dreamed of Andari dancing in the palm of his hand.

He awoke to a shout. Sleep clung to him, but still he rose.

"—ados, Sun!"

This again? He thought and went out to meet what would surely be shadows.

Shadows indeed. In the dark of the hallway, clothed in black and weapons dusted with ash to dull their shine, Sun could hardly see them. The glow of his exosuit's full battery was barely enough to distinguish one amorphous blob from another.

Andari had not lied. Desperados were among him. He laughed, boisterous and challenging. The shadows waited.

Sun strode up to them, his muscles loose and languid like a prowling lion. It was always good to show off, he thought. Prove that you're untouchable. A hint of fear was always useful. To his right, a shadow brandished a trembling cudgel, an ash-stained band of metal wrapped around the meaty end. Sun smiled at him. The shadow swung, and Sun let it hit the middle of his chest, all but pitying the men.

A heavy feeling in his gut. Hard. It made him think of a hammer striking an anvil. (He'd come to call this type of pain *dull.*) He bent over, shocked and breathless. He didn't hear anything but the wheeze of his breath leaving his lungs. *What was happening?* Another dull strike on his back. He felt every bit of it and fell to his knees.

More pain, a different type. It made him think of skinning an animal, of his skin being sawn with fire. (He'd later call this type of pain *sharp.*)

His legs were pulled out from under him and he landed on his back, head smacking into the floor with a *crack*! The light of his exo-suit died as the shadows swarmed over him, bound his feet and arms, and gagged him when he tried to bite. The pain continued, sharp and blunt and fiery.

. . .

His bones had ossified over the screws of his suit that had been set into him—removing the suit had taken hours. They brought in an electric wrench and did not give up until his bones had shattered at the ankles, the wrists, the hips. The pain, sharp, was nothing to the noise.

The grind of his own bones breaking in his ears. The whirr of the wrench. The hiss as the bolts grew red-hot from the friction and burned his flesh. The men's shouts of victory.

When the suit was removed, they sat him up and turned on the lights. They held the suit in front of his face, shaking it. Such a silly thing. Straight rods with tiny pistons and pumps. It looked like a stick figure a child might draw.

"See the source of your strength, Sun! Gone forever! May it be the last thing you see."

He turned to the voice but did not recognize the face from which it came. It didn't matter. Was Sun to know the face of all his enemies? He did not think so.

A knife, red-hot, was put to his eyes. So hot he thought that the water of his eyes boiled away before the knife even touched them. They seemed to rupture at the smallest pressure—but his tormentors did not give in. They carved them out and let the air and sand sting and torment him as good as any blade. And when the sun had risen, he was put in a cage outside Kosmoa's temple to hear their revelry and taunts while the day cooked him.

. . .

Night was soon. Sun had felt its coming as the cold began to take over. And still the temple's party gave no sign of stopping. In fact, by the sound, it seemed the night only made their dark worship fuller.

He slept. It is not fair to say he dreamed. Memories are not dreams. Dreams are flights of fancy. Memories are a prison of the mind.

To dream is to be free.

To remember is to be fettered.

Sun slept. He dreamed. He remembered.

A sharp pain in his side woke him. His pride, the little of it he had left, was destroyed by the whimper that escaped his lips. All their torment of him, and he had not cried out. Until now, when sleep he did not even want was taken from him.

"Who's there?" Sun asked and groped blindly for the foot that kicked him. He found it, only to bring his hands to his chest as the boot came down on his fingers.

"Get up."

The voice did not wait for Sun. Hands grabbed under his armpits and hauled him up. They shackled him again, but it wasn't necessary. Blind, abandoned, a prisoner of his own mind. Where could Sun run to?

On a chain they led him into the temple of Kosmoa. When Sun crossed the threshold, he felt the evil of that place stick to his skin like a thin veneer of oil. They paraded him through the halls, taunting him and throwing things. Sun never knew when the next blow would hit. Would it be soft, a handful of scat thrown into his face? Would it be sharp, a dinner fork flung from the feast table? Would it be solid, a stone chucked? There was only a stone—or some other hard object— thrown once.

"Don't kill him yet!" the man who'd kicked him awake yelled. Sun almost laughed.

The parade finally stopped. They spread his arms so they nearly left their sockets and chained him to the altar. Sun was certain it was the altar. He could feel wickedness like hot breath, like pulsing blood, and strongest at his back.

"Where's your strength, Sun? Your eyes? Your god?" laughter and cheers from the worshippers. "How about a game? You tell me where I am going to hit you. If you guess right, I'll release you. May Kosmoa strike me if I don't. Ready?"

Did Sun want to play this game? Would it matter if he played? No. Rationality came to him: a sudden (and rare) inspiration. *At least you choose what hurts. Play. Save yourself from pain.*

He ignored rationality. *Hurt more. Maybe you'll get lucky and they'll kill you by accident.*

"Body," Sun said. His words were barely intelligible through the mess of broken teeth, swollen lips, and macerated tongue.

The fist slammed into his face. "Care to try again?' The voice said to screeches of laughter—hyenas watching a lion fall.

"Body."

Face.

"Body."

Face.

"Face!"

Body. Sun coughed blood. He felt hot streams of it drip from his face, felt them splatter on the ground and splash his feet.

"Oh, this is *very* fun! Andari, give this a try."

For a moment, Sun's mind was entirely blank. Eternity lived in a moment. Time could have passed him by entirely.

"Guess, Sun," she whispered. Her fingers were cold on either side of his face. He had the mental image of his blood running from her fingertips down her forearms. Her forehead touched his, and he whimpered at the pain of it. And at the hurt it caused to his face, too.

"Guess," she repeated.

Despite himself, Sun hoped. She would set him free. This mercy for the love they shared. Whatever they had done to press her into betraying him, it was over. She could set him free. Everything would be forgiven if she just *set him free oh please, Donum.*

"Body," he mumbled. "My body."

Eternity in a moment.

She slapped his face.

His scream tore his throat and rattled stones. It echoed to the gate on the hill. They continued their torment of him. They took turns, coming up and hitting him. Sun did not play the game. He hung there and if he wept, his tears were not from pain or mockery. Not from pride. Tears of heartbreak. His tears were of weakness. Of perfect, beautiful weakness.

• • •

Andari kept close to Sun, silently sending away the men and women she knew would slit his throat in an act of "mercy." Death was no mercy. What was more important than his life?

She would have set him free, she *would* have! But his life would have cost her own. And what was more important than her own life?

Andari kneeled down to where Sun hung limp. His lips moved, but she heard no sound.

"What did you say, sunshine?" she cradled his head in her hands, lifting it up to look at his busted, bruised face. Nothing. She put her ear close to his lips, and could feel his breath tickle the hairs at the back of her neck. She heard him, barely. The same thing repeated again and again.

"Lord remember me. Avenge me. Release me from this prison. Give me death."

Andari looked at him with pity, tears half in her eyes. Poor man. Donumdonair could not reach him here—not where Kosmoa reigned. No one could save him.

She smoothed his hair. She squeezed his hand. He squeezed back.

She pulled her hand back, but he did not release it. His grip increased in strength around her. She watched in horror as her skin tore and blood began to drip from her hand, bones ground into dust and muscles to mush. Shock held her scream. She looked up at the mob, but none paid her any attention.

When she looked back to Sun, she saw him begin to glow like a knife fresh from the forge. She blinked, and now he was blazing, blindingly bright. And now she did scream as he grew brighter and brighter until her eyes burned, and she fell off the altar platform, scrambling blind for some exit she could not see with her mangled hand clutched to her chest.

. . .

Though he did not breathe, his chest felt full of crisp, clear, life-giving air. He was no longer thirsty. He knew he would never thirst again. Sun smiled, and rolled his shoulders. Muscles burned in euphoria, the effort a holy cleansing. Joints sang in holy worship. He felt his skeleton would rip out of his skin and begin dancing. The altar shattered. Shouts, blades, and lite-bolts all bounced off of him. They couldn't stop him. No. They couldn't stop *HIM*. The earth trembled. Men and women scrambled to escape, but blinded by glory they found no freedom.

The temple of Kosmoa fell in the heart of the city.

The gates stood tall on the hill overlooking it.

Find the story of Sampson in Judges 16.

Orders
Katelyn Flatt

Eyan and his brothers flew across the sand in formation, with two at the front and two behind. The electric whir of their hoverboards sounded like locust, and the dry, hot wind, whipped through their light weight tunics. The harsh sunlight glinted off their black-tinted goggles. In the distance, the Desperado camp stood, rippling in the heat.

Eyan leaned forward on his hoverboard, shifted his weight from side to side, and followed the fluid curves of the sand. His board was long and sleek, stolen straight from a general of The Order of Kosmoa. A single welded gash ran from its tip to its center. He didn't have the proper boots to clip his feet into place, but he made do with two thick bands of leather.

Beside him, his brother Sorian flew over the desert with equal ease, his weight shifting with the sand beneath and his faded blue scarf billowing behind him like flags on a ship's mast. The blue light emanating beneath his hoverboard swelled as it traveled over each ridge of the sand dunes. Although his board was the same as Eyan's in make and model, only the mechanics still matched. The exterior had been destroyed in an explosion and completely reconstructed with scraps of mismatched metal. Yet every piece was meticulously cut to match its neighbor, outlined with perfectly even welds, creating a beautiful spiderweb-like pattern across the entire board. Sorian casually leaned his tall, muscular frame toward Eyan, and his hoverboard drifted closer until they were only a hand-width apart.

"Are you alright?" Sorian's low voice was dampened through the scarf, but he spoke clearly.

"Of course," Eyan growled. He faced forward, his red, dust-streaked scarf trailing behind him as he leaned to the side to swerve around a boulder. "We've scouted hundreds of times. What's one more?"

"That's not what I mean," Sorian said flatly. He clicked his rear heel against a switch on his hoverboard. The nose of his board shot upwards with a low boom, carrying him over another boulder. It landed close to the ground and hummed louder, then settled back up to its normal height. "I haven't seen you that angry in a while."

"Yeah!" Eyan's brother, Jarrka, zipped forward from behind them. He had pulled his bright yellow scarf away from his face, exposing the gap in his toothy grin. "I thought your head was going to explode!"

"Or that you'd kill Uncle Aarav," Tipa, the youngest, said. But as he spoke, his voice cracked. Jarrka cackled, and Tipa pulled his green scarf away from his mouth to tell him off.

"I'm not going to wait around and do *nothing* while those nubfaced roaches take everything we own!" Eyan shouted to be heard over the hum of the hoverboards. Jarrka's laughter and Tipa's squabbling cut out as they eyed their two older brothers. Eyan balled his fists and felt his face grow warmer than it already was.

"Uncle said he's waiting for the messengers," Sorian said.

"Yeah, that's *all* he's doing," Eyan shot back. "If he was sending out scouts or fortifying our village in the meantime, I could handle it. But he's just waiting for the Desperados to strike first. I can't let that happen, so long as there's something I can do about it."

"Like disobeying a direct order," Sorian mused.

"When necessary," Eyan said.

"Well, better alive than obedient," Jarrka said with a chuckle. "Isn't that your mantra?"

"I'm still alive, aren't I?" Eyan allowed himself a smirk.

· · ·

Short red and blue tents, each stolen from a Journeymen camp and hastily pitched, loomed ahead as they approached the Desperado camp. Slightly taller purple tents decorated with intricate silver and gold hourglasses, all stolen from The Order of Kosmoa, poked above the others sporadically through the camp. Leather covers made from sand-rat hides protected some of the tents from the sun and sand, but only a few.

Though he couldn't see it from his position, Eyan knew after many years of fighting Desperados from the Osk'oa Clan that their camps were built like ripples in a pond, with the leader's tent in the center and his soldiers surrounding him in ever-widening rings.

Eyan and his brothers shot across the sand, low to the ground and close to one another. Eyan whistled a single short and piercing tone. He jabbed a finger towards a sandstone outcrop that overlooked the camp. Sorian and Tipa glanced at each other, then nodded at Eyan and veered off toward the sandstone outcrop, their green and blue scarves whipping back and forth behind them. Jarrka fell beside Eyan, and they both crouched low on their hoverboards and approached the camp.

They came to a stop and slipped their feet from their hoverboards just out of earshot of the camp. Eyan flipped his hoverboard up over his head, and it connected to the magnet strapped to his back with a satisfying clang. Jarrka followed suit. He flicked his toe and his hoverboard snapped in half and folded down the middle. He snapped it to the magnet on his back. The two brothers, keeping low to the ground, darted silently toward the closest tent. Eyan hovered inches from the tent, the fabric tickling the edge of his ear. Deep inside, he could hear the rough snoring of a Desperado. They glanced around the edge of the tent, then darted behind the next tent to the right. Inside, he could hear someone rolling over on a leather mat.

It was common for Desperados to sleep off booze and women late into the heat of the day. After skirting nearly a quarter of the outer ring without any sign of Desperado guards, the two brothers stepped inside the perimeter of the camp. The two snuck to the next ring of tents and crouched low to the ground.

They sat, listening. Not a sound could be heard from within these tents. Eyan turned to see Jarrka's shoulders rapidly rising and falling, his eyes wide and hands clenched into fists. He waved to get Jarrka's attention. Then he theatrically puffed up his chest, held his breath, and lowered his hands with a slow exhale. Jarrka nodded, and after a moment, his breathing slowed.

Eyan crouched down and lifted the edge of the tent beside him, peering within—empty except for two wooden tables on either side.

Eyan rolled inside, the purple fabric dropping back to the ground as he jumped to his feet. The hot, stuffy air of the tent caught in his throat as he looked around.

On the table, he found a couple dozen lite-rifles. Some had been repaired with heavy, inconsistent welds, and each one was coated in a thick layer of dirt and grime. But the oil-stained metal tubes twisting around the barrel caught Eyan's attention most. One end of the tube ended in a jagged cut close to the muzzle, while the other looped once around the stock and connected with a silver canister. Two wires ran along the side and wrapped around the trigger.

Just as Eyan picked up the modified lite-rifle, the fabric over the doorway of the tent swished open.

Eyan dropped down behind the table, heart hammering, rifle still in hand, as two Journeymen women walked in. Each had a bulging leather sack slung across her shoulder—dark braids woven with silver beads twisted into a knot atop each of their heads. And though the tent was dark, Eyan could see that their arms were cut and bruised. One of the women dropped her bag onto the ground beside the table. As the bag settled, a couple of lite-cartridges tumbled out onto the sand.

Eyan glanced up at her and caught her gaze. She stared at him, white knuckles clutching the fabric of her dark blue dress, eyes wide. Yet she remained silent, watching Eyan. The other woman glanced at her, eyebrows furrowed. Then her eyes trailed to Eyan, and her hands flew to her mouth as she gasped.

Eyan slowly lifted a finger to where his lips were underneath his scarf, then crawled out underneath the tent wall. He reemerged into the bright sunlight, and a moment later the two women passed by them, keeping their eyes forward. Eyan and Jarrka continued to move through the Desperado camp, pausing before each stretch of open space, their leather shoes gliding soundlessly over the sand. As they neared the center of camp, they saw more and more Journeymen slaves, each marred with slashes and bruises across their exposed, burnt bodies. The bleating of sheep and goats and the lowing of cattle rose up through the heat as they reached the center of the camp. Beyond the last row of tents, they found pen after pen of rough hewn logs stuffed full with cows, sheep, and goats. Every animal had its tongue hanging from its mouth and white saliva caked on its lips.

Nearly thirty slaves shuffled in a line toward the center of the camp and a massive unlit bonfire. Sweat glistened across the slaves' foreheads and backs. Four Desperados stood guard, barking orders and cracking whips above their heads. The Desperados each stood a full head's height above the Journeymen slaves, and their bulging muscles could be seen even under layers of leather tunics and spiked metal armor. The Journeyman slaves flinched with every snap of a whip.

One slave, his eyes half closed and jaw slack, staggered forward, and the four logs in his arms tumbled to the sand as he collapsed.

The nearest guard lumbered towards him. The other slaves cowered away, and their line moved to the side, giving the fallen man a wide berth. As the Desperado approached the fallen man, he raised the whip high above his spiked helmet.

Eyan felt the sand behind him shift. As he turned to look, something slammed into the hoverboard on his back with a deafening clang, and he fell, face first, into the sand with a grunt. He rolled aside just as a Desperado slammed a wooden club with metal spikes into the ground right where he had been.

To his right, another hulking Desperado wrapped his arms around Jarrka's neck and lifted him from the ground. Jarrka's feet kicked about wildly, and he clawed at the Desperado's head, his hands small in comparison. The burly man chuckled and punched Jarrka in the face. The boy's goggles shattered, scattering into the sand. Jarrka hung limp.

The Desperado with the club reared back his leg. Just before his spike-studded boot could make contact, Eyan kicked off the sand into a backward summersault..

As his feet were in the air, he disconnected his hoverboard from the magnet on his back and switched it on. The low, steady hum filled the air as Eyan landed on his board, slipped his feet beneath the leather straps, and kicked his heel against the boot switch. He dug his fingers into the burning sand, and his hoverboard spun around, spraying sand at the Desperados.

He crouched low on his board and shot away, circling the nearest tent at lightning speed. He shifted, coming around the tent behind the Desperado holding Jarrka. Eyan slipped out his dagger and plunged it deep into the Desperado's neck. As the man cried out, he dropped the boy. Eyan slowed his board and caught Jarrka around the middle, then put on a burst of speed toward the center of the camp. Shards of black glass stuck out of Jarrka's face, just missing his eyes. Blood trickled from the cuts and ran down his face and over his closed eyelids, pooling in his dark lashes and staining his yellow scarf orange. Jarrka was only a few years younger than Eyan, nearly sixteen, and just about the same height. But Eyan held him like a little child—his arms wrapped around his brother's shoulders and under his knees.

Somewhere close by, a horn sounded. Then another.

Adrenalin coursed through Eyan's veins as he zipped past the pens of animals. Slaves cried out and leaped from his path, scattering in every direction. He glanced to his left and right to see Desperados running after him, clubs and lite-rifles brandished. Nothing new. He'd escaped worse. He weaved through the horde of Desperados, dodging falling clubs. Bolts of light whizzed past him, burning the edge of his scarf, and leaving black burns on the sand. The tents flickered past him one after the other, colors blurring together.

Through the spaces between the tents, he saw Desperados streaming toward him. He glanced around feverishly. A piercing electric cry split the air as a sizzling white lite-bolt missed him by a fraction of an inch and hit the sand to his left. It exploded in a bright green flame. Eyan's eyes grew wide and he could feel the heat through the scarf around his mouth. He leaned backward to avoid the huge blast and twisted his feet underneath of himself, shooting back the direction he came. He looked back and saw a Desperado lowering a modified lite-rifle, just like the one Eyan had seen earlier in the tent.

Waves of Desperados closed in around him, but out of the corner of his eye, he saw a tent that had partially collapsed. He jerked his body toward it.

He dodged each Desperado's claw-like hands reaching toward him, traveled up the fabric like a ramp, and clicked his heel. He boosted up over the tent, soaring through the air and over the Desperados, holding Jarrka close to his chest as his scarf flapped in the wind.

His hoverboard fell and collided with the ground with a thud. His knees buckled, and the board bounced, skittering across the sand. Eyan gritted his teeth and brought his knees up to his chest, the board lifted from the sand underneath them and straightened. The Desperados behind him cursed and fell far behind him. Yet more streamed from the tents as he passed between them.

He darted around tent after tent, weaving between Desperados, dodging weapons. He shot through another line of tents, and he caught a glimpse of the open desert. He swiveled his heel to click the boost. Another piercing electric cry echoed in the air, and the tent beside him exploded in hot green flames.

The blast rocketed Eyan from his hoverboard and into the tent on his other side. The purple fabric wrapped around him as his shoulder hit something solid. He lost his grip on Jarrka and they tumbled to the ground.

Eyan lay on his back, unmoving. His chest rose and fell as the fabric settled over him like burial linens. He could feel the vibrations in the ground as Desperados circled around him, and he could hear their muffled jeers and hollers. He lay with his eyes closed, mind racing, fingers grasped around the daggers sheathed on his thighs. His whole body buzzed with adrenalin and dread. The goggles on his face felt different. Crushed. A stickiness by his eyebrow began to itch—he and Jarrka would have matching scars. Eyan swore under his breath.

All at once a corner of the fabric over him pulled away, and four meaty hands grabbed his neck, hair, and arms. Someone ripped off his goggles and scarf, and Eyan squinted in the glaring sunlight.

"Well, ain't this cute," a Desperado chuckled.

Eyan blinked until his eyes adjusted.

A horde of Desperados surrounded him. Their studded armor and swords glinted wickedly in the sunlight, and the stench of sweat and ale engulfed him like a cloud. His arm and hair were caught in the grip of the Desperado on his right, while his other arm and throat were held tightly by the one on his left.

"Two spies, is it?" the Desperado who spoke before continued. Scars ran across the man's eye and nose, and a festering, goopy sore clung to the side of his face, dripping into his bushy brown beard.

The man leaned in close, his sour breath turning Eyan's stomach. Eyan turned his face away and saw Jarrka held by another Desperado. Jarrka's eyes were open but not focused. His knees were bent together, and he leaned heavily on his captor.

The Desperado with the scars grabbed Eyan's face with his thumb and middle finger and forced his mouth open. He studied Eyan's cheekbones, his smooth skin, his hairline, his eyes. He stuck his filthy forefinger into Eyan's mouth and pulled back his lip to study his teeth. Eyan pulled away, but the two Desperados on his sides gripped his arms tighter. He shuffled his feet and felt the familiar metal of his hoverboard beneath the tent fabric.

"What'cha reckon our leader be wanting with these here pretty little prizes?" the man spit. Eyan flinched as droplets of saliva sprinkled his face and lips, and the Desperado grinned a big, black smile. He released Eyan's face.

"Where are you from, worm?"

Eyan swallowed as best he could with the sweaty hand pressed against his throat. He leaned forward, shuffling his feet until they were right above the boot indents of his board.

"Rike you," he hissed.

The Desperado smiled again and punched Eyan in the gut.

Eyan coughed and doubled over. The Desperados holding him loosened their grip ever so slightly.

Eyan grinned.

He yanked the daggers from his thigh sheaths and plunged them into the Desperados at his side then leaped forward and sent an uppercut into the jaw of the man in front of him. The Desperados staggered

175

back, and Eyan clicked his heel against the start switch on his board beneath the fabric. Instantly his board hummed to life and lifted off the ground. Eyan spun in a tight circle, dragging the daggers through the tent fabric, ripping it to shreds. Just as the Desperados lunged for him, he leaned forward, clicked the boost, and shot out into the open desert.

Eyan held onto the edges of the board and the scraps of tent fabric twisted in the wind behind him. He tore across the sand, hardly daring to look back.

• • •

"We can't just sit here doing nothing!"

Eyan's fight with his uncle from earlier that day flashed across his mind as he zipped across the sand. He'd ditched the fabric a while back and could now pilot the hoverboard with his feet securely in their place. Hot air and dust rushed past him, and he flew with his sleeve pressed against his nose and mouth, eyes squinting through the wind and sand.

"We're *not* doing nothing. We're *waiting*."

"For what? An invitation?"

His own harsh tone echoed through his head, and he grit his teeth.

"*I* am the chief, and *I* am the one who speaks with Donumdonair. And if He tells me to wait, *you will wait too*."

Eyan's village, made entirely of sandstone huts, blended into the surrounding desert, made invisible by the mirages. But as the distance between him and his village shrank, the outlines of the buildings emerged. Smoke rose from the corner gathering square where most of the ovens were built, and as he crossed the threshold of his village the smell of freshly baked bread and roasted lamb wafted over him.

"If we wait another day, we're dead." Eyan's voice echoed in his head.

He clicked off his hoverboard and settled to the ground. Yet he stood there, feet still connected to the board, unmoving. His uncle's final blow hummed in his ears.

"And if you don't wait for orders, you're done."

Slowly, mechanically, he pulled his feet free from his board. He lifted it to his back and winced as he stretched the shoulder he had landed on earlier. The board connected to the magnet on his back with that familiar clank, and after taking a deep breath, he headed into his village.

He made his way to the gathering square. People milled about the square with baskets of food or stood by tables stirring bowls of dough and talking in small groups. Children ran about, screaming and laughing, chasing each other.

A father chased a small boy around a table. He grinned as he caught the child in his arms and pressed a scruffy kiss against the boy's cheek. The boy shrieked with glee as the duo walked back toward the long banquet table set up in the middle of the square. The groups of families and friends sat around the table, eating and talking amongst themselves. As Eyan approached, he found his uncle sitting at the head of the table, eating bread and deep in discussion with one of his advisors.

Eyan's heart hammered against his ribcage. Jarrka's bloodied face flashed across his mind, and he forced himself to step forward. As he passed a family, their chatter halted. To his right, two women gasped and stepped back, giving him a wide berth. Though his feet brought him towards his uncle, he studied every face in the square. Dread rose higher in his chest and throat. Sorian and Tipa were nowhere to be seen.

"Nubatou, Eyan, what happened to you?" his uncle's advisor yelped as he came to a stop at the head of the table.

Eyan glanced at his uncle as the man turned to face him, but he found it difficult to keep his eyes from drifting to the ground.

"Eyan?"

His uncle's tone was cautious yet firm.

"Chief Aarav," Eyan started. His chest felt tight and he forced himself to breathe.

"By Donum, you're bleeding." His uncle stood and tilted Eyan's chin with a gentle grip, studying the side of his face. "Hada, get me a rag," he called to his advisor. The man jumped up and ran towards the ovens.

Chief Aarav did not take his attention off his nephew.

"What happened." It wasn't a question.

"Chief Aarav, I-I riked it all. I did what you said *not* to do, and now Jarrka—"

A hush fell over the table, and many eyes turned toward the pair. His uncle held up a hand and grabbed Eyan by the shoulder.

"Not here." His Uncle shook his head.

Hada ran up with a soft linen cloth, which Aarav took. He led Eyan to one of the sandstone buildings that bordered the gathering square and stepped through the open doorway.

The room was typically used for eating when the weather was too harsh. Inside the small room, they found a wooden table with four stools. Aarav took the hoverboard off Eyan's back, set it against the wall, and directed Eyan onto one of the stools.

"Talk," he said, joining Eyan at the table. He wiped the blood off his nephew's face, careful to avoid the shards of goggle that were still lodged in his cheeks.

"Chief Aarav, I'm an idiot." He took a deep breath and closed his eyes. "I went to the Desperado camp. It was just a scouting mission—we've done hundreds of them, and—" His voice caught in his throat, he squeezed his eyes shut. His heart hammered in his chest and he clenched his hands into fists.

Chief Aarav wiped the blood away a little more forcefully as Eyan confessed, but he remained silent.

"I have no defense," Eyan sighed. "Chief Aarav, I went scouting with my brothers against your direct orders. We split up before the camp and Jarrka and I got caught. *He* got hurt, and *I* got away. And, if Sorian and Tipa aren't here, then they're caught too. If not worse." His eyes burned. "Uncle Aarav, I messed up and now my brothers are in trouble. And I can't save them on my own." He couldn't bring himself to look at his uncle. He sat on the wooden stool, his hands clasped like he was once more a small child.

"I said if you disobeyed, you'd be done," Aarav stated, his voice flat and measured.

"After what I just did, I deserve it," Eyan said, his eyes on the dirt floor. "You can demote me, disown me, Rike, even kill me. I'm guilty. But don't leave them there."

Aarav sat opposite his nephew. He wiped one last bit of blood from Eyan's face and leaned back. Eyan glanced up to see his uncle staring off into the corner, rubbing his chin with his thumb and forefinger. After a moment, he nodded his head, then sighed deeply.

"Alright," his uncle said. "Here's what we're—"

Screams erupted from the gathering square. Eyan and Aarav leapt to their feet and raced to the doorway. Outside a band of at least a dozen Desperados with torches in their hands zipped around on hoverboards, igniting everything in sight. An old man raced away from the square, a wailing child clutched in his arms. A green blaze consumed the banquet table. Two women scurried away from one Desperado, only for their path to be blocked by another. He grabbed one woman by her hair and flew away, dragging her through the sand beside him as she shrieked. The Desperados circled the entire square, herding the people closer and closer to the burning table. The cries of children filled the air mixed with the crackling of wood flame and the laughter of the Desperados.

Aarav snatched a lite-pistol from his waist and fired four bolts. Each blast hit a different Desperado square in the head as they flew by. All four went limp. One slammed into the side of a building and his board exploded in a brilliant flash of white and orange. The others crashed into the ground. At the sound of the lite-pistol blast, the other Desperados dove for cover behind burning barrels and smoking buildings.

"That you, Chief of Slaves?" one called out from behind a stack of wooden crates full of fruit. "You sent scouts to our camp. That's war!" The Desperado fired a shot toward the chief. Brilliant green flames fell as the bolt of light struck the doorframe.

In response, Aarav fired twice at the crates. They exploded into tiny splinters. The Desperado hiding there leaped backward with a yell, his face engulfed in white smoke. He beat at his beard and ran off between buildings. Eyan jumped forward, hand on his hoverboard, but Aarav grabbed his shoulder.

"You didn't check that you weren't followed?" Aarav snapped.

"Why should I have? They're already here every day to claim their precious tribute. They *know* we're *here*."

"But they didn't know *you* were from here," Aarav said. He pulled Eyan back into the building and shoved him down onto one of the wooden stools. "Stay here."

"What? No, you need me. I'm your best soldier!"

Somewhere further into the village more screams erupted followed by blasts from the modified lite-rifles. Aarav held up his hand.

"A soldier can be trusted to follow orders."

Eyan opened and closed his mouth, but no sound came out. More screams came from outside, along with the deep rumble of a building collapsing.

"Stay here," Aarav said. He turned and ran through the doorway, lite-pistol raised.

The little building had no windows, so all Eyan could do was sit in the corner, alone with his thoughts and the horrified shrieks, watching the glow of the flames dance along the sandstone wall.

Eventually, the glow dimmed and dusk turned to night. Eyan stayed where he was told, picking at the glass in his face and massaging his shoulder. Silently, he prayed for his brothers' lives to be spared. Aarav walked back in. Soot and what looked like blood tainted his hands.

"What'd you do?" Eyan asked.

"Hunted down those other Desperados," Aarav replied. He walked up to the table and lit three candles, then pulled another stool up in front of Eyan. From his pocket, he fished out a small pair of metal tweezers. He sat down, and in the light of the candles, he began to pick the smaller bits of glass Eyan had missed. "Do you know why I told you to wait?" Aarav asked. His voice was as calm and steady as his hands.

"No sir," Eyan murmured.

"Does that mean I had no reason?" Aarav glanced into his nephew's eyes.

When Eyan remained silent, Aarav continued.

"I have wanted to take those Desperados down since the moment our scouts saw them," he said. He pulled one last piece of the shattered goggles from Eyan's eyebrow, then extracted a small pouch from his pocket and unwrapped it, exposing a small lump of what looked like grey clay.

"When I told Donumdonair of my plans, I expected his usual reply. I expected him to tell me which of my soldiers to bring on our raid and which day would be best to attack. I even hoped for some insight on this particular camp since sometimes Donum provides that." He pulled off a small piece of the clay and rubbed it between his fingers until it softened to a paste. He gently rubbed it against the cuts on Eyan's forehead. Eyan winced, but he relaxed as the salve cooled his face. Aarav continued to speak.

"Instead, Donumdonair said to wait. I figured I had misheard, but he remained firm. I asked him over and over, every single day, for his reason. And when the Desperados found us and started demanding tributes, I cried out to Donumdonair that we could have avoided this if he had only let us. All he did was repeat his command. *Wait.* Eventually, I asked him how long I was to wait. And do you know what he said?" Aarav chuckled quietly as he rubbed the final bit of salve against Eyan's face. "He simply said, '*wait until I tell you to go.*' We don't always get to know his reasons, Eyan. Nor should we. He allows a hundred years of suffering to bring a thousand years of peace. He will close the queen's womb for decades, then gift her the child that conquers nations. He holds every person, animal, and green leaf in the palm of his hands. He designed the path of the sun and moon and he has woven the fabric of our history. And *you* are arrogant enough to feel *owed* an explanation for his '*wait*'?" he shook his head.

"I see now," Eyan murmured.

Aarav studied his nephew. "Are you ready to follow orders?"

Eyan blinked. "What do you mean?"

"On my way back to you, Donum told me to go. Let's go get your brothers."

$$\bullet \ \ \bullet \ \ \bullet$$

A few hours later, Aarav, Eyan, and just over four dozen men and boys ran silently through the desert. They had scraped together and dispersed between themselves twenty-seven lite-weapons and thirty-two swords. They left just a handful of weapons with the men who had stayed back to guard the village. They had also found seventeen working hoverboards, most of them scavenged from the Desperados' earlier attack. Eyan wore his own hoverboard strapped to his back. Most men carried unlit torches and tinderboxes. The last items they carried were twelve ramshorns.

As the army reached the camp, Aarav raised his fist and their group halted. From within the camp, drunken shouting and wicked laughter mingled with the beating of drums. Desperados were patrolling the open spaces between the tents, modified lite-rifles in hand. The flames of the bonfire in the middle of camp flickered high into the night sky, towering above the tops of the tents. Aarav held up one finger, then two, then motioned towards one side of the camp. Then he held up three fingers, then four, and motioned toward the other side. He held up five fingers and then pointed to the ground.

Two groups of men went left, and two went right, each careful to stay far outside the light that emanated from the camp's torches and bonfire. The final group, Eyan included, stayed with Aarav.

They waited in the dark, unmoving and silent.

Minutes passed as they listened for the signal. Eyan fought to keep his fingers from tapping or his knee from bouncing. He watched his uncle sit so still that he could have been carved from the sandstone on which he sat. They waited and Eyan had to remind himself to breathe. They waited, the muscles in Eyan's leg cramping as they crouched. Then a distinct chirp of a desert bug broke the silence. A few seconds later, another one. Closer. Then another. A man behind Aarav answered the call with his own chirp. Eyan quietly pulled his board from his back and set it on the ground. He slipped his feet into place.

Aarav stood and looked over his men. Then to Eyan. He tilted his head and raised his eyebrows.

Eyan nodded. He was ready.

In one smooth motion, Aarav unholstered his lite-pistol and fired a bolt into the camp. It flew through the night like a shooting star and collided with the top of the bonfire with an explosion of burning wood.

Instantly, the Journeymen surrounding the camp blew their horns, blasting a song every Journeymen in their village knew, no matter how young. It was the song of freedom their ancestors had sung when they had left their own bonds of slavery behind.

In the same instant, every single hoverboard hummed to life. Eyan, along with the other sixteen men on hoverboards, darted straight into the camp. With a sword brandished in each hand, he crouched low on his board and zipped around the tents. He rocketed towards the center and sliced every tent rope he came across.

He turned a corner and a Desperado leaped into view, lifting a modified lite-rifle. Eyan ducked low against his board, and the green blast sailed past him, singeing the edges of his hair. A Journeymen behind him screamed as it exploded, and sand pelted Eyan's back. Eyan kept his eyes forward and pressed towards the center of the camp.

The circles of tents collapsed from the outside in, one after the other, as the Journeymen flew towards the center of the camp. The Desperados inside the fallen tents thrashed their way out as the rest of the Journeymen army ran through on foot with a battle cry, their lite-rifles blasting into the unprepared Desperados. As Eyan flew into the center of the camp, the drums had ceased and were replaced by a warning horn, the tone low and haunting as the Desperados scrambled for their weapons. Desperados fought against the Journeymen, slaying the slaves and free alike.

With all the tents in his pathway chopped down, Eyan raced through the chaos, dodging swords and modified lite-rifle blasts. The clamor of metal striking metal and fiery green explosions threatened to overwhelm his senses, but then he saw them. A group of maybe fifteen Journeymen tied to posts around the bonfire. He crouched low and leaned forward on his board, darting around weapons and fallen men.

He reached the first post, where a boy of about thirteen wearing only a loincloth stood tied. Eyan sprang from his hoverboard and attached it to his back.

"Let me go! Let me go!" the boy cried. Eyan dropped a sword and grabbed a dagger from his thigh sheath. In one slash he severed the ropes around the young boys wrists. Without hesitation, the boy swooped up Eyan's sword and raced into the thick of battle. Eyan watched as he joined a group of older Journeymen slaves setting the animals loose.

Eyan zipped over to the next post, then the next, cutting loose each slave until everyone had been freed. None of these prisoners were his brothers.

He spun around, peering through the chaos. With clenched teeth, he ran into the battle. He whistled two loud blasts, then listened. No response. He skirted the animal pens as the Journeymen broke down the last gate. He whistled those same two quick blasts, hoping the stampede's thundering hooves weren't loud enough to drown him out. He darted past a row of black fabric tents and whistled again.

Two quick whistle blasts came from somewhere inside the tents.

He flipped around and ripped aside the fabric doors. The first few tents were empty, but inside the third, he found them.

His brothers each lay in a separate corner of the tent, their arms tied above their heads. They wore nothing but their undergarments, which were tattered and bloody.

"Eyan!" Sorian cried.

Tipa's cracked lips spread into a grin, yet in the far corner, Jarrka lay still.

Eyan slashed the ropes above Sorian's wrists. With his arms free,

Sorian pulled Eyan into a tight hug. Eyan wrapped his arms around his brother's muscular shoulders for just a moment before he stepped over to free Tipa.

"What happened?" Eyan asked.

"We were getting the overview of the camp up on that outcrop, like you told us to," Tipa explained, his voice cracking weakly. He rubbed his wrists as Eyan freed him. "We saw you two get caught. When we turned to go home, they had us surrounded."

"When did you get free?" Sorian asked as he ran to Jarrka and dropped to his knees beside his brother. He pressed his fingers against Jarrka's neck. "We saw the tent collapse around you two, and then we were caught. We thought you were dead."

"I got away, but they followed me back to the village," Eyan said. He grabbed Tipa's narrow shoulders and spun him around, exposing the long, swollen lashes across his back. He cursed and pulled his youngest brother into a hug. "They burned the market square."

Eyan turned and raised his dagger as the tent flap rustled behind him.

"Praise Donum, you're all alive." Aarav rushed inside the tent, immediately stepping to free Jarrka's hands with his dagger. The young man moved his head from side to side, but his eyes remained closed. As Eyan looked closer, his breath caught in his throat. His brother's body had been whipped beyond recognition. The glass from his goggles still protruded from his face and the skin around it had turned red and swollen. His nose was crooked and purple, with dried blood caked down to his lips.

"When he came to, he fought back," Sorian explained. "He wouldn't listen when I told him to stop, to just bear the torture. So they beat him more."

187

Aarav swore, then looked at Eyan.

"Your new mission is to get your brother home and stay with him until we return." Eyan could hear the clatter of weapons just outside of the tent, the anguished death cries of Journeymen and Desperados alike rattling the tent posts. The skin of Eyan's fingertips itched as they caressed the hilt of his dagger, but as he looked down at the dried blood crusted around his brother's face, he nodded.

"Yes, sir."

Find the story of Othniel in Judges 1 and Judges 3:7-11.

The Mark, Part I

Chris Babcock

The bard wrapped his bandana tighter around his mouth, bracing himself against the first lashes of the sandstorm. The orange glow of two beacons cut in and out a few hundred yards ahead as the dust devils danced around them.

He could feel the sand biting into the fabric of his clothing and glancing off his goggles. He hadn't been in a storm like this since his youth.

The angles of shanties began to fuzz into view. The old maps showed a copper mining town on this road—the last twinkle of civilization before the true desert began. He'd have to be careful. Border towns housed more than just Journeymen.

Limping his way into the square, the bard made for a saloon and ducked under the porch. The sand still licked at his heels, but he pulled the bandana down an inch and breathed through his nose.

Adjusting the hood so it shaded his brow, he rapped on the scarred door. Inside, booted feet stomped, and glasses clinked to the tune of an electric banjo.

The door opened a crack and a woman with a crooked nose peered out. "We're full. Try Kolsun's down the street."

The bard inclined his head. "Peace be with you. I was told this is a safe place for Journeymen. I can pay well."

The woman shifted. "Pardon. Thought you were a Kosmoan priest. Better be careful with that cloak of yours." She opened the door wide, ushering him in. "Got some wildebeest stew and yeast loaf if yer hankering."

"That would be wonderful." The bard surveyed the room, adjusting the hilt of a lite-lash beneath his cloak. The Desperadoes used the long electric whip to herd cattle—but he found it served better than a knife at close quarters. He picked his way around a table of rough Kosmoan men who seemed to be robbing a freckled girl of her life's savings at a game of nine-scratch. The men scowled at him, tipping back shots of petroleum vodka.

The bard settled on a divan against the far wall. It gave him a full view of the tavern, including both entrances. Lighting a waterpipe, he sucked in a mouthful of bittermint mist. It soothed his parched lungs.

Across the room, a group of children concluded a game of knuckle-buckle. One of them spotted the bard and pointed. The others turned.

The bard groaned, pulling his hood lower over his eyes. *So much for this being the best disguise.* His mouth twitched as the children floated toward him. They avoided eye contact—were they afraid of scaring him off or spooking themselves?

Five children settled around in a wide circle. Three others joined, hanging on the outside like tethered moons.

"Excuse me, sir?" The eldest child pushed a curtain of brown bangs from his eyes and finally looked directly at the bard. "Do you tell stories?"

"Only scary ones," the bard grunted around his waterpipe.

"My mother says I shouldn't listen to stories from Journeymen," piped a small child. Her sardonic accent and the leather patches on her overalls marked her as a Desperado.

"Well then," the bard said with a smile, "I suppose you should all run off to bed."

The children exchanged a web of glances, then scooted forward all at once.

"Tell us about The Mark!" the eldest said.

The bard's stomach tightened. "Oh, that's a dark story."

"My pops says The Mark was a coward," said one Kosmoan child.

"Was not!" cried a Journeymen girl. "Was the bravest of all! Ma said so! He beat up the Eastern Kosmoan armies so bad they di'n't never come back!"

Both children looked to the bard as if settling the matter before a judge.

"Well," the bard murmured, "perhaps you are both right." He settled back in the divan. "In those days, though, he wasn't called The Mark. His name was just Gilly. And he grew up in a small border town not much different than this one."

The children cocked their heads and listened.

"In those days, the Journeymen didn't control the rivers and the mountain gorges. We had no outposts. We had no rifles. Kosmoan-folk would swarm across the fords and through the passes with their herds and their hovercraft. They would take our harvests, topple our walls, and burn our vineyards." Old anger burned through the bard's veins like whiskey. "They slew any elder who upheld The Ancient Mandates. And they took every eldest son as a sacrifice to Kosmoa."

The bard fingered the lite-lash under his cloak. "In those days," he murmured, "many of the Journeymen worshipped Kosmoa. I suppose we thought that if he made the people in his Order powerful and tech-rich, maybe he would do the same for us. But instead, his priests came to our lands and killed our sons on the very mountain peaks where we had prayed for Kosmoa to protect us."

As the bard continued to speak, the children fell silent, woven into the tapestry of the tale.

• • •

Gilly pulled Miri after him through the sand-hewn cavern walls. Their footsteps echoed like thunderclaps as dark clouds brewed in the narrow sliver of sky far above.

"Love, where are you taking us?" Miri sounded calm. Quiet. Naive.

"I have a stash," Gilly said. He squeezed her hand, not daring to look her in the eyes. He couldn't let her see his shame. His grief.

"A stash?" Miri stopped in the middle of the chasm and their fingers parted.

"Yes." Gilly turned, resting a hand on the chasm wall. "I was worried they would come for our clan. I've been saving up some supplies. Canned food, desert-grade rebreather filters, a rifle, and some cartridges—"

"You're organizing a rescue party?" Miri's eyes shone with pride and hope.

"What? No! We're getting out of here, Miri. Those supplies will get us all the way to the Riverine cities."

Miri took a step back. "But I thought—"

"No, Miri!" Gilly felt directionless anger well up inside him like crude oil from a jammed pipe. "What do you want me to do? Kosrike it. If those Kosmoan roaches catch me interfering, they'll string me up, too."

A beat of silence passed between them. Miri tilted her chin up. "He's your nephew."

"He *was* my nephew." Thunder rumbled overhead. "He's probably dead now, and there's nothing you or I can do about it. Kosrike it, the boy's sniping father should cut him down if he really cares. He's the eldest of us now, and it's *his son.*"

"The son has a name, Gilly. His name is Divvo. And he's *your nephew.*"

"I don't give a roach's—" Gilly caught himself. He had to hold back the tide of his grief. He loved this woman. She was not the problem. He wanted to burn something—he wanted to kill someone. But it wasn't her fault. She just didn't know how to make hard choices. That was his job. He took a step forward, touching her elbow. "I love you, Morning Flower." A sudden tightness in his throat made him pause. He moved his hand down toward the small bump of her stomach, feeling for the kick of the child inside her womb. He hadn't yet felt it. "I love you, Miri. I just—I can't—won't leave you alone. If they catch me, what will they do to you?"

"Oh, Gilly." She reached up, cupping his cheek with her small hand. "Do you remember what the prophet said?"

"They killed him, too."

"But not his message." Her eyes shone, reflecting a flash of lightning as it lit up the sky above. "Donumdonair is with us. He saved us from bondage in the Riverine Empire. He made water from sand and sank Kosmoa's army."

"We were strong back then. Now we are weak." *I am weak.* "If we don't leave, Kosmoa will take everything from us."

Miri took a deep breath, and in that moment, Gilly knew he had lost the fight. "Do what you want to, Gilly. But I'm not running." She turned, striding uphill and toward the hidden entrance that concealed this branch of the canyon.

Gilly swore under his breath, turning away from her. Perhaps he could still convince her later tonight. He ran deeper into the cavern, picking his way by feel. He'd been down this path hundreds of times, mining the last seams of an abandoned cobalt shaft.

The Barbwire Constellation rose overhead as he ran, its twelve distant red suns dancing above the lip of the cliff like fireflies.

The canyon walls turned abruptly, then ended in a sheer wall. The hungry gate of the mine bid him come and be swallowed—one last time.

Gilly stepped inside the tunnel entrance, groping for the lantern he left hung inside. "Just get the gear," he murmured to himself. "Get the gear, take the back road home, then convince Miri to get out of this kosriking country." He found the lantern and ground the igniter switch. On the second try, it flared to life, washing the tunnel in orange light.

He ventured deeper into the dark, taking two left turns and then entering a wide underground quarry the size of a misshapen temple. A partial collapse had filled in one corner of the vast cavern; the rocks piled in a slope like the seats of a boxing pit. Gilly made for the pile of rubble, which hid his treasure trove.

The swing of the lantern cast odd patterns on the jackhammer-hewn walls, and his footsteps wobbled as if he had drunk too much wine.

The light seemed to grow as he climbed the mountain of rubble. He squinted his eyes, glancing down at the lantern. Its light seemed frail in comparison to—

The lantern blew out. But the light grew.

A stranger sat on the rocks at the top of the heap, directly above Gilly's hidden stash. On the stranger's brow rested a crown that radiated light as deep as the ocean and as full as a bushfire. A sleek chrome rifle twinkled on his back.

Fear pierced Gilly like the rays of a neutron star. He shifted, pebbles tumbling out from under his feet. *They found me,* he thought. *Kosmoa is here to play some final trick.* He scrambled down the slope, expecting a rifle bolt to split his spine.

"Peace be upon you, warrior of Donumdonair," the voice said, echoing through the cavern. It halted Gilly as if his feet had been set in quick-stone.

Gilly turned, shielding his eyes against the light with the crook of his elbow. "Who are you?"

"Your king is with you."

"What king?"

The stranger tilted his head, his eyes shining like the moon. "The one you serve."

"Is this how the priests of Kosmoa try to catch us now? By seeking a sign of rebellion? Surely you are aware that we have no leader to follow."

"I am." The stranger rose, the crown on his brow casting his shadow around his feet like a dark cloud.

"Are you a demon of Kosmoa?" Gilly's voice sounded thin in his ears.

"I am with Donumdonair."

Gilly put a hand on his thigh to still the shaking in his knee. "Then why do you bear a star upon your brow?"

"*We* set the stars in the heavens long before men worshipped Kosmoa. They are not his to plunder." The voice rang between the walls of the cavern, strong enough to crush bones. "The victory is ours, and we will give it to you, Gilly Thorntree."

The fear and bitterness in Gilly bubbled up into a harsh laugh even as he trembled. "What victory? Where are the armies that our ancestors spoke of? Where is the god who turned sand into water? Where is the faith that split the mountain pass and crushed the Riverine Army?"

A sad smile drifted across the stranger's face as he took a step down toward Gilly. "Where indeed? And yet we give it now to you, mighty warrior. Go in strength and save the Journeymen from the iron grip of Kosmoa and his pimping priesthood."

"I am the youngest of six brothers, of the weakest family in the Clan of the Forgotten. Do you know what you are asking?"

The stranger descended. Each of his steps on the broken stones echoed through the cavern.

Gilly considered running, but a new emotion rooted him to the spot. Not fear—not even disdain. He saw for the first time that this stranger did not carry himself like the haughty priests of Kosmoa or the foolish young warriors of the Journeymen who rushed to their deaths.

This stranger held his head high without seeming to look down on Gilly. He strode as if he bore the weight of the stone ceiling and yet as if his feet bounced on moss. His hands bore scars but seemed gentle enough to cradle a child. He carried himself like a king.

The crown sparkled brighter in shades of ruby, emerald, and amethyst—a *king among kings.*

The stranger stopped in front of Gilly, resting a hand on his shoulder. "I know what I am asking of you, Gilly of the Forgotten Clan." The man smiled, as warm as a grandmother and as strong as a judge. "I know what I ask, and I know what I give. The rest, I leave to you. Will you rescue our people?"

Gilly fell to his knees, ignoring the pebbles that bit through his pants. "Sir—forgive me. I have heard of phantoms in these hills. Old spirits. Allow me to bring a meal and eat with you, to know if you are truly—*my king.*" He whispered the last words. Could this be a deliverer sent from Donumdonair?

The stranger's laugh drove back the shadows. "Go, Gilly. And speak with Miri. She will have things to say."

• • •

The children looked up at the bard through the haze of bittermint mist that hovered in front of his face.

"Was The Mark very afraid?" the small Journeymen girl asked in a hushed voice.

The bard smiled. "He wasn't even The Mark then! He was just small Gilly from a clan nobody cared about. He was *very* afraid."

The brown-haired Kosmoan boy smirked. "I knew it." Then his nose wrinkled as a new thought seemed to occur to him. "Who was it in the cave? The stranger with the star on his crown?"

The bard took another long draft on his pipe, letting the question hang in the air.

"Must'a been the Journey-folk spirit," the Desperado girl said in a whisper. "Maw-maw says he roams the desert sometimes. She says he's deadly. Like a fire you can't see."

The bard mulled over those words, keeping one eye on the far table as the freckled young lady committed a previously-hidden bandoleer of rifle cartridges to another round of gambling with the Kosmoa men. "Your Maw-maw sounds like a wise woman."

The Journeymen girl's brow scrunched up in betrayal. "You sayin' the spirit was an evil one, Mr. Bard? I thought 'e was a messenger from Donum!"

"I didn't say evil now, did I?" the bard asked. "Some good things are dangerous. And some evil things don't seem so bad at first lookabout."

The children shifted. He laughed. "Aye, you must be careful with strangers. Even old men with funny beards and good stories." He wiggled his eyebrows.

One child giggled, and the others followed.

A moment of silence ensued. Two twins scrunched their toes in unison as they waited for the story to resume. At the gambling table across the room, a bearded thug made obscene gestures at the unfortunate lass.

"But was Gilly brave?" the Journeymen girl asked.

The bard clenched the pipe between his teeth. "Well," he murmured, "that remains to be seen."

And the bard continued his tale.

· · ·

Miri pulled Gilly back down the tunnels. Her pigtails bumped on her shoulders, and her overalls swished through the dead air. "Do you think he'll help save Divvo?" she asked, breathless.

"I—I didn't ask, love." Gilly allowed himself to be pulled along. "Are you sure we shouldn't bring a meal?"

"There was no way I was going to cook while you met with a seer-spirit! You have *canned food* in that stash of yours, Gilly. Real canned food!"

Gilly felt silly. He hadn't thought of that. Perhaps the whole trip back to his house had been meaningless. But no—now *she* was with him.

That introduced a new fear. What if it had all been a delusion? Or worse—what if he were leading Miri into some awful trap?

"How did you know he is the one, Gilly?" Miri asked. She slowed from a run to a walk, looking up at him with her big brown eyes.

"I didn't at first. But Kosmoa and his people have an…aura."

"Like when they killed Killiam," Miri whispered. "They seemed almost—hungry."

Gilly kept his eyes on the ground but squeezed her hand. She had been there with him. They were only kids when Gilly's oldest brother had been strung up to the steel tree, hanging there for three hours until the lightning finally struck. The Kosmoan priests had eyed the assembled villagers as if one death wasn't enough. As if Kosmoa demanded more and someday they would return. *When you worship the god of sky and space,* Gilly thought, *there will never be enough to satisfy his void.*

"And this man is different?" Miri asked.

"You'll see." He could tell she asked not because she doubted, but because she *knew.* She saw hope in him and wanted to join. For the first time in years, he had something to share with her. Something that truly mattered. He had expected to feel her pride when he showed her his survival stash. But now that seemed silly in light of *this.*

They turned a corner and a soft purple light drifted up from the cavern. Gilly felt the pulse thundering in Miri's wrist as they rushed down a set of rough-hewn steps.

The stranger knelt at the end of the cavern.

Miri paused, edging closer to Gilly. Fire shone in her eyes.

"Please, come in. I was praying to my father." The stranger rose and inclined his head toward them. "You are Miri."

"Yes, sir," Miri whispered. She took several hesitant steps forward, and the stranger came to meet her, fire dancing on his brow. His footsteps made no noise as he glided over the floor. The stranger took Miri's hand and squeezed it, then looked over her shoulder, his eyes piercing Gilly. "You have a brave wife. Many would not have followed you into these depths."

"I know," Gilly said, tears suddenly pricking his eyes. "Sir," he began, voice faltering, "forgive me, but I didn't bring a meal."

The stranger only smiled. "Was the meal for my sake or for yours?"

"I remembered—Miri reminded me—that the finest food we own is in the cans in my stash. Please, allow me to serve you."

The stranger's eyes softened, but he said nothing.

After a moment's pause, Gilly made for the rubble pile on the other end of the chasm, eying a large slab of stone that concealed a pit with his supplies hidden inside. His footsteps echoed in the cave as he bounced up several boulders. He placed his lantern next to his feet, then heaved the slab aside.

Lifting the lantern again, Gilly inspected his treasure. Dusty metal gleamed up at him. Cans of food, ammunition packs, rebreathers, sand goggles, a pair of binoculars, a slash-tent, radiation cream—and his rifle.

He pulled out the rifle and ran a finger over the olive-wood stock before laying it to the side. Rubbing the dust from the cans, he inspected the labels and chose four: fig jelly, glider worms in balsamic vinegar, honeyed mulberries, and even a can of corn from the Far North. Slinging the rifle over his shoulder, Gilly carried the cans in one arm and held the lantern with the other as he made his way down the rubble pile toward the stranger and Miri. The two talked in low tones, Miri's face glowing like it had behind her wedding veil. Somehow, he felt no jealousy.

Not far from where Miri and the stranger stood lay a large boulder that had fallen to the floor during the partial cave-in. Gilly made for it, laying down the cans on its marbled surface. Blue-green streaks of cobalt glittered in the light of the lantern.

The stranger turned toward Gilly, then touched Miri's shoulder to guide her over to the meal. The two of them smiled like long-lost friends, and Miri held a hand to her womb as if sharing this moment with her child.

The stranger knelt down in front of Gilly's offering, making approving humming noises as he looked over the cans. He held up the can of mulberries toward Miri. "You have been craving these, haven't you?"

Miri gaped.

"They'll be good for your child." The stranger pulled out a plasma knife and cut through the top of the can before flicking it away. He handed the can to Miri and she held it like a massive diamond in her cupped hands.

The stranger met Gilly's eyes. "Thank you for this offering, Gilly. But I sense that you wish for more than a shared meal."

Gilly blushed, staring at the floor.

"You wish to know if I am more than a messenger or a prophet. Speak your mind, son."

Gilly opened his mouth, hesitated, and then spoke. "Few people will sell their lives for a prophet, sir. But for a king..."

The stranger nodded. "Put your rifle on the stone along with the food, Gilly."

"Sir?" Gilly touched the stock of his rifle. It had been his prize since he was thirteen and had dreamt of avenging Killiam's death.

"Will you give me your food but not your weapon? Put it on the stone."

Gilly swallowed, then did so. His fingers lingered before they left the stock.

"Now step back, both of you."

Gilly held Miri's hand as they took three steps back like uncertain children.

The stranger knelt and touched the stone with his hand. A blinding light roared up around the stranger, and white fire consumed the cans and the rifle. The stranger's crown burned brighter, harder, and his face became like pounded bronze even as the flames rose around him.

Then it ended, leaving a corona of light burnt into Gilly's vision.

The stranger stepped back from the stone, which was now split from top to bottom and textured with molten steel and tin that still glowed in shades of orange and purple.

Miri fell to her knees, pulling Gilly with her. "My Lord," she cried. Gilly felt doom crash down around his ears as if the ceiling were caving in. "Oh my god," he murmured, resting a hand on the stone. He felt dizzy. *I have seen Donumdonair's spirit. And I questioned him.*

The stranger's footsteps drew near like the beat of an executioner's drum. The stranger pulled the rifle from his shoulder. And then—he knelt.

"Go in peace, Gilly and Miri," the stranger murmured. "Go in peace." He pressed his sleek chrome rifle into Gilly's hands and set a plasma knife atop it. "You will need these. Now, listen carefully to what I am about to tell you to do."

• • •

The bard paused his story to order a pint of beer. The serving girl—Yeema, according to her name badge—held her pencil with shaking fingers. "Will that be all, sir?"

"Only one question—that girl in the corner with the men. She's losing. What is your establishment's position on bad bets and debtors?"

The girl's composure cracked as she looked away. "Don't got a policy, sir. Only rule is that trouble happens on the streets, not in here. If Izza wants to make bad bets, the M'am won't stop the men from making her pay in…other ways."

"Ah." The bard noticed for the first time the resemblance between the girl at the table—Izza, apparently—and the server. *Sisters.* "And would you let that happen, Yeema?"

Yeema looked as pale as cheese. "I'll get your beer, sir."

"Mmm." The bard looked back down to the children, who seemed confused by the exchange. *Kosrike it,* he thought. *Why me? Every single time.*

"I think Miri is pretty," one girl said.

"You don't know that," another boy argued.

The bard wished he could share their levity. Instead, anxiety pooled like bourbon in his stomach as he kept an eye on Izza's table.

"What happened after they saw the spirit of Donumdonair?" the Desperado girl whispered.

"Mmm?" the bard asked. "Oh, yes. The story. Well, the spirit of Donum told Gilly and Miri to go cut down Kosmoa's tree and save little Divvo. It would be Gilly's first test, just as he tested Donum."

The Kosmoan children gasped, and the Journeymen children leaned forward in awe.

"You can't just do that," one Kosmoan boy objected. "The priests would kill you!"

"Hence the plot of our story," the bard said dryly.

"Cut down the tree all by themselves?" the Desperado girl asked.

The bard shook his head, beard dragging against his chest. "No. They went to Gilly's brothers for help."

"And *did* they help?"

The bard snorted. "His brothers were all roach-faced drunk." At the far table, the men jostled poor little Izza as she lost *again.* "And roach-faced drunk," the bard said gravely, "is not a good place to be."

• • •

Gilly strode out of his father's pub, the *Black Lung.* He wanted to scream as he met Miri's eyes. She had stayed outside—the men of the *Black Lung* had a reputation for treating women's bodies like they treated their snuff boxes—never more than a quick grab away.

"Too drunk?" Miri asked. She cradled the new chrome rifle.

"They were probably too drunk three hours ago. Agor is barely conscious. Kosrike it!" Gilly slammed the base of his hand against the stone wall of the tavern. "All their drinking will earn them is guilt. Divvo will still die. Alone. What does Donumdonair want us to do by ourselves?"

The tavern door creaked, and the bouncer, Shadd, peeked out. Despite the *Black Lung's* reputation, Shadd had bucked Gilly's father on several occasions to be kind to half-legs who had lucked out in the minefields. "Gilly, boy," Shadd boomed. Then he glanced back into the bar and stepped outside. The door creaked shut behind him. "I saw you speak with your brothers. You look like a man with a plan." His gaze wandered up to the dark peak where Kosmoa's tree glimmered in the moonlight. "Are you thinking of a little action?"

"We are."

Shadd chuckled. "You never did inherit your father's poker face."

"That's because I never lost my conscience."

"Aye." Shadd bit his cheek. "Most of the Kosmoan lads should be down at the pass, not guarding the tree. Live long enough with hovercraft and you forget that Journeymen can still climb. We'll want a third man to belay us on the ropes, though."

"I'll go," Miri murmured.

Gilly's stomach clenched. "Love, you're pregnant. You are carrying a *child.*"

"I suppose that'll be four of us, then."

"You can't put our child at risk. I won't let you."

Miri touched her stomach with one hand even as she handed him the chrome rifle. "This will be our firstborn, Gilly. If we don't do this, they'll string him up just like Divvo."

"You shouldn't have to fight." Gilly felt tears welling in his eyes. *Kosrike my brothers.*

"No," Miri said. "But maybe Donum doesn't give these jobs to people who have to do them. Now, come on, we're wasting time."

• • •

Gilly went first. One hundred meters of thin rope spooled out behind him, growing heavier with each meter that he climbed. The rope was for Shadd and Miri—it would do nothing to break his own fall. The rough stones cut into his fingers, and the cliff side offered him a devil's dilemma. It would be easiest to use the deeper crevices and hand-holds. But he might discover a snake or scorpion coiled in the rocks.

He decided to take the risk. Divvo's life mattered more than his own, and time was no longer on their side. He paused, his leg hooked around a natural stone gremlin, and surveyed the dark sky. Storm clouds obscured the stars, but the moon twinkled near the horizon. *One hour until dawn.* If they were still on the rocks at that time—*Donum help us.*

Gilly pulled up a hundred meters of rope, his back aching as he held himself cramped against the cliff. With the rope in hand, he tied it around the stone gremlin and then let it drop back down. "Clear for you to start climbing!" he called down to Shadd and Miri. A muffled reply echoed back to him and he continued upward.

Halfway up the cliff, Gilly found a sycamore tree and once more wrapped the loose rope around it. Lightning split the bruised clouds. Two small forms struggled up the rope below him, their faces tight with exertion. They weren't as confident as him. Gilly had grown up climbing in the mountains with Killiam before—before the nightmare started. With renewed vigor, he strained toward the top of the cliff, arms burning and pulse pounding in his forehead. Thunder rumbled as if Kosmoa were trying to shout them down. A high-pitched tone reached his ears as the thunder quieted. Was that a child's cry he heard?

Rain droplets began to spatter against his forehead. *No, no, no.*

Pulling himself up and over a curved boulder, Gilly found himself at the top of a flat mesa.

Kosmoa's tree glimmered thirty paces ahead, taller than any tree Gilly had ever seen in the desert. Lightning struck a nearby mountain peak, closer this time. It illuminated the dark spells carved into the steel branches. The trunk was formed of snakes that curved around each other as if in lovemaking, constricting toward the sky.

In the uppermost branches hung a dark form, strung between bole and limb like a fly in a spider's web. Wires grasped Divvo's hands and feet, curling around his little stomach in hundreds of tight loops.

"Help me, please!" Divvo cried, voice hoarse. "Someone, please!"

In the last flicker of light, Gilly looked around for enemies. There were none. *Arrogant nubatous*, he thought.

Gilly raced over to the tree, tying the last section of rope around its trunk as a final anchor for Miri and Shadd. He dropped his rifle to the stone and then began to climb. Hand-holds and foot-holds appeared in fortuitous places; no doubt meant to help the priests of Kosmoa string up their victims.

Gilly felt cold. Cold and angry. Rain spattered his face even as a dark fire burned within him. Divvo whimpered and shook in the branches as thunder rolled overhead like the sonic boom of a Kosmoan fighter jet. *They. Will. Not. Win.*

Cannot. Let. Them. Win.

Not. This. Time.

Plasma knife clenched in his teeth, Gilly scaled the tree like a ladder, then shimmied out along the branch that held Divvo.

"N'uncle Gilly?" Divvo asked, his voice raspy.

"I'm here, lad." Gilly expected his voice to shake, but instead, it came out harder than the steel of Kosmoa's tree. He pulled out a plasma knife and slashed through the wires binding Gilly from below. They were meant to channel the electricity through the boy's body when the lightning struck. Gilly sliced through two more, gritting his teeth. Divvo screamed as the web of wires shifted and cut into his wrists.

Riking idiot, Gilly thought. *You can't cut him down without a plan.*

The first head peeked over the cliff face, illuminated by a flash of lightning. Shadd's face twisted, and he pointed to something in the air behind Gilly.

Gilly turned, stomach clenching. Water dripped from his brow.

Another flash of light—and then he saw a hovership hanging in the air only one hundred meters away. It bore the hourglass mark of Kosmoa, lord of time and space. No doubt Kosmoa's priests waiting to see their sacrifice devoured.

"They've seen us, Gilly!" Shadd shouted up through the howling wind. "We have to get out of here! Leave the boy." Miri scrambled onto the mesa behind him, no more than a shadow among shadows.

"No!" Gilly screamed. "Help me cut him down! The lightning is getting closer."

Shadd exchanged a glance with Miri, then raced over to climb the tree. He carried a satchel of miner's TNT on his shoulder.

"Miri!" Gilly called. "My rifle is near the base of the tree. Guard our backs."

Shimmying further down the branch, Gilly counted the strands of wire he would have to cut. *Seven.* "Shadd! Hold the wires below the places where I cut so that we don't drop him."

Shadd grunted as he made his way up the tree trunk. Slinging his satchel of TNT over a nearby branch, he scooted towards Gilly on the limb that held Divvo. He grabbed two wires in his fists and held tight as Gilly sliced through them with the plasma knife. *Snap! Snap!*

A whir overhead marked the movement of the hovercraft. Wind buffeted the steel branches of the tree, and the whole structure began to sway violently.

"Miri!" Gilly shouted. "Keep them off us!"

"On it," Miri shouted back. Gilly spared a glance toward her and saw her sighting down the rifle with one foot up on a boulder. She pulled the trigger, and several bolts of light streaked through the sky, pinging off the ship's electro-shields. The flashes gave Gilly just enough light to work by.

Snap! Snap! Snap! Snap! Snap! Shadd grunted as the wires cut into his hands and he held Divvo up unaided.

"He's free!" Gilly said. "Pull him up!"

Shadd yanked on the wires, and Gilly helped him lift. Soon, they held the small, shaking boy in their hands. With surgical precision, they cut several remaining wires from around his stomach.

"Get him down," Gilly said. "I'll deal with the satchel."

"Roger," Shadd said, tucking the boy under one arm and scampering down the tree.

Reaching out for the explosives, Gilly pulled a wire out of the pack and attached it to one of the wires that had held Divvo. He let that dangle, then climbed down to the branch below.

Stone screeched fifty paces away as the hovercraft landed on the mesa.

Flashes of rifle fire lit the sky. "Gilly!" Miri screamed. "Get out of that tree. They're coming."

"Get the kid home!" Gilly gritted his teeth. "I'm finishing this whole sick tradition." He reached up for a wire dangling from the satchel of explosives, then tied it to the wires that had bound Divvo from below. A bundle of explosives now hung where Divvo had.

Floodlights lit the mesa. Lite-shots cracked through stone as men poured out of the ship and rushed forward with rifles raised.

Gilly scrambled down the trunk, watching as Miri handed the rifle to Shadd and scrambled down the cliff with Divvo secured to a carabiner and a braking mechanism. Their heads disappeared from view even as Shadd knelt near the edge of the cliff, picking off Kosmoan soldiers as if they were desert fowl.

Gilly hit the ground, sprinting toward Shadd. The burly man picked off another Kosmoan thug, then clipped himself to the rope and began to repel. *Twenty paces.* Water splashed under Gilly's boots and flashes of light lit his steps as the men behind fired. *Ten paces.*

Light split the sky, thunder cracked the earth, and an explosion tore the air. It hit Gilly with the force of a collapsing tunnel, tumbling him over the stone. Everything went black.

• • •

A corona of purple light beckoned Gilly. He saw the stranger's face, but now the crown was not of emeralds and rubies but of desert thorns. Blood ran from his brow.

The stranger reached down and took Gilly's hand, pulling him from the darkness. *"Do you trust me?"*

"To the end," Gilly whispered.

"To what end?" the stranger asked, pain in his eyes. *"To your end or to mine? To your glory or to my own?"*

"I—" Gilly hesitated. The vision ended.

• • •

Pain erupted like the blossoms of a volcano. Boots and clubs slammed into Gilly's ribs. Light stabbed through his eyes as he fought to breathe, curling into a ball. A steel toe slammed his skull, and another crunched into his front tooth. He heard voices as if they came through thick mud.

"Enough," a familiar voice said. *Father.*

Sharp pain replaced the grinding ache and the nauseating terror. With it came clarity, as if every sense were sharpened by a whetstone. Gilly curled tighter around his stomach before forcing open one swollen eyelid.

A wall of a dozen leather boots confronted him, backlit by a fading fire. Rain lashed the twisted remnants of the steel tree.

"He has to die," a silky Kosmoan voice said.

"Nah," his father drawled, spitting tobacco onto Gilly's leg. "We'd make our Lord Kosmoa look weak. Like we have to fight his battles for him."

"Do you have an alternative?"

Gilly rolled over, blinking mud from his eyes as he stared into their faces. His father stood next to a Kosmoan priest and four Enforcers.

"Brand him," Gilly's father said. "Put Kosmoa's hourglass on his forehead and let him contend with the boy. Folks will know he is marked—and sooner or later, he'll disappear." He winked. "Killing someone is easy. The timing is the hard part."

The priest considered this. "Hold him down."

Gilly screamed as four men grabbed him, and his father pulled out an electric cattle brander. "Father, no! Please!"

The brand descended.

• • •

The bard broke off the story, pulse pounding in the crook of his neck.

"So The Mark *was* brave," the Journeymen girl said, casting a glance at the scowling Kosmoan boy.

Across the room, several people shirked away as two men grabbed little Izza and dragged her toward the door. She made no noise—only struggled in silent horror, her face as pale as coal ash. How old could she be? Maybe nineteen? There was no reason to intervene. It would mean, at best, sleeping on hard rock tonight. At worst, it would mean he died a few days sooner than expected.

The bard heard an old voice in his head. *To your glory, or to my own?*

He rose from his chair. "Stop." His voice rang across the room. The men turned, then sneered when they found themselves confronted by an old man. Three of their friends rose from the table, approaching the bard.

"Time to leave, children," the bard said in a firm voice. The kids scattered to the corners of the room but kept watching.

The three men encircled him, alcohol and madness swimming in their eyes. "Why don't you just look the other way, Journey-roach?"

"Donumdonair is not blind," the bard said, "and neither am I." He whipped the lite-lash from under his cloak, whipping it across their throats in a single swipe. Their eyes bulged as they fell to the floor.

The two men holding Izza let her go, taking a step back. They reached for their holsters.

The bard pulled two knives from behind his shoulder blades, the hood falling from his brow. He flung the knives end over end. They soared through the air and sunk deep into the knees of the two remaining men. Each cried out, clutching their legs, and sank to the wooden floor.

The bard crossed the room, putting a hand on Izza's shoulder. "My hoverbike is parked in a cave in Ashor's Vale. You know the place?"

Izza nodded, lips quivering.

"Good." The bard handed her a set of keys. "Go. Find your way to my son Jochan in Tar'im. He will keep you safe."

Izza trembled, her eyes wide as she clutched the keys to her chest. "But—"

"Go!"

The girl fled out the double doors.

The bard turned, breathing hard. The room sat in deathly silence, save for the scrabbling of the wounded men on the floor.

The children stared at his uncloaked face. The bard laughed, "the

213

story is finished, children." He lifted his hand to caress the hourglass scar on his forehead. "At least, this chapter of it."

He strode toward the door but stopped as he tucked the lite-lash under his cloak. He turned, finding the gaze of the small Journeymen girl. "The Mark wasn't brave. He just learned to do the right thing even when it scared him."

His mind wandered back to the echo of an army. *For Donum-donair and for The Mark.*

"Sometimes." He rested a hand on the door. "He did the right thing—sometimes."

The bard disappeared into the storm.

Find the story of Gideon in Judges 6.

The Mark, Part II
Jonathan Babcock

Gilly grabbed the sandstone ledge, hauling himself up to the top of the ridge. Loose scree tumbled away down the barren red hillside. He wormed his way onto the flat rock surface, his head down, cheek pressed to the rock.

The two men with him did the same. The roar of machines grew as they crawled towards the far side of the ridge. Rust-colored sand whipped at them—the first warnings of a storm.

They paused just short of the edge. Cold dread pooled in Gilly's gut. Finally, he worked his way a few inches farther, peering over the cliff. Desert vehicles swarmed up the valley. Heavy jeeps and motorcycles with wide wheels threw up dust clouds as the invading army advanced.

Gilly squeezed his eyes shut, willing the Kosmoans to disappear.

"We need to know their numbers," Shadd murmured, voice hoarse. Thunder crackled in the distance, churned up by the static of the sandstorm. It echoed through the valley, seeming to expand in volume.

"It doesn't matter. We can't face them," Gilly shot back. Bile rose in his throat as his own screams echoed in his memory. He'd been unable to stand up against the small group of Kosmoan Enforcers before, let alone an entire army. "We need to get back." He began to pull away from the edge.

"We're not leaving," Shadd said. "Not until we know their numbers." His voice came out more forcefully this time. An order, though technically, they didn't have a command structure.

Jez grabbed a battered spyglass from its holster on his thigh. It had been a scope for a lite-rifle once. None of them had the good fortune of possessing the actual rifle. He began to search the valley with it, peering beyond what the rest could see.

"Their forces stretch out of sight," Jez's voice warbled as he spoke. Gilly swore.

Sand pelted at the unhealed burn on his forehead. He reached up to touch it, then pulled his curly dark hair down to partially cover the brand. His own father had suggested they stamp the shape of an empty hourglass there—a grisly reminder that his time would run out. Sooner or later, the god Kosmoa would take revenge, they said.

His hand dropped down, brushing past his rebreather. Not an advanced model, but better than a bandana. *Could this army be the end?* he wondered. Could they have been right?

"We're doomed," Jez murmured.

"No, we're not," Shadd snapped. "We just need a strategy."

Jez tucked his spyglass away, eyes hollow. "There's at least five thousand soldiers within view."

"The first report of their army came in, what, three hours ago?" Gilly said. "At the rate they're going, they must have around twenty-five thousand troops already here. With more coming."

Lightning flashed, striking a lone tree on the other side of the valley. Gilly flinched, nausea invading his gut.

"We need to warn our village," Shadd said. "We can escape into the hills."

"And do what?" Jez asked. "Slowly starve to death? There is nothing for us in the wilderness. There will be nothing for us when we return to our destroyed homes."

Shadd stared out at the swarming army. "We have to *try.*"

Gilly swallowed hard. He'd offered up some of his stash to Donum's messenger, but the remainder would be enough to survive in the wilderness, for a little while at least. His stomach churned as he eyed Shadd and Jez. His own people would kill him for those supplies. He was already an outcast. No one would hesitate to secure their own family's future by destroying his.

They needed to get out fast. Make for the hills before anyone else could. The thought of Miri giving birth to their child out there made his palms sweat.

"Donumdonair has deserted us," Jez said. He rose to his knees. "There are no more deliverers." He wrapped his arms around himself, rocking back and forth. "Hope deserted these lands along with Donum."

Jez gradually stood. He swayed in the harsh wind, then took a step towards the edge.

A violent shudder ran through Gilly. *Rescue. Our. People.* The words drilled into his mind.

"Stop!" Gilly's voice rang out clear. Authoritative.

Jez froze. "Nothing is left for us, Gilly." He stared down at the army, one foot half over the cliff.

A chill ran down Gilly's spine. Cool and refreshing in the desert heat. Strength settled over him. "The clans can stand and fight."

Below them, two jeeps swerved out of the flow. Sand sprayed out in a semi-circle as they drifted to a halt, facing the cliff. The men inside pointed up at Jez as the heavy mounted guns in the back began to swivel.

Gilly scrambled to his feet. "Jez, get back!"

Jez shut his eyes. "You're just a man, Gilly Thorntree. You don't have the power to stop the Kosmoans."

Gilly grabbed Jez around the waist and threw himself backwards as the crack of the lite-bolts split the air. They landed in a tumble, Jez screaming.

Gilly rolled out from beneath him. The young man writhed, clutching at a burned gash on his shoulder.

"I'm going to begin the Summoning," Gilly announced, steel in his voice. He pushed himself up onto his knees, careful to stay below the sightline of the gunners. "I may just be a man, Jez. But Donum *has* sent a deliverer. Me."

With that, he rocked back on his heels. *Rike, what have I just said?*

• • •

The dripping of water sounded an unsteady counter-beat to the rhythmic crunch of Gilly's boots. His lantern swayed, casting flickering shadows through the mine. He couldn't shake the crawling sensation of rock-spiders on his skin. Everything felt wrong. Off-kilter.

The afternoon had passed in a dazed blur, but already, young warriors were arriving. On pain of death, the Summoning called all able-bodied Journeymen in the outer settlements to fight. Only the

Summoner could release them from the bond, as dictated by The Ancient Mandates.

Gilly had fled as people arrived. What if Jez was right, after all? Did Gilly really know that he would be the deliverer?

Weeks and a lifetime ago, he'd met a shining stranger in these tunnels. "Donum, if you are for us, send your messenger again." His words bounced back to him in the empty tunnels.

Gilly gritted his teeth. The scent of damp, sandy rock assailed his nostrils. He couldn't remember a time when the abandoned tunnels here had ever been this wet.

His pace increased as he neared the tunnel where he'd met the stranger. He still couldn't describe him. It felt almost dreamlike. If not for Miri meeting the stranger, he could almost believe he'd imagined it.

If nothing else, these tunnels contained his stash. He would bring the supplies to Miri. She could escape. They could set a meeting point in case things went badly.

He turned a corner and stopped in his tracks. A pebble that he'd kicked plunked into the lapping water in front of him. The jet-black liquid filled the steep entrance to the tunnel. In the near distance, it rose to the ceiling, fully blocking off any hope of entering.

His stash was gone. As was his meeting place with the stranger. Slowly, he sank down to his knees.

Hope is not gone.

Gilly stilled. The word felt like a whispered shout. So clear, yet… not audible at the same time. Had he imagined it? No echo reverberated off the walls.

"Donumdonair?" he asked, breathless.

Hope is not gone. And neither Am I.

Again, no echo sounded. Yet Gilly heard it as clear as day.

No shining radiance accompanied the words. No stranger with the light of the stars upon his brow appeared. Water continued to drip off the walls. His lantern cast only a small pool of flickering light on his surroundings.

Gilly waited, blood thundering in his ears.

He dimmed his lantern, searching the darkness in front of him for any sign of light. Time ticked away with each splash of water. He couldn't bear to return outside to the gathering armies. Thankfully, Shadd was organizing them.

Finally, he struggled to his feet. Every joint in his legs screamed from kneeling on the cold stone. "Donum," he called, his voice echoing."Your messenger asked that I would rescue the Journeymen. If that was from you, then make it so that this tunnel is drained of its water by the end of the day. Without your sign, I will not march the army. Will you save the people by my hand?"

The tunnels gave no answer.

· · ·

A young warrior stepped forward to shake Gilly's hand, the last light of dusk peeking over his shoulder. Freckles dotted the young man's face along with some scruffy fuzz that Gilly thought might be an attempt at a beard. He couldn't be older than twenty-one. "I'm Ahiyah. I lead two hundred men from Sarinak."

The number surprised Gilly. So many had answered the call from a single village? "We'll need every man we can get." He tried to exude confidence. "It's good to meet you, Ahiyah. My name is—"

THE MARK, PART II • J. BABCOCK

"Oh, I know," he cut in. "You're The Mark."

Gilly paused. "What?"

Ahiyah's confidence faltered for a split second. "Is that…not a name you wish to be called? I heard the men in camp calling you that."

Gilly swept his hair back and pointed at the ugly burn. "Do you know what this is?"

Ahiyah nodded, grinning. "That's the mark of Kosmoa. They say that you received it after cutting down one of Kosmoa's sacrificial trees. It's a mark of rebellion." Excitement shone in his eyes.

Bitterness tinged Gilly's laugh, though he tried to hide it. "Call me that if you like."

• • •

Gilly found excuses to arrive at the mine alone later that evening. He stopped a little distance in and let his eyes adjust. Things slowly came into focus, and he found the lantern he'd left the night before.

He struck a piece of flint, spraying sparks towards the fuel-soaked lantern wick. The shaking in his hands made it harder than normal. The lantern flared to life after several tries, and he quickly dimmed it. Running out of fuel while underground would end him before the Kosmoans even got the chance.

He set out at a jog, the light spinning crazily off the walls as the lantern swayed. His pulse quickened as he realized that less water dripped off the walls today.

Off in the distance, he heard the clank of machinery. He picked up his pace, flying past broken carts and dusty tunnel offshoots.

He pulled up short at the entrance to the tunnel he wanted. No water. He sucked in gulps of air through his rebreather, mind spinning. He'd wanted to meet the messenger again. He'd prayed for a sign. And the waters had disappeared.

He forced himself to walk as he entered the tunnel. He didn't want to be a mess when he met with the stranger.

The rumbling of machinery grew louder as he proceeded. The source of the noise finally struck him. Water pumps. They would kick on automatically in the event of a flood as soon as the water hit a certain point. His stomach roiled.

Trembling, he reached the chamber where he'd met the stranger. Nothing. He'd worked himself into a frenzy just to see a hall of wet rock, exposed by the machinations of a rusty water pump.

His scream of frustration reverberated through the underground quarry. He stood there stiffly while the echoes died down around him.

He walked over to where he'd hidden his stash in the rock slide. Gone. All of it. The supplies should have been scattered throughout the quarry and up into the tunnel, but he couldn't spot any sign of them.

"Donum," he whispered. "I...don't know if this was from you." He shook his head in disgust at his own stupidity. "Please, don't be angry with me. But I would ask you for another sign." He couldn't shake the quivering in his bones as he spoke the words.

"I would ask that by morning tomorrow, these tunnels would once again be flooded." For the tunnels to be unflooded so quickly today and then flooded again tomorrow *while* the pumps ran would be nearly impossible.

Unless Donum made it happen.

• • •

Miri squeezed Gilly's hand. He hated the way his fingers shook in her grip. He should be strong for her.

"Take a deep breath, love," she murmured.

A short, panicked laugh escaped him. His wife, nearly eight months pregnant, was the one telling him to breathe. He'd made the short trek back home to spend one final night with her before they marched.

He tried to take her advice, but a violent tremor cut him off. They sat together on the edge of their bed, the night pressing in on them. He leaned forward, putting his head between his knees. "I can't do this," he gasped. "I can't lead these men into battle."

Miri held tight to his hand. "Yes, you can. I know who I married, Gilly Thorntree."

"I'm not even sure if I can trust myself," he said. He looked up at her, trying and failing to see her eyes in the darkness. "I thought I heard a voice in the tunnels yesterday."

"Sometimes, trusting yourself isn't what's important," Miri whispered as she rubbed his back."The better question is, do you trust Donum?"

He squeezed his eyes shut in the darkness. "I—I don't know."

"Then pray that he will make himself clear to you," she said.

Gilly swallowed hard. He pushed himself up on trembling legs. Miri stood with him and wrapped her arms around him, her forehead pressed against his collarbone.

They held each other for a long moment. The child inside of Miri's womb kicked hard enough that Gilly could feel it. He fought back the sudden tears that stung the corners of his eyes. Everything in him still wanted to run.

Finally, Miri pulled back. "Go and find the answers that you need," she said. "Donum will make a path for you."

. . .

Gilly cupped the water, then let it slide through his fingers. He couldn't stop the ridiculous grin on his face. The muted sound of the water pumps sounded in the depths.

Donum still heard the prayers of men.

Gilly rose from his crouch. Time to go. He'd waited long enough. Today, they would strike the Kosmoans. And they would strike hard.

He jogged out of the tunnels, emerging into the pre-dawn cool of the desert. A few stars still clung to their fading existence. But the sunlight would win out.

Shadd met him as he returned to the mass of tents. "Where did you disappear to?" he whispered.

Gilly ducked into his tent, holding up the flap for Shadd to follow. "Seeking answers." He kept his voice low, trying not to wake the slumbering warriors around them. They would need their strength for the day ahead.

"Did you find them?" Shadd asked.

Gilly nodded. "Donum marches with us."

Shadd raised an eyebrow.

"How many men have arrived?" Gilly grabbed a lite-rifle off of a cot in the corner. A warrior had gifted it to him the day before after discovering their leader marched without a proper weapon.

"By my best count," Shadd said, "around thirty-thousand."

Gilly froze, an energy-mag halfway into the gun. "That many?"

"Aye." Shadd seemed almost shaken by the number. "But Gilly, I need to know. Are you able to lead them?"

"Yes." The confidence in his voice surprised him. It felt the same as on the cliff. A power not fully his own coursed through him.

Shadd dipped his head in deference. "I will follow you faithfully, then. You're no longer the lad I grew up with, eh?" He grinned wryly.

Gilly smiled. He sat down on the cot to pull on a pair of desert boots that rose to his midcalf. "How equipped are the men?"

"Some? Well. Others? Not so much," Shadd replied. "We've got about nine thousand rifles between us. Then, about seven thousand sidearms. Others came equipped with older weapons. Crossbows and the like. I don't have an exact count on those. But you can count on sixteen thousand well-equipped warriors, plus others as reserves."

"Good. We'll need every one of those men," Gilly said. It shocked him that so many Journeymen out here possessed weapons like that. Their small village had chosen a strategy of passive appeasement towards the Kosmoans. Apparently, not everyone shared that ideology. "What about heavy armaments? Vehicles?"

"Not much for heavy armaments," Shadd conceded. "We've got no vehicle-mounted guns or energy cannons. We do have hundreds of desert bikes and dune buggies, though. Scrappy stuff, mostly, but enough for a mounted contingent."

Gilly grunted. The latest scout reports put the Kosmoan forces at fifty thousand troops. "There will be three Kosmoans to every Journeymen with a weapon," he mused.

"Does that scare you?" Shadd asked.

"Yes," Gilly admitted. "But also no. The thoughts...the doubts are still there." His brow furrowed as he sorted his thoughts. "But somehow, they're muted. I can ignore them for now."

"Well, whatever works for you," Shadd snorted. "I'm just hoping I don't nub my pants once the fighting starts."

They quietly finished their preparations, then exited the tent together to begin rallying the men.

An hour later, Gilly stood on a jeep's roof, facing the masses of warriors. He wiped the sweat from his hands on his khaki trousers as he faced thirty thousand sets of eyes.

"Journeymen!" he shouted. His voice only carried so far, but criers further out would repeat his words every time he paused. "Brothers in arms! Today, we're gathered to strike a blow against the Kosmoan scourge."

The sun slanted through the smoke of a thousand cooking fires. Tents scattered the rugged terrain, pitched wherever a flat spot could be found. Cacti littered the area, making it difficult to move through some areas in the camp. They'd gathered by a hill just outside the tents.

"We are gathered under the protection of Donumdonair," Gilly announced. "For too long, we've wilted under the destructive power of the Kosmoans and their false god." He paused to let the criers carry out his words. "But today is the day that Donum has ordained for us to be set free. To break off the chains of our oppressors!"

Scattered cheers greeted his words. Would that be enough of a speech? He couldn't tell.

Dismiss some of the men. The voice spoke into his mind, startling him. A chill radiated up his spine, spreading outwards. It felt the same as when he'd decided to begin the Summoning.

"Donum?" He mouthed the word, too soft for anyone else to hear.

226

You have too many men. When you win this battle, you will say that it was your own skill that brought victory. Dismiss anyone who is afraid to march against the Kosmoans.

He tensed, unease eating at his gut. He wanted to ignore the voice as some Kosmoan trick, but the chill spread to his limbs, cool and refreshing.

"*Men,*" his voice warbled out at an odd pitch. He cleared his throat. "Warriors of the Journeymen clans!" Gilly called. "Today, among you, there are those who are terrified of the coming battle. I would bid you leave with Donumdonair's blessing. The victory is still assured for those who choose to fight."

Silence greeted his words. Then, the shuffling of feet. Men cast anxious glances at each other.

Finally, one man called out from the crowd. "We are released from the bonds of the Summoning, should we choose to be?"

"Yes," Gilly said. "I would only ask that those with weapons give them to those without."

The uneasy silence lingered again. Then, one man split off from the group. He propped a lite rifle against a rock, saluted Gilly, and shouldered a pack. With that, he started walking off through the tents.

The dam broke. Men began to mill about, some leaving immediately, others conversing quietly, and then leaving in groups. With each person that left, the fear on the faces of the others grew.

Gilly got down off his perch just as Shadd stormed over.

"What was that?" he snapped. "You said you could lead these men." He poked an accusatory finger at Gilly's chest.

Gilly shrugged, then squared his shoulders and raised his voice. "I can't deny the voice of Donum."

"Rike." Shadd looked out at the crowd. "We've lost at least half."

Coldness seeped through Gilly. Not the reassuring chill but the bone-freezing pain of dread. "Get the leaders to bring status reports. Any groups that have lost their leaders will need to find new ones. We can't delay our march."

Shadd looked at him, askance. "Do you realize the organizational chaos you've just created? And you expect us to continue with the march?"

Gilly met Shadd's eyes. "We're running out of time, Shadd. The Kosmoans were delayed yesterday, but we need to strike before they can fully leave the valley."

The bulk of the Kosmoan forces had camped in a flat area near the top of The Ardus Valley. Hills and bluffs ringed it on most sides, but in hours, they could pass through it and take settlements like Hosel and Bresh. From there, they would spread out, crushing neighboring towns and villages. Gilly's own village would likely be conquered in less than a day.

Shadd shook his head and stalked off.

Two hours later, they marched. About ten thousand walked or rode with the army. They'd lost more than two-thirds of their numbers. *I made the right decision*, Gilly reminded himself.

Gilly rode in a light dune buggy that Ahiyah drove. The young soldier had lost all but twenty of his men. Several of his remaining fighters hung off the back of the buggy, hitching a ride for a little while before swapping out with the others.

They rode in almost complete silence, save for the roar of the engines. An hour passed, then two.

Stop the army. Donum's voice popped into Gilly's mind, making him sit bolt upright. Once again, a chill accompanied it. Ahiyah cast a glance at him but kept driving.

Why? He tried to think the question as clearly as possible. How did that even work? Did Donum hear all of his thoughts or just the ones sent to him? Or none at all? The Ancient Mandates were lost to most of the Journeymen, but Gilly suspected that perhaps such things would be answered in them.

Your army is still too large. The answer came back.

Gilly slumped back against the interlocked leather straps of his seat. *What if I say no?*

I chose you, Gilly Thorntree. Do you trust my promises?

"Bring us to a halt," Gilly said.

Ahiyah did as instructed. They were the leading vehicle, and the ones behind followed their example. They came to a halt on the rim of a shallow gully. Rocks lined the bottom.

Gilly carefully climbed on top of the open buggy. He perched awkwardly on top, legs hugging one of the exposed roll bars. *What now?* Did he just repeat what he'd done earlier?

Have them find water, Donum answered.

We already have water, Gilly shot back.

I know.

A suspicion nagged at Gilly. Three times, he'd put Donum to the test. First, the test of the meal, then twice in the tunnels. Donum had tested Gilly with the tree of Kosmoa in response to the first. Now, he put two more tests before Gilly. It didn't feel like a coincidence. Three for three.

Gilly took a deep breath, then yelled out to the assembled crowd. "You are to find water."

Confusion greeted his simple statement. Slowly, shouts rippled outwards through the crowd as people began repeating the order. Nearly all of the men began to pull out canteens and hold them up. Strangely, however, a few wandered down into the gully. Ahiyah himself jumped out of the buggy and scrambled down the slope.

Shadd walked up with his canteen. "Why did you call a halt for this?"

Gilly shrugged. "Not sure yet."

A few more men headed down into the gully. Oddly, they began digging. Gilly let it go on, waiting for further instructions from Donum.

Minutes later, Ahiyah jogged up the slope. "We've found water," he announced. True enough, wet sand clung to his hands.

Set apart those who dug to find water. They are to be your army. The rest may go home.

No. No, no, no. Gilly fought the swelling panic in his chest. Far, far fewer than a thousand men stood in the gully.

His arm shook as he raised it for the Journeymen to see. He would pass Donum's second test. But at what cost? "Journeymen!" he hollered. "The word of our maker, Donum, has come to me. Those who have found water in the gully are to continue onwards. The rest of you may be dismissed to your homes."

Shadd's canteen thumped into the sand at his feet. "What?"

Gilly took a deep breath and looked down at his friend. "I'm sorry." He swung off the buggy and landed in the sand. He couldn't stop the shaking in his body.

Shadd picked up his canteen and turned to leave. Then, he turned back to Gilly. "May Donum bless you." He wrapped Gilly in a hug, the emotion thick in his voice. "I'll do what I can for Miri if…if… *Bah.*" He pulled back. "Stay alive. Don't do anything stupid."

Shadd slipped away, disappearing into the milling mass of confused warriors. It felt wrong for him to go. He'd assembled and organized this army. Yet he'd also doubted it.

He watched for a moment longer, then headed down into the gully. Ahiyah fell into step beside him as he began organizing the men. In total, two hundred and ninety-eight warriors remained. Gilly split them into three groups.

Their three columns roared across the desert on motorcycles an hour later. While few in number, they'd been left with the best of the equipment. They all carried lite rifles and pistols. The motorcycles, while somewhat cobbled together with bits of loose tin and metal, would carry them well.

I've delayed the Kosmoans. Donum's voice came into Gilly's mind. *Bring your army close to their camp. Do not attack until I tell you.*

"Thank you," Gilly murmured. With so few men, their only hope lay in controlling the pass. Once the Kosmoans spilled onto the plains, the small Journeymen army would be easily encircled and destroyed.

Gilly eventually called a halt about a klick from the rim of the edge of the valley. He ordered the men to pitch their tents, then found a rocky outcropping that overlooked the Kosmoan camp. He settled in to wait for Donum's voice, trying to ignore the frantic pace of his heartbeat.

Ahiyah strolled over to join him as dusk fell. The young warrior took a seat next to Gilly, swinging his legs off the edge of the rock ledge. They sat in silence for a while, watching the sun fade into the desert horizon.

"I want to believe we can do this," Ahiyah finally said. "I'm not sure, though."

Gilly shrugged. "You're not the only one with doubts. Are you still with me?"

Ahiyah nodded. "To the end. I won't stand on the cusp of history and walk away." He sighed, long and heavy. "Imagine telling your grandchildren that you walked away hours before the battle that freed the Journeymen. Even if we don't win, at least I'll die honorably instead of being hunted down in the hills."

"You're wise for someone your age."

A pained smile slipped across Ahiyah's face. "The Kosmoans took my parents from me when I was young. That ages you."

"I'm sorry," Gilly said.

"Not every hand in cards is a winning one," he replied, shrugging. "I've done the best I could." He cleared his throat and looked out over the plains. "You know, this is the place where The Great Marshal, Eliana, defeated the Kosmoans decades ago."

Gilly's eyebrows shot up. "I had no idea," he admitted. "Donum stood with his people then," he said. "Let us pray that he'll do so again."

"Mmm."

A shot rang out and echoed, shattering the stillness. They both bolted upright. The sound had come from the direction of the Kosmoan camp, within sniping distance. Gideon glanced out at his troops. They hunkered down, waiting and watching for another shot. No cries of pain sounded in the camp.

The now familiar chill trickled up his spine. *I have given the Kosmoans over to you,* Donum said. *You are ready to attack. If your fear is too great, however, go towards their camp where you heard the sound. There, you will be encouraged.*

Gilly swallowed.

He clenched his fist, nails digging into his palm. Part of him wanted to just attack. Even if Donum failed them, at least it would be over. No more wondering.

He slowly unclenched his fist, blood rushing back into his knuckles. He glanced at Ahiyah. "Are you willing to join me for some scouting?"

"Where you lead, I'll follow."

Gilly nodded.

They left instructions for the others to stay put, then set out. They ran low across the sand, out of view of anyone on the ridge. While the Kosmoan equipment would need to go through the pass at the top of the valley, nothing stopped light foot soldiers from climbing up the ridges. The last light of the sun lit them from behind, so at least it would be in the eyes of anyone trying to sight in on them.

The sand sloped up to the short mesa that ringed most of the valley. They arrived at the sharp ridge of the mesa just as the sun fully slipped below the horizon. A chill swept across the desert, intensified by the light wind. The two figures climbed to the lip of the ridge and carefully checked for picketed soldiers.

Together, they inched their way onto the flat surface at the top. Immediately, voices from the other side of the ridge gained clarity. Gilly and Ahiyah crawled on their elbows to the cliff's edge and peeked over.

"You say you shot this?" a robed priest of Kosmoa crouched over a dead antelope, shining a light at it.

Gilly and Ahiyah were no more than twenty meters from them.

"Yes," a guard responded, bowing. "I saw something moving and spooked. There's something bad in the air tonight."

The priest scoffed. "You're a fool."

The guard shifted from one foot to the other. "Eh, with respect...I shot it through the intestines. Bad luck before a battle. Could you take a look at it?"

The priest sighed. He accepted a plasma-knife from the guard. He clicked it on with a twitch of his finger, sending flickering light out along the blade.

The acrid smell of burning flesh drifted up to Gilly as he watched the priest cut into the animal. The priest began to pull out various organs from the antelope. Each time, he would hold it up and inspect it, trying through divination to learn something. Finally, he pulled out the heart.

Gilly watched as the man's hands began to shake, his light sending out twisting shadows from the movement. The priest flung the heart away and stood up.

"What is it?" the guard asked.

"The heart contained an ill omen," the priest said. "Our...our army will not meet the success we expect. A...different god marches against us."

A strange mixture of awe and euphoria stirred within Gilly. Even the priests of the enemy acknowledged the victory of the Journeymen.

They silently withdrew a few hundred meters before Gilly dropped to his knees. He bowed face down in the sand. Emotions overwhelmed him, swirling in a powerful cacophony within his chest. Praise flowed out from him, yet he couldn't find the words to express it. Time spun out of meaning as he worshiped Donum.

At last, Ahiyah touched his shoulder. "What's our next move?"

Gilly slowly rose to a kneeling position. "Attack." His voice felt hoarse from lack of use.

Stars now shone brightly overhead, twinkling in the night sky.

"I like the sound of that."

Ahiyah flicked on a small light, and together, they jogged back to the Journeymen camp. Anxious soldiers flocked to them as they returned.

"To me!" Gilly shouted. "Warriors of Donum, the victory has been guaranteed to us this very night. We march immediately."

A ragged cheer went up.

"Gather the motorcycles," Gilly ordered. "Rip off any mufflers. If any of you possess powerful lights, bring them."

"One of the buggies carried floodlights in the back," Ahiyah said. "They were intended for security in the camp."

"Bring them," Gilly said. He pitched his voice to carry further again. "Carry your weapons with you, but don't expect to use them," he announced. "Follow my lead and copy what I do."

The men scattered to go about their tasks. Minutes later, they wheeled their motorcycles across the sand. Many of them carried floodlights strapped to the back. They kept totally silent, save for the swish of boots through sand and the occasional creak of their leather clothing.

They split off into three companies as they neared the ridge. Gilly stayed in the center while Ahiyah and another leader each took a company. The men worked in teams to carefully hoist every motorcycle up onto the flat of the ridge. They operated in the dark, carefully coordinating in silence.

The Kosmoans still hadn't posted any sentries out on the ridge. Lights lit up sentries guarding the pass far to their right, but that seemed to be the only real point from which they feared attack.

Eventually, the Journeymen were fully stretched out along the ridge—ten warriors with their motorcycles in between every floodlight. Gilly stood silently for a long moment, looking up at the heavens. No moon graced the sky tonight—the stars shone brightly. His warriors waited around him for the signal.

At last, he stepped to the nearest floodlight. He inhaled deeply, then flicked the switch.

"For Donumdonair," he roared, "and for The Mark!"

His men took up the cry. "For Donumdonair and for The Mark!" rang out in the night as they bathed huge portions of the Kosmoan camp in light. Their motorcycles growled to life seconds later. They revved the engines, the roar consuming the valley below them.

Dazed Kosmoans stumbled out of the tents below. Terrified screams sounded as they prepared to meet an oncoming enemy onslaught.

The roar of the motorcycles echoed off of the canyon walls. The valley amplified the sound to incredible levels, mingling with the screaming of the Kosmoans. It thundered around them, continuing to build on itself as it shook the ground.

Energy blasts began to light up the night below. Gilly crouched for cover, but no energy bolts passed near them. The Kosmoans were firing on each other. Gilly rose to his feet and whooped.

Something streaked a burning trail through the sky, momentarily distracting Gilly. He tracked the falling star, then glanced back at the battle.

The fighting below them intensified. Kosmoans began to clamber into their vehicles and roar across the battlefield with guns blazing. Tents collapsed as jeeps tore into them, and scattered soldiers tripped in the confusion.

More stars began to fall. Gilly watched openmouthed as the sky itself seemed to come crashing down. Thousands of burning meteors lit the night, casting a ghostly glow over the chaotic battlefield.

Near the far side of the canyon, a munitions cache exploded, adding to the cacophony. It set off a chain reaction of other explosions around the camp. Huge chunks of shrapnel and metal blasted into the sky, then crashed back down atop Kosmoan soldiers.

A jeep overturned as it swerved to miss falling debris. Another jeep opened fire from close range on the exposed underside, sending the first vehicle up in a mushroom cloud of flame. A random energy bolt struck the driver of the second jeep in the chest, and he fell forward on the controls. His jeep plowed through a squad of terrified footsoldiers before slamming into another parked vehicle.

Stars continued to rain down. One meteor slammed into the center of the Kosmoan camp, throwing up a wave of dirt on impact. The noise continued to mount, building on itself and overlapping. Gilly could see soldiers screaming and shouting orders, but the sound never reached him.

Bodies littered the ground, the scale of the destruction staggering. Already, fewer and fewer energy blasts lit up the night.

As the cacophony fell silent, the lights of vehicles lit up the valley further down and Gilly's heart leaped into his throat. Reinforcements? He squinted, trying to make it out. The vehicles were driving *away* from them. A full-scale retreat.

The Journeymen began to cut their engines as stillness settled over the piles of bodies and mutilated equipment down below. The warriors' cheers rose towards the sky, even as the meteors stopped raining down.

Ahiyah ran along the ridge to Gilly. He tackled him in a hug, slapping Gilly on the back. When he pulled back, the light of the fires reflected off of his eyes. "You did it!"

Gilly laughed, breathless and overwhelmed. He'd done it.

Ahiyah turned to the gathering Journeymen and raised his fist into the air. "Victory! For Donumdonair and for The Mark!"

Three hundred voices roared back in response, echoing across the bowl and into the night sky. "For Donumdonair and for The Mark!"

Find the story of Gideon in Judges 6:33.

Steelhounds of Mercy
Nicole Gusto

In the calm afternoon, Makir read stories to the girl. Moments ago, he had just killed a man. *I should've wiped my hands first.* Dried blood stained the bounty hunter's fingernails.

But the girl didn't mind.

She grasped his calloused hands, her earth-brown eyes as mesmerizing as a mirage, urging him to keep reading.

To the outsider, she appeared like a skinny boy. Her hair had been sheared into a buzz cut. She had a strong nose and a knife scar on her ruddy cheek. A cloth jacket swallowed her small frame. *Only men survive out here.* Makir insisted that she look like a boy to stay alive. *Are you fourteen years old? Fifteen?* She was barely a woman, but too solemn—too exposed to the horrors of Covenant—to be a mere child.

A L Z I O R.

She had written her name in crooked letters. She didn't know how to write anything else, couldn't say anything either.

"Kid, I've read you enough stories." Makir flipped his hands, their sign for *stop.* The rectangular holopad glowed in his palm, illuminating their tent with blue light. The Kosmoan device emitted ghostly holographic text.

Outside, the world sprawled with desert plains and cloudless skies. Motorbikes and refurbished trucks bordered their site, welded with scavenged Kosmoan tech. The temporary camp looked like a haven for mechanical beasts, smelling of gunmetal and smoke. Men clothed in protector coats and wide-brimmed hats kept watch, each fitted with rebreathers that masked their rugged faces. To a traveler, Makir's squad looked like bloodthirsty road pirates.

Only survivors in the wasteland knew—the Steelhounds were worse than pirates, especially when one's name was on their hunting list.

Alzior settled beside Makir in the tent. She signed with her fingers, "more." Then pointed to the text.

"Calix's been teaching you more signs, huh?" Makir tapped the rusty holopad. "If that nub-head can get you talking, I'd give him extra rations."

Months ago, a merchant posted a bounty for a runaway female slave. The notice simply read: *She sliced his throat—stabbed him in the chest! Find the snipe who murdered my son!*

The Steelhounds discovered the runaway in the outskirts, unconscious and skinnier than the desert lizards. A serrated knife rested beside her, glinting like a beast fang. In an instant, Makir pieced her story together: *Torn dress. Bruised neck. Pale calves lined with scarlet.* She was no murderer. She was a survivor. Makir covered her with his jacket. The moment she stirred awake, she seized her knife and stabbed her own cheek. He had to pin her down. Whenever his victims saw him, their first instinct was to *run,* to *live.*

But not her.

"*Rike* it." He swore in the tent. "Fine. I'll keep reading. We're still tracking our next guy, so we've got time." Makir touched the Kosmoan holopad. Folklore and history were hard to come by. Though Makir barely believed in The Ancient Mandates, he hoped that reading could help Alzior communicate.

"*In a span of time, in an era between wars, divine mercy will come.*" Makir read, "*Mercy shall atone. Mercy shall set free. Tell the men of flesh; proclaim it to the souls in darkness, that mercy shall shatter their shackles...*"

He was uncertain if Alzior could truly hear him speak, but the girl watched his finger moving along the text. Her curious eyes poured over the moving illustrations beside the words. Holographic lines swirled and scattered between them, forming the digital figure of a swordsman hacking down chains.

She pointed at the illustration, then at him.

"Me? A man of mercy?" Makir grimaced. "Kid, I am *no* such thing."

She didn't break her gaze.

"I let you stay with us because you're useful," he said. "You're riking good with those medic tasks and tracking drills. If Calix didn't ask for an apprentice, I would've left you in the wasteland to rot."

She shook her head, a flicker of light in her eyes.

Her presence should've soothed the hunter's conscience, but a cruel weight slowly slithered into him and gripped him tight. Memories as dark as an abyss. Memories he'd been failing to bury in the sands of time.

His real daughter was around Alzior's age. *Mercy.* He scoffed quietly. *If divine mercy were true, she would've lived.*

"Captain!" Calix, the Steelhound tracker, entered the tent. He lifted his goggles over his dark hair, lite-rifle hanging beneath his sand-dusted coat. "We found him."

"Signal the men," Makir said.

• • •

Makir had rules for bounty hunting. The first of which was the most crucial.

Secure the area. Render escape impossible.

"The guy's in the pub. Second to the rightmost stool." Calix removed his rebreather and tan boonie hat. The young man's beard had yet to thicken, but his tracking skills were as good as a desert wolf's. "I'm telling you, Captain. This guy's got the cleanest hands."

Should be easy. Makir had brought ten of his squad members. He placed a group to the south of the pub and another behind the back gate. As their technician rigged the traps, Makir, Calix, and Alzior approached the iron-wrought doors in the front.

Of all the men in his squad, Calix was the one who knew how to communicate with Alzior, though she was still learning to use signs. "Are you sure you want to go with us?" Calix's hands moved in specific gestures. He dragged his finger to his throat. "We're collecting someone today."

Alzior nodded. She thumbed the hilt of her serrated dagger.

"Stay close," he signed. He buttoned her jacket to hide her blade and then he placed his boonie hat on her head.

"I swear, Captain," Calix said. "This kid's gonna be a killer apprentice one day."

"As long as you teach her to wield that knife." Makir eyed him.

"Make sure she doesn't get herself killed."

"Of course." Calix flashed a wolfish smile, fingers twitching over his hidden pistol. His unruly hair fell just above his olive eyes, making him look feral. "Have I ever disappointed you?"

"Don't get too cocky." Makir pushed the doors open. Lamplight spilled over his gray hood, darkening the shadows on his face. "Focus."

They entered the bar. The ceiling hung low, the lights a mix of lanterns and sun-powered bulbs. Floors creaked. The walls bore stains. And the men inside feasted like sweaty animals. Liquor drenched their beards and trousers. Desperado dice clattered over gambling tables, and half-masked women danced on a platform, their clothes thin and flowing.

Someone caught Makir's eyes.

A young slave girl wiped vomit from a table. Jade-green eyes with a familiar depth. Black hair framed her face.

He had to tear his gaze away.

The stranger looked like his daughter.

She's dead, he reminded himself.

"Over there, Captain." Calix's sharp eyes trailed to a raven-haired man. The target hulked over the pub bar, his back against the patrons, face towards the cluttered shelves. On his side, a post-war pistol gleamed.

Makir sat next to him. "Gershom Eli."

No reaction. The man sported a trimmed beard and sky-gray eyes. Leather coat. Black scarf. And hands—hands that were washed too clean in a filthy desert.

"Stop pretending you can't hear me," Makir said. "I know it's you, *Gershom Eli.*"

Gershom took a swig from his mug. His words slurred. "Don't know anybody with that name."

"Then maybe these ones sound familiar: Salome Havria, Jem Hodesh, Michal Noa, Yellan Day…" one by one, Makir counted them on his fingers, the dried blood underneath his nails a contrast to Gershom's spotless ones. "They were someone's daughter, someone's wife, someone's grandmother—did you really think you could wash their blood from your hands?"

The man glared at him, his breath like rotting meat. "Who's asking?"

Makir leaned close. "Heard of the Steelhounds?"

"You're *Makir.*" Gershom's eyes widened as if he'd seen a ghost. "*Captain* of the Steelhounds."

Makir caught the movement in time.

Gershom's hidden blade swiped for his temple. Makir raised his fist, parrying Gershon's strike. He captured Gershom's arm, elbowed his ribs *hard.* The man grunted, his knife clattering over the bar. Makir caught his head, brought it down—*Smash!*

Gershom's face met Makir's knee. *Drip. Drop.* Scarlet splotches stained the floor. Gershom stumbled by the stool, his nasal bones flattened.

Slave women screamed. Drunken men halted in their gambling. *Bam!* A blastfire scorched the upper roof, dampening the patron's stirring rage.

"Anyone who's not friends with the bleeding fella' over there, you're welcome to leave." Calix had raised the lite-pistol over his head, its barrel glowing at a non-lethal charge. Alzior stood by his side. "Anyone who happens to *be* friends with that bleeding fella' over there, *please*, do stay. We'd love to have your guts on the floor, too."

People began their frantic exit. The pub owner hid behind the bar.

Get bystanders out of the way. Another golden rule in Makir's book. *Eliminate fools who stay.*

Gershom Eli stumbled for the back exit, his face a broken mess.

"Captain!" Calix yelled. "We have a runner!"

Alzior threw her dagger. *Thwack!* The blade stabbed Gershom's boot. The man fell through the exit door, crashing on top of their trip wire. His body convulsed. Electricity coursed through him like a million terrible needles.

"*Dasmon!*" Makir called the Steelhound technician. "That's enough! Kill the electricity."

The technician emerged from the storeroom, his gloved hands clenched around the trigger device. The older man loved to take his time. He slowly turned the switch. He adjusted the lens on his specialized goggles. Gershom twitched at his feet.

"Interesting." Dasmon watched with morbid fascination. He had the look of a scientist who dissected vermin for fun. "The shocks weren't enough to kill him yet."

He clicked the trigger device off. Gershom's body stilled.

"*Alright!*" Calix threw his hands up. "We caught him!"

Within moments, the rest of Makir's crew entered the pub. The fugitive hung between their strong shoulders, his body limp, chin drenched with fluid.

"Do we stun him to sleep first?" Dasmon grasped Gershom's hair, tilting his face to observe his injuries. "Or do we just neutralize him?"

Makir glared at the murderer. He thought of Gershom's victims, the weight of their lifeless bodies against his. "No, he deserves to suffer. You know what to do, Dasmon."

The Steelhounds left the room, dragging Gershom out the back exit.

The pub owner peeked from the bar, shaking like a tumbleweed. Makir forced the gentlest smile he could muster despite the specks of blood on his own cheek. "Do you have wash basins in the back?"

The pub owner nodded, pale with fright.

"We'll borrow it." Makir strode to the storeroom and grabbed a mop. "Alzior, Calix, get some rags. Let's help the bartender clean this place up. Gershom's riking blood is everywhere."

. . .

The pub owner stared at Alzior. "The sound doesn't bother her?"

From the backyard, Gershom's tortured screams rattled the wooden walls, only to be drowned out by the screeching whir of an old chainsaw.

Swoosh! Thud! Alzior aimed her knife at a dartboard on the wall. Focused. Unflinching.

"She's deaf." Calix plopped down on the bar stool. He and the men had packed up the rags and indulged in free drinks. "I used to have a little sister like her. She only responded to Kosmoan ship blasters—riking ear-splitting things."

Beyond the walls, Gershom's final wail echoed, and then—silence.

Makir sipped his drink, ignoring the dark weight creeping over him. *Gershom is worse than me.* He remembered his daughter's face, her lovely eyes devoured by the flames. *He's worse than me.*

Rike it. Every hunt helped wash his conscience clean, but for some reason, this one couldn't.

"A toast to the Captain for leading a successful hunt!" Calix said. "What would we do without you, Captain? The Great Donum knows we would've been rotting nub in the desert by now." He placed his filthy boot on the stool, shouting, "*To the Captain!*"

The Steelhounds raised their sloshing drinks. "*To the Captain!*"

Lucky nub-heads. Faint amusement played on Makir's lips. He raised his mug. "To the Steelhounds."

Makir's crew occupied all the tables by now. Half of them were young, just past the rites of manhood, with beards still growing. The other half were seasoned fighters, old enough to be their fathers. Ex-prisoners, runaway slaves, clan outcasts—they all joined him, chasing survival in the merciless desert. Years of roaming and hunting bonded their souls together like molten iron.

But their celebration was cut short.

Bam! Bam! Fists pounded the locked entrance doors.

"We're closed!" the pub owner wiped the counter.

"Must be our Kosmoan clients." Makir stood. "They're too early for the body." Then he *heard* it—the buzzing sound. The electric charge of a lite-pistol set to max.

"*Get down!*" Makir tackled the pub owner.

Rounds of blastfire speared into the bar.

Calix covered Alzior with his body. Men flipped the tables over to shield themselves. The blasts lasted for seconds, chipping the beams and shattering glass mugs. Stray shots nicked arms and legs, staining the floor with blood.

The darkness in Makir's mind swelled—he was back in that old village. The rifle in his trembling hands. The civilians at his mercy. *Searing blastfire. Stray shots and weeping children.*

An ionic discharge melted the iron door from its hinges.

"*Kosrike,*" Makir swore under his breath. He recognized the man who dismantled the door, the man with a dagger on his belt. Inscriptions spiraled the metal pommel, bearing the language of a clan he knew too well—and hated.

"*Rike,*" Makir said. "It's the Aeronians."

"After all these years, you still swear by the name of my clan." The man's speech had a harsh accent, consonants pressed to the point of spittle flying. He approached as the door crashed behind him. The visitor could have been a typical Journeymen. Same sun-tanned skin and light eyes contrasting like gems against dark hair. But he was no typical Journeymen. The weapons on his person were those of a hunter, too.

Behind him, his armed men pressed into the pub.

The visitor unsheathed his dagger and then pointed its death-sharp edge at Makir. The same blade had shined on him before, its owner roaring at him. *You're a merc for the clans, Makir! You swore a kosriked oath!*

"Makir, bastard son from the Clan of Thaelin." The man's accent turned his z's into th's. Whenever Ronen or any of his men uttered the name of Makir's clan, Zaelin, it sounded like *Thaelin*—rugged and distorted. "Look at you now, the exile got himself a loyal squad!"

"Ronen, spawn of Aeronian dung pile," Makir said. "It's been too long, and you still can't pronounce clan names right."

"Who is this, Captain?" Calix said. Though some bled, the Steelhounds stood up, their hands hovering over pistols and rifles, barrels glowing to a low charge. Alzior had gone over to Makir's side, her gaze haughty.

"Ronen is my old..." Makir clenched his teeth, "...colleague."

"You mean *competition.*" Ronen sheathed his knife.

"*Please, please!*" the pub owner cried behind the bar table. "No shooting indoors! Take your fight outside!"

"Yeah!" Calix yelled. "We just cleaned up the place!"

"*You son of a snipe.*" Ronen loomed closer to Makir. "The Kosmoans first approached *us*. The Clan of Aeron tailed Gershom for two days—and here *you* are. Collecting *our* kill! He was our bounty first!"

Makir shrugged. "You were too slow."

"Blast that! We're taking Gershom with us!" Ronen shoved Makir aside, making his way to the back exit.

Dasmon stepped out, his apron stained like a butcher's, goggles flecked with scarlet. "I'm sorry," the old technician said. "That won't be possible. Gershom is dead and well-packaged now."

"*What?*" Ronen's face darkened with rage.

"The Steelhounds collected the quarry first," Makir said. "You Aeronians slacked off. No wonder the Kosmoans contacted us."

"You'll be punished for this." Ronen seethed. "I'll wipe that smirk from your face. You're still showing off, stealing all the glory for yourself!"

"I'm better than you at this job."

"You were *nothing* without me!"

Slivers of darkness wrapped Makir's heart. A lifetime ago, he would've agreed with Ronen. The Clan of Aeron took him in, gave him a job when the Clan of Zaelin exiled him to the wasteland. But he remembered his daughter in the fire, the soot coating his trembling hands. His finger pulling the trigger. *Beautiful face. Burned face.* Scattered beads and blood surrounded her. *She was too beautiful for that hell.*

"I'd rather be *nothing* than to have ever met you. My daughter would've lived." Makir faced Ronen, nose to nose, gaze filled with fire. "*Leave!*"

"Not until you *repay* me for stealing my bounty!"

"I'm guessing a free drink won't be enough?" Calix muttered.

"I want a body in exchange for the body you stole." Ronen seized Alzior's nape, bringing her close to him. She shrieked, slammed her palm on his arm, but Ronen was as unmoving as a boulder. "This small thing will do. Do you cut its face every time it displeases you, Makir?" The Aeronian clan leader smirked. "Well, aren't you pretty for a boy, even if you have that scar on your cheek—*aagh!*"

A narrow blast seared Ronen's ear.

Calix lowered his lite-pistol. Alzior scrambled to his side. "I would've blown your skull to bits, but Alzior's been through much. Can't let her see your brains, right?"

The Aeronians stirred behind their leader. Ronen's ear welted and bled. But then, his shoulders heaved. Sardonic laughter escaped him, rising into utter hilarity.

"What in Donum's wounds is *this*?" Ronen howled. "You have a child amongst your recruits, a sharpshooter who talks like he's killed more than you have, and—what is this? An old snipe!" He pointed at Alzior, Calix, and then Dasmon. "Are you playing *family?* Is this what a Steelhound does when he abandons his clan? Is this what a hunter becomes when he loses his *baby?* He plays pretend *family?* And with pitiful renegades!"

"*Renegades?*" heat erupted inside Makir. "You calling us fugitives?"

"Don't tell me." Ronen flashed a disgusting smile at Alzior. "This kid's a riking replacement for your dear Eyra, isn't she? "

Click.

Makir's lite-pistol touched Ronen's abdomen. "I dare you—call us renegades again. Go on, say my daughter's name too."

"You'll kill me now, in front of *your* men?" Ronen pressed close to Makir's ear, his voice a humid whisper. "Your Steelhounds are loyal to you now, but only because they don't know you like I do. They don't know what you're capable of, what barbaric acts you lowered yourself into. You're just as corrupt as the criminals you hunt."

Makir's grip on the pistol tightened. *Father!* He heard broken slivers of her voice. *Father?* Lovely eyes watched him from a distance, eager to find him. The same beloved gaze turned glassy.

Lifeless.

Hollow.

As the flames licked away her flesh, he wrestled with the questions. Did Eyra see him press the trigger? Did she see his hand on the rifle that set her world on fire?

Makir snapped back to the present.

He felt the Steelhounds crowding near him: Alzior, Dasmon, Calix, and the rest of his men. Their hands hovered over their weapons, ready to tear the pub apart—for him.

"We have ninety seconds to vacate the room," Dasmon announced. "Leave now, or you Aeronians will be buried alive with us. I happen to have the roof rigged."

"Y-you *what?*" the pub owner burst into tears.

"Watch yourselves, Steelhounds." Ronen gritted his teeth. "The Clan of Aeron is moving. *You'll* have a bounty on your heads soon enough."

The men of Aeron left, but not before they knifed the parked motorbikes and shot the windows. As the sound of their truck roared away, Dasmon deactivated his trigger device.

"You were bluffing, right?" Calix sighed. "You're not *really* blowing this place up, yeah?"

"Unlike you, I don't do warning shots," Dasmon said.

. . .

The pub turned into a medic bay. The stray shots had nicked some legs and arms, so Alzior fetched fabric and liquor for their wounds.

Renegades. Makir hung his head in his palms. *I'm not the same as you anymore, Ronen. I'm not—*

He couldn't stop seeing her. Eyra and her beaded bracelets. Eyra in that cursed village. Eyra—

Alzior grasped his hand. "Hurt?" she signed.

Ignore me, kid. He didn't know how to make his hands say it. He didn't deserve her care, didn't deserve the way she looked at him with compassion.

Mercy. Words from the Mandates whispered to his heart, otherworldly and soft. *Mercy for those in shackles.*

His hands trembled. Makir wanted to believe the Mandates' words, but his mind pounded with the image of hellfire.

"Swear it on Donum's throne." Ronen's voice clutched his memory, his accent heavy. *"We'll destroy the enemies and their allies! No one escapes from this town. No one lives. For the sake of Thaelin and Aeron!"*

"Father, look at what I made." The bracelet in Eyra's palm glimmered with colors and textures, beautiful beads of glass and shell and clay. A myriad of materials to color the dull desert. *"I will trade pelts for this."*

The Aeronians didn't tell him that she was trading in the town of Maw. Eyra didn't tell him that she was visiting that town's merchants. There he was, blindly blasting away houses with his rifle. And there *she* was, her lifeless body in the marketplace. Colorful beads scattered around her, making her look like a doll that slept on broken gemstones. It shouldn't have mattered. He was a merc under a sacred oath, and she was a mere bystander, a pitiful sacrifice to their cause.

And yet her name would haunt him forever.

With Ronen reappearing, it felt as if his past had caught up, swallowing him alive like quicksand. *Is this punishment for sacrificing Eyra at the crossfire?*

Rike it all.

He had rebuilt his life in the desert, created his own castle over sands that buried his guilt. He looked at his Steelhounds and their bleeding limbs.

What if Ronen toppled everything he rebuilt?

"Dasmon," Makir said. "We're regrouping."

Dasmon wiped his goggles clean. "Are we retrieving another bounty, Captain?"

"No." Makir donned his rebreather mask. "We're doing something more important."

Something personal.

• • •

Two days later, the Steelhounds prepared for battle.

"Calix and Alzior should've been back by now." Makir inspected the equipment in their trucks. "Where the rike are they?"

"If they don't return by sunfall, we'll send another team." Dasmon counted the Kosmoan rifles they acquired, along with a crate of ten thousand chips, fifty disrupters, and four hundred cans of treated meat. The Steelhounds charged their pistols and divided the rations.

Two days ago, Kosmoan clients traded it all for Gershom's head. Their sweeping robes had billowed around unblemished ankles, solemn hands folded beneath loose sleeves. The Kosmoans were a strange lot. Their metal sky-ships looked like dolphins soaring over the dunes.

"The Journeymen aren't known to be privy to our tech," the Kosmoan had said. "Your clan is an exception."

"We're not a clan." Makir had cocked his head, appearing half-machine and half-human beneath all his equipment. *We're more than one.*

Dasmon inhaled a sharp breath as he unpacked the tech, marble-blue eyes going wide with delight. He held the new rebreathers: matching bronze masks with the latest Kosmoan disc filters. One set was smaller than the rest—*for Alzior.*

"We'll scout for you, Captain." Calix had said. "Find out where Ronen hides."

Makir's holopad had emitted a schematic of the Okivian plain. Five X's marked the holographic map. Five X's for the bustling towns of the Aeronian clan.

Alzior's face had lit up when she saw the map. She had yet to learn the signs to express why she was excited, but she kept pointing at the 'X's, then pointed at the horizon, west from their blazing firepits.

"Alzior knows this road." Calix's smile was feral. "I'll take her with me. She could learn a thing or two."

"It's dangerous." Makir looked at Alzior. If only he could communicate it to her directly. *Don't be a nub-head, kid!* But Makir didn't have the signs.

"Want to go with me?" Calix's hands spoke for him. "We'll visit those towns."

Alzior poured over the map. "Go," she signed with two fingers.

Fine. Makir conceded. *If this assignment will teach the kid to be more useful, then so be it.*

As dawn sliced the sky between darkness and light, they donned the rebreather masks that were the color of old bronze. Leather-strapped goggles protected their eyes; they looked like creatures with insectile faces. Calix, Alzior, and two more Steelhounds revved their motorbikes. In minutes, they claimed distance on the broken concrete highways.

"Sunfall is in three hours," Makir said. "That sharpshot better be back with the kid."

"Captain, why are we ambushing the Aeronians?" Dasmon's hands skittered over the rebreather with calculated intelligence. "Ronen and his men have no bounty."

"They called us *renegades*!" Makir said. "They threatened to post a bounty on us—that's enough of a reason."

"I know you only accept missions for material benefits, but our current operation is an anomaly in your habits. I want to understand—what happened between you and Ronen? Were you that same merc—son of Shiloh, from the House of Zaelin—the merc who stormed the town of Maw?"

Merc.

Renegade.

Bastard.

"Unearthing my past won't be good for you." *And for me.* "It's not something I'm proud of."

"Captain, you're not the only one with a past to be ashamed of—all your men are like that." Dasmon ceased in his tinkering. "You offered us a chance, turned us into the Steelhounds. We're all the same. We all craved mercy and found it here."

"Dasmon, that's—"

"*Captain!*" A Steelhound at the lookout point yelled. "They're back!"

Makir ran to the camp entrance, only to be met by one motorbike and two Steelhounds. One of them had a shattered rebreather, the other a bleeding lip.

"They captured them, Captain," The Steelhound said. "They got Calix and Alzior."

• • •

The Steelhounds located the Aeronian camp before sunlight could invade the mountains. From a distance, the ruins of Halina looked like a city of broken giants. Towering walls crumbled as if they were half-eaten by flying beasts. Metal spikes stuck out of toppled columns like shattered bones. Rusty vehicles lay submerged in layers of sand and dust. Above all the dirt, weathered trucks were parked away from makeshift firepits.

"Pre-war vans. Standard lite-rifles. Daggers, of course." Dasmon spied the Aeronians through rusty binoculars.

He and Makir hid in the fifth floor of an old mid-rise building. The ruined concrete buildings either stood or leaned against each other, forming an open square area for the Aeronian camp.

Dasmon said, "Their numbers are twice our squad, but they're not as equipped as we are."

"Ronen's been speaking nub then," Makir muttered. "He never owned the guns to match his blasted tongue."

The Steelhounds hid amongst the north and south quarters, rigging mines along the exit roads. A support crew climbed up the empty buildings, silent and swift. One signal from Makir and his assault team would attack.

The depraved things Ronen does to women and children. The memory made Makir's fingers tremble over his rifle. He wasn't the type who prayed, but he mustered two requests to the great Donum. *Keep Calix alive. Please spare Alzior.*

The darkness inside transformed into a new monster, accusing him. *You never should've sent them out for recon. You should've ended Ronen in the pub while you had the chance.*

Dasmon struggled to keep his voice low. "It's Calix—he's alive! He's with Alzior!"

Beneath them, the Aeronians organized themselves into several groups. Ronen stood before his men, firelight writhing on his face like an awful mask. An Aeronian guided Calix and Alzior from the shadows. Their old rebreathers and goggles still covered their faces, and wires bound their wrists.

They forced Calix to kneel—the position of a war prisoner.

A blade flashed.

Ronen raised his relic dagger. A merc pulled away Calix's cherished boonie hat, then gripped his hair. His throat lay exposed for one clean swipe.

"*Kosrike,*" Dasmon swore. "He's going to kill him!"

Makir grabbed the lite-rifle and fired. Electric heat exploded—Makir *missed*.

"Steelhounds!" Ronen shrieked. Metallic heat scorched the ground between him and Calix. "They found us!"

The Stealhounds opened fire.

Dust flew. Sand exploded. Concrete burst into pieces. Screams roared through the ruins. From their hiding places, the Steelhounds lit up the kill zone, and in the flurry of running Aeronians, Calix and Alzior vanished.

Ronen yelled incoherent orders. Men dragged a pre-war machine gun and aimed indiscriminately at the buildings. Dasmon and Makir ran downstairs to the lower floor before—

Crash!

Bullets shattered the room above. Seconds later, an ionic charge blasted the machine gun and it fell to silence.

Beyond the firepits, bodies scattered. The injured dragged themselves away.

"Bullets and blades." Makir dusted the grit from his shoulders. "That's all they got?"

"They're all runners." Dasmon glanced over the dusty balcony. "Scattering like ants."

"Then we round them up. Take them down one by one."

Makir shot a blastfire to the sky. The assault team marched into the square. Bronze rebreathers and goggles obscured their human faces. They moved in like synchronized soldiers, alight with the glow of laser rifles. As the morning sun arrived, Makir slipped out toward the battle line, leading the carnage.

Aeronian defectors raced to the endless sands. *Boom!* The mines cut them down. A fortunate few escaped through the narrow alley-ways, riding on swift bikes.

Where's Ronen?

A wind rose, cloaking the ruins in a haze of dust and sand. *There! Eastern side!* Makir scrambled over chunks of concrete. He ducked under resurfaced pipelines. Ran through the broken sidewalks. He spotted the silhouette of a tall man dragging a smaller body towards the outskirts. *Twelve feet away.* Makir adjusted his goggles, the Kosmoan lens picked up the shadows in the dusty wind.

The larger man hefted the petite body over his shoulders like a ragdoll. *Alzior?* As the dust settled down to his boots, Makir caught sight of their faces.

Tier 61 Rebreathers. Upgraded goggles. Boonie hat.

Calix and Alzior!

"*Calix!*" Makir roared over the blastfire. "*Calix!*"

"Captain!" the man swiveled back. "I got Alzior!

"*What are you doing? Where are you running to?*" Makir shrieked, his voice a metallic cry behind his rebreather. He ran as fast as he could manage into the scorching sand. Something was off in the way Calix moved, in the way he ran.

He ran from the battle like a deserter.

Makir screamed, "*Calix, come back!*"

"*Stray fire!* "A Steelhound shouted from a top level. Scorching blast-fire pummeled the path. Makir flattened himself beside a concrete house. Calix lunged for cover under a dilapidated roof, Alzior in his arms.

The moment the blasts halted, Makir sprinted. Ten feet of dangerous open space stretched out before him. Calix leaned against the fallen tiled roof, blood staining his coat.

259

"Calix—*you nubhead!*" Makir crouched next to him. "Give me Alzior, *kosrike,* you're bleeding!"

But Calix held on to Alzior's unconscious body, holding her upright by her shoulders. Her head nodded against his arm, a bruise on the side of her temple. Calix kept her in front of him...like a human shield.

Makir screamed, "Are you riking crazy!"

"I'm leaving, Captain." Calix's voice was distorted through his rebreather. "Ronen let us go. So Alzior and I, we're leaving."

"What in Donum's wounds are you saying? You're betraying me now?"

The young man looked at him through his tinted goggles, the boonie hat covering his messy hair. *"Goodbye*, Captain. It will be better for Althior this way."

It rang in Makir's ears.

Amid the blastfire, he *heard* it.

"Say that again." Makir's fingers neared his pistol. "Swear it on my clan, on the House of Zaelin, that you're hell-bent on leaving with Alzior—that *she even* consented to this!"

Three laser shots pierced the sky, bursting into hellish gold—the victory signal for neutralizing all enemies in the ruins.

"You've got your victory, Captain. The House of Ronen is dust now," Calix said. "We'll be off to find our own way. I swear it on the house of Thaelin. I swear it on Althior's life."

"Of course, Calix." Makir listened to his voice, his speech. The way his consonants slipped around Alzior's name. Only one clan spoke with their z's turning into th's.

"You're not a good liar, *Calix*," Makir said. "Her *name* is Alzior."

Makir seized his pistol and fired. Calix's head snapped back, a hole carving through his forehead. Makir caught Alzior in his arms. Her chest heaved with steady breathing. *She's still alive.*

But the man at his feet wasn't.

Makir wrenched the rebreather from the corpse's head, blood pooling around his knees like a fountain.

Ronen. The Aeronian's red-stained face greeted him behind the mask. *Not Calix.*

. . .

Tears streaked Alzior's cheeks as she cleaned Calix's wounds. Right before the night conquered the sky, they found the young man crumpled near the debris, half-naked and maskless.

"I would've taken him down in one shot..." Calix mumbled. "He took my clothes and my rebreather...riking snipe..."

Ronen's dagger had missed his neck and swiped across the meat of his chest instead. Calix wasn't going to die of the bleeding. It was the infection that would end him soon.

"There were survivors." Makir convened with his squad outside the medic tent. A blue road shimmered on the holographic map. "They're escaping through this route. If they make it back to their villages, and their townsfolk welcome them—"

"They'll instigate another battle against us," Dasmon said. "Must we go as far as capturing a road? What if civilians or travelers were—"

"*Again* with the questioning, Dasmon?" Makir clenched his fist. "You saw what the Aeronians did to Calix. Those snipe-heads didn't fear us enough. As long as Ronen's men live, they're a threat."

"But we've seen their equipment. Their threats are mere words."

"Those Aeronians are a blasted infection! They're small now, but they'll spread if we don't cut them away."

Inside the medic tent, Alzior sobbed, her voice a deep, broken sound. Makir watched from the tattered tent entrance. Calix placed a weak hand over Alzior's head, affection in his gaze. He signed one phrase, "I'm sorry." Then, in the next stretch of silence, his hand fell limp. His breathing ceased.

A wail tore through Alzior's throat. She pounded Calix's chest with her fists. Desperate. Hysterical. Her cries shook the tent, breaking Makir.

Those blasted Aeronians. Makir clenched his fists. *They haven't paid for their sins in full.*

How much more would they take away from him?

Makir stepped into the tent to comfort Eyra—no, *Alzior.*

This was Alzior.

Not Eyra. He chided his exhausted mind.

"Come here, kid." He offered his arms, and she buried her face on his shoulder. He didn't know enough signs to declare his new oath. *We'll get them, I promise. We'll do it for Calix.*

We'll do it for us.

• • •

Makir strode over a cracked asphalt road like a reaper for the dead. A dark, threadbare hood fell over his head. Tinted goggles, the shade of steel, hid his eyes. War paint decorated his rebreather, jagged like serpentine fangs.

"No, no! We're not Ronen's men!" that was their targets' common excuse. "We're only travelers!"

"Spare us! Please!" their usual spiel.

"Answer us one question, and we'll let you live." Makir glared at the escaping mercs. "Which clan am *I* from?"

"You're from the clan of…" they hesitated. "The clan of Thaelin."

"Right answer." Makir charged his lite-pistol. The barrel glowed hell-orange. "Spoken by the wrong tongue."

Their Aeronian speech, their z's collapsing into th's, was always their undoing.

The Clan of Thaelin. Makir fired. *Sounds foolish.*

• • •

Three days later...

"*Murderer.*" An Aeronian boy spat at Makir, a relic dagger on his belt. An old woman accompanied him, walking in a shapeless dress and a heavy veil. The boy shielded his grandmother with outstretched arms. "The god of this desert will curse you!"

Three Steelhounds surrounded the pair.

"We warned your towns." Makir stepped into their circle. "No one walks in. No one walks out. One foot on this road and you single yourself out as Ronen's follower."

"Forgive us, great Steelhound." The old woman threw herself at Makir's boots, her veil falling past silver tresses. "We're mere travelers beyond the Okivian road. We know nothing of the clan's dealings with you."

A strange exhilaration alighted in Makir. Here was a woman begging for their lives, a woman who could've been a spy for Ronen's allies.

"So, you recognize us." Makir helped her up on her shaking feet. "Then tell me, what is the name of my clan?"

"*Alzior!*" Dasmon stumbled from their trucks. Makir turned as Alzior's arms reached out to him.

She tackled him.

Makir backpedaled, catching her weight. She stood on her toes, wide-eyed and frantic. The girl looked around, beheld the desert mountains, the winding road, the travelers, the pile of bodies behind the motorbikes...

Kosrike. Makir covered her face with his hands. *You weren't supposed to see that, kid.*

He had locked her away in the truck cabin for this reason. She was lucky enough that she couldn't *hear* what they were doing, but now—

She freed herself from Makir's grip. His hands sought to hold hers, but for the first time, she shirked away, gasping at the sight of his bloody fingernails.

"What's wrong with you, kid?" Makir grabbed her elbow. Alzior dropped to her knees and clung to his legs, yelling a deep, halting sound. She held on, stopping him from facing the Aeronian travelers.

"Why can't you just *tell* me what's wrong?" Makir screamed. "Let go of me, you snipe!" he raised his fist—then stopped. *Rike it.* He breathed, one shred away from slapping her face. *Maybe she's going mad about Calix dying.*

"Take her back to the tents," Makir ordered. "Lock her in the truck."

Dasmon pried Alzior off Makir's legs and held her by the waist.

"But Captain! Alzior is—"

She threw her weight against Dasmon's hold. A snarl escaped her mouth. She smashed her heel into Dasmon's knee, and the technician buckled.

She flashed past Makir like lightning.

Makir dropped his pistol. A blood-red gash appeared on the back of his hand. Red welled up and spilled in rivulets, scarlet lines that pointed back to the girl.

Alzior stood before Makir, death-pale and quivering, her back against the grandmother and the boy. The dagger in her hand glinted with his blood.

"Alzior!" Makir thundered. "What the *rike* are you doing? You're defending the enemy!"

Dasmon staggered to Makir's side. The other three Steelhounds hesitated, their grip on their rifles faltering at the sight of their young Steelhound.

"Captain, I've been trying to tell you." Dasmon said. "She is—"

"*Althior?*" The grandmother's voice speared through Makir.

The boy cried out, "By great Donum's hand! It's really her—it's *Althior!*"

"How do you know this girl?" Makir waved his pistol at the travelers' faces. "Answer me!"

But they ignored him. They embraced Alzior fully, saying her name again and again, as if she were a loved one who crossed valleys and wastelands and finally returned. "We thought you were dead. We thought the road pirates got you." The old woman captured Alzior's face in her wrinkly hands. "How we missed you, Althior!"

Alzior.

A l t h i or

The sound of her name assaulted Makir.

The way the vowels of her name truly flowed. The way the consonants glided around the sound of 'z.'

The same way that Ronen had said it.

Donum's wounds. "She's Aeronian, isn't she?" Makir said. "This whole time?"

"Yes." Dasmon leaned on his leg. "I figured it out when she was looking at your map. I doubt she belongs to Ronen's House, but she's Aeronian. These travelers might be her relatives from the fifth village."

Alzior is Aeronian.

"Mercy." The girl faced him, signing the word. Her whimpers were louder than the throbbing in his head. *Aren't you a man of mercy?*

"Stand aside, Alzior." Makir charged his pistol. "If we let any of them live, they'll keep hounding us."

"Captain," Dasmon said. "Please think about this. The Aeronians *are* Journeymen like us. Not all are like Ronen."

A mumbling sound left Alzior's mouth—and then a heart-wrenching wail. She tossed her dagger at Makir's feet.

You were merciful once to me, Makir. Her eyes—like Eyra's—looked at him. Longed for him.

Makir raised his pistol, aiming, hand shaking.

Alzior stood her ground.

She faced his pistol, the last line between his judgment and mercy.

Makir couldn't let go of it just yet.

"Mercy, mercy." Alzior signed it over and over again. Her silent tears screamed at him. *Please have mercy.*

As he looked into her eyes—the eyes of Eyra, the eyes of *Althi-or*—his pistol dropped to his side. He fell to his knees in the dust. And finally, Makir wept.

Find the story of Jepthah in Judges 12:1-7.

Beyond Brothers
Anita DeVries

My brother's right fist halted in midair at the sound of rapidly clanging bells. He squinted as his glacier-green gaze shifted from my face up to the smog filled grey sky. Eddie relaxed his handful of my ripped leather shirt. It was a hand-me-down from Eddie, though the worn shirt *he* was wearing would've fit me better. I was broader in the shoulders but still a good six inches shorter than my older brother. At nine years old, I was a better fighter than my peers. I guess I had Eddie to thank for that.

At the slight relaxation of his fist, I slipped out of his grasp and ran from the dusty, flat field we called a 'playground' and took off around the co-op down the main, and only, street of our village to our little two-room cow-dung home on the edge of town.

"Where is your little sister?" Mom's thin frame shook as she stood holding the thin wooden door open against the dust-filled wind. Her light blond hair was pulled up into a bun, little whisps escaping around her ears.

I stumbled and flipped around, rushing back towards town. I bent my face down and narrowed my eyes as tiny grains of dust and sand pelted my face. It was hard to see more than five feet ahead.

Eddie burst out of the sand cloud, running towards the house. "What are you doing? This isn't a drill—get to the house!"

The dust stung my eyes. "Gotta get Suzie!" my voice choked on the particles of sand. Coughing hard, with squinted eyes, I ran down the street, turning at the small co-op building. I scanned the flat playing field, hands cupped around my eyes. Through the swirling grey clouds, the bottom of a great beetle-shaped spaceship approached. Its six thin landing legs were out. Along the belly of the ship was a black hourglass. Frantically, I searched the ground. Behind me, up against the back wall of the co-op, Suzie sat struggling to pull her bandana back over her nose as tears smudged her dirty face. I ran to her.

"I'm here, it's okay." I swung my thin sister up into my arms, holding her face against my chest, shielding her from the atmosphere. Behind us, the long, spindly landing gear of the ship touched the ground.

"Donumdonair, hide us," I prayed as I swerved around the co-op. Frantically, I ran the two hundred meters out of the downtown to our home nestled against the upward mountain slope. Mom still stood in the doorway, though my dad, Anuth, had his hand on her elbow and was ushering her inside. When they saw me, he ran towards me and took my crying sister from my tired arms. We hustled into the house together.

Mom and us kids rushed to the corner of the back room where we descended into a grave-like hole in the floor that was barely big enough to hold all four of us. We tried to still our heavy breathing as we lay curled up together in the dirt. Dad shoved the straw mattress that they used as a bed over the opening. The mattress dipped as he lay down on it, further collapsing our space, the air instantly suffocating.

Heat filled my face. I tried to steady myself against the anger that raged in me. I hated hiding from our enemies while they plundered our town.

Bang! The shot reverberated powerfully through the soil, jolting us together. Hobnobbed boots pounded the ground, closer with each movement.

Our bodies melded together, and my ears pricked for any indication of the enemy's location. A squeaking of the bedroom door. Dad shifted on the mattress that covered us.

"What do we have here?" the slow, gruff voice of a Kosmoan speaking through his rebreather.

My dad used to sit at the kitchen table to meet them when they came. He would sustain their taunts, a few punches, and then they would take whatever they wished from the house. A few of the townsmen had found that playing sick saved their bodies from being abused.

My dad's thin voice replied, "Please, I have the plague. All I have to live on is there in that corner. Take it, it's yours."

"Ha! A few turnips, that is not enough, you lazy dog. This village is behind on its sacrifice." The Kosmoan spoke in a gruff, sneering voice. "Get out of your bed!"

"I'm sick." Dad coughed.

A thick voice spoke, "Don't I know you?"

"No, no, sir." Dad's hacking worsened.

I could hear the snap of fingers. "Yes, yes, I remember you. On my last mission here, remember when I was stationed here to lead you into the righteous paths of our god Kosmoa, a god you little snipes would not accept nor enjoy all his glorious benefits? It was about ten years ago." He paused, and I could hear a boot step forward. The earth against my back shook. "You had a beautiful whore of a wife." He laughed.

My mom's breath caught in her throat.

Everything above went deathly still.

"Where is that whore? Or is she out pleasing another man?"

Mom's body contracted beside me.

The booted foot stepped closer. "Or do you have her hidden?"

Suddenly, the bed was overturned and light entered our hole. My dad yelled in pain. I heard a scuffle and a shot. Eddie was first out of our hiding place. He ran to attack the legs of the closest Kosmoan.

I scrambled after him but froze at the sight. Dad was lying on the floor, the boot of a Kosmoan guard on his back and a laser gun aimed at his head. Dad's nose gushed blood. A second Kosmoan, still wearing his old rebreather, lay face down in a pool of blood from his exposed throat. The third Kosmoan kicked Eddie hard into the wall of the small room and he crumbled to the ground.

A Kosmoan Captain stood in the doorway and pulled off his rebreather, letting it hang to one side of his chiseled, cleft chin, and called, "Hands up everyone, stand against the wall nice and slow or your father will be killed."

The Kosmoan guard that held Dad dug his boot deeper into his back. The barrel of a lite-pistol dug into the back of his skull, pushing his head half-sideways into the ground.

Mom led the way to the wall. Suzie clung to her knee-length leather tunic. I backed up to join them, feeling the rough old cow dung against my thin shirt.

"You have been a busy little whore, haven't you?" the Captain looked down at my sister, then back up at Mom. His sharp brown eyes studied her appreciatively, a sinister smile on his lips.

She shifted her wide blue eyes from him over to her husband on the floor. Dad held her gaze with his glacier-green eyes. I watched as she focused on him. Her thin frame straightened and her breath deepened.

I looked back at the Kosmoan Captain. His presence and strength swallowed the room. A lecherous grin lit his brown eyes with evil mirth. He turned to face me, "You are not like your brother and sister, are you?"

One black booted foot stepped toward me, then the other. He towered before me. His light brown face was scarred and dirty, framed with long, wavy black hair. A bow and the tails of arrows seemed to grow from his left shoulder. My eyes dropped down, taking in the Kosmoan technology that covered his whole body. His military vest was decorated on the left side of his chest with the emblem of an hourglass. Beneath were pockets on both sides, hiding tools of war. His mail-armored legs looked mighty powerful, as did his thick boots.

A rough hand lifted my chin to look into his hard brown eyes. He turned my head one way then the other. His frown lifted, and he grinned at my mom, eyebrows raised. "You did well. He has the makings of a strong and handsome man, like his father." He laughed at that.

I was confused. No one said I looked like my father, with his straight, thin, blond hair, slim frame, fair skin, and glacier-green eyes. Even at nine years of age, people called me stocky and mocked my thick black wavy hair, deeply tanned skin, and brown eyes.

The Captain turned toward Mom, just to the left of me. He took a step towards her. Suzie's lower lip trembled as she moved further behind Mom, hiding behind her worn, knee-length tunic.

"Hmmmm." His half-gloved hand came up to Mom's face as he let the skin of his uncovered fingertips brush the side of her cheek. She twisted fiercely from him. He grabbed her chin and tilted her head toward him. She spat in his eyes. He released her and backhanded her face. She almost fell on top of my sister but gained her balance and faced him again.

From the corner of my eye, I saw my father push off the ground, dispelling the foot of the Kosmoan. Dad ran towards the Captain, digging his thin shoulder into the tormentor's side, shoving him away from his wife. The Kosmoan he had just jilted grabbed him from behind. Eddie flew up from the floor, running toward the man, but the Kosmoan easily elbowed him to the ground while twisting Dad's arm around behind him and shoving him face first into the wall.

The Captain shook off the attack, though his face was flushed. "You Journeymen are more trouble than your worth. We should kill you all."

Breath caught in my lungs. My mind raced. I looked at my dad against the wall. The Kosmoan punched him in the right lower side of his back and he crumpled to the ground. From the corner of my eye, I saw Eddie rise from the ground. A Kosmoan kicked him back down. Eddie writhed in pain on the dirt. Mom's eyes were wide, trembling, and my sister cried as she hugged Mom's legs.

The Kosmoan Captain again stepped towards me. This time, rage compelled me to hold his brown eyes. He looked away first, turning towards Mom, "I'll make you a deal. This boy will come with me, and you will all live. He is my son after all, is he not?"

Anger seethed in me. How dare this roach call me his son? I threw a punch at him, but he blocked it easily, twisting me around and locking me in his arms.

Mom glared at him. "Leave him alone. He is the son of Anuth."

"No, my name is Thorold." He turned me around, holding me at arm's distance as I flailed my fists at him. He smiled, then suddenly grew deathly serious. "Stop now," he commanded.

My body betrayed me by obeying. I stood still, caught between the power of my loathing and the weakness of my flesh.

Calmly, he studied me. "What's your name?"

"Gharib." I raised my chin in pride as I said it. "*Son* of *Anuth*."

"Your mom's been keeping a secret from you, Gharib. I was stationed here for almost a year, and I was here at your birth. I named you. You're my son, and your destiny is with us."

"No! I am not one of you!" I looked at my brown hands. Frowning, I looked up into his brown face, then around at the fair complexion of my parents. They looked silently back at me. *Could it be true?*

Thorold reached an open hand towards me and I knocked it away. He remained calm, "Don't be afraid. Your life will be much better with me. I'll make you a strong ruler." He looked to where my dad was crumpled on the dirt floor. "Not a coward."

I looked over at my dad.

His face grimaced, "Remember my name and Donumdonair's, son."

Bang!

The shot reverberated through me as my dad slumped to the floor. I ran to him, holding his bloody head in my hands. Hot tears seared my cheeks.

Thorold's voice broke into my thoughts. "He's not your dad, and he may not claim you as a son. You're *mine*."

Rage bolted through me. I turned and ran at Thorold, punching his hard vest. One of the other two Kosmoans caught me from behind, laughing. Thorold aimed his gun at Mom. "Shall I kill her too?"

"No," I screamed, struggling to free myself.

He nodded, "Then be a good son and come with me. Our god will love you, I promise."

"No," pleaded Mom.

Bang! The gun went off. Mom still stood, but some of the ceiling shattered above her head, dust raining down on her and Suzie.

"I'll go," I yelled, my body shaking. "Leave my family alone."

Mom's eyes closed for a moment, tears streamed out, and she looked pleadingly up at the Kosmoan, "Please, keep him away from Kosmoa, I beg you."

"I am his father, and I will do what is good for him."

Tears were spilling from Mom's eyes. "May I hug him goodbye?"

Thorold nodded and the man released me. I ran into her open arms.

"Take courage, son. Donumdonair will go with you." She kissed my wet cheek and whispered, "Do not worship Kosmoa." She released me abruptly. I hugged my sister and said goodbye, with a lump in my throat the size of my fist. She was trembling. Eddie was still lying on the ground. I walked over to him and hugged his limp body. His eyes fluttered open, his jaw bruised. With difficulty, he spoke, "You don't have to go with them. We are your destiny."

"Hurry up, let's go," Thorold demanded.

I turned from my brother and stepped over to place a kiss on the cheek of my lifeless father. The lump burned in my throat. I squared my shoulders but could not stop the tears from spilling down my cheeks. With Thorold leading me, I walked out of the bedroom. I turned back to glimpse my family for the last time and saw the other two Kosmoans pick up their dead comrade. As they walked past the kitchen area, they shamelessly took whatever they saw, even our one nice plate, placing it in a sack hanging from their shoulders. *What kind of animals were these enemies, these people whose blood ran through my veins?* Bile rose in my throat. I ran outside, hurling what little I had in my stomach onto the dry earth. It pooled there, unable to seep away.

The two Kosmoans came behind with their cargo. One of them pushed me forward and I stumbled behind Thorold. From all points along the road, Kosmoans were returning to their ship from the raid, full of the town's meager possessions. Wheelbarrows full of vegetables that would have helped the town survive the winter, an ox, the only one for miles, a few goats, and some jugs of milk. Together, we walked up the ramp and entered the back end of their spaceship.

An oppressive darkness hit me as I left the comparative light of the outdoors and entered the hold of the ship. My body grew hot as I looked around at our town's few animals being led into pens on either side.

"Hey! Give those back!" I yelled above the engine at a tech-covered Kosmoan directing the loading of the livestock and produce. "The townspeople need them."

The man barely turned his rebreather and goggle concealed face towards me.

Thorold was just a few steps ahead of me. His head rotated to me, his face completely concealed, voice muffled. "They will find a way to survive. They always do. We can never find all their hidden bounty."

A jab in my back forced me forward. I pushed back and found a laser gun in my back. "Keep moving kid!" the armored Kosmoan said, shoving me hard. I stumbled into the large main area of the spaceship. A steel staircase led to the next floor; above it was the gruesome face of some kind of beastly half-man with wicked squinting black eyes that seemed to watch me. Thorold ascended the stairs in front of me. I was halfway up when I heard the "*baa*" of a lamb. I turned around and saw one of the Kosmoans enter the large back opening of the spaceship carrying a little lamb. There was only one in our whole town, and it belonged to Suzie.

Hot blood pounded through my veins. I turned completely and jumped on the rail, sliding quickly down and ran up to the man. "Take that back!" I demanded. His hand shot out and struck me hard in the face, knocking me into darkness.

• • •

When my eyes opened, I was lying on the lower bunk in a small room with a sink, toilet, and one closed steel door. The air was clean. I breathed in deeply and noticed a foreign scent in the air. I couldn't decide if I liked the smell or not. At least it was not dusty. I got up and looked out of a small window. Far below, I could see the bare, mountainous area of Covenant. Somewhere in there was my little village, my people…or not my people.

Sadness choked me as I walked from the window to the door and tried to open it. No success. I inhaled deeply, the air caught in my throat, and I coughed it out as I looked around. There was no other exit. I focused on the image of my bloody face in the mirror above the sink. I turned on a tap and a thin stream of water splashed into a steel bowl. I rubbed my hands together under it and then splashed it on my face. My throat itched every time I swallowed. Tentatively, I cupped my hands under the running water, then slowly brought it to my lips. The cool liquid soothed my throat. It was far cleaner than the town water I was used to. Quickly, I ducked my head under the faucet, greedily sucking in gulps of water.

A whirling sound came as the door behind me rose from the bottom up. A young man around Eddie's age, but dressed far better in thick leathers, stood smiling at me. His wavy black hair looked like mine, and his brown eyes were friendly. He held no gun, however, a handle of a dagger was sticking out of a sheath on his belt. "Hi! I'm Arnuld—I'm your brother! I have to take you to our good father, Thorold."

My brother? He looked more like me than Eddie, and his disarming smile seemed genuinely kind, not like Eddie's mocking grin. But a brother, one who calls Thorold '*our good father*'? Mutely, I nodded and followed behind Arnuld's confident gait down a thin aisle. Sleek steel doors lined both sides of the hallway. We came to a stop at the end of the hall and stood before a larger door. Arnuld stepped in front of a small circular sensor. It moved to look into his eye as he tilted his head up and stared into the lens. He blinked twice and the door opened. A thrill filled me. I had never seen anything like that before. We ascended three flights of steel stairs leading to a spacious common room with gleaming steel tables bolted to the ground and steel chairs erupting from the floor around them.

"How many people are on this ship?" I asked as Arnuld led us past the rows of tables through another door that opened to a much wider hallway.

"Capacity is six hundred, and we're full. Impressive, isn't it?" he opened another door and there stood Thorold. He looked much smaller and less formidable without his battle garb on. Just a comfortable grey cotton shirt with an hourglass emblem on the left side of his chest, and leather pants with a number of pockets, all of which enhanced his physically fit body. He stood beside a large, ornate wooden desk. Behind him were floor-to-ceiling windows that revealed an impressive vista of the mountainous desert of Covenant.

"You may wait outside," Thorold addressed Arnuld. When he was gone, Thorold smiled at me. "You need to learn your place before you start making demands, Son."

Anger thundered through me, "You promised my mom would live if I left with you, but if you take all the food and livestock, she'll die."

"Next year, I will go back and make sure they have enough. But you need to prove yourself to be a worthy son first. Then your town will be prosperous."

"What do you mean by that?"

"You must learn our ways and follow them. Be one of us. It is your destiny, and your birthright is to be part of the ruling people, not a poor servant."

There was steel in his voice. *Did he speak truth?*

When I was dismissed, Arnuld was waiting for me, leaning against the wall. He grinned as I approached and pushed himself up. "I know how you must feel, just taken from a dirty little town…"

"You don't know how I'm feeling!" I clenched my fist, eyes narrowed. "My father was killed today!"

Arnuld's eyes hardened. "Today, you learned who your *true* father is, and you have been given an opportunity to become a leader—a prince among men."

"All I want is my family." Instinctively my hand came up and wiped away a few tears. No matter how hard I scrubbed, they wouldn't stop flowing.

"Hey, it will be okay."

Arnuld put an arm around me and I cried against his shoulder.

"Come," he spoke gently into my ear, "let's go back to the mess hall and have a snack. You'll feel better."

He led me quickly through the steel halls of the ship, his hand on my shoulder and my eyes cast to the ground. When we reached the mess hall, there was a smorgasbord of snacks waiting for us. Everything from fruit to dried meat and even various sweet cakes. We ate and chatted about all things young boys like: weapons, mechanics, and favorite treats.

"If you think this food is good, wait till tonight. It'll be a big feast, a worship celebration." Arnuld grinned through a mouthful of chocolate.

"What will it be like?" I said, swallowing another big bite of cake.

"You'll see." A twinkle lit his eyes, and the excitement grew in me. "Come on, I need to get you familiar with the ship so you know where you're going without me dragging you along all the time."

He brought me down to the bottom floor of the spaceship where I had entered. A few horses were neighing, and the low moo of an ox drifted behind us from the stalls that lined the sides of the room. The sounds followed us as we walked up a few steel steps at the front of the dank area. I cast a quick glance around, eyes searching for Suzie's little lamb, but didn't see it. The door lifted, and I was struck with the sight of a million strange levers, buttons, lights, keyboards... things I had never seen before. All sides of the room were lined with rows of computers. Arnuld brought me to a man. His eyebrows were scrunched together and tiny beads of sweat clung to his fat upper lip. He grit his teeth as he swore under his breath, attention on the machines he was working on.

"Rike!" the man pulled on a rusty wire, and it disintegrated off of a knob. The lights cut out. In the darkness, I backed up against the wall. The lights came on again. The engineer had replaced the wire in the dark.

"Is everything okay?" Arnuld was hanging on to a large red lever marked "Emergency Reset". The engineer ran over and swatted his hand away.

"Rikes! Don't touch anything! Do you want to crash this ship?" the man glared at him, black eyes flashing, "What are you doing here?"

"I—I just need to get Thorold's son, Gharib, registered in the system so he can open doors and get to where he needs to be."

"Well, go over and do it then. You know where the scanner is. I'm busy." He turned back to his work, cursing as he tapped on a keyboard. "This ship isn't going to last much longer," he grumbled. As if in response, the floor jolted, and I stumbled into Arnuld.

"Kosrikes!" the engineer cursed, turning a wheel and setting a lever, which he propped up with a steel pole. The ship steadied. The beefy Kosmoan held a microphone to his lips, "Descend to lower altitude. I repeat, descend to a lower altitude."

A voice came back through the speaker, "Acknowledged. Preparing to descend."

"She'll make it to the depot." The engineer's voice was tired and thick.

"Setting new course." The words came through. I could feel the ship descend.

Arnuld led me to the far side of the room. No one was around. "Usually, there are more people working," he gestured. "Must be getting ready for the celebration."

"Seems like the ship is in trouble," I said.

"Oh, we've had worse before. The engineers always figure it out. Good parts are hard to come by, but our god Kosmoa always leads us victoriously." He turned his attention to a scanning machine, a large computer with a retractable arm holding an eye scanner. He touched a lever and the arm gave a mechanical whir and knocked into the side of his head. "Rikes! I've never done this by myself before."

"Maybe we should wait for help." I leaned up against a bank of computers. A beeping sound erupted, and I jumped away. The sound stopped, and the two of us stole a glance at the Kosmoan engineer. He paid us no mind and we turned back to the machine.

"No, we need to get this done and be on time for the worship service and feast tonight." Arnuld tapped on a keyboard and hit a series of buttons. At one point, he had me stand in front of the lens and told me to wink at it.

• • •

In the evening, I went up to the top floor of the spaceship into a glorious room that had windows all around, displaying the heavens. The tables were decorated with lamps and incense and table ornaments made of gold and silver. I was ushered to the front of the room. There was a ten-foot-high statue of a figure that had the face of what looked like a beastly man but the curvaceous body of a woman. They told me to bow to the idol Kosmoa, and obediently, I did. A sick feeling instantly arrested my motion, and I stood quickly.

I was given a seat before the idol at Thorold's overflowing table. There was not enough room for all the food, strong drinks, and sweet-smelling hashish. Thorold held up a gold cup, "We declare to-day another victory for our great god Kosmoa. He alone has the power of war, love, and fertility."

The crowd cheered.

"Our god is more powerful than the god of the Journeymen. We know this, for we hold the power over them, not only in war but also in love, for we care about people and share our bounty with those whom the Journeymen would call 'reprehensible.' We do not cast judgment on others. *Everyone* feasts tonight."

Again, the crowd erupted in praise, shouting, "Great is our leader, Thorold, and great is our god! There is none like Kosmoa!"

Thorold quieted the crowd and spoke again. "Kosmoa is great, not only in war and love but also in fertility. This day I introduce to you my son, Gharib. Born for Kosmoa's glory!"

Jubilation filled the ship. Applause shook the room. I was beck-oned to stand. A smile played on my lips—never had I been so es-teemed. A drink was put in my hand. Thorold commanded everyone to drink to me and Kosmoa. Someone shoved the cup up to my lips, and I took a gulp. The deep brown liquid burned, and I spit it out.

Everyone laughed as they drank liberally. Then, a smoking glass with a straw-like appendage near the bottom was put to my lips. I was told to inhale. The strong smoke caught in my throat, worse than the swirling dust of my hometown. I shoved it away, coughing heavily.

"Bring in the dancers!" Thorold yelled.

Glittering, scantly dressed women exploded into the hall, dancing in an intoxicating display of rhythm and sensual movements.

When the music stilled, a steaming hot plate of food was put in front of me, with large slices of meat on a bed of rice, exquisitely arranged with other vegetables around it. I breathed in deeply of the succulent aroma. Arnuld was already eating, so I took a piece of meat and popped it in my mouth with my fingers—it was the most succulent piece of meat I had ever had. I could not even tell what animal it was.

Arnuld tried to persuade me to drink some more, but I adamantly refused. I ripped pieces of flat bread from the basket in front of me and scooped up the rice and veggies with it. My head hung close to the plate as I grabbed extra food from platters, hardly setting it on my plate before devouring it.

"Hungry?" Arnuld laughed. "One day, you will be used to eating like this and will take time to actually taste it before swallowing."

"I don't think I will ever get used to this."

We laughed together. I stopped and looked around. All of the Kosmoans were seated below us, laughing and talking with one another. An old man looked up to catch my eye, and he smiled and nodded, practically bowed towards me. A grin stretched my lips.

Drums started rolling and the grand doors at the end of the room opened. More dancers, flame-throwers, and acrobats came bounding into the center of the room. I lifted my head as juice ran down my chin, enthralled by it all. Arnuld pressed the pipe to my lips again. This time, I was not surprised by the smoke but coughed it out anyway as soon as it hit my lungs.

"You get used to it," Arnuld shouted to me over the noise. He winked and patted my back.

I laughed without restraint.

The room seemed to dance to the rhythm of the music, and my

head swam as if all of the hatred and fear I'd held inside of me was poured out—only mirth remained. I could not shake the smile from my face as I reached for my cup.

The doors at the end of the room opened again, and I turned to see a naked man led in, a noose around his neck. My heart clutched within me, and my smile dropped. The man was bruised and bloodied, but that shock of blond hair I would know anywhere. He was one of our townsmen.

"What are they doing?" I shouted to Arnuld over the erupting cheers.

"It's just part of our celebration, to showcase our power," he clapped me on the back as we spoke, his eyes bright, "We take one of the prisoners, and the generals are given a turn to…"

Thorold stood from our table, clapping his hands with a barbaric howl, thrusting his thumbs through his belt loops, and making his way to the idol of Kosmoa, where the man was tied by his guards.

My body tensed. The smoky air forced its way into me, threatening to burst me open. I couldn't take anymore. I started to run for the door. I stumbled around a person taking a bite of meat. "That lamb is delicious."

My food turned foul in my stomach and rushed out, splattering some of the people close by. "Get out of here!" someone yelled. I rushed away, blindly stumbling out of the room, trying to find a place to heave out the food. I made it to the stairs and leaned over the cool steel railing, stomach retching every bit of food and drink onto the stairs below. My body continued to heave bile, retching little bits of green mucus over the railing until my stomach felt like it was lodged in my throat.

I ran down, circumventing the slimy, chunky mess as I passed it.

I descended to the bottom of the ship where the livestock was held. The smell of dung and hay greeted me. Thoughts of home swirled in my mind. I entered the first stall and slumped against our town's ox. I buried my face into the warm side of its large black neck.

The ship still swayed as I leaned against the ox, but slowly the world stopped spinning, and I could feel my breathing return to a normal rhythm.

"How do you like being a Kosmoan?"

I looked around. On the other side of the ox, in the dim light of the stall stood a familiar figure in a too-tight old leather shirt. I flung myself into Eddie's arms, and he held me. "It's alright, brother." His voice was low and soothing. "I'll bring you home."

A picture of our grieving mom, deceased dad, our broken home, looted village, and sweet lamb-less Suzie overtook my mind. I took a step back and looked up at him, "I don't have a home, Eddie. I'm cursed."

His lips twitched, "Have those evil Kosmoans deceived you so quickly? You have a home; you're my brother." He smiled, then straightened his stance, put his right hand on my shoulder and said, "Donumdonair blesses you, and you are blessed forever."

"Dad used to tell us that." I wiped a tear from my eye, stepping backward to look up at Eddie. "I believed it when I was little. Now I know it's not true."

"Don't say that! It *is* true!"

"No, Eddie! I did the unthinkable," I cried violently.

"What?"

His arm was around me. I looked up into his bruised face and confessed, "I kneeled to Kosmoa."

Eddie thought for a moment. His arm stayed around my shoulders.

"In your heart, do you honor Kosmoa? Would you like to be a Kosmoan or Journeymen?"

I grimaced and dropped my head into my hands. "I would rather starve with the Journeymen than live in the wealth of a Kosmoan."

Eddie nodded, "Then Donumdonair forgives you, and He will lead us home."

"Do you realize we aren't anywhere near our home or solid ground? Even if by some miracle I made it back, everyone knows the truth about me... I would be an outcast."

"Most of the town knew the truth already."

His words stunned me. "They did? Did you?"

Eddie laughed, "Of course!"

I crossed my arms and stepped back. "No wonder you hated me."

His glacier-green eyes looked at me oddly, "Why would you say that?"

"We fight all the time!"

"We're *brothers*. That's what brothers do. If I didn't love you, I wouldn't even want to be around you. I certainly wouldn't have boarded this ship to save my little brother from a bunch of unclean roaches."

Warmth flooded me, and the term 'little brother' lingered in my ears. "But how did you get on the ship?"

"Believe it or not, I prayed to Donumdonair to hide me." He looked down as he said it, as if he was embarrassed a little. "And I entered the ship, along with this ox, just walked right in beside it. I tried to find you, but I couldn't open the doors to get out of here."

"It's an eye sensor. They scanned my eye, and I can open some of the doors now."

Eddie nodded. His face was bruised, and his lip cracked. He massaged around his lips with his fingers as he thought.

"Let's get off this ship—with the help of Donumdonair, of course. He got me here," Eddie shrugged, "I'm sure he can get us back."

Relief and hope flooded through me. We leaned our foreheads together and asked for Donumdonair's help. A warm sensation came through me, and my muscles felt strengthened. We turned to walk out of the stall. An oxgoad was just outside the door—a pole about eight feet long with a steel spike at the end for directing livestock. I grabbed it. "You let all the animals free. I'll go up where all the raiders are feasting and getting drunk."

Eddie studied me, a smile on his lips, "What are you going to do, little brother? Kill them all with that?"

I looked up and down the pole, then back at Eddie, "If I have to."

"Maybe we should make a better plan," he smirked. We sat in the dust in silence beside the ox. I thought through all of the things I had seen on the ship.

"I saw an emergency reset lever," I told him. "What does that mean?"

Eddie's face lit up. "That might do it," he smiled at me and raised his eyebrows. "Show me."

Wordlessly, Eddie and I released the animals. Then he followed me up the stairs to the mechanical room. I blinked my eyes in front of the sensor, not sure if it would work, but the door whizzed open. We didn't see anyone and crept over to where the red lever was.

"Rikes, who's there?" The voice was the same one as before. We split up and hid behind some computers. I still held the oxgoad. Eddie went to one side of the room and me on the other. The Kosmoan was headed towards Eddie. I hit the ground with the goad and stood up. He turned towards me. "What are you doing back here?"

"I forgot something."

"How did you get in here?"

"The usual way, I blinked."

"Go on out! You shouldn't have been given access to this door."

I backed up to the door, oxgoad in hand, staring the engineer down. As he took two powerful steps toward me I saw Eddie reach for the red lever.

Everything went dark. A crush of silence as the engines stopped.

Almost by instinct, in the darkness, I lowered the oxgoad to the height of a man's belly, the nail end sticking forward like a halberd.

The ship tipped toward me, and I stumbled another step backward toward the door. The blunt end of the oxgoad caught behind me on the bulkhead and supported my weight.

Then I felt the weight of the oxgoad shift, I heard something like canvas split, and I immediately smelled something like feces and blood.

"Kosrikes!" I heard the engineer say with a deep guttural moan.

The ship leveled and the emergency lights flickered on as his body twisted away from me, the oxgoad stuck deep in his gut. I stumbled up away from the haunting sounds of the groaning man. I watched aghast as the engineer pulled the oxgoad out of his body and stumbled to his feet. Hunched over his wound, he staggered toward the reset lever and gasped as he weakly pushed it up.

The engines roared back to life. Full lights came on and the movement of the ship steadied.

I grabbed the bloody oxgoad from the floor just as the engineer eyed Eddie.

"Kosrikes!" He lurched for Eddie with one hand while the other hand gripped his bleeding gut. Eddie stepped aside, and the engineer fell atop a console, the blood pooling into the circuits, sparks flying from the controls as the ship lurched once again.

Eddie lunged around him and pulled the lever down again.

I looked into his eyes for just a moment before darkness filled the chamber and the ship began to spin. I felt Eddie's arms envelop me in the dark, and he and I held each other—brothers in a world spinning out of control, banging against everything in the turmoil, until we fell into the embracing our destiny.

Find the story of Shamgar in Judges 3:31.

The Stars Stand Witness

Drake McDonald

I AM ZERU, son of Lurra, of the Clan of Naritha, and this is the story
of how I lost my little star.

Hutsa arrived at dusk to take her away. I had walked out to the
mag-dome control box to wipe down the coils when I saw him coming. His speeder, at first a black speck on the setting sun, grew larger
as the sky faded from fire to night.

"Hail, Apprentice," I said as he pulled up, putting my hand over
my heart and bowing my head slightly. The speeder stopped just short
of the copper line that marked the mag-dome's perimeter. If you hadn't
known it was there, you'd have missed it in the red dirt of the desert.
On one side: me, my land, and the mag-dome controls, on the other:
dirt, tumbleweeds, and Hutsa.

He'd brought a driver with him, a young man in black coveralls
and cap with a green scarf wrapped around his face. Hutsa vaulted
out of the backseat of the speeder and landed lightly on his feet.
"Hail, Narithan," he said, hand on heart, bowing deeply. His voice
was so muffled by the scarf wrapped over his nose and mouth that I

291

almost didn't hear him when he added, "and hail, father."

So he is *here to take her back*, I thought. "Hail, son," I said.

Hutsa straightened back up and pulled down the scarf. Dark hair, green eyes, skin red from the desert dust. He looked like he'd lost weight since I'd last seen him, and his jawline was dark with scruff. He was dressed in the white tunic of his office, cinched at the waist with a red sash that trailed behind him to the knees. He'd augmented this with a pair of thick, dark brown cargo pants patched at the knees and a heavy coat of old, crumbly leather that reached to his ankles. He wore it all rather poorly, like it was a size too big for his frame.

"Is she here?" he asked.

"Where else would she be?" I replied, turning back to wipe down the coils. Izara had been here four months, and he was only *now* looking for her?

Hutsa sighed and almost seemed to deflate—a tension dropped out of his shoulders, loosened his knees. "Thank the Giver," he said.

"Yes," I agreed, closing the lid on the control box with a clang, "the desert is a dangerous place for a woman traveling alone without her *husband*."

Hutsa blushed. "Listen," he said, "it was a...*complicated* situation...and yes, I should have come after Izara a lot sooner, but..." he buried his face in his hands and sighed again, long fingers massaging his forehead. I noticed that he had purple patches under his eyes.

"Look, I'm sorry," he said, crossing his arms. "I'm sorry I let Izara cross the desert by herself. I'm sorry I didn't come looking for her sooner—I just...can I *talk* to her?"

My finger hovered over the mag-dome's ENGAGE button. For a moment, I thought about leaving them in the desert. Let Hutsa and his driver sit out here overnight, and if they were still here in the morning, maybe *then*... But no—it would be wrong to disrespect an Apprentice like that. After all, Journeymen are bound by The Ancient Mandates to offer hospitality to one another.

"Apprentice, did you bring your sacred implements?" I asked.

Hutsa looked up, confused, then realization dawned—"Yes, yes! I did!" He turned around and pulled a hefty black satchel from the back seat of the speeder, holding it up for me to see. "I can offer sacrifices for you and lead you in prayers—it'll take a few days to do all the purification rites and prep an altar—unless you already have one, but—"

"We have an altar," I said, "and I'd like you to offer sacrifices for me and my wife."

"Of course," Hutsa said, suddenly grave. He bowed deeply. "It'd be my honor."

He straightened up again and motioned his driver to advance across the mag-dome border. He climbed back into the backseat of the speeder as I engaged the mag-dome, a faint hum thrumming through the air as the protective shield shimmered up from the copper line in the dirt. Far off in the center of the property, over the main house, a brief spark flickered as the field closed.

• • •

"Ibaia, we've got company!" I said as I threw open the door to the one-room homestead.

"Company?!" my wife looked up from setting the table to shoot me a look that was half "who-is-it?-we-didn't-invite-anyone-for-dinner" and half "how-dare-you-spring-this-on-me-last-minute?" I stepped aside to let her see the men behind me.

"Hail, Narithan. Hail, mother!" Hutsa shouted as he entered, carrying his bag of sacred implements.

For a moment, I saw Ibaia's mouth drop open, but she quickly recovered. "Hail, Apprentice. Hail, son!" she said, coming around the table with open arms and a smile. "It's been too long since you've come to see us, Hutsa!" she said, kissing him on both cheeks. "Do you like roast cliox? Zeru just slaughtered it today..." She took Hutsa's bag from him and led him over to the stove, gushing about dinner. It gave me a minute to locate Izara stretched out on the couch, reading. She had her mother's blue eyes and my russet wavy hair and by some trick of Donum's, was taller than both of us. That night, she was wearing a yellow dress spotted with red flowers that seemed to glow against the golden tan of her skin.

"'Zara," I said, tapping her arm, "look who's come." Izara lowered her book and propped herself up on her elbows, gazing over the back of the couch. Her eyes settled on Hutsa for a moment, and I thought I saw passion flicker in them—but it vanished before I could tell if it was anger or love. Then her gaze turned to the door and the driver who'd just entered.

"Evening, Criat," she called, lifting a hand in greeting and smiling.

The driver pulled down his scarf and tipped his cap. "Evening, Izara," he replied, waving back.

"Hail, wife!" Hutsa rushed up to the couch and tried to hug Izara, but she turned away and stood.

"Hello, Hutsa," she said.

Izara had returned to live with us after almost eighteen months of what we thought was happy marriage with Hutsa. She'd said they had a fight, and she just wanted to take a week to cool off, but when the week ended, she stayed another, then another, then four months passed.

The dinner conversation was bland. Hutsa and Criat told of their trip across the desert. It's usually a two-day journey from their homestead to ours, but they'd left very late the night before and pushed through the whole trip in a single run rather than stopping in Pau or Turo or a smaller village. Hutsa asked about the harvest and how my cattle were doing. Izara sat silently, only occasionally asking Ibaia to pass the salt or asking Criat to cut another slice of cliox.

I was gathering the plates and utensils for washing when Ibaia said, "So, Hutsa, it's been a while since an Apprentice came by, and we were able to offer *proper* sacrifices. I mean, Zeru will occasionally burn fat offerings on the altar, and we always offer the first basket of the harvest, but…we're not *you*. We read The Ancient Mandates, but *your* line is appointed by Donumdonair to lead our worship. So all of this is to ask…is there anything we need to do to prepare?"

"Yes, actually," Hutsa said, pushing back from the table and reaching for the bag next to his seat, "There's a few cleansing rituals and prayers…" he pulled a small black leather-bound book, dog-eared with a broken spine, from his bag. I saw Izara roll her eyes as I turned to drop our dishes in the pot of water warming on the stove.

"…and I'd recommend you read chapters ten through seventeen of the Mandates," Hutsa continued. "And the prayers in chapter thirty-seven, hymns one-oh-eight, one-thirty-five, two-fifty-seven through two-seventy—"

"And then you *still* won't be good enough." It was Izara's voice, low and hard, almost spitting the words. The intensity made me turn.

Hutsa hunched over his little black book, frozen in surprise. Ibaia was seated next to him, eyes wide, forehead furrowed, mouth slightly open—overwhelmed by the flood she'd just received from him. Izara was across the table from Hutsa, leaning back in her chair with her arms crossed over her chest. The passion was back in her eyes, and this time, I knew it was anger. The driver, Criat, seated next to Hutsa, pulled the brim of his cap down over his eyes and sank in his chair, curling in on himself.

"That's what you're *not* telling them, right?" Izara said. Ice in her voice. "They'll recite the prayers, sing the songs, read the chapters, and even after *all of that,* they still won't be pure enough, right?"

Hutsa's mouth opened and closed a few times while he searched for the words he wanted. "Zara," he said at last, "this book is the foundation of our worship."

Izara rolled her eyes again and massaged her forehead.

"It is!" Hutsa continued. "The Ancient Mandates are Donumdonair's *specific* revelation to the Journeymen, handed down on the crossing to Covenant over a thousand years ago. He chose *us* out of all the peoples in the universe and gave us *this land* as our inheritance."

"And we've done a real good job keeping it," Izara said. "Between the Kosmoans and the Desperados—no offense, Criat." The driver sank lower in his chair.

"You're absolutely right," Hutsa said, "we haven't done a very good job keeping it—and you know why? Because we've strayed from The Mandates." He closed his book and gripped it in both hands. "The *only* way to worship Donumdonair is by following the *specific* methods and rituals in this book. We *must* follow the Mandates—"

"And just being present with him isn't enough?" Izara asked. "Pondering the depths of his mystery, giving him all we have, that's not enough?"

"No," there was finality in the word. Hutsa lowered the book to the table and gazed at Izara with an intensity that was almost frightening. If she hadn't also had fire in her eyes, I might have said something to ease the tension.

"We *must* be pure if we are to be acceptable to Donum," Hutsa said. "We must follow the Mandates if we are to have intimacy with him."

Silence. Then Izara pushed her chair back and stood. "No one can keep the Mandates the way you want them to," she said, "and no one will ever be worthy." She crossed the room in a few strides and vanished out the door.

"Izara, please, it's—" Hutsa called after her and started to get up, but I put a hand on his shoulder.

"Let me talk to her," I said. "I know where she's going."

Hutsa nodded and lowered his head, turning back to the table. Beside him, the driver straightened back up and lifted his cap. Now I could see the hardness in his jaw, the ghost of old tension in his muscles—how had I not seen the Desperado in him?

"So Criat," I heard Ibaia say as I turned to follow Izara out the door, "did Izara say you're not a Journeymen?"

"No, ma'am," the man said, "I was born a Desperado..." His voice faded as I stepped outside.

· · ·

297

Izara was standing beside the altar, a gentle night breeze ruffling her dress. She had her arms crossed against the cold as she gazed out to the horizon where the dark ground rose to meet the deep purple of the sky, speckled with white, red, blue, yellow, and green stars.

The altar wasn't much, but I loved it. That stack of stones and beaten metal had stood since before the house was even built. It started as a single large flat stone I could burn offerings on, but as the farm grew, as my family grew, I added a few embellishments: an ash grate, a tinderbox, and even a few ornamental horns at the corners.

I scuffed my feet on the ground as I approached so she would hear me coming. "I don't want to fight again, Hutsa," she said.

"You don't have to, my little star," I said. She turned with a puzzled look on her face. She looked down at the dirt, shaking her head.

"I'm sorry, Papa," she said. "I know you don't like fighting."

"Oh, I don't know," I said, "there's always room for healthy *discussion*." She smiled at that, and I did, too. She looked up and caught my eye, then shook her head again. "Is this what you left him over?" I asked. "His dedication to The Mandates and purity requirements?"

"It's not just that, Papa," she said. "He can't..." Her mouth held open for a moment, words lost. *"He can't see the stars."* Her voice cracked as she looked up, catching my eye again. Tears were glistening in hers.

"It's not that he's dedicated to the Mandates. It's that *they're all he sees.* He's never looked up at the sky and felt Donum standing near. He's never seen his glory in a sunrise or felt the pleasure of singing a hymn. I mean, he sings, but it's just words and noise to him! He's never reveled in his breath or felt joy in his sight! I just..." she trailed off, searching for words. "Everything he believes feels so different from everything I've seen, and living with him was so hard…"

The tears fell. I closed the space between us and wrapped my little girl in a hug. "Donumdonair has gifted you with so much love for this world he's made," I said, letting her go and lifting her face, wiping her tears away. "It's a beautiful gift to see his presence in everything because then you are never alone." That made her smile.

"But not everybody can see that," I continued. "And your husband's not wrong about the Mandates. We need to remember our history—how Donum led our ancestors across the lands to Covenant, how he led us to victory over the Desperados and Kosmoans—even if we didn't do a very good job of *keeping* that victory. Did you know the Journeymen were once mighty? You'd never guess it from looking at us now. That's why we need the Mandates—to remind us of who we are and who Donumdonair has called us to be."

Izara ran a hand across her cheeks, drying her tears. "But still, Papa… It's hard living with someone who sees the world so differently, even if we both follow Donumdonair."

"Did I ever tell you how your mother and I chose Hutsa to be your husband?" I asked. Izara shook her head. "It wasn't an easy choice. I wanted only the best for my little star, and your mother was determined that you should marry a Journeymen. We both knew that you loved Donumdonair, and we knew you had a gift for loving his creation, so we went looking for a good, devout man who also loved Donum and could help grow your gifts. We prayed for months, interviewed over two dozen men, all of them strong, faithful believers, but none of them *clicked.* They didn't feel right for *you*—until Hutsa.

"I thought the interview went very well, but when Hutsa left, your mother turned to me and said, 'He's the one.' When I asked her why, she said she'd had a vision. That she'd seen him raising you up in front of our Journeymen brothers and sisters, a multitude, from every clan, and you'd united them. Like during the Conquest. For the first time in over a thousand years, our people—a single nation united under Donumdonair. And you were going to be the one to do it. When she told me that…"

"But Papa," she started.

"Marriage can be hard," I said, cutting her off. "It's hard when different people come together. Compromises have to be made—hearts, minds, and routines have to change. Do you think it was easy for your mother and me when we got married? We slept on opposite ends of the house for a full year!" I laughed, and she laughed too.

"Hutsa is going to offer sacrifices for your mother and me, and in a few days, he'll head home. I love you, little star, but you'll have to go with him. It's time for you to outgrow this nest and make your own. That's no easy task, but I know you can do it." I wrapped her in another hug and held her close like I used to when she was my little girl—my little star.

A few days later, after the sacrifices were made, the hymns were sung, and the fellowship feast was over, Hutsa and Izara climbed into the back seat of the speeder, and Criat drove them off into the late afternoon as the sun sank towards the horizon.

I never saw my little star again.

• • •

My name is Criat. I have no clan. This is the story of my home-coming.

We left the homestead way too late. When Hutsa and I made the drive down there, we had pushed the speeder hard to make the entire trip in one day. We almost blew a coil a couple times. When we left the homestead, it was late afternoon—almost sunset—and there was no way we were going to make it all the way back home in one trip. That's why Zeru offered to let us stay another night. But Hutsa was ready to head home. Said we'd overstayed our welcome.

So we left the homestead way too late. And that's why we had to stop in Turo.

Though we didn't *have* to stop in Turo, we could have stopped in Pau. The sun was sinking into the horizon when we left the homestead, turning the desert a scabby blood color. We drove for a few hours, then had to stop to refill the coil-baths, so we pulled over at a well. There was a junction there. I told Hutsa that we should turn off the main road and go to Pau. Sure, it would take us off the road home, "but Pau's way closer than Turo," I said. "We'll get there way before dark."

"But Pau's still a Desperado city," Hutsa replied. "Turo's filled up with Journeymen—and I'd like to stay among our people if we can."

I didn't argue with him—he didn't pay me to argue with him. He gave me a loft in his barn, food to eat, and a speeder to drive, so I didn't argue with him. I should have.

I was born in Turo back when it was still a stronghold of the Des-perados. My mom and dad weren't in love—she was the daughter of a wealthy merchant who liked to spend her daddy's wealth on *plazzera*. He was her dealer. They used to get hopped up on the drug and do the nasty, until one day, bad timing, she got pregnant. Her dad was furious. Kicked her out of the house and told her to never come back. My dad wouldn't take her in, but when she died in childbirth nine months later, the midwife left me on his doorstep. He loved me at first—he would let his female clients play with me while he measured out their *plazzera*, and sometimes the men would bring me candies. Eventually, though, his business dried up as the market shifted from *plazzera* to *indarkeria*, and his patience ran out with his money. He got hooked on the *dark*, and one day, when I was about six, he traded me for a bottle. I cried as he walked away, then the dealer slapped me, and I stopped because I didn't want to get slapped again.

The dealer ran a brothel, and I lived there for almost seven years. Then the owner moved me from the brothel to an underground garage on the other side of the city, where I learned how to drive and fix speeders. It felt good to slide into the steering rig of a speeder, *powerful*—I loved it. The boss of the garage let me fix up a little mag-lev rust-bucket I found on the smelting heap and let me take it out on deliveries sometimes.

One day, I came back from a delivery run to find the garage blazing. Doors locked—men screaming inside. I was so horrified I didn't stop my bike to try and help them. They were already goners anyway. I gunned my little speeder across town to the brothel where my owner lived, but the house was already ash.

For the first time in my life, I felt a strange sensation—*freedom*. For all I knew, either my owner had died in the brothel fire or he would believe I was dead from the garage fire. *I could leave Turo* and no one would ever know to look for me.

So I pointed my bike towards the edge of town and gunned it as fast as I could. When I reached the line where the hard-packed dirt road gave way to desert sand, I kept going, setting a course for any-where but where I was. Eventually, I ran across a road and followed it until my little rust bucket blew a coil. Then I walked until my legs gave out.

That's where Hutsa found me, lying in a ditch, blistered with sun-burn and dehydrated. He pulled over, loaded me into his speeder, and brought me home. He gave me water, food, a place to sleep, offered to *pay* me if I'd help out with his farm. No one had ever done that be-fore. He taught me about his god, Donumdonair, the giver of gifts. He taught me how to read The Ancient Mandates. Taught me how to work numbers. I owe so much to him, but he's never called the bill due. Not in the almost six years I've worked for him. And I don't think he ever will. Hutsa's not someone to ask for something in return for his gifts.

It was nearly dark by the time we reached the outskirts of Turo. The city was brighter than I remembered it. In the last few years, Turo had become a city of Journeymen—the Decandran clan. There were solar panels on all the buildings now, and every alley was strung with wiring and lights. Shops had signs that glowed green, pink, and blue. As we made our way to the city center, we even passed through a dis-trict where all the streetlights glowed bright red.

Underneath the facade, however, some things were still the same. A tag scraped on a wall, a vagrant reeling under some dark drug. A gang of mag-lev bikers rumbled past us, flashing dirty looks. They wore leather jackets with a Desperado scimitar embroidered on the back, though their faces looked like Journeymen.

I pulled the speeder over at the edge of the city center. Around the square, the shops were starting to close up for the night. Chains clat-tered on doors, locks clicked on windows. In the center of the square was a pile of stones that, at one point, was supposed to be an altar where the people could gather to offer sacrifices for themselves and their families. But now the stones were cracked and the whole pile was dark, not with soot from the sacrifices but decaying growths.

"I don't think this is a good idea," Izara said as Hutsa climbed out of the speeder.

"No, no, it's the custom!" Hutsa replied, pulling his Mandates from inside his jacket. "These are our Journeymen brothers and sisters, and The Ancient Mandates commands them to offer hospitality to travelers. I'm sure someone will come through shortly and offer us refuge."

Izara sank low on her seat in the speeder. "I'm not sure they follow the Mandates around here," she mumbled.

I don't think Hutsa heard her. "I'm sure we'll be fine, you'll see," he said.

I also climbed out of the speeder but didn't go far because the sun had just set, and I didn't want to leave Izara alone in the square after dark. Hutsa walked over to the altar in the center of the square, rummaging through his bag of sacred implements.

I saw the kid half a second before he made his move. He was barely a shadow—a thin, wiry teenager in a sleeveless leather jacket and pants—and he moved fast. He darted out of an alley and grabbed for Hutsa's bag. Hutsa yelped in surprise but kept his grip, which made the kid stall. That was all I needed to lower my shoulder and charge into him.

He sprawled down hard on his shoulder, scraping his arm bloody on the gravelly pavement of the square. "The rike?!" he yelled.

"Get on out of here," I said, standing over him with my fists clenched. "We don't have anything you want, and this man is an Apprentice. Don't you have any respect for Donumdonair?"

The kid spat in his hand and rubbed his bleeding arm as he scrambled to his feet. "Rike Donumdonair," he said, "he hasn't given a rike about us for years." He spat again, this time aiming for Hutsa's feet. He missed. I watched him limp back to the alley he'd come from.

"Come on," I said to Hutsa, putting an arm on his shoulder. "We can't linger here." He didn't argue as I led him back to the speeder.

I was about to start the engine and make for an outskirts inn when I heard a voice call out, "Apprentice? Hail, Apprentice!" I looked around for the source of the voice and saw a white-haired old man hurrying towards us.

"Hail, Journeymen," Hutsa replied, uncertain of the man's clan.

"Aztarna, son of Fidela, of the Decandrans," the old man said. He took Hutsa's hand and clasped it in both of his. "Apprentice," he said, "you can't stay here. It isn't safe. Please, come and stay with me. I have food, and a garage for your speeder, and warm beds for yourself and your wife, and your protector here." I think I might have blushed at that.

Hutsa accepted the man's offer and helped him into the front passenger seat of the speeder. He gave me directions to a small house not far from the city center, a little hutch with bars on the windows and a code pad on the garage. As he lowered the garage door behind us, I glanced back and thought I saw the slightest movement of a shadow on the far side of the street. Then the door was closed, and the old man was inviting us inside for dinner. I was sure that we were safe in Aztarna's house.

I was wrong.

• • •

My name is go-rike-yourself, son of some-roach-who-didn't-give-a-nub, and this is the story of how I made an Apprentice my snipe.

My real name is Berekoi, and I used to be a Decandran, but when my dad kicked me out of the house, I said rike that. Rike him, rike the Journeymen, rike Donum, and rike all his "gifts." Nobody's ever given me a riking thing, least of all the flying roach-man in the sky. I've had to *work* for every riking thing I have. I've had to scrabble and steal and swindle and *take* every *riking* thing. And then I've had to fight to keep it—which is why when that nub-head of a Desperado floored me in the square, I had to track him and his Apprentice friend down.

I didn't start the night wanting to rike them up. In fact, we'd have probably left them alone if Hil hadn't tried to edge in on me. And the *dark*—kosrike, that was some good nub—that *indarkeria* was *killer*, you get me?

My gang's about fifteen guys strong—not so small we're ignored, but not so big we can't get away quickly when the Enforcers show up. I've beaten every one of these rikers to a pulp at least once because I *own* these nub-heads. They're *mine*.

We start every night in the alley behind Zoa's shop—Arazoa is my right-hand man—and they were already drinking the *dark* when I got there.

"Hil brought a new blend," Zoa said when he met me at the alley entrance. "Stronger than usual and plussed up with something."

"And they didn't offer me the first cup?" I asked. The rike did these nubheads think they were?

"There's a…*situation* you'll need to deal with," Zoa said.

I shot him a look that said, "the rike is this *situation?*" but he just nodded down the alley where the rest of the gang was assembled around the stack of crates I use as a platform when it comes time to give assignments. Hil was sitting on the stack. The riker was sitting on *my* throne.

The rike?

I walked down the alley to join my gang, shouting to announce my arrival. Smiling. Happy, even.

"The rike is all this?" I said when I reached the stack of crates—and Hil. I wasn't angry. My guys were happy, so I was happy.

Hil was grinning ear to ear, sitting next to a crate of bottles filled with black liquid. "This," he said, pulling a bottle from the crate and popping the cap off, "is the latest shipment of *dark.*" He held out the bottle. "It's good stuff."

I'm sure it is, I thought, *but the rike if I'm gonna drink it from you.* I reached into the crate and picked up a bottle for myself. "I see you didn't think to hold the first bottle for me," I said, glancing around at the guys drinking around us. Smiling daggers.

Hil's grin got wider as he took a sip from his bottle, "Yeah, well…" he said, "I thought you were too busy eating gravel to care."

The atmosphere shifted around us. Conversations started to fade as the gang felt the tension rise.

"You mean when that Despo riker ran into me in the square?" I asked, taking a sip of my *dark.* Zoa was right. It was way stronger than usual—and there was something else in it, something really *riking strong.*

"I mean when that Despo *laid you out* in the square," Hil said, chuckling to himself. "And then you turned tail and ran like a *rik-*

ing roach." He glanced around at my bleeding arm, which was half-scabbed over by now. "Does that hurt, little Berry?"

The gang had fallen to silence around us, tensed like roaches. Ready to pounce. *Rike these nubheads.* I kept grinning my signature nub-eating grin and took a step back from the crates, lifting my bottle to Hil. "Race you to the gravel?" I said.

Hil hopped off the stack of crates and lifted his own bottle. "To the gravel."

We clinked our bottles together and went bottoms up. The *dark* was like ice running down my throat. Hil had the advantage because he'd been nursing his for a minute, while mine was new—but I could out-drink, out-rike, out-fight anyone, anytime.

I finished my bottle and swung for Hil's head. The riker tried to be clever and ducked, but I was expecting it and aimed low. The bottle shattered as he went reeling, shards of glass carving up his face and leaving me with a jagged stub in my hand. He groaned as he hit the gravel, his own bottle spinning out of his hand.

"Alright, alright!" he said as I knelt over him, "you win, Berekoi!"

"Rike that," I said and shoved my broken bottle into his throat.

The *dark* had started to buzz in my brain. Pounding rhythm in my pulse. I could feel my temperature rising. Electricity was starting to tingle on my skin. THE RIKE DID THIS RIKER THINK HE WAS? I pulled the bottle from his neck and buried it in his chest, his gut, his groin, again again again. My hands were coated in sticky red liquid that stank like death. At some point, I started yelling.

By the time I had finished with Hil's body, I was coated in filth, but I didn't care. The *dark* had taken me. I thrust my hand into the gaping hole at Hil's neck and smeared my face with his blood, screaming to the stars. The guys around me took up the call, gathering to smear themselves in their own *dark*-fueled ecstasies. By the time the last man had put on his war paint, the *dark* had started speaking to me—saying clearly with every pound of my pulse: RIKE. THE. APPRENTICE.

The night came in flashes.

I led my gang to the old riker's house. We beat the door. There was shouting inside.

The old man opened a small hatch in the door. I demanded he give me the Apprentice. I didn't want to kill him—that would be too simple. I wanted to rike him raw. Dominate him. *Own him.* What could his god do against me? Against the *dark*?

The old man threatened to call the Enforcers.

RIKE THE ENFORCERS. I WANTED THE APPRENTICE.

I ordered my gang to break their way into the house, whatever it took.

More shouting inside, sounds of a fight.

The front door swung open and the woman stumbled out. The Apprentice's wife. Her husband was behind her, but the door swung shut before my guys could grab him.

RIKE HER! I DIDN'T WANT HER!

But the *dark* whispered she was a fine prize, so we took her, and that night I learned that Donum was indeed the giver of great gifts.

• • •

I am Hutsa, son of Gurtza, of the Apprentices, and this is the story of my grief.

I didn't sleep the night Izara was taken. None of us did.

I don't know what came over me.

There were men beating on the door, on the windows, calling for me. Why did they want me? I had only arrived in the city today. And they wanted to *defile* me.

I just don't know what happened.

One moment, I was at the door, then Izara was there, then Criat was there, then the door was opened and closed again, and Izara was gone, and Criat was on the floor with a bloody nose. The old man Aztarna was over by the kitchen table, the remains of our dinner not even half finished, his mouth open in shock. Then the gang went away, and we were left in silence.

It was all so fast and strange.

It was still quiet when the sun came up, and the light gave me the strength to go looking for Izara. I asked Aztarna to open the garage, and when the door went up, there she was.

Her yellow dress was orange now. Her skin almost black with scabs. Her hair was matted and thick with clotted blood. All I could think to say to her was, "get up."

She didn't respond. I knelt and held a hand in front of her mouth—not touching her, but close enough to feel breath. There wasn't any.

It's against the Mandates for an Apprentice to touch a dead body. I called out for Criat and Aztarna. Criat's nose had stopped bleeding, but it was swollen and purple and looked incredibly painful.

I'm not sure what came over me.

When they got her loaded into the speeder, Criat handed me the power stick. He said he was staying in Turo. When I asked him why, he just shook his head and looked at Izara's body in the backseat. His jaw flexed.

The journey home took the whole day. There was something meditative about the experience. Red dirt stretched out in all directions, the blue dome of the sky overhead, plateaus standing like monuments against the horizon. I traveled miles and miles without seeing another speeder. It gave me some time to think.

When the gang came knocking, they came knocking for me. To defile me.

But I couldn't give myself to them. I am an Apprentice. I'm set apart. I must be pure before Donumdonair—not only for myself but for my fellow Journeymen. How could I offer worship for others if I myself have been defiled? If I am unacceptable, then how can I hope to lead others into Donum's presence?

I never should have opened the door—that's true.

But I also shouldn't have been in a situation where my purity was in danger. The gang should never have come knocking.

Yesterday, I made the decision to travel on to Turo instead of Pau because I thought we'd be safe among our fellow Journeymen, but the Decandrans had betrayed us. They didn't deserve to call themselves Journeymen after this—even those who weren't part of the gang. They had allowed this disease to fester within themselves until the pus oozed out over me and mine.

They were impure—and they *must* be *cleansed.*

At any cost.

· · ·

I am Izara, daughter of Zeru, of the Clan of Naritha, and my story isn't finished yet.

I was dead. My body was lying on the kitchen table where I once served Hutsa and Criat in our homestead that I hadn't seen in months. Hutsa carried it in himself, breaking one of his dearest Mandates. It would take him days to perform the purification rites. Something must have snapped inside him.

Now Hutsa was rummaging through our kitchen, looking for something. He'd taken off his jacket, his white tunic stained with my blood. His hands were shaking.

He stopped, his hand hovering over an open drawer. Uncertainty flickered across his face, then hardened into resolve. His hand disappeared inside, then reappeared holding a large plasma-knife. The blade was triangular with a curved edge, used for dicing vegetables. He flicked the switch on the handle and a razor-thin wire of blue light glowed to life mere millimeters from the edge of the blade.

I wasn't living inside the body anymore, but I still winced a little as the blade bit into my arm. Hutsa lowered the knife through my elbow, careful not to cut so fast he nicked the table. When the joint was severed, he took my hand and placed it on the counter behind him, moved on to my shoulder, my legs... I watched this man I had married butcher my body.

Suddenly, the doorway to the kitchen grew dark, and I saw a man standing there—dark hair, bright, golden eyes, dressed in white, haloed by the sun setting behind him.

"Who are you?" I asked.

The man glanced at the table, then stepped into the room. "I'm a friend," he said.

It occurred to me that this man had responded to *me*, who was dead. And Hutsa didn't react to the man's entrance. "Are you a spirit?" I asked.

"Of a sort," the man replied, "though most Journeymen know me as Mezulari—"

"The Messenger of Donumdonair," I said. Suddenly, I felt very uncertain of how I should react. Should I kneel? Or at least bow?

The man laughed, "You're fine just as you are," he said. His eyes glanced back at the table where Hutsa was carving up my torso. "You know, you're going to be a powerful witness," he said.

"What do you mean?" I asked.

He took a step closer to the table and me. "Your broken body will become the seed of a unified kingdom for the Journeymen—born out of blood, yes, but tempered and strong," his eyes settled on Hutsa for a moment, then returned to mine. "Hutsa is going to send a piece of your body to each of the clans, and they will rally around you. They will exact justice from the Decandrans, though they might be a little too harsh on their brothers and sisters...but this will birth a new unity and eventually a kingdom for the Journeymen to call their own. They will be united as they haven't been since the conquest of Covenant, and their kingdom will lead to a new age of prosperity not only for Covenant but for the whole world."

I wasn't sure how I felt about this. It's great that the Journeymen will be reunited, but last night... I could still feel Hutsa's hand on my back—the teeth, the knives in my skin. The fists in my hair. The blood...

"Does Donumdonair know how painful this was for me?" I asked.

He smiled again, this time with sadness. "Yes," he replied, "he does. One day, we will be humiliated, beaten, and killed by a gruesome mob. They will break our body and leave us naked on the side of the road, lifted up for all the world to see. But then, as now, that death will not be the end of the story, and that brokenness will become the seed of a new kingdom."

I received this in silence, and then realization dawned on me. "Wait..." I said, "*we?*"

He smiled again, extending a hand. "Come," he said. "It's time to go home."

I took his hand and gazed into his eyes, and felt an intense joy rising in my chest so powerful that it brought tears to my eyes. Perhaps it was the light of the setting sun, but as I blinked away the tears, his face blurred into a sea of stars, brightening into the glory of eternity.

Find the story in Judges 19.

Acknowledgments

Thanks for spending some time in the land of Covenant and taking this journey with us. I hope that these stories came alive for you!

So much went into this project, so first and foremost, I'd like to thank you, the reader, for taking the time to read each of these stories. You can support this project by sharing the book with a friend and leaving an honest review on your favorite site like Amazon or Goodreads.

I'd also like to thank everyone who supported this project in big and little ways. Thank you to everyone who prayed for the project, applied to be an author, and shared about it on social media. This project wouldn't be the same without you.

I would like to give a special thanks to Thirzah and Lindsey Backen for helping us imagine the land of Covenant and its people in the early stages of brainstorming the universe.

Thank you Shelby Little for being there through every overly excited info-dump I gave you about this project—even though I'd definitely told you everything twice already. Your patience is a gift and mystery to me.

And a big thank you goes to Brad Pauquette. Thank you for keeping your hand on my shoulder and driving me forward to bring this project to completion. Without you, none of this would have been imaginable for me, let alone possible.

Thank you, reader, for spending this time with us.

-Alli Prince
Project Manager

| Author Biographies

Chris Babcock's adventures have taken him from the Thar desert of India to the rainforest slopes of Malawi. He loves sci-fi and fantasy, especially books that deal truthfully with difficult topics. If you think it must be awkward for him to write about himself in third person—he thinks so, too. Join the journey: chrisbabcockauthor.com

Jonathan Babcock was born in Canada, raised in Malawi, and currently lives in New Zealand. Jonathan has a passion for seeing new places, trying new things, and living life as an adventure. In his spare time you can find him devouring fantasy books, climbing mountains, playing the guitar, or glowering at a blank page.

Abigail Bales is a Jesus-lover and writer from Indiana. When she isn't writing stories or poetry, she's probably sipping coffee, strumming a guitar, or looking out a window. She graduates high school in May 2024 and is excited to see where Jesus takes her next. To follow her journey, join her mailing list at LadyBluebird.me

Anita DeVries's goal is to write in a way that encourages personal faith in Christ. She holds a Journalism Diploma and an Honors Degree in English and History. Her employment has been in print media and business. Currently, she is in The Company's Arche Year program and works for a political advocacy group.

Elijah Fitz lives in New Hampshire with his wife. Sometimes, he writes. Soli deo gloria.

Megan Flahive refused to take naps as a kid, so her preschool teachers taught her to read instead. As a lifelong learner, she has a love for travel, fairy tales, and food. She lives in Indiana but her imagination takes her on innumerable adventures elsewhere. Follow Megan and her writing on Instagram at @meganiswriting_

Katelyn Flatt has multiple published works, including a short story published by *The Pearl*, and her first novel when she was sixteen. She loves writing big-picture stories that explore new technologies and is always asking "what if...?" She lives in Las Vegas, NV with her husband.

Nicole Gusto is a dreamer and storyteller from the Philippines. She often writes about broken things—mostly robots, oftentimes human hearts. When she's not writing, she's a speech pathologist who loves helping kids tell their own stories. Nicole is an Academic Teaching Assistant for the Young Writer's Workshop, has been published in *One Voice Magazine* and *The Rebelution*. You can visit her website at www.nicolegusto.com

Vannah Leblank grew up traveling across North and Central America and used to hate writing. But, somehow, by the end of sixth grade she was writing her first novella and she hasn't stopped writing since. She is currently majoring in Psychology, working on literary projects, and seeking to praise God through every aspect of her life. Follow her on Instagram @vannah_leblank_author

Drake McDonald is a storyteller. He makes videos, designs art installations, and writes short fiction and poetry. His work is previously published in *The Pearl*, *New College Review*, and *A Coup of Owls*. You can follow his blog at live-between.com

Matthew Sampson writes science fiction and fantasy, draws comics at work for a bit of office humor, and makes stop motion movies on YouTube under the original name of Matthew Sampson Bricks. He currently keeps a careful watch on a prison library in New Zealand.

Thirzah was born in the Netherlands but grew up in Southern Maryland. When she's not writing books, she's reading them. As the former managing editor of *The Pearl*, Thirzah has worked with many writers to help them improve their work. Learn more about Thirzah on her website, ThirzahWrites.com

Editor Biography

Alli Prince

Alli Prince has been creating stories since she could form words and has been writing since long before she learned about sentence structure and grammar (her editors think she could still learn a thing or two about grammar). She's been published to *The Pearl* and was the project manager for *Lawless*.

Alli is currently attending a writing trade school called The Company. She is learning everything she can about writing, editing, and marketing. She hopes to use these skills to influence the world of Christian literature and bring glory to God's name.

Alli lives in Cambridge, Ohio but is originally from Las Vegas, Nevada, where her family of twelve (yes, you read that right, twelve) cheer her on and encourage her to pursue the dreams God has placed on her heart.

To learn more about Alli, check out her Instagram @alliprinceauthor or visit her website alliprince.com.

Editor Biography

Brad Pauquette

Brad has worked in the publishing industry since 2009. He is the editor of many books and anthologies and a published author. As a publishing consultant and developmental editor, Brad has coached award-winning and *New York Times* bestselling authors to produce exceptional books and reach new audiences.

Brad is presently the director of The Company, a community of Christian writers on a mission to change the world. He personally mentors The Company's writing and publishing apprentices as part of The Three program.

Brad lives in Cambridge, Ohio with his wife, Melissa, and their six children. Learn more about him at BradPauquette.com. He'd love to hear from you.

Brad welcomes invitations to speak to churches, events, and podcasters. Reach out to him via his website.

About The Company

The Company is a trade school for bang-up Christian writers.

Aspiring writers move to Cambridge, Ohio from all over the country to attend our two-year, full-time apprenticeship program. Apprentices improve their writing craft, develop their business skills, and grow spiritually. Upon graduation, these writers are fully equipped to professionally publish their work and reach real audiences with the stories God has placed on their hearts.

As part of The Company's program, apprentices use real-world projects to grow and develop their skills. *Lawless* is one such project, developed by a second-year apprentice, Alli Prince, under the mentorship and supervision of Brad Pauquette.

Aspiring writers who are ready to make big steps towards their publishing goals are encouraged to apply to The Company's apprenticeship program.

The Company also offers a variety of part-time and online opportunities to help aspiring writers take action and get to work.

Learn more at
Writers.Company

Don't Stop Now!

More great stories are just around the corner.

New short stories, essays, and poetry posted weekly.

100% free. 100% worth it. All the time.

Read and subscribe today at

PearlMag.co

Made in the USA
Coppell, TX
19 February 2025

46140033R00194